Bury the Dead

BURY THE DEAD

Peter Carter

Oxford University Press 1986
Oxford Toronto Melbourne

Oxford University Press, Walton Street, Oxford OX2 6DP

Oxford New York Toronto
Delhi Bombay Calcutta Madras Karachi
Petaling Jaya Singapore Hong Kong Tokyo
Nairobi Dar es Salaam Cape Town
Melbourne Auckland

and associated companies in
Beirut Berlin Ibadan Nicosia

Oxford is a trade mark of Oxford University Press

British Library Cataloguing in Publication Data
Carter, Peter, *1929*–
Bury the dead.
I. Title
823'.914[F]   PR6053.A739
ISBN 0–19–271493–7

Typeset by Fontwise
Printed by
Biddles Ltd., Guildford

For E. P. Hodgkin

'Let the dead bury their dead.'

Jesus Christ

Prologue

On a bright autumn day two men met in a popular tourist resort in the Harz mountains of Germany. They were elderly and prosperous: well fed, well dressed, well preserved, and travelling in glossy, expensive cars.

One of the men was not alone. He had two companions. They were young, muscular, and watchful.

The two elderly gentlemen had lunch together. The young men did not eat. One of them stayed in the restaurant bar, by the door, and the other sauntered in the garden at the back of the restaurant.

After their lunch the two elderly gentlemen ordered brandy with their coffee, lighted large cigars and, in a cloud of cigar smoke, leaned forward companionably: two old cronies reminiscing, about the War perhaps, enjoying a tax-deductible lunch, possibly their last in the mountains before the winter closed in.

One of the men blew smoke in a vague spiral towards the ceiling. He was tall and spare and, despite his years, ramrod straight.

'So you travel alone?' he enquired.

'Yes,' the other man, silver-haired, pink, with a scar on one plump cheek, sipped his brandy.

'Is that wise?'

'Why not?'

'Oh,' the tall man shrugged. 'One hears of old people being attacked.'

The silver-haired man was mildly dismissive. 'I take good care of myself. I don't wander the streets at night—or during the day, come to that.'

'And your home?'

The silver-haired man smiled, showing dazzling white teeth. 'I find it difficult getting in myself at times. And I have dogs. Excellent dogs.'

'Yes,' the tall man nodded. 'You always were good with dogs.'

'Besides,' the silver-haired man said, 'there is one advantage to being elderly. There comes a time when nobody is really interested in you. A blessing in disguise, really—for the likes of us, that is.'

'I wouldn't be too sure,' the tall man said. 'Some swine have long memories. A friend of ours in South America had a nasty shock recently.'

'South America.' The silver-haired man waved his cigar. 'Anything can happen there. It's why I stayed in Germany. In any case, who remembers me?' He crooked a finger for more drinks.

'Hmm.' The tall man paused until the waiter had poured the brandy and then, casually and without any attempt at concealment, he slid his hand into his breast pocket and took out an envelope. 'I thought that you might want to see this.'

The silver-haired man opened the envelope and fished out an official-looking document. He stared at it then, carefully, placed it on the table, face down. When he looked up his face was no longer pink but white. 'Where did that come from?'

'One guess,' the tall man said.

The silver-haired man placed a manicured finger on the document. 'It doesn't mean much.'

'There are more.'

'Oh?'

'Yes, a complete file, so we are told.'

'Reliably?'

The tall man paused, judiciously. 'The impression is, yes. That is why we paid a high price for that. The matter was carefully discussed before the money was drawn from the Fund.'

'Thank you,' the silver-haired man said.

'Oh, don't thank me. We are all concerned about the welfare of our old comrades. Besides, there are others involved.'

The silver-haired man knocked an inch of ash from his cigar. 'Have you met the, er, vendor?'

'Certainly not.' The tall man was slightly offended.

'But we know who he is?'

'Of course. He isn't a professional, you understand. Just a greedy little bureaucrat without honour or loyalty.'

'Then it should be easy,' the silver-haired man said. 'We just buy everything he has.'

'I'm afraid that it isn't quite so easy.'

The silver-haired man lost some of his composure. 'What do you mean? Don't say it's the price, there must be plenty of money in the Fund.'

'No, no. Calm yourself.' The tall man made a warning gesture. 'You know us better than that. Let me explain. The vendor has access to the rest of the file—and other papers. It seems that after the War masses of documents were dumped in the State Archive which haven't been looked at since. Typical inefficiency.'

'Typical,' the silver-haired man agreed.

'Yes, well. The vendor has been working in an Archive and he found that'—he tapped the document—'and the rest of the material. He wants money, of course—our money—but he is frightened. He wants guarantees that we will get him out and he wants to meet one of us, someone important. In fact,' he coughed, 'in fact he wants to meet that man.' He tapped the document again.

'That man is dead,' the silver-haired man said flatly.

'Of course, of course.' The tall man was soothing. 'But still, the vendor insists on meeting him. And really, you know, we must get to those files before someone else does, some fanatic brooding on the past who won't want to sell, who might hand them over to other madmen obsessed with revenge. You follow me?'

'So far,' the silver-haired man was chilly.

'Good,' the tall man smiled. 'The other thing I ought to mention is that we really must have the original documents. I mean we need them here, in our hands, not simply destroyed over there. They will be of inestimable value to us, raising money, influence . . . but you know this.'

The silver-haired man nodded. 'Of course. But what do we do?'

'We have thought of a scheme.' The tall man leaned forward and spoke softly, although not in a whisper, his voice pitched just below the level of the noise in the restaurant. He spoke for some time and then leaned back.

The silver-haired man stared balefully at him, the scar on his right cheek white against his flushed face. 'Is that the best you can think of?' he demanded.

'I'm afraid that it is.' The tall man finished his brandy. 'I should say two things. First, it is an order. Second, if you come back without the documents it would really be better for you if you don't come back at all. Of course, if you can think of a better idea do let me know, through the usual channels. Now I'm afraid that I really must go.'

He stubbed out his cigar and waved for the waiter. 'I'll pay the bill. Really, the food here isn't bad at all.'

They walked to the car-park, the young men flanking them. At his car the tall man held out his hand. 'Well, goodbye, my dear fellow. We will send you all the details. I do wish that you would find yourself a companion.'

The silver-haired man ignored the offered hand. 'About this bureaucrat. The vendor.'

'Oh,' the tall man seated himself comfortably in the back of his car. At a touch of his finger the sepia-tinted window slid down. 'Yes, him. Use him, of course. In fact you have to. Then kill him. *Auf Wiedersehen*.'

Chapter 1

ERIKA NORDERN stood poised, one foot forward, rocking on her toes and heels, taking deep, slow, rhythmic breaths, focusing on the black and white fibreglass bar, 7 metres away, and exactly 1 metre and 70 centimetres from the ground.

She had been jumping for an hour now and was glistening with sweat but she had driven the bar up to this, above her best ever height, and now she was ready to jump into the unknown.

There were no other athletes in the gymnasium, but her coach was standing against the wall, and high in a shadowed corner of the gallery there was a man.

The man had been there for the hour that Erika had been jumping. He had not spoken, or even moved, but his very immobility was disturbing, detracting from the absolute concentration the bar demanded. At a mere 1 metre 46, a child's jump, Erika had twice brought the bar down; but then the silent, unmoving presence had become a challenge and she had begun to leap like a deer, clearing the bar with ease as it edged up, 3 centimetres at a time, at each jump, hoping for a response from the gallery. But each jump had been met with the same enigmatic silence.

But a jump of 1.70 should bring applause and Erika took that final breath and ran forward, curving in to the bar, driving explosively off her right foot, twisting her body, clearing the bar with her head and shoulders, and hips, but clipping it with her left heel and bringing it down as she fell on to the landing bed.

There was a clap of hands but a disapproving one as the coach came forward. 'Your heel is trailing again, Erika!

The approach was good, and the take-off, but you lost your concentration. You have to think of *all* your body, not just the trunk and legs. Everything, from the top of your head to the tips of your toes. And you must *think*. Think and jump. The unity of theory and practice.'

The coach's voice was raised, almost shrill, and Erika felt uneasy. 'She is not talking to me,' she thought. 'She is speaking to the man in the gallery.'

'I'll go again,' she said.

The coach's eyes flicked away, a quick glance at the gallery, and then, almost imperceptibly, she relaxed. 'No,' she said in a normal tone. 'That won't be necessary. You have done enough. I will see you on Monday. Don't forget to do your exercises tomorrow.' She turned and walked away. Erika looked up at the gallery. The man had gone.

Erika showered and changed and wheeled her bicycle out of the school. It was dark and cold with a thin biting wind bringing snow from the East. She swung on to the bicycle track. Here, on the edge of the city, there was little traffic and no pedestrians, not even by the new electronics factory glittering behind its steel mesh fence. She pedalled steadily on, wondering about the man in the gallery: who was he and what had he been doing, sitting so silently in the darkness? She had not asked, of course. Authority in the person of her coach would tell her when, and if, it was necessary.

At the corner of her street, where the new flats began, she skidded to a halt and dismounted by a huge beech tree. Behind the tree, half hidden by bushes, there was a granite boulder.

It was not forbidden to look at the boulder, but it was not encouraged, either. It was only the presence of the beech tree which, when the flats were built, had saved it from being dynamited out of existence.

Erika looked around. Lights from the windows of the flats stained the street red and green. A man on a noisy motor bike wobbled past. From far away, tugs on the river moaned. A dog barked madly into the night. Then there was silence and solitude.

Erika stepped through the bushes and knelt by the boulder. Already the snow had covered it in a white shroud. She brushed at the snow with her gloved hand. As mysteriously as an image developing on film, letters appeared:

MEN OF THIS PARISH.

FALLEN FOR

FATHERLAND AND GOD.

1870—1871

And then there were the first names: Hans Arp, Peter Breitner, Johann Müller. And then there were two more dates, as ominous as those of Doomsday: 1914–1918; and more names. Many more names. A register of a cataclysm. But there were no dates beginning 1939. It was as if the mason had grown weary of carving the names of the dead.

Crouched in the darkness and the cold, Erika peered at the memorial and then with her gloved finger she scribbled a name in the snow: Colonel Erich von Ritter. 1945. Then she backed away to her bicycle. Already the snow was obliterating the name.

Under the cold yellow glare of the sodium lamps she pushed her bike across the street, locked it in the rack at the back of her flats, and ran up the stairs, taking the steps easily, three at a time; six flights, twelve stairs to a flight except for the final one which, for some reason no one had ever discovered, had thirteen, and which led to a door with a neat aluminium plate which read, 'Family Nordern'.

Erika pushed in, dropped her satchel in the tiny vestibule which was a source of some pride to the Norderns, and went into the sitting-room. Her brother Paul, two years younger than Erika, was sprawled on a small sofa watching a Western on television. He made a vague grunting noise which could have meant 'hello' or 'don't disturb me'.

'Where are they?' Erika asked.

'Mother's out. He's in there.' Paul jabbed his thumb at a door. 'And she's in there.' Another jab at another door.

Erika went into the kitchen, which was merely part of the sitting-room fenced off by a ledge and a plywood lattice which bore a cluster of artificial ivy, and made coffee. She sipped it, letting the mug warm her tingling fingers, then edged through the crowded sitting-room and into her parents' bedroom. Tucked in beside a double bed was a desk. Her father was sitting at it, typing with two blunt fingers. He raised his head and stared at Erika through heavy, silver-rimmed spectacles.

'Erika.' He nodded. 'You are all right?'

'Yes. Can I get you anything?'

'No thank you.' Herr Nordern nodded at a mound of papers piled on his desk.

Erika tilted her head to look at them: tables of statistics, incomprehensible to her although clear to her father who was a planner in the Ministry of Economic Development.

'I'm busy, Erika.'

'Sorry,' Erika backed away.

'Excuse me, I didn't mean to seem sharp. We're short-handed at the office.'

'It's all right, Father.' Erika retreated into the sitting-room. The cowboys and Indians had gone momentarily, replaced by a grinning blonde in an improbable dress who was spraying a kitchen with a deodorant and assuring the viewers that domestic happiness lay through the use of the spray after every meal.

Erika sidled past the sofa, and Paul, and into her own room. It was tiny, scarcely large enough for the two narrow beds jammed into it and the hard upright chair on which, her back as upright as the chair, her grandmother, Omi, was sitting, listening through earphones to a record-player.

Erika placed her hand on the old woman's shoulder. She turned and a smile illuminated her face.

'Ah!' she cried and fumbled with her earphones. Erika gently disengaged them, smoothed down the grey hair, and placed one of the earphones against her own ear. The music was Mozart, the aria from *The Marriage of Figaro*:

> '*Say, ye who borrow*
> *Love's witching spell,*
> *What is this sorrow*
> *Naught can dispel?*'

Omi picked up her spectacles. Her hands were dappled

with the spots of old age and her knuckles were twisted with arthritis. It was a long time since she had fallen under Love's spell but, with all its sorrows, the spell still held her in enchantment although its caster had been dead for forty years.

'So.' Omi put on her spectacles. 'How is my Erika?'

Erika sat on her bed. 'Well, thank you.'

From the sitting-room came the crackle of gun-fire and the bugles of the United States cavalry.

'I'll tell Paul to turn it off,' Erika said.

'No,' Omi waved her down. 'Let him enjoy himself. When I was young all the boys were mad on Westerns. They all read Karl May's books. Winnetou, the noble Indian. I read them, too.' She smiled. 'That was a long time ago.'

'They still read him,' Erika said.

'So they do.' Omi made to rise. 'I'll get you some soup, Dear.'

'Not just yet.' Erika stretched out on the bed. 'I'll wait until Mother gets back from her meeting.'

'Meetings!' Omi tutted with disapproval. 'It should be men who go to them.' She picked up a piece of crochet-work and old and gnarled though her hands were they manipulated the hook with surprising delicacy; a skill learned in the years after the War using unravelled baling cord. 'And what comes from all these meetings? Tell me that.'

'A new Germany, Omi.'

'Ah, new, new! Everything has to be new. Like this flat. We were better off in the old one.'

Erika smiled. She, too, had preferred their old flat in Central Berlin, which had escaped Allied bombing and Russian artillery. It had been comfortable, with its big rooms and solid walls, until it had been knocked down to make way for a government building. But the new flat, with its central heating, was at least warm, a real blessing in a German winter.

But still they had possessed space, room for her things and for Omi's, too. She glanced at her corner of the room. Her books, the wooden bear with a convincing growl which her father had brought from Moscow. Her poster of the great Olympic team of 1976, in Montreal, with their forty gold

17

medals, more than the United States, a signed photograph of the great Rosie Ackermann in Montreal, clearing the bar at 1 metre 93 to become Olympic Champion . . . and in the other corner Omi's possessions. Not that she had many. All that she had owned had gone in the war—and there was only one item from before that catastrophe, a creased and wrinkled photograph of her husband, Colonel Erich von Ritter, dashing and upright in the uniform of the Artillery, the weaver of that spell which still held Omi enmeshed. Throughout all the horrors she had suffered, Omi had held on to that.

The front door slammed. The television fell silent. The voice of Frau Nordern could be heard through the thin walls. With a lithe, supple movement, as though gravity were suspended in Berlin, Erika rose from the bed.

'I'll help get supper,' she said.

Chapter 2

FRAU NORDERN, in her forties, stout and formidable, was already bustling in the kitchen. Through the ivy came the rattle of plates and peremptory commands:

'Paul, lay the table, Erika, cut the bread, Omi, tell Father five minutes.'

Five minutes precisely and the soup was being ladled into the new Czechoslovakian bowls which were Frau Nordern's pride and joy. The Norderns had a quantity of new things, Herr Nordern having recently had a couple of excellent bonuses.

'So.' Frau Nordern's spoon caught the edge of her plate as if it were an order to begin eating. Herr Nordern poured out wine for his wife, Omi and himself, and apple-juice for Erika and Paul. Omi murmured a grace and took a tremulous sip of her soup. How she relished it, Erika thought. Although she ate little how, even now, she relished every drop and morsel. But then she had lived through days, months, years, when there was no food, when she had lived in rubble and, like wild animals, men had fought each other for rotten potatoes. No wonder she enjoyed her food and, although of course it was a mere superstition, no wonder that she thanked God for it.

Her mother was speaking. 'Paul, did you get better marks for your technical drawing this week?'

'Yes,' Paul muttered into his soup.

'See that you do! How can you hope to become an engineer if your technical drawing is bad? Going to the disco won't get you into university. Do you want to end up a common labourer? What marks did you get?'

'Sixty-five.' Paul pushed his apple-juice away. 'Can't we have Club Cola?'

'Cola!' Frau Nordern recoiled. 'Do you think I'm going to have that rubbish in my house? It is full of acid which rots your teeth away. . . .'

She launched into a defence of good, honest, German apple-juice. Erika looked sideways at her brother. 'He's lying,' she thought, with a touch of amusement. 'He's got bad marks again.' The Cola was a mere diversion, although not a bad one at that. Of course, the issue of the marks would come up again, but Paul had postponed it, as he did everything if he could.

Having exhausted her onslaught on the demon Cola, Frau Nordern turned to Erika.

'And you, anything special today?'

'I had a training session,' Erika said.

'Yes?' Herr Nordern prompted.

Erika was prone to blushing, and she blushed now. 'I was on my own. For an hour.'

'An hour?' Herr Nordern put down his spoon.

'Yes.' Erika blushed more furiously. 'I had the gym to myself.'

'So.' Herr Nordern pursed his lips. 'They wouldn't give you an hour to yourself unless. . . .'

The 'unless' was unstated. Erika and her father and mother knew perfectly well that an hour of individual coaching with a whole gymnasium reserved would be given only to an athlete of real talent and real promise; a genuine outstanding prospect, one worthy of the utmost the State could give, and one for whom the sports field could lead to vistas of national fame and honour.

For a moment there was a profound silence as the Nordern family contemplated that future, then Erika said:

'There was a man there.'

'A man?' Frau Nordern broke away from her reverie. 'What sort of a man?'

Erika shrugged. 'I don't know.'

'What was he doing?'

'Nothing. He just sat in the gallery.'

'Watching you?'

Omi gave a scandalised 'tut' and Erika's blush crept back.
'I suppose so.'

'Did he speak to you?'

'No.'

Herr Nordern peered through his thick spectacles. 'Let me get this clear,' he said in his calm, precise voice. 'You were training. A man was watching you, and your instructor, Fräulein . . .?'

'Silber,' Frau Nordern said.

'Of course, Fräulein Silber. She said nothing?'

'No.'

'But she knew the man was there?'

'Yes. I think so.'

Paul guffawed. 'Probably old Silber's boy-friend. Who'd want to look at Erika?'

His guffaw died away as his mother stared coldly at him. 'Do you think this is a laughing matter? Do you?'

'All right,' Paul was sullen. 'Only a joke.'

Herr Nordern coughed. 'He could have been an inspector. Inspecting Fräulein Silber, I mean. They do that, you know.'

'With only one girl present?' Frau Nordern was contemptuous. 'How was he dressed?'

Erika put a finger to her mouth, trying to remember. 'I think that he had a hat on, and a suit.'

'Not'—Herr Nordern's spectacles gleamed across the table—'not athletic clothing?'

Erika shook her head. He hadn't been wearing a track suit, and wasn't there something a little strange in that, something incongruous? Wouldn't an inspector have been wearing one? Or would he? She looked up. Her father was toying with a piece of bread and her mother was frowning into her empty bowl.

'Is there something wrong?' she asked.

'Wrong? No, of course not. Why should there be?' Frau Nordern bustled into the kitchen, came back with a bowl of stewed plums and disregarding Paul's mutinous scowl gave him an extra large portion.

'Eat!' she said in a voice which left no room for argument. Very much the tone of voice, in fact, with which she terrorised errant mothers at the Health Centre where she was a social worker.

Like the mothers, or some of them, the Norderns meekly obeyed, finished their supper and then, a little reluctantly on Herr Nordern's part, very reluctantly on Paul's, the males obeyed the democratic rules of the household and washed up. Afterwards, coffee made and a little plum brandy poured, Herr Nordern put on the television for the News, switching from that other Germany to their own as Paul beat a retreat into his tiny room.

Erika stretched out her long limbs as the News brought its disparate tales: unemployment, racialism, warmongering in the West; peace, progress, and prosperity in the socialist countries. As usual, there was a cloud over Poland but that was not unexpected, especially by Omi who was openly contemptuous.

'Slavs,' she said. 'Never any discipline. Never.'

But then Omi did have a certain unprogressive attitude towards the Poles; inexcusable, of course, but understandable since the home in East Prussia where she, and her ancestors, had grown up, was now a holiday centre for Polish steel workers, that particular part of the old Germany having been handed over to Poland after the War.

The news ended and Herr Nordern stood up, stretched himself, and stubbed out his small cigar. 'Ah,' he said, 'we're lucky to live here. Security, yes, security.'

He looked around the flat with modest pride: the new wallpaper with its bamboo motif, the new carpet, the real, hand-painted oil-painting of the Tatry mountains where they had spent their summer holiday. It was a pity that there wasn't room for a piano but he and Erika made passable music, she on her flute, himself on a recorder. Yes, they were lucky.

'But I must work,' he announced.

'So late?' Erika asked.

'Yes. It's because of Steinmark being away.'

'He's *always* going away,' Frau Nordern snapped. 'Where is he this time?'

'Dresden,' Herr Nordern said. 'Going through old files. Well, I must finish my report.'

'The brown coal production?' asked Frau Nordern.

'Yes, it really is most interesting,' Herr Nordern said, a little improbably. He nodded and went into the bedroom and within a minute or two the uneven tapping of his typewriter told that he was indeed immersed in the projected figures for the production of brown coal over the next five years.

Frau Nordern took out a bulky file of reports and began annotating them with a steady, unnerving energy. Omi caught Erika's eye and she found a channel on the television with a light orchestral concert from the Hamburg station.

Contented, Omi carried on with her crochet-work, nodding in time to the music. Erika opened a novel by Christa Wolf which had been commended to her. It was a quiet, peaceful, and typical evening in the life of the Norderns.

At 10.30 Frau Nordern yawned, a wide, face-splitting yawn which revealed broken and jagged teeth filled with grey metal. 'Bedtime,' she said, in a voice that meant it.

'Yes,' Omi was ready for her bed. She went to the bathroom and then Erika helped her undress, slid a night-gown over her frail body, and eased her into bed.

'Good-night, Omi,' Erika said.

'Good-night, *Liebchen*.' Omi offered her face for a kiss then took hold of Erika's hand. 'I don't like that man watching you,' she whispered. 'When I was a girl. . . .'

Erika smiled down. 'It's nothing, Omi. Nothing at all. Really.'

'I suppose not,' Omi sighed, unconvinced.

'Will you sleep now?'

'Yes, my Dear. Will you pass my Bible and the Watch-words?'

Erika handed over the Bible and the Watchwords, a collection of biblical texts the Lutheran Church circulated for daily reading and study.

'I miss our old Bible,' Omi murmured. 'It had all our family names in it. Mine, my mother's, father's, grandmother's. . . .'

Erika sat patiently as Omi slipped away into her dream-world. The cistern in the bathroom gurgled three times. Gently she disengaged her hand and tiptoed into the sitting-room. Her mother was there in a florid dressing-gown. Mysteriously, she beckoned Erika into the kitchen.

'On Monday,' she hissed, 'when you go to school, ask Fräulein Silber about that man. Do you hear me?'

'Yes,' Erika was impatient. 'But it's nothing.'

Her mother took her by the elbow. 'You do as I tell you. Now go to bed.'

Erika used the bathroom then went back into her bedroom. Omi was sound asleep, her breath as light and dry as the rustle of withered leaves, although as Erika leaned over her to remove the Bible and the Watchwords, she murmured something.

'A dream,' Erika thought. What could it be? What masked images were stealing across that old mind? Surely nothing as strange as the epoch Omi had traversed, and no nightmares stalking through the darkness could reveal such horrors as those she had seen in the broad daylight of the twentieth century.

Erika slid into her night-gown, switched off the bedroom light, and, as she always did, peered through the window. There were not many lights on in Klara-Lettkin-Strasse. Only here and there a glowing window told of a night-bird or a shift worker. The late train to Dresden sounded its klaxon as it always did, exactly at that time; an owl hooted in the beech tree, the red lights on the Television Tower gleamed in the distance, and beyond that there was a lurid glow in the sky where, with all its mysteries, that other Berlin simmered.

Chapter 3

ERIKA WAS showered and dressed by 7.00 but her mother was up before her, sitting at the table in her amazing dressing-gown, drinking coffee as she went through more reports on her mothers.

As Erika joined her, Frau Nordern shook her head. 'Some of these mothers!' She made a vehement cross on a report with a red pencil. 'This one, picking up her baby at the crèche and she was drunk! She may be deserted and having a bad time but if she doesn't pull her socks up I'll have her before the People's Court.'

She picked up another report and scowled at it as if it were an American plan for the destruction of the German Democratic Republic. 'What are you going to do today?'

'I'm going to see Rosa,' Erika said.

'Not training?'

'Not today.' Erika spread a little jam on a roll. 'Just exercises.'

'And homework.'

'And homework,' Erika said, dutifully.

The bedroom door opened and Herr Nordern came out, muffled in an overcoat and carrying a bulky brief-case. He gulped some coffee, patted Erika on the head, and barged to the door. 'Back at 7.00,' he said over his shoulder—'I hope—meetings on Sunday!'

The door slammed. From Paul's room came the muffled wailing of a rock group on a West German wavelength. The phone rang.

Erika stretched out her arm. 'Nordern.'

'Ah,' a sharp voice squeaked. 'Erika? Aunt Bertha here. Let me speak to your mother.'

Erika handed over the phone and listened absently as her mother spoke.

'Yes. . . . no . . . might be . . . yes, we'll look, but are you sure? Pink and purple?' She rolled her eyes mysteriously at Erika. 'All right then . . . what was that?'

Erika poured herself more coffee. The family had relatives scattered across the country. Bertha was her father's sister, married to a railwayman and living in the dismal new town of Eisenhüttenstadt.

'What!' Frau Nordern's voice rose a scandalised octave. 'Bodo?'

Erika pricked up her ears as her mother gave a series of 'tuts' before putting down the phone.

'Bodo,' Frau Nordern said bitterly. 'In some sort of trouble again. It's not funny, Erika.'

Erika suppressed her smile. Bodo was her father's brother. He was a genial, devil-may-care sort of man who liked a song and a drink and female company. He was a self-employed builder who made ten times the official wage by building week-end bungalows in the woods in Hoppegarten, and plenty more by various shady deals which sometimes brought him into collision with the authorities—although he always managed to escape unscathed. But although he lacked the true spirit of selfless, socialist cooperation, Erika liked him.

'Mark my words, he'll come to a bad end,' Frau Nordern said. 'What a disgrace.'

'Yes, Mother.' Erika was dutiful but she wondered whether her mother was more concerned about the disgrace to Bodo or to herself for, although she was certainly a loyal citizen of the State, there was, at times, more than a whiff of old class attitudes about her, as indeed there was about Omi, their family having been *Junker*, Prussian aristocrats, wielders of the sword and masters of the countryside, until the German Democratic Republic had removed from them their swaggering grasp of both land and sword.

Frau Nordern nibbled at some cheese. 'Bertha wants to know if there are any chair covers in the shops. There's nothing in Eisen. Pink and purple! Can you imagine it? Anyway, keep your eyes open.'

Erika said that she would, finished her breakfast, helped

Omi dress, then settled down to her homework. Paul shuffled into the room, had his breakfast, washed up with an exaggerated air of martyrdom, and began *his* homework, spurred on by his mother's sharp comment that if he didn't do it, and do it properly, he would not go to the cinema that night—if ever again.

Omi came in, took her favourite seat by the window, and sat with her Watchword for the day. The others sat industriously around the table. Erika went into her parents' room, the only one big enough for her to do her aerobic exercises. The phone rang, twice, but each time there were only clickings and hummings.

'Wouldn't you think that they could get these things right,' Frau Nordern said. 'Men on the moon and the phone doesn't work!'

After lunch, Erika, smart in a leather topcoat and fur hat, caught the fast train, the *S-Bahn*, into the centre of Berlin. A pale sun was shining from a brilliant sky on to streets lightly powdered with snow, making even the gloomy area around Ostkreuz look attractive. The huge square of Alexanderplatz was full of bustle and already men were at work preparing for the great Christmas fair. There was the usual cluster of people around the Television Tower, the quick snack stalls were doing good business, there was the usual quota of seedy types wandering in and out of the bars, and the usual groups, too, of Turks who had come across from West Berlin to take advantage of the cheap alcohol the G.D.R. supplied.

Erika peered through the windows of the Centrum Store which dominated one side of Alexanderplatz but there was no sign of chair covers, of any colour. She shrugged and went back to Alexanderplatz station to get the underground railway for the two or three stops to Pankow, where her friend Rosa lived.

She went down into the dingy concrete cavern which led to steps which in turn led to a gloomy green-tiled platform whose gloom was not lightened by, on the curved wall across the rails, a line of identical posters, showing a skull above a huge array of graves and with the message, '*Raketen raus!*'—'Missiles out!'

Erika stood looking at the posters and then a man walked

along the platform. He was not drunk, or if he was then he had it well concealed, but suddenly he began shouting. Pointing to the posters he shouted, 'The Mirror Wall! The Mirror Wall!' And, as he came abreast of Erika, he shouted, 'Look Fräulein! Take a good look! It is the Mirror Wall!' and then he walked off, in a mad, brisk way, as the *U-Bahn* train came in.

Erika sat in the train thinking about the man. Berlin had plenty of odd types, people still suffering from the War. Around the park where she did her morning run a man wandered, shouting incoherently, and nobody bothered, not even the Police; but then that man *was* mad, a harmless lunatic. But the man on the platform . . . there had been a sinister and ominous sense in what he shouted: a mirror wall, and the long line of skulls . . . it wasn't a pretty thought and she deliberately shook it off as the train ran into Pankow.

Rosa lived in a high-rise flat which, although suffering from inefficient heating and no lift, and which was scheduled for demolition one day, Erika rather admired for its view. She made light of the twelve flights of stairs, passing several grunting and complaining women as she ran up, came to the top floor and banged on the door.

Rosa was a class-mate of Erika's, a good, although not outstanding, sprinter. She was glowing with pleasure both at the sight of her friend and because her parents had gone out for the afternoon.

'Ah!' Erika smiled with deep satisfaction for, whatever benefits living in the German Democratic Republic might bring and, as Erika was told every day—virtually every hour—it brought many, privacy was not one of them and simply to be alone in a flat with a friend was a pleasure, a luxury. And the central heating was working.

Not having Frau Nordern's ideological objections to Club Cola, Rosa's parents kept a stock in. Rosa poured two glasses and the girls stood by the window looking at the panorama of Berlin—both Berlins.

Rosa, for whom the view was so familiar that she scarcely gave it a glance, sipped her Cola. 'How did your training session go yesterday?'

Erika was mildly startled. 'How did you know about it?'

'Aah!' Rosa raised her finger. 'I have spies everywhere. No, seriously, I heard Fräulein Silber mention it to the caretaker on Friday. A private session!'

'I don't want to talk about it,' Erika said.

'Why ever not?'

'I don't know. I just don't.' Erika was uncharacteristically abrupt; she did not even want to think about the session and the mysterious man. But Rosa was not easily put off.

'You're marked out for special treatment—oh yes you are. First the Indoor Championships, then next year the Spartakiad. . . .'

Erika shook her head, but the thought was not easily shaken out of it. The Spartakiad was the great national athletic competition and to win that was really something.

'You could win,' Rosa said. 'You could be Victor Ludorum!'

Erika laughed. 'I won't even win the Indoor Championship.'

'You'll win that.' Rosa was emphatic. 'A month from now you'll be Berlin Indoor Champion, then, July, German Champion.'

'There are girls ahead of me,' Erika said. 'I know that. It was that year. . . .'

'Yes,' Rosa's responsive face looked grave. Erika had made a bad landing when she was jumping two years previously and it had taken a year for her leg to mend, and six months for her to recover her nerve. 'But still you've done it. You have come back and your heights are good, you can't deny that. And remember Rosie Ackermann!'

Erika didn't need reminding of that name. Every girl in the Republic had it branded in her heart; a girl fifteen years old plucked from a regional competition, sent to the Olympic Games, and winning the gold medal for the high jump.

'And then there's travel,' Rosa said.

'I have travelled,' Erika said. 'I've been to Czechoslovakia, and Hungary.'

'Oh yes,' Rosa shrugged. 'We've all done that. But over there.' She pointed through the window.

Dusk was creeping in from the East and across the pale grey line of the Anti-Fascist Barrier; beyond the huge swathe of razed and desolate wasteland where the arc lamps burned and the guard dogs roamed, and beyond the second wall which sealed that off, the brazen towers of the other Berlin were beginning to glow, neon signs in red and green flickering on and off like silent messages from an alien and hostile planet.

Rosa leaned her elbows on the window-ledge and cupped her chin in her hands. 'I wonder what it's really like,' she said.

For one profoundly deceitful moment Erika was tempted to say that they both knew very well what it was like. Every day the television, the newspapers, teachers, told them the litany of Western woes; the West German television told them of its joys; people did come and go, the old and the young and the privileged. But still, when all was said and done, that information was only a substitute for the real thing. What would it really be like to cross that pale barrier which, for all of her fifteen years, had cut them off so irrevocably from the lives led over there.

'A strange thing happened to me today,' she said, and told Rosa of the man in the underground.

Rosa whistled. 'That is strange,' she said. 'Creepy. What could he have meant?' She shivered. 'Like looking in a mirror and seeing . . . ugh! It's like Snow White.'

'What do you mean?' Erika asked.

'You know, "Mirror mirror on the wall, who is the fairest of them all?" but the wrong way round. Or like those things in the fair with those mirrors which distort you. A real crackpot. Best not to think about it. Have some coffee.'

Erika stretched out on the floor as Rosa made the coffee, and chattered on about films, the boy in school who had been making eyes at her, the last dreary meeting of the F.G.Y.—the Free German Youth movement—the new dinghy her father was planning to buy so that they could go sailing on the Berlin lakes next summer. Erika listened dreamily, but at the back of her mind was the silent observer in the gym—and the mysterious message the man on the underground had shouted. . . .

The Kleists' cuckoo clock called 5.00. 'I'd better go,' Erika said.

'Oh,' Rosa was disappointed. 'Are you coming to the cinema tonight? They say there's a good film on at the Kosmos.'

'I might,' Erika said. 'But I've got to have early nights.'

'Ha! ha! Strict training. For that gold medal—' Rosa waved Erika's protests away. 'I'd be doing the same. I'll look out for you at the cinema anyway.'

The radiator gave a strange gurgle. Rosa banged it vigorously and it gurgled again. 'That means the heating's going off. Thank goodness I'm going out.'

Erika took her train home. At Hain a man got in the compartment with a bicycle. He was old, mildly drunk, and dressed in an amazing variety of clothes—a tattered woolly hat, a purple anorak covered with badges and tied around the waist with a yellow scarf. His bicycle was not much younger than he was and as oddly coloured, daubed with all the hues of the rainbow. 'It's a good old bike,' he announced cheerfully to the compartment at large. 'Solid steel. I painted it myself,' he confided.

A man opposite Erika burst out laughing and Erika laughed with him.

'Laugh away,' said the old man, laughing himself. 'It's nice though, isn't it, Fräulein?'

'Yes,' Erika said. 'Very nice.'

'Two kilos of paint went on this bike,' the man said, 'and I didn't pay for any of it!' He placed his finger against his nose in a cunning gesture and fell on to a seat, still laughing.

When Erika got off the train at Biesdorf he was still laughing and telling an enraptured audience that next year he was going to enter for the Peace Race and cycle to Sofia, although modestly admitting that he would be lucky to actually win.

Erika smiled all the way up Oberfeldstrasse. The cheerful, battered old man with his indomitable spirit, drunk or not, had brought a note of genuine, carefree enjoyment into the bleak evening and had done something to eradicate the slightly chilling incident at Alexanderplatz. But as she turned into Klara-Lettkin-Strasse some of her smile slipped a little. Parked by the beech tree opposite her flats was a car, and unlike the battered old bangers which littered the streets of

Berlin, it was a large, shiny, new car, and cars like that meant *official* in the German Democratic Republic.

But the car could hardly have anything to do with her so she shrugged and turned into the entrance of the flats, and then paused.

A man was standing inside the doorway. He was muffled in a huge overcoat and wore a hat which shaded his face. He was staring at a piece of paper. Erika walked to the stairs, giving the man a sideways glance, but as she put her foot on the first stair he spoke.

'Nordern,' he said.

Chapter 4

'FAMILY NORDERN?' The man stepped forward, taking off his hat, and holding up his piece of paper as if it were a passport to unknown territory. He had sleek silver hair over a pink face from which good living had smoothed away the lines of age, but not a scar on his right cheek.

'The family Nordern,' he repeated. 'Please.'

Erika nodded and the man smiled. He had fine, white teeth. 'Which floor do they live on?' His voice was quiet and patient as if he were talking to a nervous animal.

'The sixth,' Erika said.

'The sixth. Thank you.' The man made no effort to move, standing holding his hat and piece of paper as though he had all eternity to spare. 'There is no lift?'

'No.' Erika turned and darted up the stairs. On her landing she halted and leaned over the bannisters. Shuffling footsteps echoed up the well and, preceded by a long shadow, a gloved hand crept up the stair-rail.

Erika ducked into her flat. Her mother raised her head from her reports, took one look at Erika, and with unnerving astuteness said, 'What is it? What's wrong?'

'Nothing,' Erika said. 'Really nothing, but a man just asked me where we lived.'

Frau Nordern stood up and Omi lowered her crochet-work. It was as if an early-warning system operated in the Nordern household and had given a first, faint, sinister blip.

Frau Nordern looked at the clock. 6.00 p.m. Not the most popular hour for visitors in Berlin. 'A man?' she said, in a tone of voice which strongly suggested '*another* man', and that Erika was responsible for his coming. 'What sort of man?'

Erika shrugged. 'Just a man, old,' adding, as there was a knock on the door, 'and here he is.'

Frau Nordern patted her hair and straightened her shoulders, buxom, robust, and a pillar of society, but there was the slightest note of apprehension in her voice as she said, 'Well don't just stand there, answer the door.'

Without enthusiasm, Erika stepped into the vestibule and opened the front door. The man was there, caught raising his hat, surprised to see Erika, blue eyes wide in his pink face.

'Excuse me, Fräulein,' he said, 'I thought that you. . . .'

Erika blushed. 'Excuse *me*. Downstairs . . . I should have said. . . .' her voice died away as her mother's bulk loomed behind her.

'What is it?' Frau Nordern demanded. 'What do you want?'

The man looked over Erika's shoulder. 'Frau Nordern?'

'Yes.'

'Who was Fräulein von Ritter?'

'And if I was?' Frau Nordern spoke with the aggression which comes from half-conscious alarm, but the man answered with easy smoothness, as if he was all too familiar with talking to people in whom a knock on the door, and a stranger on the doorstep, could give rise to such fears.

'I'm your uncle,' he said. 'I'm Uncle Karl.'

The blood drained from Frau Nordern's face as the man smiled at her and gave a bow, his heels clicking together almost imperceptibly.

'But—' Frau Nordern took a step backwards and her hand went to her breast. 'But you're . . . you're. . . .'

'Dead.' The man said.

Across the landing a door opened and Herr Schneider who lived at number twelve peered through and then closed the door hurriedly.

'Dead, yes.' Frau Nordern shook her head, shaking away the belief of years.

'I've startled you,' the man said. 'Forgive me.' He moved forward into the vestibule, discreetly closing the door behind him. 'I would have given you warning but circumstances. . . .'

'Yes, circumstances.' Some of the colour returned to Frau Nordern's cheeks. 'I must tell mother. Break the news . . . the shock. . . .' She stopped speaking as the man raised his hand.

'Permit me,' he said, 'please.' Mysteriously he was behind Frau Nordern and Erika. 'Allow me to be the first. My sister, you know, my dear sister.'

And then he was in the sitting-room, among the bamboo wallpaper and the plastic ivy and, as the Orchestra Bonn played Strauss waltzes, he was bending over Omi, kissing her old, lined cheeks—his as fresh as a boy's—and kissing her hands with their blue veins like a relief map of a railway to death, and assuring her that he was, that yes, yes, indeed he was, her very own brother Karl who, a lifetime ago, had gone into the fire and furnace of war, and into the frozen circles of snow and ice, in far-away steppe lands where men with skin swarthy, quite unlike his own pink cheeks, and hair dark, unlike his golden locks, and with teeth broken and blackened or mere bands of aluminium, scratched to show symbolic molars, incisors, canines, who had. . . . Ah! what memories Uncle Karl brought with him into the bamboo wallpaper and ivy. What memories for Omi of her family: burned, blasted, mutilated, imprisoned for years on end in those steppe lands by the men from the East who, with their swarthy skins and aluminium teeth had finally stood triumphant in that very city of Berlin, in the heart of the Reich, raising their flag, red with a golden hammer and sickle, over bleeding, smashed, hammered, and prostrate Germany.

'Karl,' tears spilled from Omi's faded eyes on to her brother's manicured nails. 'Karl, is it really you? Really?'

'Yes, really me!' Karl laughed delightedly, showing his brilliant teeth, and slid from his beautiful overcoat lined with red silk, and sat in Herr Nordern's chair, a huge cigar suddenly in his mouth, a polished shoe gleaming as he swung his foot. 'Now, now, no more tears! You're glad to see me, aren't you? So!' Magically a bottle appeared in his hand. 'Whisky! The finest Scotch malt.' He caught Frau Nordern's eye. 'Should we?'

Frau Nordern supposed that they should and in her turn produced glasses, which were filled, and toasts then drunk: to

Omi, Frau Nordern, Erika, to Paul, absent at the cinema, Uncle Karl himself.

'And Herr Nordern?' Karl said. 'Can we expect him?'

'Any minute,' Frau Nordern said, and proving her correct the door opened and Herr Nordern, solid and impassive, stood in the frame, blinking through his heavy spectacles.

'Hans,' her face slightly flushed from the whisky Frau Nordern stood up. 'Guess who this is?'

'Guess?' Herr Nordern stared solemnly at Uncle Karl. 'I've no idea.'

'It's—' Frau Nordern began but stopped as Karl rose, beaming, and held out a plump hand.

'Von Bromberg,' he said. 'Karl August Herman von Bromberg, your mother-in-law's brother and, I know, I'm dead!' He laughed his jovial, infectious laugh. 'But as you see, not! No, very much alive and delighted to meet you, my dear sir.'

'But. . . .' Herr Nordern placed his hands on the table. 'But where . . . how—oh, forgive me,' he took Karl's hand and shook it.

'I know, I know,' Karl cried. 'Many questions, quite so. But please, sit.'

Erika, although fascinated by Uncle Karl, nonetheless felt a mild spasm of resentment as he waved her father to a chair, gave him a cigar and a light from a gold cigarette-lighter, offered him a drink and said, as if he were the head of the household, 'Another glass, Erika.'

But she got the glass as Herr Nordern meekly sat down and accepted the whisky and joined Karl as he raised his own glass in salute.

'A little treat,' Karl said. 'Not that you seem short of anything,' looking around the room. 'But forgive me for not giving you warning. I only found out today where you lived! But where, how, why–yes? Well, I'm afraid it is a long story and I mustn't keep you from your supper.'

Frau Nordern and Omi clamorously denied that Karl was keeping them from anything and Herr Nordern shook his head in agreement. 'Of course not, take your time.'

'So,' Karl leaned back, blew out a stream of cigar smoke, and took a long drink of his whisky. '1945,' he said.

The room went still and the cigar smoke hung under the ceiling like thunder clouds before a storm; 1945, that year with the face of Janus, looking both ways, to the hammering years of victory—and the hammered years of defeat.

Uncle Karl cocked an eyebrow, nodded as if the silence confirmed what he already knew, and addressed himself directly to Herr Nordern. 'Of course,' he said gravely, 'of course my dear Hans—I may call you that? Thank you. Of course I do realise that 1945 meant the end of the rule of, of. . . .'

'Of the Fascists,' Herr Nordern said flatly.

'Exactly! The Fascists. And what a good thing that was, those awful gangsters, Hitler, Himmler, Bormann, the sweepings of the gutters, but it was a hard time.'

'It was,' Omi cried, her voice trembling. '*Schrecklich! Schrecklich!*' She covered her face with her hands as if to blot out those terrible years.

'There, there.' Karl balanced his cigar carefully on an ashtray and leaned forward and patted Omi on the shoulder. 'Don't distress yourself, my Dear. It is all over. Over and done with. Finished. Isn't it, Hans?'

Herr Nordern took his time answering. He gazed for a long moment at Omi, and for a longer one at Karl, before saying that yes, he supposed it was.

'So.' Karl poured out more whisky. 'At all events, February, 1945, I was with Army Group IV in Silesia. We were retreating, of course. The Russians were crashing at us, in Poland, Hungary, Romania, and the Reich. . . .'

Erika stirred uneasily. Into the cosy room, stirring the ivy leaves, shaking the bamboo on the walls, had come images of death and destruction as vivid as the terrible resurrections of old news-reels, where men fell dead over and over again, cities burned, tanks reared and fell on gun-pits, men and women and children were burned, blinded, mutilated, the dead lay unburied, and the smoke from the death camps disfigured the heavens.

But Uncle Karl was talking smoothly on and it was hard to believe that the untroubled blue eyes in his bland pink face could have seen such horrors. Indeed, it was comforting that such a face could have seen them. It distanced them, pushing them back into the ghastly dark age before the triumph of socialism in the new Germany. Not that one should totally forget the horrors, of course. Indeed, as a matter of State policy, Erika was frequently reminded of them in school and had been to a death camp as a salutary reminder of what could happen again unless the peace-loving forces of the world were forever vigilant.

But still, relieved by Karl's presence, Erika attended to him again.

'My unit fell south,' he said. 'I desperately wanted to get to Bromberg—home, you know—but war is like that.' He shrugged ruefully. 'I dare say that there were men in the north who wanted to be in the south, hey? But still, we fell back towards Dresden. Of course, there is no need to tell you what happened there.'

No need at all. Everyone knew that. Two air raids. One at night by the British, one the next day by the Americans. A fire-storm and, well, nobody knew for certain but at least 100,000 dead.

'But I will be frank,' Karl said, nodding at Herr Nordern. 'We knew that the war was over and we were merely trying to slow down the Russian advance. Yes, to be absolutely honest, that is what we were trying to do. The High Command—the Army High Command that is—I'm not talking about the madman in the Bunker—it was hoping that the Americans would come in before the Russians. That is the truth, but in the front line, well, we were obeying orders, that's all, doing our duty as soldiers. You know, *Befehl ist Befehl*, orders are orders. Not that it mattered much to me, really, because I was wounded.'

Omi gasped and Karl smiled at her.

'It wasn't too serious, as you can see, ha! ha! That was in Königsbrück, just north of Dresden and there. . . .' He paused and looked thoughtfully into his glass. 'There I did something rather disgraceful.'

Almost absent-mindedly he refilled his glass, and the others too. Omi raised her fine head and peered over her spectacles as though Karl had used a coarse, vulgar word.

'Disgraceful?' she said. 'A von Bromberg?'

'Ah!' Karl bowed stiffly, leaning towards his sister, and

between them there was a subtle interplay of shared and charged feeling. 'Not that sort of disgrace,' he said. His voice was clipped, and he seemed to Erika to have exchanged his elegant brown suit for the field-grey of the world-shaking Wehrmacht. 'No, not a disgrace of that sort. You see—' he turned to Herr Nordern, the field-grey slipping away as he spoke and a confiding chuckle replacing his tone of command. 'I was an officer. That is a fact of my life and a consequence of my history—Prussian history I might say. I was a major, an acting colonel to be precise, and, with the utmost respect to your Russian allies, then—I emphasise *then*—the troops of the Red Army were, how shall I put it? They were a little undisciplined. Of course not all of them, some were splendid chaps, but they had been without leave for three years, and they had taken very heavy losses—you see Hans, I do understand—but I did know that they were in the habit of shooting officers, and so I took a different identity.'

He sighed, drained his glass with the relieved air of a man who has made his confession, and filled it again.

'A different identity?' Frau Nordern asked.

'Yes, I took a corporal's uniform and his identity card. And then I was taken prisoner. To Russia.'

Russia! For a moment it seemed as if an icy breath from those far-away steppe lands came into the room, breathed by the ghostly mouths of those millions who had gone there and never returned. Omi shuddered. 'Terrible,' she whispered.

'Well, terrible. . . .' Karl pursed his lips judiciously. 'Hard, yes, it was hard. Winter, you know; *winters*, I should say, because I was there for some time. But then those years after the war *were* hard, for all of us. And, in a way, I suppose we deserved it. Terrible things were done in the East. Of course, not by the Wehrmacht. I must emphasise that no German soldier would do such things. That was the S.S. And then there were the murder squads—and not all those were Germans, far from it! There were Poles and Latvians, yes, Russians, too, but I prefer not to think about it, really.'

He gazed at Herr Nordern. 'I'm sure that you will understand that, Hans. The tragedy of war.' He shook his head, ruing the waste and folly of it all. 'But still, I did get out, after ten years. I went to West Germany and started a business—in electronics. I have been quite successful, I might say rather successful. In fact your Government has invited me here for discussions. I may become an agent for them, advising, and buying western technology; not that yours isn't excellent, ha! ha! but that is why I am here tonight, sitting with my dear sister, and my new-found family.'

Omi and Frau Nordern dabbed their eyes and Erika stared at Karl quite openly. Herr Nordern, in his slow deliberate way, sipped his whisky.

'So that is why we couldn't trace you. You were under a different name.'

'Ah, you did try, to trace me?' There was an odd note of alertness in Karl's voice.

'Of course,' Herr Nordern said. 'You were the only one of Omi's brothers left.'

'Yes,' Karl was grave. 'We paid a heavy price, didn't we.'

They had, Erika thought, indeed the Brombergs had and the Ritters. Dead in the Russian inferno, in France, in the Western Desert, in the bombing . . . and now there was only Omi left, and Karl, miraculously risen from the grave.

'And did you try to trace us?' Herr Nordern asked.

Karl's beaming poise suddenly slipped. He actually squirmed with embarrassment and then, with the air of a man squaring up to a hard decision he said, 'No, I did not. I'm sorry, my dear family, but that is the plain truth. When I got back I wasn't too well, you know. But really, I just wanted to forget, to wipe out the past. That may not be a nice thing to say but I am prepared to say it. But now I have had to travel here on business I simply had to find my family.'

'And how did you find us?' Herr Nordern asked.

'The authorities! I asked my friends in the Ministry and they were most helpful.' He beamed at the Norderns as if they were personally responsible for the helpfulness of the Ministry of Economic Development.

'I would expect that,' Herr Nordern said. 'But what is your identity now?'

'Ah! Of course I have my own identity, my real self. I am a von Bromberg again. I went to the authorities in Bonn and made a clean breast of everything. They were helpful too, most helpful and understanding. I find that people are, you know, if you trust them. But—' he pushed back the cuff of his fine silk shirt and glanced at his watch—'but I must go,' he raised his hand, stilling any protests, 'I really must. I have to see some officials. But we will meet many times. Yes, and allow me, dinner tomorrow night. All of us, at the Palast. I absolutely insist. Shall we say 7.30? Then we can have a long talk and find out everything about ourselves.'

He shrugged into his overcoat. 'No, there is absolutely no need to see me out. I have a car waiting for me. Good-night, dear family.'

He kissed Omi, Frau Nordern, and Erika, shook Herr Nordern's hand, discreetly disengaged himself from Omi's grasp, and then he was gone, as mysteriously as he had arrived.

Chapter 5

THE DOOR clicked behind Karl and the Norderns sank back into their chairs and stared at each other.

'Well,' Frau Nordern broke the silence. 'It's incredible.'

There was no dissent as she shook her head and said again, 'Simply incredible. I mean, you read about these things in the papers, but to come back from the dead after forty years. . . .'

'Yes indeed.' Herr Nordern took off his spectacles and polished them with his handkerchief. 'Perhaps we could talk about it over supper.'

'Ah!' Frau Nordern threw her hands into the air. 'Supper! Of course! Uncle Karl comes back and I'm forgetting the food.'

Herr Nordern peered at his spectacles and removed a last speck of dust. 'I just thought that it would be nice to eat,' he said mildly. 'But if you would rather wait. . . .'

'We'll eat. We'll EAT!' Frau Nordern clapped her hands, the family machine went smoothly into action, and within minutes they were all sitting around the table.

Herr Nordern raised his eyebrows as if to ask what the fuss had been about and said, 'How old was Karl in 1945, Omi?'

Omi unclasped her hands and raised her head from prayer. 'He would have been . . . let me think . . . twenty-four. Yes.'

'Twenty-four.' Herr Nordern nodded. 'And he has been away forty years. Another lifetime. What is it?'

Frau Nordern was on her feet. 'I've forgotten to tell Bertha. I'll phone from the bedroom.'

She brushed aside Herr Nordern's protest that the news could wait ten minutes and went into the bedroom. Herr Nordern gave one of his rare smiles. 'The wires will be buzzing tonight. Would you put your mother's food in the stove, Erika? Thank you.' He turned to Omi. 'I am glad for you.'

'Thank you,' Omi said, formally. 'But he hardly stayed at all.'

'Not his fault,' Herr Nordern said, 'if he had an appointment. And he might have been looking for us all day, Nordern isn't the most uncommon name in Berlin. It's lucky we weren't called Schmidt. But, of course, he would have been looking for you, Omi, for a Ritter.'

'Yes,' Omi raised her chin. '*Von* Ritter, that is a name still.'

'It's not his name, though, Omi,' Erika said, taking her place again.

'No, he has our family name of course, von Bromberg. Another great family. Twenty-seven generals our family gave the State. We served under Frederick the Great, Frederick William, the Emperor William II . . . there was a statue to my grandfather in Potsdam. . . .'

She wandered on, recalling the martial glories of the houses of von Ritter and von Bromberg. Erika was curious. Usually her father discouraged Omi from talking about her family, not discourteously, but deflecting her, obliquely showing his, and the State's, disapproval of Prussia's military past—and the role played in it by the *Junker*. But tonight he leaned back, letting her talk, indeed prompting her a little.

'Most interesting,' he said. 'And when was the last time you saw Karl?'

'Now let me think.' Omi tapped a gnarled finger on the table. 'It would have been 1943, in the summer, here in Berlin. He was on sick leave. He had been wounded out . . . out there.'

'In the Soviet Union?'

'Yes, in Russia.'

'That's odd,' Herr Nordern said.

'What is?' Omi asked.

'My father was in Berlin then, on sick leave, too. He was going back to the Russian Front. He might even have bumped into Karl.'

'Yes,' Omi was distantly polite. 'But not socially.'

43

No indeed, Erika thought. Sergeants did not mix socially with majors in those days.

'What regiment was he in?' Herr Nordern asked.

'The Brandenburg,' Omi left the 'of course' unspoken, but it was there all the same, it being inconceivable that a von Bromberg would serve in anything other than the élite of the German army.

'Ah!' Herr Nordern nodded as if he, too, accepted that. 'My father was in the Engineers, being a carpenter.' He stood up as Frau Nordern came from the bedroom. 'I must do some work. Excuse me. We will talk about this for a long time to come.'

'We will,' Frau Nordern said as her husband retreated into the bedroom. She bustled into the kitchen and came back with her soup. 'Yes,' she said, attacking her meal with her usual gusto. 'I can't get over it, I really can't. Bertha almost fainted when I told her. Omi, I got through to Maria, and Frida Sackheim, and the Belows,' she reeled through a list of cousins, discreetly dropping the aristocratic *von* from their names. 'Some I couldn't raise but I'll try again tomorrow. We must have a party, a real celebration, everyone together. We'll take a room somewhere like we did when you were seventy, Omi. That would be nice, wouldn't it?'

'Oh yes,' Omi smiled and then, disconcertingly, burst into tears, holding her face in her hands and sobbing the bitter tears of old age, sadder even than the tears of childhood.

Frau Nordern put her arms around Omi's shoulders. 'Now don't distress yourself, Mother.' She rolled her eyes meaningly at Erika. 'She's tired, poor thing, and the shock—and it's late. Come along.'

'I'll do it,' Erika said. She helped Omi into the bedroom, undressed her, and put her into bed.

'It's real, isn't it?' Omi said. 'Karl was here, just now?'

'He was, yes.' Erika smoothed Omi's hair.

'Pass my Bible child, and the Watchwords. What is the text for today?'

Erika opened the text and read: '"Jesus said unto a man, Follow me. But he said, Lord, suffer me first to go and bury my father. Jesus said unto him, Let the dead bury their dead: but go thou and preach the kingdom of God."'

Erika frowned at the words as she read them. What on earth could they possibly mean. How could the dead bury the dead? And for Jesus to forbid a man to bury his dead father, it was just callous. She looked sideways at Omi but her grandmother was lying on the pillow, her tears wiped away with joy and her face suffused with wonder.

'Ah,' she said, 'the Gospel of Luke. I know it.'

'But what does it mean?' Erika asked.

'Mean?' Omi raised her old hand. 'One day I will tell you, *Liebchen*, but it is a commandment I have broken many times, may God forgive me.'

Erika half-smiled, thinking that Omi could not have broken many commandments, and certainly not any serious ones.

Omi smiled back. 'But God has forgiven me. Yes, he has sent Karl back to me. The others, all dead, what grief! I could endure that, but Karl, not knowing whether he was dead or alive, that was hard to bear and, it has been a great sin, Erika, sometimes I wished that he *was* dead and that I knew it. Yes, even that rather than the uncertainty. Not that we were ever very close. Boys and girls weren't in those days, even brothers and sisters.'

'What was he like as a boy?' Erika asked.

'Oh, a little wild. Once he took one of our colts and raced it round the village and spoiled it. Papa was very angry. He whipped him in the stables in front of the grooms. That was a great humiliation. And he had some trouble in the cadet school, gambling, but Papa forgave him because he fought a duel.'

'A duel!'

'Yes, with sabres. Didn't you notice the scar on his face?'

'What was it about?' Erika pulled her chair closer to the bed.

Omi chuckled. 'Some nonsense, I hardly remember. But cadets were always duelling in those days, and students, too. It was a mark of honour to have a sabre slash on the face. You would think it would be the opposite, wouldn't you? But no, all the old officers had their scar. And he was a great horseman. His ambition was to ride in the Olympics but he had a fall and broke his arm. He was bitter about that. And then the War came . . . but I am so happy tonight.'

'And I am happy for you, Omi.'

'Thank you, child.' Omi's eyelids flickered and drooped. Erika kissed her and patiently waited until her faint breathing fell into a regular rhythm. Then she went into the sitting-room.

Her mother was at the table, her arms folded, the errant mothers forgotten. 'How is she?'

'Asleep, but she is so happy.'

Frau Nordern shook her head. 'What a night. I can't get over it.'

'I know,' Erika said. 'Should I make some coffee?'

Frau Nordern nodded. 'Yes, I can't concentrate on anything now.'

Erika made the coffee and sat with her mother. 'Did you remember him?'

Frau Nordern shook her head thoughtfully. 'I can't say I did to be honest. I was only an infant then, you know, and lots of officers came to our house.' She smiled ruefully. 'Not that they stayed long. They preferred Berlin with all the bombing. Making up for lost time. I'd given him up years ago.'

'Uncle Karl?'

'Yes. There were so many missing, for ever. And we've never spoken about him, you know.'

Erika did not miss the significance of the latter remark. Little was said in the Nordern household about the past of the Brombergs, or the Ritters. It was as if a curtain had been drawn across the stage of pre-1945 Germany and only selected figures were allowed to make their appearance before it. But now, with Karl coming, it was as if the curtain had been lifted and one could see some of the cast—and some of the scenery.

Frau Nordern drummed her fingers on the table and then looked up as Herr Nordern came into the room. 'Finished?' she asked.

Herr Nordern shrugged as if to suggest that his work was never finished which was, in fact, the case. 'I smelt coffee.'

'Sorry father.' Erika poured out a mugful.

'You'd forgotten all about me,' Herr Nordern said. 'Never mind poor old Dad.'

'Don't talk nonsense,' Frau Nordern said. 'Drink your coffee.'

Herr Nordern meekly obeyed, and took a small tot of plum brandy with it. He lighted one of his small cigars. 'Talking about Karl?'

'Who else?' Frau Nordern said.

'He fought in a duel!' Despite herself, Erika was fascinated by the thought of that bland figure slashing away with a huge sword.

'Oh yes,' Herr Nordern's voice was colder than before. 'They did that in the old days, the aristocracy, but they took good care not to get hurt. Don't think it was like those romances on the television. They were padded up and they had masks on so that only their cheeks were exposed and they had to stand still, hacking away at each other with sabres over ridiculous points of honour. Huh, barbarism! It was nothing to be proud of.'

'No, father, of course not.' Erika was contrite, ashamed of her sudden interest in duelling. 'I'm sorry.'

'There's no need to apologise,' Frau Nordern said sharply. 'Omi is bound to want to talk about Karl. I do myself,' she said, with a flash of defiance.

'Did I say you shouldn't?' Herr Nordern said.

'Well, no.'

'So.' Herr Nordern stubbed out his cigar. 'I just don't want your getting any romantic rubbish into your head, Erika. The *Junker* were ready to join up with Hitler when it suited them, remember that, and to smash the working class. Anyway, bedtime.'

'All right.' Frau Nordern was subdued. 'Where is that Paul?'

'He's probably on the *S-Bahn* now,' Herr Nordern said.

'Hanging about Alexanderplatz, more likely,' Frau Nordern said. 'I'll give him a piece of my mind when he gets in.'

Erika collected the mugs, washed them, made her goodnights, and went into her bedroom. When she had undressed she went to the window. Heavy snow was falling, huge swirling flakes spinning against the street lights. How strange it was, Karl coming from the past, his dapper air of well-being and affluence evoking those days when the von Ritters and von Brombergs had lorded it over acres—a strange and eerie contrast to the memories of war and death which he had brought with him. . . .

The night train moaned, the front door rattled as Paul crept home, the owl hooted in the beech tree, Omi gave a little uncertain snort, and Erika joined her in sleep.

Chapter 6

HER MOTHER'S rap on the door woke Erika. Omi was already awake, smiling as Erika got up.

'It wasn't a dream,' she asked, 'was it?'

'No.' Erika smiled back. 'It wasn't a dream.'

The family did its usual morning minuet around the flat. Having put the coffee on, Frau Nordern disappeared into the bedroom to dress, Erika darted into the bathroom before her father could claim his rights there, poured the coffee when he did, and was laying the table when Paul made a belated, dishevelled entry.

'What was he like?' Paul demanded, without preamble.

Erika laid out bread, jam, cheese, ham. 'Nice. Very smart. White leather jacket, real American jeans, cowboy boots.'

'Yes?' Paul's eyes widened.

'Yes. Did you get the records he brought you?'

'Records! For me?'

'Plenty. Rock groups. British and American.'

'Ah!' Paul threw his hands in the air. 'Where are they?'

'Mother has them. Ask her.'

'Terrific!' Paul said. 'Wonderful!' But he thought it less wonderful when, as his mother bustled in and he asked for them, he got a withering rebuke.

'Rock records! Do you think Karl would bring you such rubbish? Are you going insane?'

'But she—' Paul rounded on Erika only to be sharply cut off.

'Never mind Erika. Just don't you forget to bring your technical-drawing book home tonight. Your father wants to look at those marks for himself.'

Paul, who had fondly imagined that the passing of the week-end would have somehow made that topic vanish, was taken aback by this onslaught, and any further protest he might have made was blocked by the appearance of his father who gave emphatic approval to Frau Nordern's demand, and who further added that he did not want to listen to idiotic chatter about rock records—or anything else—while he was having his breakfast, thus squashing both his children.

Breakfast was a brief meal in the Nordern household, and before Omi was dressed, the plates were washed and stacked and the family were struggling into their overcoats. Herr Nordern had to go out of Berlin for a meeting and was taking his car. Looking at the snowy streets he said, somewhat reluctantly, that he would drop his wife off at work, and his children at school, for that one day only.

'Two minutes,' he said, and since, when he said two minutes he meant it to the last second, and if you missed that second that meant, instead of going in a car, freezing at the bus-stop, he was taken with the utmost seriousness and all conversation stopped—even Uncle Karl being forgotten—as brief-cases were gathered up, Omi kissed goodbye, and the rush downstairs took place.

There was the usual breathless, nerve-racking crisis as the second-hand Lada coughed and spluttered, died, whined, and coughed again, but the indignity, not unknown, of the Norderns' pushing the car was avoided as it settled for starting, and they belched their way down Klara-Lettkin-Strasse.

Although it meant an inconvenient detour, Herr Nordern had to drop his wife off first. He ground down the main road, busy with heavy lorries feeding the factories in Hain, and then, to the accompaniment of gasps from Frau Nordern, never the most tranquil of passengers, pulled into Siegfriedstrasse, passed the Lindenhof Children's Hospital, and stopped in a warren of flats at the bureau where Frau Nordern dealt with her mothers.

Frau Nordern heaved herself out of the front seat and, as Erika wriggled forward to take her place, hissed, 'Erika, don't forget to ask Fräulein Silber about that man. Paul, don't you dare forget that exercise book, and if you don't have a good mark you won't come to the Palast.' And, to all and sundry and totally unnecessarily, 'Remember Uncle Karl tonight.'

She slammed the door and, as nothing in the old Lada worked the first time, slammed it again. Herr Nordern drove off, the windscreen wipers whining feebly as they scraped ineffectually at the plastered snow on the glass.

Herr Nordern cursed their inefficiency as he peered through the windscreen, then said out of the corner of his mouth, 'Don't take this Fräulein Silber stuff too seriously. Nothing to get worried about.'

'I'm not worried,' Erika said, not altogether truthfully.

'Good.' Herr Nordern tooted at a couple of teenagers on scooters who were wobbling precariously across the road. 'It's not like the old days, you know.'

'The old days?'

'Yes.' Herr Nordern pulled up at the traffic-lights on Lenin Allee and fished a cigar out of his pocket. 'There were times, back in the fifties, when you had to look over your shoulder every ten minutes and watch how you spoke and there's no denying it. I've seen people jump at their own shadows. But that's over. As long as you're a good citizen the authorities won't bother you.'

He let the gears in as the lights changed and a huge lorry loomed over the back of the car and growled menacingly. 'But ask Fräulein Silber anyway, it will ease your mother's mind.'

He half smiled and then fell silent as he threaded through the traffic and pulled up at the corner of the school, letting Erika and Paul out, not forgetting a final ominous warning to his son, before he roared off in a huge cloud of exhaust smoke.

Paul had already joined the gang of slightly raffish students who, even in the worst of weather, hung about outside the school until the last possible moment. As Erika pushed her way through them, ignoring the inevitable, mildly salacious remarks, Paul was in the middle of a group talking excitedly: 'Terrific, a real big shot from the West. Rich!' Erika tried to catch his eye, failed, shrugged, and walked through the glass doors of the Egon Schultz school.

The school was a standard ten year polytechnic and,

although it was dedicated to the memory of a member of the Border Police who, it was claimed, had been murdered by agents from the West, it had a distinct, although unobtrusive, leaning towards pupils like Erika and Paul, the children of government functionaries. There were two leaving points, at eighteen for university or, ominously, at sixteen for a vocational school or work. Erika was in the seventh year and Paul was, precariously, holding on to a place in the fifth year. Hence his parents' concern for his grades.

A warning bell pealed as Erika walked through the crowded hall under the eyes of Marx, Lenin and the President of the G.D.R. who stared down from huge portraits. She glanced at the notice-board which was crowded with appeals from the various school clubs to JOIN THEM NOW, and from the Free German Youth movement an exhortation with more than a hint of desperation, to support it, walked past an improbably idealised bust of the late Egon Schultz, and into the huge cloakroom.

Erika had a locker next to her friend, Rosa, who dashed in at that moment.

'Late this morning,' Rosa said. 'The snow, brrr! Done all your homework? Russian! Who made up that language?'

She rattled on cheerfully as other pupils bawled and bellowed and jostled each other, some trying to get out and their tardy colleagues trying to get in. The bell pealed again, a final imperative call, bringing in the loafers from the gates and choking the cloakroom even further.

'Come on.' Rosa took Erika's hand and drove through the mob like an ice-breaker. In the Hall she turned, rolled her eyes, pointed to a poster urging the pupils to remember their socialist duty and study hard, and dashed up the stairs.

Erika went to her class-room and her first tribute to her socialist duty which was a maths lesson. Her next, where Rosa rejoined her, was compulsory Russian, a lack-lustre lesson, although pupils with an eye to their future ploughed doggedly through it. But there was an appreciable lightening of the atmosphere in the third lesson in which a Herr Voss, one of the few male teachers in the school, took German literature. Voss was an easy-going man in his fifties, coasting to retirement. He was ready to joke, to turn a blind eye to minor transgressions of discipline, was not too heavy-handed marking grammar, and he had a knack of making every member of the class feel that they had something of value to add to the lesson. So it was an agreeable time, leading to the midday break.

'Off you go, *Kinder.*' Voss waved his dismissal. 'Don't leave anything behind: jewels, bottles of wine, valuable notes on the Russian Five Year Plan of 1935 and *don't* make a racket outside the Principal's office.'

The class clattered out and made an undisciplined dash for the canteen. Erika took her time, disliking the hurly-burly and knowing, anyway, that Rosa would have saved her a place. And Rosa was there, on a good table by a radiator, with soup and rolls, fiercely defending a free chair against all comers. But she did not pay much attention to her lunch as she waved a spoon at Erika and said:

'And what is all this? Rich uncles coming from the West? Aha, you've been keeping him dark.'

Erika made an impatient gesture. 'How did you know about that? Oh—Paul. I suppose the whole school knows.'

'You can't blame him,' Rosa said. 'A rich uncle coming.'

'Not uncle. He's our great-uncle. My grandmother's brother.'

Rosa dismissed the genealogical details. 'What's he like?'

'Well,' Erika succumbed to the allure of telling about the wealthy, and faintly mysterious, Uncle Karl.

'So!' As Erika finished, Rosa clapped her hands. 'It's exciting. Like a novel. Oh yes—' she raised her finger— 'everyone has got relatives over there, and a lot of them are rich, but they haven't come back from the dead, have they? And he's taking you to the Palast! Have you been before?'

'No, it's terribly expensive.'

'I should say so. We had dinner there just after it was opened, and the bill! But, er, tell me,' Rosa dropped her voice, although that was hardly necessary in the tremendous din. 'Don't mind my asking, but did he bring you anything? You know, presents.'

Erika blinked. 'No, he didn't. I mean, he had whisky and cigars but nothing else. I don't mean for me—' she added quickly—'I don't care at all. But he didn't bring anything for Omi or Mother. . . .'

'Ah well,' with her usual cheery good nature Rosa dismissed the matter. 'I dare say he'll make up for it tonight at the Palast. Not that presents matter, anyway. I didn't mean that, you know.'

'Of course not,' Erika agreed, but, still, she was thoughtful. Gifts were important, flowers especially so in Germany in the winter. She herself would no more think of visiting a relative without taking some than she would miss a training session for a disco.

She was still thinking about the flowers as she sat in her class on German history, and her attention was somewhat lacking as the teacher, Frau Gerhardt, delved into the intricacies of the Class Struggle in Germany in the days of Bismarck.

'And so,' Frau Gerhardt concluded, 'in the late 1840s the new German capitalists allied themselves with the *Junker* in order to defeat the democratic aspirations of the working class. Next week we shall see how this alliance led to German Imperialism and the Prussian-Austrian War. Dismiss.'

The class rose quietly, and left quietly, too, as Frau Gerhardt was a ferocious disciplinarian.

'Just like those old *Junker*,' Fritz Kott, a friendly class-mate of Erika's, whispered as they left and she was so abstracted that she did not feel the usual blend of defensiveness and pride which remarks about the *Junker* usually aroused in her. And then it dawned on her. 'Of course,' she thought, 'Uncle Karl could not have known that we were the Norderns he was looking for and he would hardly have wanted to wander around Berlin calling on other Norderns with his arms full of gifts. How stupid of me not to have realised that.' And feeling more cheerful she went down the covered way which led to the gymnasium.

The gym was big, superbly equipped and immaculately maintained, because, whatever else the German Democratic Republic stinted money on, it was not sport. At the far end of the gym, surrounded by a circle of adoring girls, Fräulein Silber was doing amazing things on the parallel bars. As Erika joined the group she somersaulted backwards on to the floor and, as piped ballet music drifted through the gym, she led the group through a long series of complicated warm-up exercises before taking them upstairs to where a running-track had been ingeniously slotted in at the foot of the spectators' seats.

'Ten laps,' Fräulein Silber said. 'Long strides, even pacing. We're not after world records.'

She pipped on her whistle and the girls set off, their feet drumming on the hessian covered track but not drowning out Fräulein Silber's commands:

'Greta, keep your head up . . . Myra, arms higher . . . Eva, lengthen your stride. . . .'

Round the track went the girls but Erika was only half-aware of Fräulein Silber's instructions for every time she came to the east corner of the gallery she was reminded of the silent man who had sat so motionlessly in the darkness there a mere two days ago.

A final blast from the whistle and the girls went down into the gym for the serious, the real and earnest object of the session, the high jump.

For such a basic human activity the jump was a surprisingly complex affair. The curved run-up for each girl had to be measured in centimetres, the bar endlessly adjusted and readjusted, and the take-off point altered with it, and there were the interminable series of false starts, inseparable from high jumping, and which led to a barrage of reprimands from Fräulein Silber.

But the class settled down, took their turns, and, one by one were eliminated as the black and white bar edged upwards, until only Erika was left, the undisputed star, but the not wholly willing centre of attraction for, despite the lesson drummed into the girls' heads that life in the G.D.R. was *communal*, that all had to be shared, triumph and tragedy alike, she had a distinct feeling that not all the lesser stars were totally displeased when she failed a jump, and that the applause when she cleared the bar was, from some of her comrades, lacking somewhat in sincerity.

The practice continued for two hours until Fräulein Silber called a halt and the group went into a somewhat tedious fifteen minutes of analysis and criticism, of each other and themselves—although not of Fräulein Silber—and in which, Erika thought, some of the girls criticised others' failures with more relish than they criticised their own.

But that, too, came to an end and the class was dismissed, except for Erika.

'You've got talent, Erika,' Fräulein Silber said. 'Real talent. And you've got courage—no, don't be modest—not everyone could come back from a fall like yours, but just now . . . you weren't jumping well at all. Let me finish—' she held up her hand—'a month from now you will be jumping in the Indoor Championships and you could win, be Berlin Indoor Champion, but not the way you were jumping this afternoon. You simply weren't concentrating properly. Now is there anything on your mind? Any worries? You can tell me. That's what I'm here for.'

'Well. . . .' Erika hesitated.

'Go on,' Fräulein Silber was encouraging, sympathetic.

Erika took a deep breath. 'I told my mother about that man.'

'Man?' Fräulein Silber frowned. 'What man?'

'The man up there,' Erika gestured to the gallery. 'The man who was watching me when I was training.'

Fräulein Silber's face tightened and for an uneasy moment Erika thought that she was going to deny that there had been a man there, but instead she said, 'Yes. What about him?'

Erika blinked. Whatever response she had expected, this wasn't it and she was at a loss to know what to say next. 'Well,' she faltered, 'it's just that my mother said I was to ask you who he was.'

'Did she?' Fräulein Silber was peremptory. 'What has it got to do with your mother?'

Erika was even more confused. She shrugged and opened her hands. After all, what really did it have to do with her mother?

'Has she a complaint?' Fräulein Silber asked.

Erika wasn't sure whether her mother had a complaint or not. 'She just wanted to know.'

'Know what? What is there to know?'

Erika was worse than confused. She felt foolish, a real idiot. She could hardly ask what she knew her mother wanted her to ask, whether the man was a scout from the Ministry of Sport, and so she said nothing at all.

Fräulein Silber stared at her then clicked her tongue. 'If your mother has a complaint, Erika, she must write to the Principal. Now it's time that you changed.'

She waved dismissal, but in a mild flare of rebellion, fuelled by the thought of what her mother would say if she returned home without the mystery solved, Erika stood her ground.

'It's not a complaint, Fräulein. Just a question.'

'A question?' Fräulein Silber's voice was raised, almost shrill. 'And what gives you the right to ask questions?'

'Fräulein Silber!' Erika was deeply shocked.

Fräulein Silber changed abruptly, her shoulders dipped and she patted Erika's arm. 'Of course. I'm very sorry, Erika. I'm afraid that I've had a tiring day. But really, all enquiries about the school have to go through the Principal. Come on now.'

She put her arm around Erika's shoulders and walked her to the showers. 'Just concentrate on your jumping and don't worry about anything. Good-night now.'

Twenty minutes later Erika was standing at the bus-stop with Paul. It had stopped snowing but it was bitterly cold and the empty street was bleak and depressing, fitting Erika's mood which, despite Fräulein Silber's remarks, was none too bright.

Paul, however, was cheerful. 'Some night tonight,' he said through his scarf. 'The Palast!' He sang a few words from an ancient pop song he had heard on West German radio: '"Down town, people are crazy 'bout down town". Lots of foreigners get in the Palast,' he said. 'Big shots, chicks, broads.'

'Don't use those words,' Erika said.

'Why not?' Paul asked. 'There's no law against them.'

'They're not nice,' Erika said. 'American slang.' She stamped her feet against the cold. 'Anyway, they're out of date.'

'Huh, how do you know?' Paul muttered, but not confidently.

Erika gave a superior smile and as the bus finally loomed out of the darkness, threw another dart. 'Mother will want to see your exercise book when we get home.'

But that particular dart did not sting, because when they did get home Paul produced his book with an airy flourish and his mother was too preoccupied to give it more than a cursory glance, thus missing Paul's artful forgery which had changed a thirty-one minus, which meant fail, to sixty-four plus which meant a respectable, but not overdone, pass. And even Fräulein Silber's instruction that Frau Nordern should write to the Principal about the man in the gallery, provoked only a token explosion of anger and an ominous threat that Frau Nordern would *see* the Principal—and that Herr Nordern would be there too, although that addition was received coldly by him when he got home. 'A fuss about nothing,' he said, as he went into the bedroom to change.

Omi was already changed, and had been since early afternoon. She sat in her high-backed chair, clad in a dark blue dress with a mere trace of embroidery around the collar. Erika tried to persuade her to wear a different gown, one more suited to the festive occasion, but Omi was unmoved.

'No, my Dear,' she said. 'I'm not one of those creatures who dress as if they were girls. Why, when I was young, women my age wore black—always—and with whalebone corsets.' She smiled. 'That is one advantage of progress. No, child, Karl will want to see me dressed fittingly, like an old Prussian. Yes.'

She nodded, as if bowing to the ghostly *Junker* of the past, and, sitting upright in her distinguished dress, its high collar showing off the fine features of her proud face, she might indeed have been, still, mistress of a Prussian estate, and the carnage and revolution of the past half-century might never have taken place.

By 7.00 the Norderns were ready: Frau Nordern handsome in green, Erika in a red woollen dress, Herr Nordern in his best blue suit, and Paul, for once, out of his jeans and crammed into a suit, too.

Herr Nordern looked at his family with a certain pride. 'Good,' he said. 'A real German family. As good as any in America, or anywhere else. A glass of wine to celebrate.'

The wine was ceremoniously downed and then Herr Nordern and Paul went out to start the Lada. The others sat in a tense silence, spirits rising as the engine spluttered into life, falling as it died away, nerves stretched as it whined, relaxed as it coughed, and coughed again, and finally, with a gigantic, triumphant roar, burst into life.

Five was a tight fit, but discomfort was forgotten as they drove down the arrow-straight Frankfurter Allee, on to Karl Marx Allee, circled Alexanderplatz, and came, at last, to where, under the shadow of the Cathedral, and crouching by the River Spree, the Palast Hotel raised its chastely neon-garlanded head.

Chapter 7

THE PALAST had been built for the tourist trade but there were no restrictions on citizens of the G.D.R. using it, and some did, although not many—the price saw to that. Having dinner there was an *event* reserved for special occasions. Erika and Paul had never been in the place, and neither had Omi although, unlike them, she was unimpressed by the golden-brown décor, brushed aluminium fittings, Scandinavian lighting, and the faint whine of piped music which gave the lobby the air of an under-used airport.

In the bar, where they took seats while waiting for Karl, Omi was openly critical. 'In the old days,' she said, 'in the great hotels, there was nothing but solid mahogany and brass, and the chandeliers were real.'

'This is solid teak,' Herr Nordern said mildly, tapping the table to attract a waiter.

'I think it's nice,' Frau Nordern said. 'The colours are so restful, and look—' her voice sank to a confidential whisper—'at the bar.'

Five pairs of eyes swivelled to the bar and four pairs swivelled back, Paul's remaining transfixed by the sight of two inoffensive Japanese business men having a drink.

Herr Nordern waved for a waiter. 'How do you like it, *Liebchen*?'

Erika liked it very much. 'But it's quieter than I thought it would be,' she said.

'It will liven up.' Herr Nordern waved again for a waiter and cursed. 'I'll get the drinks myself.'

He stood up and Paul rose with him.

'Where do you think you're going?' Frau Nordern demanded.

'Toilet,' Paul muttered.

'Yes, well don't be all night, and don't go wandering around the hotel. And don't go buying Club Cola.'

'I've got no money anyway,' Paul said dolefully as he wandered away.

'No money! He had five marks on Saturday.' But Frau Nordern's indignation was half-hearted as she leaned back and patted her hair. 'It's two years since I was in here. When Hans and I came to that reception for the Ethiopian Trade Delegation. Not that they had any money to buy anything. But we went downstairs to the night-club and danced. They were good at that,' she added, a little dreamily.

Omi smiled. 'The first dance I went to was in a hotel—the Adlon. Ah! that was *luxe*. All Europe used it. It was a wedding reception. Cousin Friedrich had married Elisabeth von Traubenberg. He was in the Foreign Office and lots of people from the *Corps Diplomatique* came, *and* Prince Otto. I danced with an Englishman. They had such manners, the English. They were *gentlemen*,' she used the English word. 'But it has all gone. Yes, all gone.'

'Yes,' Frau Nordern echoed her mother's regret for the vanished past with its missed joys. 'But still, it *is* nice here, dreamlike somehow.'

Herr Nordern appeared, undreamlike, wrathful, followed by a waiter who began to casually pour out wine until sharply halted.

'I'm supposed to taste that,' Herr Nordern said. He took a sip, and, a little reluctantly, nodded approval. The waiter shrugged as if to say, 'What was the fuss about?' put the bottle down, none too gently, and ambled away.

Herr Nordern growled. 'The service in here! All the waiters hanging about hoping to serve foreigners and get big tips. Still, this wine isn't bad. Not bad at all.'

He drank and lighted a cigar. Omi looked at him disapprovingly and, to Erika's secret amusement, did something otherwise unheard of and ticked him off.

'You shouldn't smoke with wine,' she said.

'Ach, so they say. It's enjoyable though, and while we're

here let's enjoy ourselves. It isn't often we get out together.'

'Omi was talking about her first dance, at the Adlon,' Erika said.

'That place,' Herr Nordern said, contemptuously.

'But your father knew it?' Omi said.

Herr Nordern gave her a wry glance. 'Carpenters didn't go to places like the Adlon before the War, Omi. Not like Bodo, he's in and out of these places day and night. But—' he waved the point aside. 'It's livening up now, Erika.'

The hotel was, a little. Guests, mainly foreign, were coming down for dinner, G.D.R. citizens, looking more prosperous than might be expected, were coming from the street, some of the women in fashions more appropriate to Paris or New York than Berlin and causing Frau Nordern's eyebrows to rise as they swished by. Three vastly exotic Asians, attended by a whole flock of officials, came in; some shady characters who looked as if they would buy or sell anything, including their own mothers, made a bee-line for the bar, and, stepping lightly, in came Uncle Karl.

'Ah!' Omi, facing the door, raised her hands, her face suffused with joy. 'He's come!'

Come he had. He joined them, shedding his beautiful overcoat and revealing an immaculate flannel suit and a silk Burgundy-red tie glowing against a pale blue shirt. His pink, manicured hands clasped Omi's, and his pink, benevolent face gleamed at the family.

'Am I late?' he said. 'Forgive me. I was delayed at the Ministry. But here we are, and how charming the ladies look. And this—?' turning as Paul appeared.

'Our son, Paul,' Frau Nordern said with a doting air.

Karl shook Paul's hand enthusiastically. 'What a splendid young fellow. We must have a long talk one day. But first, a drink to celebrate. Yes, my dear Hans, I see you have wine but permit me.'

He clicked his fingers and the reluctant waiter, reluctant for Herr Nordern that is, popped up like a jack-in-a-box.

'Champagne,' Karl said, 'with tulip glasses, and the menu and the wine list.'

Omi nodded approvingly. 'Tulip glasses for champagne. That is correct. Of course, Karl would know that.'

Karl blew her a kiss from his polished nails. 'Of course *we* know that,' drawing the Norderns into an intimate, privileged circle. 'But I'm afraid that not all waiters do, nowadays. Although I must say, I have been agreeably surprised by the service here.'

'Surprised?' Herr Nordern said.

Karl nodded. 'I know, Hans, you think that I expected slovenliness, inefficiency, surliness, the usual tale we hear in the West; the inevitable results of socialism—no incentive to work and so on. Well, I won't deny that I did expect that, but it has been quite different. As we can see.'

The Norderns could see, as they were suddenly surrounded by a whole flock of waiters bringing champagne, the tulip glasses, the menu, and the wine list.

To the agreeable pop of a champagne cork, Karl scanned the menu, his face serious. 'Please,' he said. 'Choose.'

The Norderns sank solemnly behind their menus. Erika gazed at hers a little bemused. The forty or so items were rather more than the school canteen offered. She peered covertly at Paul who was gazing blankly at the puddings. She poked a finger at random at his menu.

'All the American stars have that,' she whispered.

Paul's eyes widened until he saw that the dish was sausage, of which he had more than enough at home.

Karl was talking intimately to the waiter and nodding approval. He looked around the table. 'Dear sister? Helga?'

Omi and Frau Nordern gave their orders, Erika said firmly that she would have what her father ordered while Paul, mildly treasonable, said that he would have the same as Uncle Karl.

'Excellent,' Karl bent his head over the wine list, throwing out suggestions to the Norderns, all of which were accepted. Then, the business finished, he sighed with satisfaction and raised his glass with a flourish.

'To you,' he said. 'Dear sister, dear family.'

Tears welled up in Omi's eyes. Karl tutted and produced a magnificent handkerchief.

'Now, my Dear,' he said. 'No tears. Remember the old days, the old ways. What would Father have said!'

'Ah, Father,' for a moment the tears threatened to spill

63

down Omi's cheeks but she dabbed them away. 'You are quite right, Karl. It isn't Prussian.'

Erika glanced obliquely at her father but he seemed quite unconcerned, lounging in his chair and sipping his champagne.

'Of course I'm right,' Karl said. 'And after all, you can't tell me anything if you are crying, can you?'

He wagged a coy finger at Omi and not for the first time Erika felt a flicker of dislike for her uncle. She had not liked his manner in the flat, and now this . . . it was, well, it was almost *ogling*; Karl was behaving like the actors in the worst old romantic films, who courted simpering girls, and, what was the word? Omi was responding, behaving almost coquettishly.

But Karl turned his arch attentions away from Omi and listened to a waiter who was whispering deferentially in his ear.

'Yes,' Karl waved the waiter away and stood up. 'Shall we dine?'

The Norderns roused themselves and led by Karl, with Omi on his arm, moved in a stately procession into the leafy, subaqueous elegance of the restaurant where they were greeted, deferentially, by more waiters and the ripple of a piano. Karl whispered to the pianist as they went by and, as the group took their seats, with a flourish the player moved into a banal medley.

Karl smiled. 'A selection from musical comedies of . . . a long time ago. You don't mind, Paul? You will allow us old folk a touch of nostalgia for one evening?'

Paul, who didn't have the faintest idea what Karl was talking about, mumbled something indistinguishable, tried his soup, and looked as though he wished he hadn't. 'Tastes funny,' he said.

'A touch of tarragon,' Karl said. 'A herb, you know. Perhaps it is an acquired taste, ha! ha! Mine is excellent, I must say. And everyone else?'

Reassured he turned to Omi. 'And now, my Dear. Your story.'

'Oh,' Omi shook her head. 'Not now, Karl. It isn't the time or the place.'

'But of course it is.' Karl dabbed his lips with his napkin. 'You can't tell me everything that has happened to you but give me an indication.' Again, to Erika's annoyance, he adopted his arch manner: 'I've told you all my secrets! Come, I'm sure that Hans won't mind, or the children. Please, just for me.'

Omi hesitated then, bolt upright, her soup disregarded, she said, not without a challenging look at Herr Nordern. 'It starts in 1945, too. My Erich was missing and the Russians were breaking into East Prussia. I took Helga to Königsberg. They said that there were ships there to take us to the Reich, but they never sailed. Then I met General Friedländer—'

'Ah!' Karl beamed. 'Friedländer! So he was there! Of course he came out of retirement in '41. Well, well, so you met him.' He might have been talking of some old crony heard of playing bridge in an obscure provincial club instead of a general battling to save a besieged city against overwhelming odds. 'But go on.'

'Yes, he promised to help us, and he did.'

'He would,' Karl said to Herr Nordern. 'He was that sort of fellow. He would do anyone a good turn.'

'He put us on a convoy heading west,' Omi continued. 'There was a corridor still open, but we couldn't get through. The convoy turned back but I didn't. No.'

There was a note of genuine, iron resolution in Omi's voice and Erika felt a prickle of pride for her.

'No,' Omi said. 'I knew Königsberg was finished, I'm not a general's daughter for nothing! I went south to Bromberg. Home.'

Erika had heard some of the tale before, although never in such detail as now, as, prodded by Karl, Omi told of the trek with her daughter through the desperate army of refugees, and the scarcely less desperate rearguard of the Wehrmacht; through endless forest in the bitter sleet and mud, an endless trudge to an elusive safety with, always, on their heels the terror from the East.

The waiters came again, plates were changed, wine brought, approved of, the main course came and Erika bent over her Wiener Schnitzel feeling profoundly uneasy at this talk of war. It was as if a foul pool had been disturbed and rotting fragments from a rotten past were floating to the surface, and coming from the mouth of her grandmother the horrors had a more horrible immediacy. She peered over her wineglass at her mother. She who, almost inconceivably, had dragged the long miles with Omi, was nodding in confirmation of the tale. Paul was not listening, his attention divided between the mysteries of Chicken Kiev and the exotic doings of the restaurant. Her father seemed to be interested only in his meal, but Karl, his plate pushed half aside, his chin on his hand, was absorbed, gazing at Omi like a sorcerer and murmuring, 'Go on,' when she paused.

'We got to Bromberg,' Omi said. 'It was wrecked, looted, and the horses were gone,' her voice quavered momentarily but then the iron showed again. 'Some of the servants were still there, Heinrich, Mathilde, old Günther, and some of the villagers. Most of those were good to us—'

'Most?'

'Yes. Some of them were unfriendly. I didn't understand it. We had always been so good to them.'

'Hmm.' Karl skewered a mushroom with a savage prod of his fork, his face no longer benign, but predatory. 'You really must let me have their names some time. But then what happened?'

'The Russians came,' Omi said bleakly. 'And then the Poles.'

'Ah yes, the Poles. The border rectifications. Not perhaps totally unjust, my dear Hans?'

'No, no.' Herr Nordern spoke casually, almost absent-mindedly.

Karl snapped at a piece of chicken. 'My sister is bound to feel sadness.' He spoke as if the loss of East Prussia to Poland were a purely personal matter, affecting the Brombergs alone. 'You will understand, our family home gone. Our home and our homeland. It is understandable.'

'Of course it is.' Herr Nordern put down his fork. 'Who said it wasn't?'

'No one, no one at all, Hans. But those territories . . . they did have a special place in the hearts of Prussians.'

'I'm Prussian,' Herr Nordern said.

'Of course.' Karl gave Herr Nordern a strange, oddly

calculating look then smiled his glittering smile. 'But of course you are. One forgets sometimes—allow me.'

He filled Herr Nordern's glass and, overriding Frau Nordern's protest that she had had quite enough alcohol, filled hers too, and Erika's and Paul's and Omi's, saying what were a couple of bottles of wine among Germans, and on such a night, and then prodding Omi into the rest of her story.

'So, the Poles came and took everything and we left, and then we met Hans's uncle.' She looked at Karl almost appealingly, 'He was good to us.' She turned to Frau Nordern, 'He was, wasn't he?'

'Yes,' Frau Nordern said. 'He was. He was good to us.'

It was another story Erika had heard before, not that it lost anything in the retelling. The long, dragging year in Bromberg, forever under suspicion by the Russians, bullied by the Polish settlers ready to pay off old scores, the threat of arrest always hanging over Omi, the dangerous journey to the safety of the west and then, like a knight in armour, Herr Nordern's uncle coming to the rescue, fighting off two drunken Latvians who were attacking them, and then guiding them across the chaos of Eastern Europe, through the vast foodless, fireless, homeless migration of desperate millions. . . .

'And so,' Omi said, 'we came to Berlin, and we stayed together, and we survived.'

'And you survived.' Karl nodded approvingly, and nodded even more so as the waiter came with a frosted pineapple, a sight as rare for the Norderns as snow in July.

'A little treat,' Karl said, shaking kirsch over the fruit, 'And—' speaking softly—'another,' as the pianist played a melody.

Karl raised his glass. 'You know this song, sister.'

Not only Karl and Omi knew the song, all Germany, East and West knew it, too. Marlene Dietrich had sung it before the War and it had echoed across the Reich ever since. 'I have a trunk in Berlin.' The trunk containing not only clothes but all the mementoes of long gone years and symbolising all the losses Germany had suffered through its ruin.

They took their coffee in the lounge. Over a cigar and brandy, Karl asked Erika a few perfunctory questions about herself, some even more perfunctory ones of Paul, and then, in his ingratiating way excusing himself to Herr Nordern, turned again to Omi.

'And did you never,' he paused, picking his words with delicate care. 'Did you never think at all of . . . of going a little further west?'

Omi gave an uncharacteristic shrug. 'There wasn't much point. The West had its own problems then, and besides, there was Helga and Hans.'

Karl raised his hand. 'Say no more. I understand. Love!'

Frau Nordern blushed, and Erika blushed with her. Why, she didn't know except that there seemed something a little embarrassing in the thought of her father and mother having been in love like two young people.

'Well, why not?' Karl smiled again. 'And no doubt your work kept you here, Hans?'

'I *wanted* to stay here,' Herr Nordern said. 'I'm a socialist, always have been. Besides, I was at the university. I couldn't have afforded to go in West Germany.'

'I see.' Karl nodded. 'Of course, a great advantage of your way of life here. Most admirable. And now you are in a Ministry. I really must talk to you about your work there, and—' he paused dramatically—'and I am glad to be able to tell you that I shall have the time to do that. I find that my business here will keep me longer than I thought.'

He beamed as Omi gasped with pleasure. 'Tomorrow I have to go to Dresden for a few days but I shall be back. Believe me, I shall be back.'

He drained his glass and glanced at his watch. 'But for now. . . .'

The Norderns took the hint. Drinks were finished, coats brought, put on, and Karl led them smoothly to the door. But there Herr Nordern paused.

'Just one thing,' he said. 'Excuse my asking. . . .'

'Ask anything you want, my dear Hans,' Karl cried. 'I should be delighted.'

'Thank you.' Herr Nordern gazed solemnly at Uncle Karl. 'I just wondered about that soldier. The corporal whose identity you took when you were captured?'

'Yes?' Karl's silvery eyebrows arched.

'His family, did they ever know? I mean, it must have been a shock when . . . when they did find out—that he was dead, I mean.'

Benevolence, as radiant as the lights from the hotel spilling across the dark waters of the Spree, beamed from Karl. 'I'm glad you asked me that Hans,' he said. 'I really am. It shows, how can one put it? Yes, a truly human and humane attitude, exactly what I would expect, and hope for, from a relative. Yes, they knew—I saw them—I should say I saw the poor devil's mother. She was the only one of the family left. I met her and confessed everything. She was forgiving, understanding and forgiving. She saw the necessity for my deception.'

'Do you see her now?' Herr Nordern asked.

'Alas, no.' Karl sighed. 'I did see her regularly, and I helped her a little, money, sympathy, and so on . . . but the poor soul is dead now. Yes, dead and buried.'

'Dead and buried.'

'Yes,' Karl gave a half-smile, contriving to look wistful and cheerful at the same time. 'But now. . . .'

With a promise to Frau Nordern that he would indeed be honoured to attend the great party as soon as might be possible, Karl ushered the family to the revolving doors and there, with much kissing of hands, left them, they to step precariously through the frosty garden, he to wave at them from the golden warmth of the hotel.

Herr Nordern had cunningly parked the Lada on an incline and so it started with no more than a token roar of protest, as if angry at leaving the luxury of the Palast for the world of bad teeth, cheap anoraks, flimsy flats, and the ghost ridden streets of the dark city of Berlin.

Chapter 8

Despite a courageous rearguard action by Paul, the Norderns were in bed within minutes of getting home.

'We'll talk about it tomorrow,' Herr Nordern said firmly, closing the bedroom door, and as by tomorrow he meant tomorrow *night*, there wasn't much talk the next morning, either, especially as the family were late rising and so, ruefully, Herr Nordern said that he would drive them to work and school before going off to his office.

The office was in an annexe of the Ministry, tucked away behind Friedrichstrasse railway station, the rail crossing point between the two Berlins, and close to the haunted wasteland where the Bunker once held its evil inhabitants.

The office was an old building, pock-marked with scars from the War, and with its western windows bricked up in order, so the Government said, that spies in West Berlin could not peer in through telescopic lenses and discover the secrets of brown coal production in the G.D.R.

Herr Nordern signed his name in the register just before the ominous red line was drawn at 7.30, and went to his office which he shared with two other middling officials. One of them, Herr Müller, was already at his desk but the other desk was vacant.

'No Steinmark?' Herr Nordern said.

Müller shrugged. 'Still rummaging through the old archives in Dresden. Sooner him than me.'

'But we're doing his work,' Nordern said, testily. 'Odd though,' he added as he seated himself. 'Someone I know is going there today.'

'Yes?'

'A relative,' Herr Nordern said. Mildly boasting he added, 'We had dinner together in the Palast, last night.'

'Did you, you lucky old dog.' Müller grinned, and began sorting his mail, casually flicking through the papers and chucking most of them, unread, into his 'dealt with' basket.

He caught Herr Nordern's disapproving eye and grinned. 'It's only junk, ninety per cent of it anyway.' He held one up and read it aloud. '"Errors in the application of forms 1098/4, sub-sections 11a and 23.1." And it's not even to do with our department. I wonder if they get this stuff over there?' He jerked his head at the western wall—unmistakable because of the crude daub of plaster which hid what had once been a window. 'Anyway, I think that I'll sneak a coffee. Want one? Go on, help me increase my consumption by one hundred per cent.'

Herr Nordern was tempted, weakened, and fell. 'All right,' he said and turned to his work, not totally displeased at being called a lucky old dog. In fact, although he was suitably censorious of some of Müller's habits, he liked the young man who brought a light-hearted quality into the office, quite unlike the rather odious Steinmark, a secretive, sly person who was suspected of informing on his colleagues. Müller would never have slid off for coffee had Steinmark been present. And, although Müller was, perhaps, a little too light-hearted in his approach to his work, even that, Nordern thought, was not a bad thing; it was, he hoped, a sign that the G.D.R. was moving to a state where people *could* be cheerful, and that, after all, was the point behind all the sacrifices that had been made—were still being made, he reminded himself as he opened his mail, conscientiously reading every word.

Müller came back with the coffee, a secretary came in with a heap of files, both men settled down to their work, laboured steadily until 12.00, took their lunch in the office canteen, returned and worked again until, at 2.30, Nordern's telephone rang. It was the secretary of the Director of the Department telling him to report to the Director's office immediately.

'Back in a moment,' Nordern said. He went up three flights of steps to the Director's office, wondering what on earth the Director, a man he rarely saw, let alone spoke to, would want with him. He went into the office where the secretary, an elderly blonde, stared at him coldly, as though he had been dawdling, flicked the intercom and when it squawked told him that he could enter the inner sanctum.

Nordern took a deep breath and went in. Sitting behind a handsome beechwood desk, under a huge picture of the President of the G.D.R., was the Director, Herr Morgner, and Nordern's Section Head, Herr Nagel.

'Ah, Nordern.' The Director beckoned him.

Herr Nordern stepped forward and stood before the desk. On the desk was a file. His name was on it.

The Director tapped the desk. 'Comrade Nordern, I have to ask you a question. Please think carefully before you answer.'

'Of course,' Nordern's mouth felt unaccountably dry.

'Good. Then the question I put to you is this.' Oddly the Director sounded as anxious as Nordern felt. 'Have you done anything wrong?'

'Wrong?' Herr Nordern blinked. 'What sort of wrong?'

Even more oddly the Director did not answer, merely staring at his desk and tapping its polished surface.

'I don't understand,' Herr Nordern said.

'I mean,' the Director said, 'have you done anything to bring discredit to this Department?'

Herr Nordern was astonished. 'Certainly not. Why should you think . . .? What is this about?'

The Director stopped his tapping and looked up. 'The Police want to see you,' he said.

'The Police!' Herr Nordern stepped forward and placed his hands on the desk. 'Has there been an accident? My family?'

The Director shook his head. 'I really don't know, but I have a duty to my Department and I must know, now, if you have been involved in anything which might affect it.'

He paused, waiting for an answer which he did not get. 'Then you are to go to this Police Station at once and see this officer—' he pushed a paper across the table. 'Report back to me the moment you return. If you—' he chopped the rest of the sentence off, although Herr Nordern knew perfectly well what he had been about to say.

Herr Nordern grabbed the paper, nodded, turned on his

heel, and walked out. But at the door he was halted by the Director's voice.

'I very much hope there has not been an accident, Herr Nordern.'

Herr Nordern hurried to his office, ignored a startled Müller, snatched his coat and hat, charged down the stairs and got into his car. Only then did he look at the paper. It simply said, 'Ostkreuz Police Station. Werner.'

He wiped his mouth and switched on the ignition. In its eccentric way the Lada decided to start as smoothly as a Mercedes. Nordern drove up Friedrichstrasse and swung around Alexanderplatz on to the vastness of Karl Marx Allee. By the State Travel Bureau the road was up and there was an interminable traffic jam, giving Nordern a little time to think. Surely the summons couldn't be because of an accident to any of his family. They would have mentioned that on the phone, or sent a man round, or given the name of a hospital. . . . The traffic lurched forward for a few yards and halted again.

Herr Nordern cursed and banged his fist on the steering-wheel. He ran through his blameless existence. Nothing there, nothing at all—well, there was that matter of the second-hand magneto which had looked suspiciously new and which Bodo had got for him for what had seemed a huge sum. But that had been a year ago and, anyway, surely the Police wouldn't call a busy official away from his work over such a trivial matter—and then it came to him. It was Bodo. That was it he thought with a sudden, treacherous, relief. The Law had finally caught up with his brother and of course, the relief mixed with bitterness, he himself was going to be dragged into some sordid law case with the effects that would have on him and his family.

The traffic moved on again and Herr Nordern banged up a gear and drove along Frankfurter Allee until he swung right into Ostkreuz, and the Police Station.

The Station was shabbily built; not old, but already some of the tiles which made up an improbable picture of a smiling policeman had fallen off leaving him curiously, but more probably, blank-faced. Herr Nordern parked his car and, sweating a little, went inside where a casual duty officer took his name and waved him to a chair.

Nordern sat on the chair for fifteen minutes in the company of various shady characters, none of whom seemed perturbed at being there and in fact, kept up a cheery, slangy *badinage* with the policeman behind the desk who seemed not only to know them all by their first names but, to Herr Nordern's disgust, to be on amiable terms with them all.

Herr Nordern stared fixedly at a poster showing the Border Police nobly defending the Frontier and was mentally composing a letter to be sent to the newspaper *Neues Deutschland*, complaining about the Desk Officer, when he realised that his name was being called, had been several times, and that the Desk Officer was frowning at him as if *he* were a criminal.

To the accompaniment of knowing leers from the criminal element, Herr Nordern stood up and went into a small office where a uniformed lieutenant was sitting at a desk drinking coffee and a stocky man with bloodshot eyes in plain clothes was lounging on a hard chair, his feet on another, reading a sports magazine and smoking a large cigar.

'Take a seat,' the Lieutenant said. 'I.D.?'

Herr Nordern handed over his identity card. 'Is your name Werner?' he asked.

The Lieutenant nodded. 'Driving-licence?'

Herr Nordern fumbled in his wallet. 'What is this about, Lieutenant?'

Werner didn't answer. He opened a bulky register, ran his finger down a list of numbers, stopped, compared Herr Nordern's licence with one of the numbers, nodded to himself, lit a cigarette, and then deigned to look up. 'Were you out last night?' he said.

'Yes. Yes, I was.' Herr Nordern said.

'Driving?'

'Yes, I was driving.'

'Whereabouts?'

'I went to the Palast.'

'The Palast?' Werner raised an eyebrow.

'Yes,' Herr Nordern said stiffly. 'Nothing wrong with that, is there?'

"Course not. Wish I could go there myself.' Werner peered at his cigarette. 'Trying to stop. Do you smoke?'

'Yes, cigars.'

'They say that they're better for you than cigarettes. Light up if you want to.'

Nordern shook his head. 'I'd like to get this over with—whatever it is. I've lost an afternoon's work already.'

'Sorry about that,' Werner said. 'You aren't worried about anything, are you?'

'I certainly am not,' Herr Nordern said, not altogether truthfully. 'Why do you ask?'

'Well, you came here quickly enough, didn't you?'

'The message said I had to.'

'Oh,' Werner clicked his teeth. 'A mistake somewhere. Message got garbled I dare say. It's always happening!' He was silent for a moment, then, 'So?'

'So?' Herr Nordern said. 'I don't follow you.'

'So you went to the Palast, but you didn't stay there all night, I suppose.'

'No, of course not.'

'So what did you do?'

Herr Nordern felt a flash of resentment. He took a deep breath and reminded himself that he was a not completely unimportant servant of the State and that he had friends in, if not high positions, then highish as it were. 'I went home,' he said. 'And I ask you again, what is the meaning of these questions? I have a right to know.'

Werner smiled sceptically, as if he had heard that one before. 'Just tell me the route you took going home from the Palast.'

For a moment, but only for a moment, Herr Nordern was tempted to say that he would answer no more questions until he knew why the questions were being put. Instead he docilely went through the journey.

'Anyone with you?'

'Yes.'

'Being?' Werner picked up a pen and held it over a sheet of paper in a way Herr Nordern found unnerving.

'Wife, mother-in-law, two children. All at my address.'

'Hmm.' Werner drew a neat line under his list. 'Been drinking, had you?'

'A little.' To his dismay, Herr Nordern found that he was

sweating. He had read of such a thing: people sweating when questioned by police even if, as he was, completely innocent of anything. And he had read that the Police saw sweat as a sign of guilt, or at least a guilty conscience. 'A little,' he repeated, acutely conscious that he had, in fact, drunk rather a lot. 'Yes, I had wine with dinner . . . of course. Now will you tell me what this is about—please,' he added, the 'please' sounding in his ears unpleasantly like a whine.

The plain-clothes man suddenly stood up and went to the office door. 'Tell him,' he said as he left the room, his voice sounding patronising, as if to say, put the poor devil out of his misery.

Werner stubbed out his cigarette and lit another. 'There was an accident last night. On Strausberger Platz. A motorcyclist was knocked off his bike. He's seriously ill. Someone saw it—the accident—and got the number of the car. Thinks he did, anyway, because he gave us your number. Said it was a Lada, too. Wasn't yours, was it?'

Relief flooded through Herr Nordern. 'It certainly was not,' he said.

'But you were there, you just said so. And it was about the time you would have been going home.'

'I can't help that,' Herr Nordern said, relief making him bold. 'And let me tell you, Lieutenant, if there had been an accident I would have reported it immediately.'

'Sure,' Werner said in his dry, sceptical way. 'Well, we'll take a statement and then you can go.' He opened a drawer, closed it, opened another—'There should be some forms,' he said. 'Ah, here they are.'

He handed Herr Nordern a form with a sinister police heading. 'Just write down briefly what you did last night, the way you went home, and say that you weren't involved in any accident to the best of your knowledge. Then sign it and put the date.'

Nordern scribbled away. As he was finishing the plain-clothes man came back with three coffees and gave Herr Nordern one. 'Soothe your nerves,' he said.

Herr Nordern finished his statement and handed the form to Werner who casually glanced at it. 'Sorry about the mystery,' he said, 'but there's a way of doing these things. Has to apply to everyone.'

'Of course,' Herr Nordern was effusive. 'Absolutely correct. But about this witness?'

Werner was dismissive. 'Probably caught sight of a couple of numbers on the plate and made the rest up. You'd be amazed how often that happens, hey, Otto?'

'Too true.' The plain-clothes man pulled his chair up to the desk and sat down. 'It probably wasn't even a Lada. Eye witnesses!' He grinned in a friendly way at Nordern. 'So you were at the Palast? A celebration?'

'Yes, a relative of mine turned up so we had dinner there.'

'Oh?' Werner looked at the form. 'You don't mention him here.'

'No.' Herr Nordern shrugged. 'I didn't think it was necessary. He wasn't with us in the car.'

'Not staying with you?' Werner asked.

'No, he's at the Palast.'

Otto whistled. 'A big shot, hey?'

'Not really,' Herr Nordern said. 'He's a business man. From the West.'

'Is he now?' Otto said. 'A business man. . . .'

'Oh.' Herr Nordern was anxious to explain. 'He's here having discussions with the Government. He's a technical expert.'

'Yes,' Otto nodded. 'But why were you having dinner with him?'

'Ah, I said, he's a relative, my mother-in-law's brother. We lost touch after the War.'

'We?' Otto said.

'I mean him and my mother-in-law.'

There was a long moment of silence which Werner broke. 'That happened to a lot of us, one way or another. Just put his name down.'

'What for?' Herr Nordern asked.

'Oh, you never know,' Werner said. 'He can testify that you weren't drunk when you left the hotel.'

'I don't see that it's necessary,' Herr Nordern said, 'and he's in Dresden, anyway.' But he wrote the name down, just the same.

Werner looked at the altered form. 'Bromberg,' he said.

'Karl Bromberg. Well, that's all right.' He nodded at Otto who in turn nodded at Herr Nordern.

'I can go?' Herr Nordern asked.

'Of course,' Werner said.

'And there will be nothing further? I mean, it's over?'

'Hmmm.' Werner was judicial. 'Can't actually say that. If the witness insists that it was your car we might need to look at it, and take statements from your family. Have to wrap the case up properly, you know.'

'My car is outside,' Herr Nordern said. 'You can look at it now.'

'I already have,' Otto said. He guffawed. 'There's more bumps than smooth bits.'

Herr Nordern flushed. 'All right. It's an old car.'

'No offence,' Otto said, sounding as if he didn't care whether Nordern took offence or not.

Herr Nordern stood up. 'I'll go then,' he said.

'All right.' Werner nodded casually. 'Drive carefully.'

Herr Nordern left the Police Station, which was fuller now, with more clients arriving. It was dark and bitterly cold, the snow turning to ice. He slithered to his car and then hesitated. Off the street, running down between grim blocks of pre-war flats, was a narrow alley, and at the end of the alley was a pink neon sign which spelled out B.A.R. Herr Nordern rarely, if ever, drank before his evening meal, but he found that he wanted a drink, and wanted one badly. He hesitated for a second and then walked down the alley.

The bar was not one Herr Nordern would have chosen, had he a choice. It was long and shabby, with splintered wooden booths full of unsavoury men and women, all drinking hard.

Herr Nordern took a seat, ordered a rum, and looked at his fellow-drinkers with distaste and contempt. The criminal element, he thought. Crooks, ne'er-do-wells, thieves, prostitutes, riff-raff, antisocial elements of all sorts and types. Even the all-powerful State, in thirty years, had not succeeded in wiping them out. Here they were, brazenly boozing the afternoon away and, by the looks of them, had been drinking the day away, the whole week, probably. It was, he thought, just the sort of place in which Bodo would be at home.

A burly waiter brought the rum in a sleazy glass. Herr Nordern downed half of it before the waiter had moved away and ordered another. In a corner of his booth a drunk in a cheap anorak with a filthy collar made of imitation fur peered at him groggily and mumbled something unintelligible. Nordern gave him a hard official glare and got a glare in return and another mumble which sounded insulting. Herr Nordern downed his rum and grasped the next one so tightly that the glass was in danger of breaking.

Herr Nordern was an uncomplicated man, if human beings are ever so. The years of hardship which he, and millions of others, had endured, had taught him to count his blessings one by one, and day by day, and anger, resentment, and doubt, were not feelings he normally permitted himself, but as he sat in the shabby bar he did feel doubt, resentment, and anger.

What a change, he thought. Last night in the Palast, cocooned in its amber luxury, tonight in this bar, surrounded by the scum of the earth; and a visit to a police station in between. He, Herr Nordern, respected official, summoned to endure an interrogation on some ludicrous charge while these . . . these *types*, each and every one of whom ought to be doing forced labour in a rehabilitation centre, were sitting knocking back the deplorably cheap alchohol which he was subsidising through his taxes. And now he came to think of it, and with another rum in front of him, he wasn't at all happy about the way the Police had behaved. Why hadn't Werner told him about the accident to begin with instead of making a mystery of it? That might be the correct way to deal with the thieves but not with a respectable citizen. It wasn't socialist. Not at all.

More seedy characters walked in, more drunks lurched out, and in came two policemen. They were Railway Police but enough to give Herr Nordern a ghastly qualm. Leaving his rum on the table, he grabbed his coat and hat and, wishing that he was invisible, sidled from the bar into the unwelcoming darkness.

Chapter 9

THERE WAS another surprise for Herr Nordern that day for when he got home, sitting with his wife and Omi he found Bodo, drinking rum and hot water.

'Thought I'd drop in,' Bodo said, 'seeing that I was round this way.'

'Doing what?' Herr Nordern asked acidly.

Bodo was impervious to acid. 'Visiting a sick comrade,' he said with an air of hideous piety. 'By the way, I got these for you.' He held up a parcel. 'New spark-plugs.'

Herr Nordern recoiled. 'I don't want them.'

Bodo laughed. 'Of course you do. That Lada does, anyway.'

'Where did you get them from?' Herr Nordern asked.

Bodo winked. 'The Minister of Transport.'

'I wouldn't be surprised at that, either,' Herr Nordern said. 'Well you can take them back to where they belong.'

'Take them back!' Frau Nordern threw up her hands. 'Whatever for?'

'Because I've had one brush with the Police today and I don't want another over stolen goods,' Herr Nordern said.

'With the Police!' Frau Nordern was horrified, and Omi drew in a shocked breath.

'Yes,' Herr Nordern was simmering. 'Some fool mistake about an accident.'

He told the story, surprised at how anxious he was to tell it to sympathetic ears, and surprised, too, at how relieved he was by telling it.

Frau Nordern was formidably angry when he had finished

but to Herr Nordern's intense annoyance Bodo burst out laughing.

'It isn't a joke, Bodo,' Herr Nordern said.

'No it isn't.' Frau Nordern glared at an unperturbed Bodo. 'To think of Hans having to sit in a police station with those criminals. The scum of the earth!'

Bodo demurred. 'They're not all that bad, Helga. Most of them are just drunks.'

'Drunks!' Frau Nordern was unutterably scornful.

'Well. . . .' Bodo took a drink of his rum. 'They take a drop too much, sure, but it's because they aren't up to it.'

'Up to what?' Frau Nordern demanded.

'You know. The pressure here . . . being exhorted, forever being told to be . . . well, to be good.'

Herr Nordern who was pouring himself a plum brandy looked up sharply. 'You're not suggesting that's wrong, are you?'

'No, not wrong exactly. You can just get sick of it.' He held out his glass for Herr Nordern to fill. 'Take Erika, say—'

'What about Erika?' Frau Nordern reared up.

Bodo held out a massive but placatory hand. 'Let me finish, Helga. Erika is a terrific athlete, isn't she?'

Yes, the Norderns were united in that belief.

'Right, and you encourage her, and quite right, too. And the school encourages her and that's right, it's what schools are for. And people should be encouraged to do what they're good at. But you don't go on at her night and day, do you? If you did she'd go off her head. That's all I'm saying. But some people, they see posters everywhere, and on the T.V. they're being told they've got to be good to prove that the system works. Well, maybe it does, in a way, but it can put too much responsibility on certain types and they hit the bottle.'

'There are drunks and criminals in the West,' Herr Nordern said, 'and a lot more than here.'

'I'm not saying that there aren't,' Bodo said. 'But we don't live there, do we?' He filched one of Herr Nordern's cigars. 'I don't know how we got into this. Who did you see at Ostkreuz?'

'A Lieutenant Werner. I suppose you know him,' Herr Nordern said bitterly.

Bodo frowned. 'Sure you've got the right name?'

'Yes, of course I'm sure. Why?'

The frown remained on Bodo's face. 'Nothing really. I've just never heard of a Werner there. Still . . . by the way, speaking of Erika, where is she?'

'At school,' Frau Nordern said. 'There's a meeting of the F.G.Y. It should be over soon.'

Frau Nordern was right on both counts. Erika was at a meeting of the Free German Youth, and it was coming to an end.

Erika belonged to the Free German Youth because it was expected of her rather than from any burning enthusiasm; but, being a conscientious girl, as she was a member, she was dutiful: attended rallies, went on camps, signed petitions for world peace, others in support of the Soviet Union's foreign policy and against various iniquities of the Western world, and when attending meetings even made notes, although these did have a tendency to drift into matchstick drawings of women leaping over impossibly high bars. She was doing that now as the Group Leader, an adenoidal and conceited youth called Herman Guttenbruk, described his experiences on a recent trip to Moscow as a guest of the Russian Young Pioneers.

'. . . I cannot begin to tell you, Comrades,' Guttenbruk was saying, 'how inspiring it was to be with the youth of a fully developed socialist country. It made me aware of how much we, *us* comrades, have to do to raise the level of political consciousness and awareness of our own youth. Just listen to the following statistics—'

But fortunately for the assembled Free German Youth, the teacher present, a Frau Zeitel, deftly intervened between them and the threatened statistics.

'Comrade Herman, I'm sure that the figures are most interesting and we must have another meeting to discuss them properly and with the attention they deserve. But I think that the time . . . so perhaps I can propose a vote of thanks to you for your inspiring talk.'

There was no dissent to the proposition and hearty thanks were given to a rather disconsolate Herman, the heartiness spilling over to Frau Zeitel, also, and the meeting broke up. Although a group of young zealots gathered around Herman, the majority of the meeting made a dash for the door, Rosa saying to Erika, 'Thank goodness we didn't have a question time!'

Erika grinned back. 'See you tomorrow,' she said, and then saw Frau Zeitel beckon her.

'Erika,' Frau Zeitel said. 'An excellent meeting, wasn't it? By the way, the Principal would like to see you.'

Erika blinked. 'Me? Now?'

'Yes, if you would.'

Erika picked up her coat from the cloakroom and walked to the Principal's office. At the door she paused, a trifle apprehensively. The Principal, Herr Lettner, was a formidable figure; a bulky man, not renowned for his intellect but an excellent organiser and a long-standing member of the German Communist Party. Pupils rarely had direct contact with him but when he did have an interview with one, he or she usually came out shaking and promising, on their deepest oath, that in future they would, they most emphatically would, DO BETTER. It was on the cards that Paul would be meeting him before too long but, Erika wondered, why should he want to see her? But of course, she thought, it was that stupid business of the man on the gallery. She bit her lip with vexation. Why had her mother made such a fuss about it? She took a breath, rapped on the door, heard a bass voice boom, 'Come in,' and entered. Herr Lettner was at his desk, a green-shaded spotlight glaring on a mound of papers, and sitting next to him was a policeman.

'Erika isn't it? Erika Nordern?' Herr Lettner turned to the policeman. 'One of our best pupils and an outstanding athlete. We have great hopes for her. Sit down, Erika. Are you well? Shedding some lessons to concentrate on the Indoor Championships? Excellent. I did want to see you, Erika, but while you are here we can kill two birds with one stone. This officer would like to ask you a question or two. You don't have to answer them, please understand that. If not, then the officer will ask you them with your parents present. But the officer had to come to the school anyway about those boys and their wretched scooters.'

Herr Lettner sounded exasperated. The pupils' scooters were a source of long-standing complaints among the people living near the school and Erika felt reassured. Scooters could hardly go with any serious matter.

'But anyway,' Herr Lettner said, 'I know what the questions are and there is nothing that you needn't honestly answer.'

Despite this assurance Erika felt a slight prickle of anxiety. Like her father, she had been brought up to believe, and did believe, that the Police were guardians of socialism, but also, like her father, she had had little contact with them and found this experience a trifle alarming.

'What are the questions?' she asked, looking at Herr Lettner rather than the policeman.

The policeman cleared his throat. He was elderly, with grizzled hair and a kindly, weather-beaten face. 'Sorry about this, Fräulein,' he said. 'It won't take a minute and, like the Principal says, you don't have to answer, but could you tell me the way you drove home from the Palast last night.'

'The Palast?' Erika was genuinely bewildered. 'How did you know I was there?'

'Don't ask me, Fräulein,' the policeman said. 'I was just told to ask you that question. If you don't want to answer. . . .' he half-closed his notebook.

Erika hesitated. 'I think you should ask my father that.'

'I dare say someone will, Fräulein.' The policeman sat immobile in a patient, policeman-like way, not looking at Erika, not looking at anything in particular, except, perhaps, some policeman's dream of a warm bar where the drinks were free—for policemen.

'But what is it all about?' Erika asked.

'Probably an accident, Fräulein. I dare say Traffic Control are looking for witnesses.'

'I don't think that there can be any harm in answering, Erika,' Herr Lettner said.

'We didn't see any accidents,' Erika said. She described the route they had taken home and the policeman slowly wrote it down.

'Thank you,' he said when she had finished. 'Not too bad was it?' He stood up and put his cap on. 'Good-night.'

The door closed behind him and Herr Lettner smiled at Erika. 'There now, not to worry. Anything you want to help you with your athletics, just let me know. And here,' he handed over an envelope. 'It's for your parents. I think that they will be glad to read it. Good-night, Erika.'

Erika took her bus, perturbed about the policeman's questions, disturbed about the letter, anxious to get home, and yet troubled about what her parents would say. 'I wish I hadn't answered,' she thought. 'I wish I hadn't.' Although another voice whispered, 'Why not?' She had merely told the truth. But still, a vague sense of guilt hung over her as she went up the stairs to the door with the neat aluminium plate on it.

It was a huge relief to Erika, when she went into the sitting-room, to see Bodo, as if his presence would act as a conductor, drawing away some of the guilt she felt, although she had hardly entered the room before she was aware of an air of tension. Omi was tight-lipped, her father, and she was surprised to see him drinking at such an hour, was gloomy faced, and her mother was sitting at the table, her arms folded, looking severely at the bamboo wallpaper. Only Bodo greeted her with a smile.

'Hi, Erika,' he said. 'How's my favourite niece?'

'Hello, Uncle Bodo,' she answered. 'All right, thank you.'

'Still jumping like a deer?' Bodo asked. 'One of these days you're going to jump right into the National Team.'

'Never that,' Erika said. She looked at her parents. 'Is there anything wrong?'

'No,' Herr Nordern said. 'A minor problem, that's all. How was school?'

'So so,' Erika said.

'Were you in the gym?' Frau Nordern asked.

'Yes.' Erika snatched at the opportunity to postpone her news. She went into the kitchen to make a drink. 'Two sessions.'

'It's for the Indoor Championship,' Frau Nordern said to Bodo. 'The *Berlin* Indoor Championship.'

'You'll win that,' Bodo said.

'I'm not so sure,' Erika called. 'They say that there is a girl at Pankow school who is terrific.'

'You'll jump the socks off her,' Bodo said. 'Did you enjoy the Palast?'

Erika snatched at that line of conversation, too. 'Oh yes, it was very elegant.'

'Well, if you win the Indoor Championship *I'll* take you out to dinner. The Stadt Berlin. How's that? A deal?'

'It's a deal.' Erika tried to smile but could not keep up her pretence any longer. 'I saw Herr Lettner tonight,' she said.

Frau Nordern swung her head around. 'The Principal?'

'Yes. There was a policeman with him.'

'A policeman?' Herr Nordern stared at Erika through his thick glasses. 'Speaking to you?'

Erika nodded. 'Yes, to me. He asked me questions.'

'What?' Herr Nordern was genuinely angry. Angrier than Erika had ever seen him before. Angrier than she had thought it was possible to be. He stood up. 'What sort of questions?'

'How we drove home last night,' Erika said.

'And did you tell him?' Herr Nordern was almost shouting. Erika flushed and her upper lip began to tremble.

'Go easy, Hans,' Bodo said. 'You're frightening her.'

Herr Nordern turned. 'Keep out of this,' he growled, but when he turned to Erika again his voice was more controlled. 'Just tell me what happened, Erika. It's quite all right.'

Erika said what had happened and her father breathed heavily through his nose and sat down. 'And Herr Lettner was with you all the time?'

'Yes, he said that I didn't have to answer anything, and that it was quite all right.'

'Did he?' said Frau Nordern in a voice which boded ill, even for Herr Lettner.

'It's abominable,' Herr Nordern said. 'Absolutely abominable. I've never heard anything like it. Questioning a girl without her parents present.'

'I'm sorry, Father.' Erika was close to tears.

Herr Nordern's manner changed abruptly. 'Now, now, *Liebchen*, there's nothing for you to be sorry about. No one is angry with you. It's just that some idiot gave the Police my car number. I'm angry with the Police, not you. But I'll make that Werner hop.'

'Hmm.' Bodo refilled his glass with an absent-minded air. 'Is it worth it?'

'Of course it's worth it,' Herr Nordern said. 'That policeman had no right to question Erika. None at all.'

'No. . . .' Bodo sounded less convinced of the limits to police powers than his brother was. 'But I don't think you'd get very far. Just a minute, Hans, let me finish. What's happened? A cop has asked Erika a couple of questions with her Principal present. She was told that she needn't answer—right, Erika? The cop and her Principal told her that. So what's the fuss? The cop didn't want to drive all the way across here, he had this other business at the school, so. . . . They were just checking out your story, and they wouldn't want you to be giving Erika a tale to tell, would they?'

Herr Nordern glared at Bodo. 'I hope that you're not suggesting that I would *collude*.'

'Not at all,' Bodo said. 'But look at it from the cops' point of view. If you *had* been in an accident you might have made up some tale between yourselves. That's what *they* would think.'

'You mean they wouldn't believe me?' Herr Nordern was incredulous.

Bodo gave a crooked grin. 'Hans, they're paid *not* to believe people. Anyway, you weren't in an accident, there's five of you to swear you weren't, so I'd forget it if I were you. They will.'

'You think so?'

'Sure,' Bodo sounded confident. 'Anyway, I'll tell you what I'll do. I . . . er . . . well, I know someone. I'll check with him—see what's happening and let you know. How's that?'

'I suppose so.' Herr Nordern was doubtful, although more than ready to have his doubts removed. 'But I'm not happy about it. Not happy at all.'

'Don't take it personally,' Bodo said. 'And hey, Erika, cheer up.'

He winked at her and, oddly enough, Erika did cheer up. 'So,' he said. 'I'd better get going.'

'You won't stay for supper?' Frau Nordern asked without warmth.

'Some other time. I'm late as it is. Don't get up. So long all.'

The door slammed behind him. Omi said, 'He's forgotten that.' That being the parcel of spark-plugs. Herr Nordern made an irresolute gesture then sank back.

'Wonderful, isn't it,' he said. 'We go out for a decent, civilised evening at the best hotel in the G.D.R. and we have the Police swarming all over us. Bodo wanders about breaking every law in the country and do the Police ever bother him? What was that he said? He knows someone. Probably the Chief of Police! Anyway, what about supper?'

'Paul isn't here yet,' Frau Nordern said.

Herr Nordern slapped his knee. 'If that boy can't get home in time for his meals he can do without them.'

'He's out with a school party,' Frau Nordern said.

Herr Nordern was struck by a sudden thought. 'I wonder if the Police have been asking him questions. I wouldn't put it past them. But all right, we'll give him half an hour then we eat. Definitely.'

In the event the half-hour was not needed because Paul came in, unquestioned, and cheerful since his evening at the Palast had made him something of a celebrity among his gang of friends.

'It was O.K.' he said over potato salad and pork, 'but they ought to liven it up a bit. The music!'

'It was excellent music,' Frau Nordern said. 'Tasteful.'

'Yes,' Omi, who had been silent for the entire evening, nodded assent. 'They used to have orchestras in the old days, but it was nice. And Karl, how handsome he looked, and elegant. But I'm afraid that it was tedious for you. I shan't bore you next time.'

'You didn't bore us Omi,' Erika said.

'I have thought about it all the day long,' Omi said. 'God is good. And when Karl comes back he and I shall have lunch together so that we shan't bore you again. Now, now,' she patted Erika's arm stopping any protest. 'I know, I remember when I was a girl the old people went on about their past. I had heard it all a hundred times, but still I had to sit and listen.' She sighed. 'But it is not correct.'

'What isn't?' Frau Nordern asked.

'Erika and that policeman. In the old days—'

She was cut off as Herr Nordern banged down his spoon. With the controlled patience of a man about to lose his temper he said, 'I don't wish to hear any more about it. And I don't want to hear any more about the old days.'

Omi and Frau Nordern spoke at once, Omi apologising, Frau Nordern defending her, but Herr Nordern cut them both off.

'I know all about the old days,' he said, with real bitterness in his voice. 'The good old days when we lived in pig-sties, the working-class, and the real pigs stuffed themselves in the Adlon. Yes—' he raised his voice—'yes, and the police beat you up because you were left-wing. And the Gestapo, my uncle was questioned by them, in the cellars at Albrecht-strasse. They pulled off his finger-nails before they blew his brains out. Those were the good old days.'

'I beg your pardon.' Omi spoke with trembling dignity. 'I think that I will go to my room.'

'There's no need for that,' Herr Nordern said, but Omi merely bowed and left the table.

Frau Nordern glared murderously at her husband. 'Now see what you've done. How dare you speak to my mother like that.'

Herr Nordern opened his mouth to speak, closed it again, then groaned. 'All right,' he said. 'I'm sorry. I'm very sorry. I'll go and bring her back.'

'I'll go, Father.' Before Herr Nordern could object, Erika had slipped from her seat and gone into the bedroom. Omi was sitting in her chair, her hands clasped, and a look of inexpressible and heart-breaking sadness on her face.

'Omi.' Erika sat next to her and took her hand.

'Child.' Omi shook her head. 'Don't leave your supper.'

'I don't want you to leave yours,' Erika said. 'Come and finish it.'

'No,' Omi was gentle but determined. 'I really don't want any more to eat.'

'But you must eat,' Erika said. 'Do come. Father didn't mean anything.'

'I know that, my Dear. Really I do.' The old hand tightened

on Erika's arm. 'It was my fault. I shouldn't have spoken.'

'But you must speak if you wish to,' Erika said.

'There are times when it is better not to. Old people should keep silent.'

Erika was horrified. 'Omi! Old people have as much right to speak as anyone. Why—' she was about to elaborate on this when Herr Nordern opened the door.

'May I come in?' he asked. 'Thank you. . . . Omi, I beg your pardon. I really do. Please excuse me.' He sat down on Erika's bed. 'I spoke without thinking.'

'No, I shouldn't go on about the old days,' Omi said. 'But I wasn't thinking of, of. . . .'

'Of *those* old days. I know.'

Erika and Omi knew, also, without being told, which old days Herr Nordern was referring to. Not the past Omi remembered through a golden veil of privilege, but the past other Germans remembered, the days of concentration camps, the torture chambers, the headsman's axe, and the gas chambers.

Herr Nordern sighed and rubbed his nose. 'It was just a misunderstanding. So much seems to have happened this week, and I was so angry about the Police. I just exploded. But do come back in, Omi. We have some cake—and cream.'

Omi half-smiled and, despite herself, Erika smiled with her. Tempting people with food was hardly typical of her father but there was a clumsy kindness about the offer which made it hard to resist, and it wasn't resisted.

The cake, good cake, with cherries as well as cream, was eaten, coffee drunk, the dishes washed, and the Nordern household settled down. Oddly enough, no more was said about Uncle Karl and the visit to the Palast.

There was an excellent film on the television. A Hungarian comedy which, as it was shown on one of the State channels, did not suffer from the maddening interruptions which plagued the programmes from the other Germany, and which, of course, were due entirely to atmospheric interference.

Even Herr Nordern, even Paul, watched the film, and when it ended the atmosphere in the flat was considerably lighter than when it had begun.

'Very good,' Herr Nordern said. 'Excellent. The world isn't all gloom and doom after all.' He stretched himself. 'Goodnight.' Meaning that everyone was going to bed which they obediently did.

It was not until Erika had put Omi to bed and was herself slipping into sleep that she remembered the letter Herr Lettner had given her but, wisely, she decided to hand it over the next morning. As one of Omi's Watchwords said: 'Sufficient unto the day is the evil thereof.'

Chapter 10

THE HUNGARIAN comedy might have eased the gloom of the previous evening, but, no matter how sparkling or witty, its effect did not last overnight, and the Norderns had their breakfast in an unpleasant atmosphere. Herr Nordern still felt aggrieved about the Police, Frau Nordern was angry with her husband, Omi was distant, Erika felt guilty of letting down her father by answering the policeman's questions, and Paul had reasons of his own for being apprehensive.

The atmosphere was not noticeably lightened even when Erika handed over Herr Lettner's letter and heard it read aloud over breakfast.

'. . . trust you will not be offended at police questions . . . assure you would not have allowed anything improper . . . duty to co-operate with the State organs . . . save them time and trouble, and I understand that you are concerned about a person present during one of Erika's training sessions. I will be happy to discuss this with you. It is a pity that neither you nor Frau Nordern are as active in the parent-teacher association as one might expect from leading members of the community. However, appointment willingly made. . . .'

'He hasn't said anything at all about that man,' Frau Nordern said.

'No, but he does have a point about the meetings,' Herr Nordern observed.

'If they had the meetings at a time I could manage I *would* go,' Frau Nordern snapped. 'I wish you had given me this last night, Erika. I would have given you a note for *him*. But look at the time!'

There was a hasty, scrambled departure as the Norderns

went their various ways. Herr Nordern had to walk more quickly than he would have wished to his *S-Bahn* station and got there sweating under his heavy clothes, despite a bitter wind whistling thinly across the platform. The train was late and when it did come in it was crowded and, perhaps reflecting Herr Nordern's mood, seemed sullen and disobliging, the passengers throwing lurid oaths at the people trying to force their way in, and the journey was not made any more pleasant by two railway policemen who elbowed their way through the jammed passengers demanding, at random, to see tickets.

One man did not have one and, notwithstanding his protests that the machine on his station was broken and so he could not buy one, could he? he was yanked off the train at Ostkreuz.

It was an uncommon event. The fares were so cheap that it was hardly worthwhile cheating. Normally Herr Nordern would have been glad to see a dodger caught but as he watched the hangdog defaulter being hustled along the platform he had a certain fellow-feeling for him.

'Perhaps the machine *was* broken,' he thought, although vandalism was almost unheard of. At any rate, thinking of his own experience the previous day, the Police might have behaved more politely.

The train lurched into Friedrichstrasse. Herr Nordern joined the anxious hordes charging down the stairs and made his way to his office. For the first time in years he signed in *under* the red line, rang the Director's office, told the chilly blonde that he was present if the Director wished to see him and settled down, unsettled, to work.

Müller came in, having also signed under the line, although, unperturbed, he winked at Herr Nordern. 'Two of us—' he began, but, seeing Herr Nordern's expression, saved any further facetious comments. 'What was your dash yesterday?' he asked as he hung up his coat on the long nail which did for a coat hook.

'Nothing,' Herr Nordern said brusquely and bent his head over his work, not raising it until 10.00 a.m. when he was summoned to see the Director. The blonde waved him in and he trudged across the carpet to the desk and exchanged 'good mornings' with his master.

'Well?' the Director said. 'Why did you not report back yesterday?'

'I'm sorry,' Nordern said. 'I didn't leave the Station until late.'

'And what was it about?'

'It was a personal matter.'

'Personal?' The Director frowned. 'Herr Nordern, affairs between employees of the State and the Police cannot possibly be personal. A man of your experience must know that.'

Herr Nordern did know it. He knew it very well. Indeed, as a loyal supporter of the regime he had spent his life saying just that thing. He remembered, with a guilty pang, how he had defended the Director's decision to sack a secretary and exile a colleague to a bleak part of the country for scandalous behaviour. 'Quite right,' he had said then. 'No such thing as a personal life for a servant of Government.' But that, of course, had been someone else's personal life.

'Yes?' The Director was waiting, and not patiently.

'Of course.' Herr Nordern cleared his throat. 'Excuse me. There was an accident the other night on Strausberger Platz. The Police had part of a number. They were checking on every car with those numbers.'

The Director frowned again. 'An accident? And you were called from this office in the middle of a working day?'

'Exactly what I said.' Herr Nordern raised his hand in agreement. 'But the Police said there must have been a misunderstanding. There was no hurry at all.'

'I see. And were you in an accident?'

'I certainly was not,' Herr Nordern said.

'So,' the Director nodded to himself, gave Nordern a long, steady look, and then, surprisingly, said, 'Sit down. Have a coffee.' He rang a bell and the blonde came in with a tray on which was an elegant silver coffee-pot and fine Dresden china cups.

Nordern took a seat, wondering what was going to happen next for, no matter how democratic the German Democratic Republic might be in theory, it wasn't every day that middling officials sat down having coffee with exalted figures such as directors.

'I suppose you saw your file on my desk yesterday,' the Director said. 'I left it there deliberately. I didn't want to seem furtive, you know.'

'I did see it, yes,' Nordern agreed.

'I read it.' The Director pushed a packet of cigarettes across the table. 'You know, I hadn't seen it before.'

Herr Nordern wasn't surprised. His file would be a matter for Nagel, the Section Head, and the Security Police.

The Director poured out coffee. 'I was interested in the file,' he said. 'You come of good stock.'

Herr Nordern felt a rush of pride. That was right. He did come of good stock. Solid Berlin working class, with a roll of honour as distinguished as any von Brombergs or von Ritters. Fighters in the trades unions and the socialist parties, leaders in the struggle against exploitation, and against Nazism— and they had paid a price for that: his uncle executed, his cousin tortured and flung into a concentration camp to rot, only the fact that his father had been in the Wehrmacht and decorated for bravery in the crossing of the Dniester had saved him from a similar fate.

'Thank you,' he said.

'It's true,' the Director said, seriously. 'But, you'll excuse me for saying so, you married a little . . . oddly.'

Nordern agreed. It was a natural remark and had been made to him all his married life, a working-class Berliner married into the aristocracy. In fact it had led to real difficulties at times. He briefly explained how his marriage had come about. 'It was the War, really,' he said. 'Everything got mixed up.'

'Didn't they just.' The Director slowly stirred his coffee. 'My father was an old communist. He was on the Hamburg District Committee, an engineer at Blohm and Voss. But he got out before those Nazi swine could get their hands on him, through Sweden and into the Soviet Union.'

'That would have been no handicap to you in your career,' Herr Nordern thought, but kept the thought to himself.

'You have never joined the Party?' the Director said.

Nordern shook his head. 'Not that it was ideological,' he hastened to explain. 'I am a communist, of course. It was just that, well, I got married, then there was university. I don't claim to be clever and it was a struggle for me, then the children came, and my work here.'

'Yes,' the Director was understanding. 'But your work is excellent. Herr Nagel speaks highly of you. In fact I would say that you are working below your true level. You haven't applied for promotion since you got your present post.'

Herr Nordern came as near to a resigned shrug as his undemonstrative nature allowed him to. 'There's a new breed,' he said. 'Young men, top-class, really well trained.'

'You're trained,' the Director said.

Herr Nordern shook his head. 'It was rough and ready,' he said. And, he reflected, it had been in those desperate years: a wracked and ruined country and the denazification programme taking place, school teachers, lecturers, managers dragged from their posts and replaced by men and women hardly knowing their subjects themselves but politically sound. And the University: half wrecked, unheated, books short, paper short, food short, and the interminable lectures on Marxism had not exactly helped his knowledge of the real world of economic affairs.

He came out of his reverie. The Director was holding his beautiful china cup up to the light.

The Director put the cup down. 'I remember drinking stuff made from burnt acorns out of old tins,' he said.

'Me too,' Herr Nordern said. 'And sharing the tin—' risking a wry joke.

The Director nodded agreement. '"Those were the days, my friend, we thought they'd never end,"' he quoted. 'But they did. Have. We've come through the worst of it, and now we have a little elbow-room. We're going to start a re-training scheme. Computers, automation, robotics.' He looked thoughtfully at Nordern. 'On full pay. Promotion. Think about it.'

'Me?' Nordern gaped in disbelief.

'Yes, you. You've earned it. *Guten Tag.*'

Nordern walked to the door in a daze but when he got there the Director's voice held him for a moment.

'By the way, did the Police treat you properly?'

Herr Nordern turned. 'Yes,' he said. 'Yes they did.'

'No complaints?'

'None at all, Herr Director.'

Herr Nordern went back to his office, his heart beating about twice as fast as it usually did. Re-training and promotion—offered on a plate! So, his years of hard work and selfless devotion to the State had not gone unrecognised. No indeed. And what a thought: a new life opening for himself and his family; a bigger flat, a new car (and he made a mental vow to return the spark-plugs to Bodo) perhaps a dinghy, sailing on the Wannsee in summer; and for himself, wider horizons, a chance to have a real say in the shaping of his country and its future. Deeply grateful, profoundly grateful, moved to the depths of his being, he went to his desk.

Müller looked up from a pocket calculator. 'All right?' he asked.

'Yes, all right,' Herr Nordern answered. 'All right, yes.' He gazed at the ugly plaster patch which hid the old window. Herr Nordern had never challenged the right of that patch to exist. It was, he thought, a regrettable necessity, like the Wall and the rest of the Anti-Fascist Barrier which stretched from the Baltic to the Black Sea. Built to keep out saboteurs, Fascist agents, wreckers, spies, murderers and, and he was ready to accept it, to keep people *in*; to prevent the flow, the haemorrhage of the population which, before it had been erected, had threatened the country with total collapse. Herr Nordern approved of that, too. Why should the State, having housed, fed, clothed, and educated people then allow them to clear off and sell their skills in the capitalistic world? If people did not know their moral duty then it was up to the State to impose it on them. And so Herr Nordern looked at the patch and said to himself, 'It is right. Keep out the West, build a socialist state, support it, support the State which knows how to reward its loyal servants, re-training them instead of throwing them on the scrap heap of unemployment.'

And, he clicked his fingers, making Müller look up enquiringly, and the Police! Of course, if it had not been for the efficiency of Lieutenant Werner, tracking down infractions of the law, his file might never have got to the Director. Yes, it fitted together like a superb orchestra. All the organs of the State working together in a perfect harmony and the end result, inevitably, being good. *Good*, that was the word. He looked across at Müller.

'This is a good country,' he said.

'Hey?' Müller looked up, startled.

'I said that this is a good country. Remember it.' Herr Nordern nodded decisively as he bent his head to his work.

Like Müller, Erika was having that same text drummed into her head in a lesson, compulsory, on Marxism-Leninism, where the teacher, Fräulein Kellerman, was explaining the difference between productive socialist work, leading to happiness, and mechanical capitalist labour, leading to crime.

'There is not, and cannot be, any contradiction between the State and the working class in a socialist country,' she was saying. 'Some criminal elements may persist but they are doomed because in no way are they related to the productive elements.'

Erika mechanically took notes although, after long exposure to it, Marxism-Leninism had long since lost whatever fascination it might once have had, and, furthermore, since it permeated every lesson taught in the school, even mathematics, it had become a background noise, like noises at a party; one was aware of it but automatically filtered it out.

Fräulein Kellerman stuck up a complicated chart which purported to demonstrate some inevitable process of economic development and rapped at it with a pointer, as if urging the green line, which showed some inner decay of capitalism, to dip downwards further and further, and the red, soaring one, which showed the vigour of socialism to leap upwards higher and faster.

'And this graph can be applied to every aspect of human activity,' Fräulein Kellerman said. 'Even sport, Erika Nordern.'

Erika started and blushed. 'Yes Fräulein Kellerman. Of course.' She held up her notebook to prove that she had been taking notes and received a curt nod from her teacher for whom sport took a long second place to Marxist theory.

The lesson ended and the class was dismissed. 'She nearly

caught you there Erika,' said Fritz Kott as they ambled down the corridor.

Erika grinned. 'I don't understand half of it,' she confessed.

'Nor do I.' Fritz leaned on the bust of Egon Schultz. 'How about coming to the Youth Club a week on Saturday. There's a dance.'

Erika shook her head. 'No dancing for me until after the Championships. If someone trod on my toe! But I might come along. I'll see what's happening at home first.'

Fritz grinned. '*Nothing* ever happens in my home. Supper, T.V., bed. What happens in yours?'

Erika opened her eyes wide. 'Gambling,' she hissed in a sinister whisper. 'Plots against the State. Undesirable films.'

Fritz opened *his* eyes. 'I'll tell you what, skip the Youth Club and I'll come to your house instead.'

'Do that,' Erika said. 'Come and watch my grandmother do her crocheting.'

Fritz laughed and walked away and Erika went to change for her training session.

The group in the gym was a small one, and select. This was the real thing. A session for the stars of the school, those who were to go into the Indoor Championships, Berlin school against Berlin school; the winners to go into the Zonal Championships, and then . . . and there were two other people there, a man and a woman. Erika did not know the woman, but the man was instantly recognisable, Johann Wolf, himself a great athlete, a high jumper, and a certainty for the Olympic team until a car crash had put paid to that ambition.

As the girls gathered around Fräulein Silber the two adults went upstairs to the gallery, leaning openly over the balustrade. Fräulein Silber clapped her hands.

'Pay no attention to our guests,' she said. 'Concentrate on your work. *Concentrate.*'

She switched on the tape recorder and the familiar music drifted through the gym as the girls began their exercises: long, gentle movements, stretching and relaxing every muscle and sinew, a rather dreamy process, freeing the mind, as well as the body, from the tensions of life. But not Erika's. As she began to jump she failed time and time again: trailing her leg

99

and bringing down the bar or, worse, getting her approach run wrong and failing to check in time, so letting her hand cross under the bar which meant that a commonplace and excusable error was counted as a jump—a mistake which could be fatal in a competition. Half in tears she turned to Fräulein Silber.

'I can't do it,' she said. 'I'm sorry.'

Fräulein Silber looked at her steadily for a moment then took her to the side of the gym.

'Now listen, Erika,' she said. 'The reason you aren't jumping well is because there is something on your mind. You can tell me if there is, that is what I'm here for. Is there?'

Erika ran her fingers through her hair. 'I don't know, Fräulein. Perhaps there is. Things seem to be happening and I don't know what to make of them, my uncle coming, the Police—'

'Police?' Fräulein Silber was sharp. 'And what is this about your uncle? Is he in trouble?'

'No, no.' Erika gulped and told Fräulein Silber about Karl, and about the Police, and the row at home. When she had finished Fräulein Silber nodded.

'I see. I will have a word with Herr Lettner. I'm sorry about the row, and you have had quite a week. But listen Erika, the real demands in sport aren't physical, they're in the mind. When you get up to the highest standards, yes, when you represent your country, the demands then! It takes courage to be an athlete, and great courage to be a great one. Show me—show them—' she pointed her finger to the balcony above them—'that you have courage. Come on. Come and jump.'

And Erika did jump, getting her run right, her balance, her poise, and she began to jump as she had never jumped before: clearing her mind of Uncle Karl and the thoughts of war that pink figure had resurrected, and forgetting the policeman, and the row, and Omi's sadness; running in a perfect arc to the bar and then, miraculously weightless as she took off, her back arching as effortlessly as a cat as she curved in the air. And she began to feel as if she was not only jumping through space but into a dimension of the mind where space and time were meaningless, where she was freed from natural laws, into a world without barriers, without walls or fences, leaping into the unknown. And, scarcely aware of it, she leaped her best ever height.

She landed after that jump, rolled off the landing bed, and realised that she was alone with Fräulein Silber.

'They've gone?' Erika asked. 'The others.'

'Yes. All gone.' There was an odd expression on Fräulein Silber's face, rather as if she had never seen Erika before. 'Get changed, Erika. And would you please come back in here?'

'Yes, Fräulein.' Puzzled, Erika showered and changed and went back into the gym. Fräulein Silber was there, talking to Herr Wolf. Fräulein Silber introduced Erika to Wolf.

'Let's sit down for a moment,' he said, suiting his action to his words and sitting on a mat. 'Now,' he said, easily, blue eyes shining from a friendly, tanned face. 'You like athletics, Erika?'

'Yes.'

'It's good fun, isn't it?' Wolf was casually amiable.

'It's. . . .' Erika wanted to say that it was more than good fun, but did not want to sound pretentious.

'Yes?' Wolf prompted, but not sharply, as if the afternoon and the evening were theirs if they wished it.

'Well, it's wonderful.' Erika looked away, embarrassed at her own remark.

'All the time?'

Again Erika hesitated. All the time? That wasn't true at all. There had been times, and plenty of them, when she had gone home in tears, and gone to bed in tears, too, when she had jumped badly, and there had been that nightmare period after her accident when she had been unable to face the bar at all, even the sight of the gym had sickened her, and there had been, still were, times when her friends were at the cinema or the disco and she was running, solitary, in the dusk. Those times were not wonderful, far from it.

But then there was that feeling of growing mastery over her body, the feeling of walking on air, the sense of limitless stamina, the ability to run to school in the heat of summer and to arrive as cool and unruffled as if she had merely walked from her room into the kitchen. And, yes, that air of effortless movement which made people turn their heads as she walked by.

'Not all the time,' she said, answering Wolf's question. 'But it's all worth it.'

Herr Wolf laughed. 'I know exactly what you mean.' He put his hands behind his head and leaned against the wall. 'You had an accident. . . .'

'Yes, I'm sorry.' Erika felt foolish for saying that, but Wolf just laughed again.

'It happens.' He held out his hand to Fräulein Silber who handed him a folder. 'Your charts, Erika,' he said, although Erika knew that.

Wolf glanced through the charts. 'You've been making up for lost time, though. 1.50—that was just after you started jumping again. 1.60, 1.70 . . . why do you think you have started jumping like this?'

'I don't know,' Erika said. 'It suddenly happened.'

'After your fall.' Wolf nodded. 'And just now?'

Erika screwed up her eyes, thinking hard. 'I . . . I just felt that . . . that I wasn't jumping over a bar but. . . .' she paused, lost for words.

'But over a psychological barrier?'

'Yes, something like that,' Erika agreed.

'I see.' Wolf glanced at the records again. When he looked up his blue eyes were quizzical. 'Do you know what your best jump was today?'

'Of course. 1.80.'

'That was the bar,' Wolf said.

'Yes, the bar.' Erika was puzzled. What else could it be?

'But do you know how much you cleared it by?' Wolf asked. 'I would say by at least six centimetres. What do you say, Fräulein?'

'At least.' Fräulein Silber gave an emphatic nod.

'So, that makes it 1.86,' Wolf said, 'and that is. . . .'

He did not need to say anything more. 1.86 was the national junior record for fifteen-year-old girls, set in 1983 and unbroken since.

'Seven centimetres to go,' Wolf said. 'Think that you could make it?'

Erika waited before answering, then said, 'I think so. Yes.'

'Every time?'

That question Erika did not answer. *Every* time—there was the rub. To make one inspired leap like Beamon in the long jump at the '68 Olympics, that was one thing. To do it again and again, on demand as it were—that was quite another.

'That is the question, isn't it?' Herr Wolf said. 'And do you know what it takes to do it?'

Another question which did not need an answer. To be able to do that meant dedication: endless discipline, self-discipline, giving up years of one's life, and even then . . . athletes had come, flared briefly, and then vanished, like Beamon himself.

'Think about it,' Herr Wolf said. 'Talk to Fräulein Silber and your parents.' He stood up. 'You know that I am with the Ministry of Sport? No? Well here.' He gave Erika his card. 'I would like to meet your parents. Do you think that could be arranged?'

It could, indeed it could. If necessary Erika would have carried her parents on her back to meet Herr Wolf. She ran from the school and was tempted to run home, too. As it was she stood all the way home, on tiptoe.

As ever, Omi was in, sitting by the window. She heard Erika's news as she made a hot drink but, although she congratulated her, there was something withdrawn about the old lady.

'Are you all right, Omi?' Erika asked.

'Yes, yes quite all right,' Omi answered. 'But it is Paul. He looks worried.'

'Is he in?' Erika was surprised as, for once, there was no music wailing from Paul's room.

'I think that he's in trouble,' Omi whispered.

Erika raised her shoulders dismissively. Paul was, if not always in trouble, then, at least, forever walking a tightrope over a Niagara of troubles.

'Go and see him,' Omi urged. 'Talk to him before your mother and father get home.'

'I don't see why,' Erika demurred, thinking that if Paul had fallen off the tightrope then that was his affair.

'I wish you would,' Omi said. 'I couldn't stand another disagreeable night. Do it, for my sake.'

That was an appeal Erika could not resist. She rapped on Paul's door and strode in imperiously, very much like her mother, in fact.

One stride was enough. Another would have taken Erika through the window and out into the street, Paul's room being just big enough to contain a narrow bed, a table-top hinged to the wall, and a few shelves. Under the gaze of various pop stars and football heroes, Paul was sprawled morosely on the bed.

'What do you want?' he demanded.

'I don't want anything,' Erika snapped. 'Omi said you looked worried. Are you?'

Paul gave a sullen shrug.

'Don't *do* that,' Erika said. 'Your manners are getting worse. Can't you speak like a normal human being?' Without ceremony she pushed Paul's legs off the bed and sat down. 'Is there something wrong? Really wrong, I mean? It's no good just lying there with a face like that. If you are in trouble you'd better tell me before Mother and Father get in.'

Paul stared moodily at the ceiling, not answering.

'All right.' Erika stood up. 'Suit yourself.'

She made for the door but Paul stopped her. 'It's old Schmidt.'

'Herr Schmidt?' Erika frowned. He was the teacher of technical drawing at the school. 'What about him?'

'He's going to send me to Lettner,' Paul said.

Erika sank back on to the bed. 'What for?'

'I altered a mark in a book.'

'What!' Erika cried.

'It was going to the Palast. Mother said that if I didn't get a good mark I couldn't go, so I altered it. I was going to change it back with some white stuff one of the lads has, but I forgot.'

'Oh Paul,' despite herself Erika burst out laughing. 'Trust you. Mother didn't really mean that you couldn't go.'

'Well, I didn't know that, did I?' Paul said. 'Anyway, they've been going on and on about those marks.'

'Not just those marks,' Erika said.

'No, but those are the worst.'

Erika sighed. 'Why don't you work harder? You really

should. It's not right the way you go on. The trouble with you is that you don't know how lucky you are.'

'Me? Lucky!' Paul was outraged.

'That's what I said.' Erika was peremptory. 'You've got a really good home, good clothes, good holidays, your own tape-recorder, and you go to one of the best schools in Berlin. All you've got to do is to stop fooling about and you're sure to go to university.'

'I don't want to go to university,' Paul said.

'Not want to go. . . .' Erika was aghast. 'But you're going to be an engineer.'

'I don't want to be an engineer, either,' Paul muttered.

'But Paul,' Erika could hardly believe her ears. 'You'll just end up as a common labourer.'

'What's wrong with that?' Paul demanded.

Erika was horrified. 'Paul! You can't mean what you're saying. You *can't* want to be a labourer. Think!'

'I do think,' Paul said. 'Everyone says I don't, but I do. I do,' he repeated, as if assuring himself rather than persuading Erika. 'I don't like school work and I don't want to go on learning for years and years and years. And there's nothing wrong with working, is there? We're all equal aren't we? That's what they're always on about at school and on the T.V.'

'Of course we're all equal,' Erika said. 'We live in a socialist country. But the State wants us all to be better. It's our *duty* to be better.'

'That's what everyone says,' Paul said. 'All the time. On and on and on. I'm sick of hearing it.'

'But what would you do?' Erika demanded. 'You can't really mean that you want to be like the cleaners sweeping Alexanderplatz at night.'

'I wouldn't be a cleaner,' Paul said stoutly. 'What do you think I am? I could go and work for Uncle Bodo. He does all right, doesn't he? He's got a better car than we have. And I'm good at woodwork. You can't say I'm not. I put all those up myself.' He gestured at the line of precarious and rickety shelves.

'Oh dear,' Erika sighed. 'I don't know what Mother or Father is going to say. But that's not the point. You can't leave school till you're sixteen anyway.'

'Can't you do something?' Paul asked.

'What on earth can I do?' Erika said.

'See old Schmidt.'

Erika blinked. 'See him?'

'Yes. Ask him to let me off.' Paul sat upright and looked at Erika beseechingly. 'You could do that, Erika. Say I'm sorry and tell him about the Palast and all that.'

'But I hardly know him,' Erika said, truthfully as she did not take technical drawing.

'No, but he'll listen to you.' Paul was eagerly optimistic. 'You're one of the best pupils in school, and you're a star—jumping and that. He'll listen to you, Erika. He really will. And I won't alter my marks ever again.'

'But they won't get any better, will they, if you won't work.'

'I will, Erika. Honest, I'll try.'

'Well,' Erika always found appeals hard to resist, and it was just conceivable that Herr Schmidt might let Paul off. He had never seemed a bad sort of chap.

'Go on, Erika,' Paul wheedled. 'Please.'

Erika stood up. 'But if you don't want to go to university what do the marks matter?'

'You know what I mean. I don't want to be caught. . . .' Paul hesitated, a hangdog look on his face.

'Cheating,' Erika said. 'I'll think about it.'

'Oh, thanks Erika.' Paul snapped his fingers. 'Thanks a million.'

'I only said that I'd think about it,' Erika said, but as she closed the door the sound of the Beatles was rising triumphantly.

Against her better instinct, and certainly against her better judgement, Erika assured Omi that Paul's troubles were trifling, found her an agreeable music programme on the television, and settled down to her homework. She was deep in the mysteries of calculus, mathematics not being one of the subjects she had been allowed to drop, when her mother came in looking bad-tempered—but that temper was thawed when, a moment after her arrival, Herr Nordern appeared bearing a bottle of Romanian champagne.

'Glasses,' he said, 'and it doesn't matter whether they are tulip or not.'

The champagne cork popped, the glasses were filled, and, surrounded by his bemused family, Herr Nordern raised his glass and gave his good news, cheered by all, including Paul who seemed not to have a care in the world, and particularly by Frau Nordern who was already running a speculative eye over the room, wondering how she would rearrange the furniture in the new, larger apartment to which they would move.

Then Erika gave *her* news, handing over Herr Wolf's card.

'Well, well,' Herr Nordern said. 'It can only mean one thing, I suppose.'

'Of course it can mean only one thing,' Frau Nordern said. 'Star treatment. STAR treatment.' She beamed on Erika and embraced her.

'I should have bought two bottles of champagne,' Herr Nordern said. 'And just think, last night. . . .'

'Forget last night,' Frau Nordern said. 'And that's who he was,' she added thoughtfully.

'Who? What do you mean?' Herr Nordern was puzzled.

'The man in the gallery—the one Erika saw.' Frau Nordern was emphatic. 'He was an observer from the Ministry, talent spotting. I thought so all the time.' She blatantly ignored Herr Nordern's sceptical glance. 'And even Paul is getting better marks. What times we have to look forward to.'

Chapter 11

AND SO a joyous evening for the Norderns, not made the less pleasant by Herr Nordern writing to Herr Wolf, presenting his compliments, and saying that he and Frau Nordern were available to meet Herr Wolf at any time.

A pleasant week followed, too. Herr Nordern was greeted at work with a certain respect which told that the news of his impending promotion had spread throughout the Department. Frau Nordern had two marked successes at work, reconciling an estranged couple and, she rather thought, reforming a bad mother. Paul escaped the dreaded Herr Lettner as Herr Schmidt proved receptive to Erika's plea and let Paul off with a severe caution. And Erika, her mind free of worries, jumped like a deer, breaking her own record time and again and forcing the bar up towards the Junior Record level.

Even the weather turned milder and Erika was able to run in the local park each morning, building up her stamina and relishing the air, returning for her breakfast glowing with health, and turning heads in more ways than one.

And then there were the arrangements for the party to be held in Karl's honour. There was a snag there as no one knew when Karl would be back from Dresden, but Frau Nordern decided to hold the party in the Budapest, a Hungarian restaurant off Frankfurter Allee which had a reputation for good food, better wine, and, most persuasive of all, reasonable prices.

This last was important to Frau Nordern who made it clear that she was not prepared to pay Palast prices even had Karl been the Holy Roman Emperor, and more to the point, neither were the relatives who were being invited, all of whom were expected to pay their share of the bill.

For, as Frau Nordern said to Erika, 'If they don't want to pay, they needn't come.' A sentiment Herr Nordern heartily agreed with, although he agreed even more with Bodo who suggested that he should hire the Building Trade Union Hall, at a very low price, and have food and drink brought in at an even lower price. But Frau Nordern would have none of that.

'Certainly not,' she said. 'Karl in a Builders' Hall, and after taking us to the Palast!' But, she added, if Bodo knew of any musicians who would not charge the earth . . . and Bodo said with a grin that he could manage that for his sister-in-law.

During the week they did hear from Karl. A letter on the florid notepaper of his hotel in Dresden. He had enjoyed a successful few days and was staying on longer to go sightseeing. His letter was doted on a little, but not as much as the other letter which arrived in an imposing official envelope, carrying the heading of the Ministry of Sport, and which said that Herr Wolf would be very pleased to meet Herr and Frau Nordern and their daughter Erika at his office in the National Stadium for Youth and Students the following Saturday at 10.00 a.m. if that was convenient.

It was indeed, and at ten minutes to ten o'clock on a bright Saturday morning, the Norderns, clad in their best, climbed, slightly apprehensively, from the Lada, walked across the car-park under the imposing walls of the Stadium, through the glass doors of the entrance-hall, gave their names at the reception desk, and were asked to wait a moment or two.

Awed, the Norderns looked around the hall with its mosaic of sports, and portraits of gold medallists of the Olympic Games.

'Look at them,' Herr Nordern said. 'Gold medallists. The best in the world. Dozens of them out of 17,000,000 people.' He put his hand on Erika's shoulder. 'And your name will be among them, *Liebchen*. Erika Nordern. A name to live for ever.'

He was brushing aside Erika's protests when the receptionist said that Herr Wolf would see them. A young man in a track suit took them to a lift, along a glistening corridor, and politely bowed them into an office.

Herr Wolf was standing by a wide window which gave a view over the sacred vastness of the Stadium. He smiled as the Norderns entered. 'My view,' he said. 'But first, introductions: Frau Nordern, Herr Nordern, Erika we know.' The 'we' referring to the woman who had been with him in the gym at Egon Schultz School and who turned out to be a Fräulein Carow, a coach of great eminence in the G.D.R. Hands were shaken, coffee offered, accepted, poured, the Norderns were seated and Wolf sat at his desk.

'No need to beat about the bush,' he said, in his pleasant, easy way. 'You know that we are always looking for youngsters of exceptional talent and in Erika we think that we have found one.'

The Norderns gave emphatic assent to this and Herr Wolf smiled again.

'I see that you agree. Now, Erika is rather older than the usual run of athletes—our athletes that is—although we knew about her two years ago. But then she had her fall and suffered a bad set-back. But, to be frank, what has impressed us is the way that she has come back.' He nodded approvingly at Erika. 'She has courage and that counts for a great deal in sport, especially at the highest level. All the talent in the world is useless without real character behind it. So. We know that Erika has talent. We believe that she has character, and she has shown her courage. The question now is, what next?'

He leaned forward and clasped his hands. When he spoke his manner was formal, stilted, even, like a person reciting a well-rehearsed speech. 'The German Democratic Republic believes that all its citizens should be encouraged to develop all their capabilities to the utmost. Indeed, that is enshrined in the Constitution.'

Having made his official preamble his manner altered and he relaxed. 'The question is, how do we best encourage Erika.' He paused, looking at the Norderns in turn. 'I dare say you know what that means?'

Herr Nordern nodded. 'A special sports school.'

'Correct.' Herr Wolf looked at Frau Nordern. 'You realise what *that* means?'

'Well . . . er . . . yes,' Frau Nordern said. 'Special coaching.'

'A little more than that,' Herr Nordern said. 'Of course

Erika would continue with her general education, but they are *sports* schools, specialised. And it might mean Erika leaving home, perhaps living with her coach.' He looked steadily at Frau Nordern. 'Not every mother—or father—takes too kindly to that. It's really why I asked you to come and see me. I like to make sure that the parents appreciate what it means.'

'Yes,' Frau Nordern said. 'I understand that.'

'We would try to place Erika in a Berlin sports school, but you would have no objections if she were to go away?'

'No,' Frau Nordern said. Although, feeling perhaps as if that sounded as if she didn't care whether Erika left home or stayed, she added, hastily, 'Of course, I would miss her.'

'That's natural,' Herr Wolf said. 'But if she did go away we wouldn't be sending her to Siberia! And you, Herr Nordern?'

Herr Nordern looked at Erika and addressed her, too. 'It would be a sacrifice,' he said, 'but a worthy one.'

'An excellent answer, if I may say so.' Herr Wolf leaned back in his chair and nodded at Fräulein Carow.

'And what do you think, Erika?' she asked.

Erika looked at the floor, embarrassed at being the centre of attention.

'Speak up Erika,' her mother said. 'She gets shy at times,' she added.

'Shy?' Fräulein Carow asked sharply.

'Very rarely.' Herr Nordern gave his wife a piercing glare. 'Just speak your mind, Erika.'

Erika looked up. 'I would like to go. Of course I'd miss home but to really. . . .' Her voice died away as she groped for the words which would express what she thought about the prospect of a genuine, first class, athletic career. And even as she fumbled for the words she was aware of the real need to find them, there and then. To show that she had brains as well as physique so that she could be a worthy ambassador of her country. But finding those words under the piercing gaze of Fräulein Carow wasn't easy.

'I would like to. . . .' she said, and then the words came to her quite naturally and sincerely. 'I would like to find out what I could really do. To discover that.' As she spoke, quite

111

unconsciously, she raised her head and shoulders and her arms, as if already soaring into unknown space.

And as she made that proud gesture Fräulein Carow raised her hands also, as if willing Erika upwards. 'That is the thing,' she said. 'To find out what you can do. Well, perhaps you will.'

That 'perhaps' brought Erika down to earth, reminding her that as yet no one had actually said that she would be selected for special training, and she wasn't going to be that day, as Herr Wolf made clear.

'You do realise,' he said, 'that nothing has been decided yet. Erika is a candidate, admittedly a promising one, but there are others, and plenty of them, I might say.'

Frau Nordern was taken aback by this. 'You mean that she's not been selected?'

Herr Wolf gave a wry smile. 'Athletes tend to select themselves, Frau Nordern. But if you mean for a sports school, then no, she hasn't.'

'Then what are we here for?' Frau Nordern was indignant.

'We have to take a first step, gnädige Frau,' Herr Wolf said. 'But other people have to be consulted, there are committees. . . .'

Frau Nordern's face fell, and Erika had a sinking feeling, but Herr Nordern was understanding. 'Of course,' he said. 'We quite understand. But at any rate you have our firm support, and Erika wants to go. If there is anything else we can do, just let us know.'

'I will let you know if there is.' Herr Wolf stood up, the interview being clearly at an end. 'Believe me, this meeting has been most useful. There is just one more thing I must say.'

He paused and the Norderns stared at him expectantly. 'Not all athletes stand on the victor's rostrum. No, but there are other rewards. So.'

He shook hands all round as did Fräulein Carow who pressed Erika's hand firmly. 'Do well in the Indoor Championships,' she said. 'We'll meet again at the Dynamo Club.' She raised her hand high, above Erika's head. 'At that level.'

Herr Wolf amiably saw the Norderns back to the foyer. At the glass doors he waved his hand. 'All yours Erika. It's just waiting for you.'

The Norderns climbed into the Lada and chugged off. Frau Nordern began to speak but Herr Nordern interrupted her. 'Let's have a drink,' he said. 'There's a decent bar near here. We'll talk about it then.'

The bar was the Silver Bear, a restaurant, really, with a bar attached, and might have been in another world from the bar Herr Nordern had been in after his meeting with the Police. It was smart, clean, full of well-dressed elderly ladies taking morning coffee although the bar, where the Norderns sat, had a quota of workmen watching a West German sports programme on a television set balanced on a shelf.

Herr Nordern ordered drinks, lit a cigar, blew out a smoke ring as if to signify that the discussion could now commence, and began it himself.

'So, *Liebchen*, what do you think?'

Erika squeezed her hands between her knees. 'It's exciting.'

'Yes,' Herr Nordern said. 'It is. I thought Herr Wolf was a very decent person.'

'I thought so too,' Erika said. She sipped at her orange juice. 'But Father, what did he mean, not all athletes stand on the rostrum?'

Herr Nordern removed a speck of tobacco from his lip. 'He was just telling the truth,' he said. 'I liked that. What he meant was that only a few athletes, only the absolute tops, win medals. A lot end up like Fräulein Silber. And that's not a bad thing to be. But you won't be like that, *Liebchen*. No, you're for the top. The very top. I can feel it in my bones. Hey, Helga?'

Frau Nordern peered into her glass. 'Of course. But nothing has happened. Nothing at all!'

'What did you expect?' Herr Nordern said. 'Erika to be whisked away on the spot? This was just a preliminary meeting. They wanted to meet us, to look us over.'

'*Us* over?'

'Certainly. It is a very serious business. The State will be making a heavy investment in Erika. It wouldn't want to do that and then have her brooding and homesick if she was away. And besides, they have to make sure.'

'Make sure of what?'

Herr Nordern looked thoughtfully at his wife. 'Helga,' he

said, as if teaching a lesson to a slow learner. 'Star athletes go abroad.'

'Of course they go abroad.' Frau Nordern laughed. 'And why are you talking like that?'

'They go to the West,' Herr Nordern said.

'Yes, and very nice too.'

Still speaking slowly, but dropping his voice a little, Herr Nordern said, 'The State is concerned that they come back.'

Comprehension dawned on Frau Nordern and a deep, angry flush spread across her face. 'You—I mean they—they wouldn't dare suggest that Erika would—' she paused, panting ominously.

'*Defect*,' said Herr Nordern. 'And keep your voice down. Of course they aren't suggesting that. They just like to make sure, that's all.'

'Make sure about us? Do you mean that they will be checking on us?'

'Of course.' Herr Nordern sighed. 'That's standard procedure. Everyone who goes to the West is checked on, except old people. I approve of it. Strongly approve.'

He clapped Erika on the back. 'Don't worry about it. You're not disappointed are you?'

When they had entered the bar Erika had not been disappointed but for the past few minutes something like it had been creeping up on her. 'Well, I didn't realise that there would be all this,' she admitted.

'And the committees. Those that Herr Wolf was talking about,' Frau Nordern said. 'Erika will be ninety before she gets chosen.'

Herr Nordern smiled ruefully. 'Yes, committees.' He spoke with the resignation of one who spent his life dealing with them. 'But believe me, once the wheels start turning in sport, they whizz round.'

'But when will they start?' Frau Nordern asked.

'They already have,' Herr Nordern said. 'From now on—' he looked seriously at Erika—'from now on it's up to you. Just keep jumping as you can and the world will be your oyster.'

'And us?' Frau Nordern said.

'What do you mean, us?'

'Will they be satisfied with us?'

'Of course they will.' Herr Nordern was indignant. 'We're good citizens. Exemplary. Not a thing against us. You're not thinking of your background are you? Forget that. It's done with. Finished. Come on,' he raised his glass. 'A toast to you, Erika. Don't blush, you will have to get used to it.'

He smiled at Erika, Frau Nordern beamed upon her, and in a friendly Berliner sort of way, a couple of men at the bar raised their glasses in salutation.

'So,' Herr Nordern drained his glass and they all stood up. As they did so there was a mild stir at the bar. On their way out Herr Nordern asked a man what had happened. The man, who was mildly drunk, pointed to the television set.

'News flash,' he said. 'West German. Some poor sod shot going over—' he jabbed his thumb in the direction every Berliner knew by heart, to the Wall.

'Poor sod?' Herr Nordern said, and he said it ominously.

''Sright.' The man's speech was blurred by drink.

'He deserved it,' Herr Nordern stared menacingly at the man, one of whose mates plucked at his sleeve.

'That's right, 'course he did,' the other man said. He elbowed his mate aside. 'That's what he meant.'

'I hope that he did,' Herr Nordern said to sickly smiles of agreement, and a loud, perhaps too loud for sincerity, 'Hear! Hear!' from the barman.

Herr Nordern glared around, meeting dropped eyes, then stared at the television set. After a moment's hesitation the barman stretched up and switched it over to another channel, a G.D.R. channel. Then the Norderns left.

'I've no time for them,' Herr Nordern said as they drove home. 'Traitors, criminals, scroungers. They won't do a day's work so they try to get over there, tell a pack of lies, and get a fortune out of the Fascists. . . .'

He was still fuming when they got home but his bad temper evaporated when they entered the flat and found Omi placidly reading by the window and, unbelievably, Paul sitting at the table industriously doing his homework.

'Now this is better,' he said, relaxing as lunch was prepared. 'Keep that up Paul. A little effort. See what that has done for Erika,' modestly omitting to add for himself, also.

Over lunch the story of the morning was told and retold, every word analysed, every encouraging nod and smile given by Herr Wolf and Fräulein Carow.

'And,' Frau Nordern said, '*and* Fräulein Carow went like this,' she raised her hand in the air, 'and she said to Erika, "We'll meet again up there." She meant at the very top; the top of the tree. Isn't that right Erika?'

Erika agreed, but she knew, and she knew that Fräulein Carow knew, and that Fräulein Carow knew she knew, that the height to which Fräulein Carow had raised her hand, with a high-jumper's knowledge, was, give or take a centimetre or two, the world record height. But she did not tell her family that.

After lunch the dishes were washed and, without enthusiasm, Herr Nordern went to his room to catch up with his work.

'The sooner that Steinmark gets back the better,' he said. 'God Almighty knows what he's up to in Dresden.' But all the same, he thought, with deep satisfaction, as he bent to his work, he's in for a shock when he does get back.

'And what are you going to do?' Frau Nordern asked Erika.

'Running this afternoon,' Erika said, 'and I might go to the Youth Club afterwards. Just for an hour,' she added hastily, as though apologising for going at all.

But Frau Nordern was amenable, pleased almost, and her pleasure was compounded when, to Erika's annoyance, Paul said that he would go too; Frau Nordern's pleasure being explicable because she believed that the club was well run and that his being there would keep Paul from the flesh-pots of Alexanderplatz.

'All right,' Erika said to Paul as, changed into her track suit, she left the flat. 'But don't think that you're going to hang around me and my friends all night.'

'I won't, Erika,' Paul said piously. 'I promise you I won't.'

Chapter 12

ERIKA RAN, mile after effortless mile around the park until dusk brought the bone-chilling mist; then, in a loping run, under the great beech tree, home. Supper was ready—soup and Bulgarian tinned fruit—eaten, dishes washed, Erika and Paul ready to go out, Herr and Frau Nordern too.

'The Beyers rang,' Frau Nordern said, mentioning some friendly acquaintances who lived a couple of streets away. 'We're going to have a drink and play cards. It will be a nice change.'

'Yes,' Erika agreed that it would be a nice change for her mother but she looked at Omi, sitting quietly in her chair.

'I don't think that I'll go to the Youth Club after all,' she said. 'I'll stay in, rest—and do some homework.'

But that ploy didn't work. Omi smiled her patient, wise smile. 'Go, child,' she said, 'go.'

Erika and Paul went, Paul politely, solicitously, opening the door for Erika and waving her through first, although it was a tight squeeze in the tiny vestibule, and at the bus-stop, in a bizarre parody of good manners, insisting that Erika stand in front of him.

Erika looked at him shrewdly. 'Are you being funny, Paul? Because if you are. . . .'

'Funny!' Paul looked hurt. 'I'm being polite.'

'Yes, that's what's funny,' Erika said. 'And what have you been looking so pleased about this week? Just because I got you off seeing Herr Lettner doesn't mean it won't happen again. And next time don't expect me to help you.'

'I know that,' Paul was odiously grateful. 'And thanks a lot for that, Erika. But you've seen me doing my homework, haven't you? I've been doing that.'

'Yes, for a week.'

'Well, a week's good. You've got to get used to these things. But listen, Erika,' Paul stamped his feet against the cold. 'Listen, when you go to the sports school you'll leave home, won't you?'

'If I go I might.'

'Well, I'll tell you what.' Paul looked down the road to where distant lights told of the approach of the bus. 'I've been thinking. When you go, Omi won't need that big room all to herself, will she? So I was thinking, when you go she could move into my room and I could have yours.'

'Paul!' Erika's cheeks flamed, with temper. 'You really are the end. Don't you *ever* think of anyone but yourself?' She swung on to the bus. 'No, go away,' she said, as Paul sat next to her.

'Listen,' Paul said. 'I *am* thinking of someone else. I'm thinking of Omi!' he urged, in one of the most improbable remarks he had ever made. 'Your room is on the street. Mine would be quieter—'

But the rest of his appeal was lost as Erika pushed past him and stood at the end of the bus, well aware that Paul would rather postpone his appeal than stand the two slow lurching miles to the club.

The Youth Club of the Paris Commune as it was officially known, or the 'Paree' as its more irreverent members called it, was a gimcrack affair, cracked concrete and cheap plastic panels, tucked beside the inevitable block of flats, and a health centre, but it was well equipped: table tennis, television, a library, a concert room, a rather more substantial annexe for weight lifting, a hall which doubled up for meetings of the Free German Youth and dancing, and a comfortable lounge where one could buy coffee and soft drinks.

A girl was playing Chopin in the concert room as Erika went into the lounge. Rosa was there drinking fruit juice with Fritz Kott and a few other pupils from the Egon Schultz School who greeted her with the same, unanimous question: 'What happened?'

Struggling not to blush, although failing, Erika told them, stressing emphatically the provisional nature of the interview. But that qualification was brushed aside.

'No ifs or buts,' Fritz said. 'You're in. *In.*'

'Maybe,' Erika said. 'But it's a big maybe. I've got to keep jumping well.'

'And why shouldn't you?' Fritz said. 'If you can do a thing once you can do it again. Right, Rosa?'

'Absolutely,' Rosa said. 'And do it better. And the way you're jumping now Erika . . . wow!' she pointed to the ceiling.

'Oh, you never know,' Erika protested. 'You can reach your peak and that's it.' She laughed despite herself. 'That has to be true, doesn't it? Otherwise people would be jumping over the Television Tower.'

'Some truth in that,' Rosa agreed. 'I know I've reached my limit. No, really. I know it. And to be tops you can lose a lot. . . .'

'And gain a lot, too,' Fritz said, with a warmth glowing beyond loyalty.

'Well, we'll see,' Erika said, 'and talking of seeing, look who's here.'

The *who* was a Herr Hocher who, with a dedicated voluntary worker, Fräulein Renn, ran the Youth Club. He was a tall, rather gloomy man in his forties, dressed, as he always and incongruously was, in the blue and white of the F.G.Y. and accompanied by Herman Guttenbruk, he of the trip to, and interminable lecture on, the Soviet Union.

Herr Hocher's long face split into a welcoming smile—or what might, charitably, have passed for one. 'Ha! ha! ha! familiar faces . . . yes . . . but not too familiar, I'm sorry to say. Ha! ha! Klaus, isn't it? and Klara—Oh, of course—' corrected—'Erika, Fritz, Rosa . . . we really ought to see you more often, ought we not? Don't you have a duty to support. . . .'

But the group had its answer to that: pressures of training, all working hard at normal school subjects, *and* attending F.G.Y. meetings at school.

'But, ha! ha! able to make time for a dance,' Herr Hocher said.

'Ah,' Rosa said, with an air of sweet reasonableness. 'We have to have some relaxation. The school doctor says that we should work hard, but not overwork,' adding a muffled 'ha! ha!' as, baffled, Herr Hocher retreated to the T.V. room where there was a noisy scuffle.

'The Louts,' Fritz said. 'I hope that they aren't staying for the dance.'

There was a general sigh of agreement. The Louts were a bunch of youths from another district who came to the club now and again and mildly disturbed the dances. There was never any real trouble, as the consequences for hooliganism in the G.D.R. could be extremely severe, but some horseplay, and the occasional illicit disc was put on the record-player, much to Herr Hocher's annoyance. Just once there had been a fight but as the then leader of the Louts had, unwittingly, taken on a junior boxing champion, he had ceased appearing. But still, the Louts were tedious, at least in the eyes of Erika and her friends, the more so to Erika who had an uneasy, and not unjustified feeling that Paul was always likely to be drawn into their orbit.

More people were drifting into the club, all of whom asked Erika how her interview had gone.

'I don't understand how they know,' Erika said. 'I didn't tell anyone.'

Fritz grinned. 'Don't you know? In this country everything is a secret—and nothing is secret.'

The group laughed as the first strains of a Hungarian pop group wailed from the hall.

'Shall we go in?' Fritz asked.

Erika resolutely shook her head. 'Not until there are more people in there.'

'Now, now,' Fritz said. 'You mustn't be shy. Just think what it will be like doing the high jump with 50,000 people watching you!'

'Don't!' Erika felt goose-pimples on her arms and the thought crossed her mind that, despite all that had been said to her about courage, perhaps she wasn't really cut out for stardom, after all. But she firmly stamped on that thought.

'All right,' she said. 'Let's go in. But I'm not dancing, remember.'

They strolled into the hall where a few couples were vaguely swaying under the glare of yellow neon, and the basilisk stare of Fräulein Renn. Rosa nudged Erika.

'Look,' she said out of the side of her mouth.

Erika looked. A girl was sauntering into the hall. She was something of a celebrity at the Egon Schultz School. Her father was a high official and had taken her with him on a trip to London and she had returned with her hair in orange stripes. She had actually appeared at school like that—once. When she came back the next day the stripes had been dyed her natural brunette, but badly, so that her hair still seemed striped, hence her nickname, Bunte. She was also something of a *femme fatale*, with the looks of a young Marlene Dietrich, and a blasé manner to match.

Bunte casually wiggled over to Erika and her friends. 'Helloo' she drawled. 'How is Rosa? How is Erika? How is Fritz? All well, yes. Athletic, yes. Democratic, yes. Socialist, yes. Healthy minds in healthy bodies, yes. Who will dance with me? In the discos in the West they darken the lights, in the East they brighten them. But come, Fritz.'

To Erika's intense annoyance, Fritz promptly accepted the invitation—obeyed the command, rather—and as Rosa moved on to the floor with another boy, she was left feeling abandoned—and foolish. She felt a rare prickle of envious hostility and in that mood, defiantly and with a lunatic rashness, accepted an invitation to dance with one of the Louts, whose approach was loutish enough: a jerk of the head and a mumbled, 'Wanna dance, chick?'

Erika moved on to the floor, keeping the Lout at a safe distance, but he was not as loutish as his manner suggested.

'You're a good dancer,' he said. 'A really good mover.'

'Better than her?' Erika indicated Bunte.

'Sure. Although she's not bad,' the Lout said. 'But what's the matter with her hair? It's all stripy.'

Erika told him the reason, expecting a sneering laugh, but the Lout was impressed. 'That's something,' he said. 'That takes some nerve you know, to do that to your hair and go to school.'

'It seems silly, to me,' Erika said.

'They do that in the West,' the Lout said. 'Stripe their hair. Cut it, too, in patterns.'

'I know,' Erika said loftily. 'It's barbaric.' Hoping to squash the Lout with that word.

But the Lout was unsquashed. 'It's individualism. Shows your personality. Makes you someone. Someone different. Yourself.'

Erika was mildly scandalised by this heresy. 'True individualism lies in the proper relationship of each person to society,' she said, primly.

'Eh? Oh, that junk,' the Lout said. 'Hey, listen, do you want to come to Wannsee?'

'What?' Erika stopped dancing. 'Now? With you?'

'Sure, why not? There's going to be a big party in the woods, real rock and roll. I've got a scooter.' He added that information with an air of modest pride.

Erika laughed incredulously. 'Go to Wannsee on the back of a scooter in this weather? You must be crazy.'

'O.K. Suit yourself.' The Lout shrugged as the music ended. 'See you around,' he said, making a bee-line for Bunte.

Rosa came across the dance-floor, her face serious. 'Erika,' she said, 'what on earth are you doing?'

'Dancing,' Erika said.

Rosa was impatient. 'You know what I mean. If you hurt your foot. . . .'

'I'm being careful,' Erika said, in a voice which meant that Rosa could mind her own business.

'But—' Rosa began.

'I don't want to hear any "buts",' Erika snapped, her eyes on Fritz who, despite competition from the Louts, was talking to Bunte.

Another disc started, Herr Hocher placing it on the record-player with his own hands, the result being a foxtrot played by a Russian orchestra, and he himself took the floor with Fräulein Renn, the pair of them going through what seemed to the young people weirdly funny gyrations together.

Finally, elbowed out of Bunte's presence by the Louts, Fritz ambled over to the girls.

'That's put the stopper on it,' he said.

'Has it? On what, might I ask?' Erika was freezingly polite.

'This music,' Fritz said.

'I think that it's very nice music,' Erika said.

'Honestly?' Fritz was surprised.

'Yes.' Erika smiled across the floor at the odious Herman Guttenbruk. 'And I think that someone would like to dance it with *me*,' she said, as Herman, lured by the smile, came across and with a ludicrous bow, asked Erika if she would do him the honour of the dance, Erika graciously accepting, to her delight leaving Fritz looking disconsolate and unhappy.

'I much prefer this music,' Herman said, doing an awkward shuffle. 'Pop music is degenerate. Don't you agree?'

'Hmm?' Erika was too occupied in looking over Herman's shoulder at Fritz to pay him any attention.

'I said pop and rock are degenerate,' Herman repeated. 'In fact I was surprised to see you dancing to pop music, and with one of *them*.'

Erika had no intention of being lectured to by Herman. 'What's wrong with dancing with one of them?' she demanded.

'Well,' Herman bumped into Herr Hocher and apologised profusely. 'They aren't good types.'

'They don't breathe all over you though.'

'Sorry. Very sorry.' Herman, whom Erika had already been keeping at a safe distance from her feet, backed away. 'But you know what I mean, Erika.'

'Do I?' Erika was aloof but seeing Fritz watching her pulled Herman closer. 'How can we dance if you're miles away?'

Herman, startled but pleased, moved in, only to be disconcerted as Erika pushed him away. 'Not that close,' she said, although pleased by the expression on Fritz's face.

The record ended and Erika walked off the floor with Herman in attendance. Herr Hocher put on another record, an amateurish jazz band.

'Shall we?' Herman said.

'I thought that you said this was decadent music,' Erika replied.

'Oh, not this. This is quite acceptable. They play it in the Soviet Union. I heard it while I was there. I went to a Young Pioneer dance in Moscow. . . .' But his reminiscences, twice, thrice told, were lost on the dance-hall air as Erika walked away round the hall, affecting not to see Fritz who was standing moodily by the door, and giving a start of surprise when he asked her to dance.

'I'm going for a juice,' she said. 'Anyway, I thought that you had a partner.'

'What? Oh, Bunte. I danced with her.'

'Really? I thought you were teaching her calculus.'

'Erika!' Fritz followed her into the lounge. 'You did say you weren't going to dance, and she did ask me. I just didn't want to seem rude. And then you went and danced with that Lout—*and* with Herman. Didn't you see me looking at you?'

'I might have done,' Erika said.

'I wanted you to stop dancing—no!—' as Erika turned on him—'because of what you said, about hurting your foot. That's all.'

'So you didn't mind me dancing with other people?'

'Well,' Fritz went red, which, Erika thought, made rather a nice change from her own blushing, and looked at his shoes.

Erika thawed, melted, forgave Fritz, for which he was pathetically grateful, and sent him for fruit juice while she looked for Paul who was happily playing table tennis. She went back into the lounge and sat with Fritz, finding out how remarkably much they had in common, until they were joined by Rosa and other friends and spent two magical hours until, at 10.00, she stood up.

'Home time,' she said. 'No,' cutting off Fritz's protests. 'I'm in training and I should be in bed now. Where's Paul?'

Fritz scurried off and returned with a reluctant Paul and they went to the door. The Louts had also had enough, enough of Herr Hocher, that is, and were on their scooters, revving them with an ear-splitting racket.

'So,' Erika said. 'Good-night, Fritz.'

'Good-night, Erika.' Fritz stared at her. 'I . . . I. . . .'

'What?'

Fritz gulped. 'I wonder . . . how about tomorrow?'

Erika shook her head. 'I can't. Really. Training.'

'Yes. Of course.' Fritz took a step nearer Erika. 'Perhaps—' then his face changed. 'Look at Paul,' he said.

Cursing Paul under her breath Erika turned. Paul was deep in conversation with a very loutish Lout indeed.

'Paul!' Erika cried over the din of the scooters. 'Paul!'

Paul did not, or affected not to, hear her and Erika walked across the yard and took him by the elbow.

'Time for you to come home,' she said, quite as firmly as her mother.

The Lout eased the throttle on his scooter and leered through the exhaust smoke. 'What's this about going home? Come with us, have a good time.'

Erika ignored him. 'Come on,' she said to Paul.

Paul actually hesitated and the Lout stuck his oar in again. 'Are you coming or not, kid? Never mind what she says.'

'Keep out of this,' Erika flared up. 'Clear off.'

'Now just a minute.' The Lout began to swing off his scooter. 'Who are you to give orders? If the kid wants to come he can, see?'

'No he can't.' Fritz's voice came over Erika's shoulder, and it sounded astonishingly determined.

'*Another* Nosey Parker!' The Lout simulated astonishment. 'The massed ranks of the F.G.Y.! Well keep your nose out of this, *Comrade*, unless you want trouble.'

'I don't want it,' Fritz said. 'But if you insist.'

The Lout hesitated for a moment but then, as the other scooters roared out of the yard, he shrugged and revved his own scooter up. 'I'll see you again,' he shouted.

'Any time,' Fritz bellowed back as the Lout drove off, tooting his horn derisively.

'Thanks Fritz,' Erika said. 'But there was no need to bother.'

'It's all right,' Fritz said. 'I know that character. His father is a big shot and he thinks he is, too. He needed taking down a peg.'

'I wasn't frightened of him,' Erika said.

'I'm sure you weren't.'

'So.' Erika shivered a little.

'So.' Fritz was solicitous. 'Better not stand about.'

'No.'

'You'll miss your bus.'

'Yes.'

Slowly, hesitantly, Fritz's hand moved forward and slowly, hesitantly Erika's hand stole forward too and touched it.

'See you Monday then.'

'Yes.' The touch of the hands became the slightest of caresses and then the hands recoiled.

'Good-night,' Erika said, and left with a sullen Paul at her heels.

The bus came and they boarded it, but to Erika it seemed less like the familiar old lumbering, lurching, yellow Berlin bus, and more a vehicle of romance, gliding through a night made mysterious by more than fog.

But even these strange raptures were forgotten when they got off and, outside the flats, Erika turned on Paul. 'I won't tell about tonight,' she said.

'Nothing to tell,' Paul muttered.

'Nothing!' Erika shook her head. 'What do you think Father and Mother would say if they knew you were even *thinking* of going off with those kids—and at this time of night! You're crazy Paul. Really crazy.' And so am I, she thought, as she ran up the stairs.

Only Omi was in, and she was ready for bed. Erika helped her prepare and, when she was safely in bed, sat by her.

'Will you do something for me tomorrow, *Liebchen*?' Omi asked.

'Anything, Omi. Anything at all.'

'You are sure?'

'Absolutely.'

Omi sighed. 'I would like to go to church. Will you take me?'

'Certainly.' Erika tucked in a corner of Omi's duvet. 'Would you like to go to the Cathedral? We could do some window shopping, too.'

'No. I would like to go into the country. I know a church in Tappersdorf. We can go on the *S-Bahn*.'

'That would be very nice,' Erika said. 'We'll go. Sleep now. Good-night.'

Herr and Frau Nordern came home contented after a pleasant evening. A last drink of coffee was had, and the flat settled down to slumber. As the owl hooted and the night train called, Erika was already slipping into the state where the real world fades and the dreamworld begins, thinking of Fritz and that last, subtle touch of two hands.

Chapter 13

THE NEXT morning Erika helped Omi dress in black, the only colour she considered suitable for Divine Service. Erika dressed soberly, too, although, in an uncharacteristic act of defiance, she pinned her F.G.Y. badge on to her lapel.

Although not approving of church-going, Herr Nordern offered to drive Omi and Erika to the church but, the day being bright and sunny, the offer was declined.

'Thank you,' Omi said, 'but, really, the fresh air will do me good.' She smiled. 'And a trip on the *S-Bahn*, it is a long time since I had one.'

Across the table Erika looked up thoughtfully from her smoked ham. With a twinge of conscience it occurred to her that it was not often Omi got out; a rare trip to the theatre or a concert, Wannsee in summer, or Potsdam, but in the winter she was trapped in the flat, passing long, lonely hours looking on to a street where little happened. 'I'll take her out more,' Erika thought, and then realised that she might not be around to do so.

Herr Nordern insisted that he should drive Erika and Omi at least to the *S-Bahn* station and stood with them until the train came, then, shaking his head, he handed Omi into a carriage.

Tappersdorf was a few stops along the line—countrified and still keeping a rural quietness: poplars masked a factory, behind pre-war houses with steeply pitched roofs fields of sprouts stretched away, the sprouts looking oddly sentient as they stood in their patient, frosty queues, waiting to be picked.

Under the inevitable power lines the church looked rural,

too: a simple wooden structure with a sharp, narrow steeple prodding at the sky as if to remind God that it was there, its bell clanking as an additional reminder and as a summons to the faithful.

There were a good number of these, the men and women solemn in their Sunday best, although the young people, and there were plenty of those, too, were surprisingly casual, wearing jeans and bright sweaters under their black leather jackets; casual and cheerful, too, in their attitude as they entered the church, calling greetings, and making good-natured jokes, much to Omi's disapproval.

The interior of the church was quite different: bare, bleak and uncompromising, painted white with a black cross standing on a simple table. If a soul was to meet God there it was without the mediation of stained glass, pictures, images or incense. It was a building for the speaking, and the hearing, of the word of God—and no distractions allowed.

But bleak though the building might be, the welcome was warm, Elders shaking hands with the congregation, delighted to see two new faces, ushering Omi and Erika to their seats. Omi not being of the school which sits as far at the back of a church as possible, Erika found herself under the nose of the Minister, who beamed upon her, and surrounded by family groups: parents, grandparents and children who made an agreeable din until a small group of musicians struck up the opening bars of the first hymn.

Erika had been to church before: with Omi, once on her own out of curiosity, and once with the F.G.Y. as a prelude to a discussion on Modern Superstitions. So the service was not unfamiliar; the readings from the Bible in the magnificent prose of Martin Luther, the prayers, the general confession, the great hymns, sung with unaffected fervour and in which Erika joined (although she was critical of the flautist) both because she liked singing and because it would have hurt Omi had she remained silent. But in the prayers, although she knelt and bowed her head, her attention was on the people in the church.

How strange, she thought, that such normal, pleasant people could bring themselves to believe in the existence of God. How extraordinary that people her own age should believe such grotesque, non-scientific ideas as that a man could be resurrected from the dead after, and a horrible thought it was, after being crucified; and how fantastic that they should believe that *all* the dead would rise from their graves—all of them, those countless millions, millions upon millions, rising from the clay into which they had, long since, dissolved. . . .

She peered sideways at Omi. Omi's old head was bowed and her gnarled fingers were pressed together in prayer. Was she praying for resurrection, asking the mysterious, invisible Maker of All Things to hasten the day when she and her dearly loved man would be united again as they had been in those golden days long past?

But if Omi was, then surely she was wrong. Erika remembered the Watchword Omi had been reading on the day when Karl had come. The Watchword had read, 'Let the dead bury their dead: but go thou and preach the kingdom of God.'

Erika was still not completely sure what the text meant but one thing about it *was* clear, people had better things to do than to dwell on the past and surely—it came upon Erika in a flash of intuition—surely the State was doing just that: not, of course, leaving the dead unmourned, and certainly not forgetting the evils of Fascism, but moving forward—preaching a socialist gospel—and not merely preaching it, doing it: making a fairer, better, juster Germany. Yes!

With a mixture of admiration at her own acumen, pride in her country, and affectionate pity for Omi, Erika politely sat upright as the Minister began his sermon.

It was not short. When the congregation of the Lutheran Church gathered to hear the Word of God expounded, they expected to hear it expounded fully, and the Pastor of Tappersdorf was ready to oblige, not merely comparing the German text for the day—a reference to the doings of an obscure Old Testament prophet—with the original Hebrew, and giving a learned half-hour to an explanation of the circumstances in which the prophet lived, suffered, and prophesied, a time in which it seemed a small group of people struggled for the truth and searched for God under the shadow of huge decadent empires to the East—and the West, but he, the Pastor, was perfectly willing to apply the prophet's message to the present day—and to present-day socialist Germany, at that. With a little of the guilty excitement of enjoying a forbidden pleasure, Erika began to listen attentively.

'Of course,' the Pastor said, 'of course, the State may properly demand our obedience in many matters: obeying its laws—if the laws are just; making us pay taxes—if the taxes are properly spent; supporting its policies—if the policies are wise. So far the Church is at one with the State. But where do we differ, as Micah differed from the priesthood and rulers of his day?

'It is in this. In the end a totalitarian state says that everything which exists belongs to it. The Church says that in the end everything which exists belongs to God.

'But what is the difference there? What is the difference between an almighty state and almighty God? It lies in one simple point. God has given us complete autonomy, that is self-government, the government of ourselves. We call that freedom, the freedom to do good—or evil—and we, the Church, say that the choice between good and evil is an individual one. Of course, if an individual chooses evil then it follows that he must be punished, but he must be punished because he, or she, has deliberately chosen to do evil.

'That is a terrible gift but it is a precious one. It belongs to us as individuals regardless of the power of the State or the claims of the State. And if the State denies us that right of individual choice then, although it might shower us with gifts, it is robbing us of our deepest, profoundest freedom, that upon which all other freedoms depend, and so the State, any State, which denies God's ultimate gift must be opposed.'

The Pastor paused for a moment and looked thoughtfully at his flock and, Erika was convinced, piercingly at her. 'There is one more point I should like to make. We are in the season of Advent which, as we know, means the Coming— the Coming of our Lord Jesus Christ—and He, as we know also, was crucified by rulers who set the claims of the State above Him. But what is the image Advent calls to our minds? Surely it is of the family of Christ, Father, Mother, and Child.' The Pastor smiled a little wryly, 'It is called a unitary family, now, and unitary families are under attack in certain quarters, but the family is at the heart of our religion and our civilisation. Why? Because there we find trust and confidence and love. Every totalitarian state has attacked the family because in that small, loving group they see a threat to the power of the State. And so, if the State sets its claims against those of the family it must be resisted.'

The Pastor gazed at the bare, raftered ceiling. 'Of course,' he said, 'of course, we are happy to live in a state where no such claims are made. Amen.'

The final prayers were said, a final hymn sung, and the blessing given. The congregation stood up and amiably shuffled out, shaking hands as they did so. At the door the Minister was waiting. Surrounded by his flock he nonetheless had an eye on Omi and Erika and, although he made no apparent attempt to meet them, Erika and Omi found themselves facing him.

'Gnädige Frau,'—'Gracious lady.'

Omi held out a gloved hand in a stately, aristocratic manner. 'Von Ritter,' she announced herself. 'My granddaughter, Erika Nordern.'

'Ah, a pleasure.' The Minister shook hands firmly with Erika, his eye resting for a moment on the F.G.Y. badge in her lapel. 'We haven't seen you before, Frau von Ritter, Erika.'

'We live in Biesdorf,' Omi said.

'I see. That will be St Mark's. Pastor Dietrich.'

'Yes. But I confess I don't go as often as I might,' Omi said. 'My age, and winter.'

'Ah, winter,' the Minister's voice had the rueful edge common to Germans when speaking of that season. 'And Erika?' He turned to her. 'Do you go to St Mark's?'

The question was put lightly but, in view of Erika's F.G.Y. badge, there was a certain teasing quality to it.

Somewhat self-consciously, Erika denied going to St Mark's, or any other church. 'I'm an atheist,' she said defiantly, although feeling rather foolish for saying so; foolish and a little ashamed with Omi standing next to her.

But the Pastor was undisturbed. 'An atheist. Quite. But you came to our church.'

'I brought my grandmother,' Erika said.

'Yes.' The Minister smiled. 'Well, that is a Christian act. Did you enjoy the service?'

Actually, Erika had enjoyed it; the resonance of the language, the communal singing and the friendly presence of the congregation had a warmth which, she had to admit, the meetings of the F.G.Y. lacked.

As if reading her thoughts the Minister leaned forward a little. 'We have a youth group. Why not come along? You could give a talk—perhaps—on atheism.'

The treacherous red invaded Erika's cheeks. 'I don't think so. I'm very busy. But excuse me, my grandmother, I mustn't keep her in the cold.'

'No, of course not.' The Minister was solicitous. 'One of us will drive you to the station.'

But that offer was declined too, courteous goodbyes were exchanged, and Omi took Erika's arm as they walked back to the *S-Bahn*. On the way there was a café, a reasonable sort of place with discreet lace curtains.

Omi squeezed Erika's elbow. 'Shall we have coffee? We've done our duty so we can have a little treat.'

Erika was ready for a treat and a moment later, surrounded by a forest of plants which gave the café an Amazonian aspect, they were seated and ordering coffee and cakes.

Omi sighed contentedly as she looked around the room which had a fair smattering of elderly ladies, like herself having a Sunday morning treat.

'Ah,' she said, 'I feel better, so much better. It is too long since I went to church—' she broke off as the coffee and cream cakes arrived. 'Dear me, when I was a child we went to church *twice* every Sunday. We girls wore starched white aprons and very uncomfortable they were too. Not that I approve of the way some of the young people were dressed today. The Creator deserves our respect.' She nodded firmly at Erika. 'But you were dressed properly. A true von Ritter.'

Erika demurred mildly. 'I'm a Nordern, Omi.'

'Yes, a Nordern too. I don't deny it.' Omi looked searchingly at Erika. 'But you take after our line. You have fine bones and eyes. The face of an aristocrat.'

'Omi!' Erika dissented quite vehemently from this heresy while, despite herself, her eyes were searching for a mirror.

'You shouldn't say such things. Besides, those old *Junker*—' she was about to say *all* those *Junker* but in deference to Omi did not—'they didn't all look nice. Some of them were awful. Take Hindenburg,' she said, mentioning the last President of the Reich before Hitler took power.

'Hindenburg.' Omi waved a dismissive hand. 'He was middle-class. All Germany may have worshipped him—but not the von Brombergs. Do you know, in the first World War, when he was Commander-in-Chief, they put up wooden statues of him in all the towns and you could pay and hammer a nail in it! It was for war charities but can you imagine anything more barbarous?'

She shook her head then reached across the cakes and patted Erika's hand. 'But you should not forget your ancestry. I know that this is Socialist Germany and all are equal, but blood counts—' she held up her hand as Erika opened her mouth in a scandalised protest. 'Yes, blood and breeding.'

'But Omi!' Erika was truly shocked. 'That is just what the Nazis said!'

'Ach! That scum.' True contempt showed in Omi's eyes. 'They talked about the glory of the family and then taught children to inform on their parents. Wickedness. Wickedness! No wonder the Almighty brought his lightning on our heads. But it is true, *Liebchen*, ancestry counts, a family line going back 600 years . . . and I see it in you.'

'Do you see it in Paul?' Erika asked, with a toughness which surprised herself.

'Paul. . . .' Omi sliced her cake. 'He takes after his father, doesn't he? He has inherited . . . what do they call them?'

'Genes,' Erika said.

'Yes. He has inherited the Nordern genes. There is something . . . crude about him. It's true, isn't it?'

Omi took a tremulous sip of her coffee. Erika watched her across the table feeling baffled. There was genetic inheritance, of course, and Paul was . . . well . . . crude, like all boys, but it didn't work the way Omi was suggesting, nothing like it. The trouble was that she wasn't quite sure how it did work. She made a mental note to listen more attentively to her lessons in biology and in Marxism, and then, to divert Omi from the views she was expressing, Erika said:

'Uncle Karl will be back soon, Omi. Then we can have the party.'

'Ah, Karl!' Omi's face lighted up in a vivid smile. 'My Karl. It is something to find a brother, *Liebchen*.' She stared into her coffee as though it were a pool reflecting the past. 'He wasn't cruel, really,' she said, as if defying an invisible accuser.

'Cruel?' Erika was astonished.

'What?' Omi blinked. 'Did I say cruel? Oh. Well boys are. I don't know why. Pulling wings off flies, killing nestlings . . . Karl was misunderstood.'

'I see,' Erika said, although she didn't see at all. She felt disturbed; thinking of the gleaming Karl with his polished manners and mannered poise, and of how once he had been a boy. 'Wild', Omi had called him the night he arrived, a wild boy, and now another dimension had been added to that figure from long ago: cruelty—a cruel boy. . . .

'But that was long ago,' Omi said. 'Long, long ago. And soon we shall all meet again for the last time. All of us who are left. . . .'

'Omi!' Erika smiled. 'You will all meet again, many times.'

'No.' Omi was certain. 'It will be the last time. We are all growing old and we shall die and be buried.'

'It's not true,' Erika said.

'It is true.' Omi pushed away her coffee cup. 'In any case, Karl will go, and then you will go away, too.'

'No, Omi.' Erika leaned forward. 'I shan't be going far—even if I go at all.'

'But you won't be at home, will you?' Omi said. 'You won't be coming home in the evening. But there, I'm just a selfish old woman, and a foolish one. You must forgive me, my Dear. And it is true what your father says . . . when I think of what it was like after the War, and when I look around now—' suiting her actions to her words she looked around the café, at the ladies, old and frail, like herself, respectable in black and grey—'these went through it too,' she said, 'and look at them, at us, coffee and cake on a Sunday morning. Perhaps it is a miracle. . . .'

'You should write it down,' Erika said. 'Write your memoirs, all your experiences.'

Omi looked steadily at Erika for a long moment, and looking back into Omi's fine, hooded eyes, Erika sensed for the first time ever, not merely that Omi was an old woman who walked rather slowly, was glad of help in undressing, and who, on days when her arthritis was very bad, needed her meat cutting for her. She was a woman from an age quite different from Erika's own; separated by a gulf, a measureless chasm of experience distancing them each from the other as surely as though they were beings from two different planets.

Omi crooked a finger for the waitress who offered the bill with subtle deference, and Omi paid it with subtle superiority. And then Omi tapped the table, once.

'Write my memoirs?' she said, and smiled, but such a smile as Erika had never seen on her grandmother's face before: wry, mocking, and, shockingly, cynical. Then the smile went and the eyes were veiled and Omi rose and said, 'I don't think anyone would want to hear my memoirs. Let us go home.'

Chapter 14

THE NEXT day or two were ones of mild confusion. The phone rang constantly as various relatives called from across the G.D.R. demanding to know the date of the party—which was unanswerable, since no one knew when Karl would be back from Dresden—and either confirming that, anyway, if it was to be on a week-end they would be present—or not.

Frau Nordern was annoyed by the refusals but Herr Nordern had a drier view. 'Most of them have hardly heard of Karl,' he said, 'and anyway, it isn't everyone who wants to be seen meeting. . . .'

The rest of the remark he left unsaid, but it did not need spelling out. There were those in the G.D.R. not unhappy at staying away from a western business man, even though he might be a temporary guest of the State; after all, they were *permanent* guests and who knew but. . . .

Although indignant at this slur on her relatives, Frau Nordern forgot it as she, Omi, and Erika became absorbed in planning a menu for the party. Herr Nordern joined in, and even Paul was co-opted although his contribution was less than successful as his views on suitable food seemed to consist only of frankfurter sausages, Cola, and, drawn from a mysterious memory of the dinner in the Palast, champagne.

In addition there was the tension of waiting for news from the Ministry of Sport and despite all Herr Nordern's warnings, based on his own profound experience of bureaucracy, he, as well as the rest of the family, found himself waiting with more than usual interest for the postman's knock.

And Herr Nordern had tensions of his own to cope with.

Despite the assurances of the Director of his Department that he was favourably looked upon, and despite the fact that there was no doubt that at his office he was being treated with a subtle air of respect, nothing formal or official about his promotion had been announced; and as he knew very well, a change of Directorship, a shift in Government economic policy, even a chill wind in international relations, could mean the end of his hopes. And always, at the back of his mind, there was the business with the Police; a mere shadow, as he repeatedly reminded himself, without substance, but there just the same and often, as he went through Ostkreuz on the *S-Bahn*, he was tempted to get off and see Lieutenant Werner, merely to get the matter sorted out once and for all but, mindful of Bodo's advice, he never did.

Erika had her own preoccupations, too. There was, of course, first and absolutely foremost, the need to keep on jumping, and to do so at the very highest level; a need which Fräulein Silber emphasised repeatedly.

'Remember, Erika,' she said, 'you are on the ladder, but only just. You have to keep showing improvement, and not just in height but in technique. Your leg is still trailing when you go over the bar. You must concentrate, wipe out everything from your mind but the leap; *everything*. And I hear that a girl in Pankow is breaking 1.80 every time she jumps.'

Erika was not too sure about the girl in Pankow, half suspecting that Fräulein Silber was using her as a means of putting pressure on herself. That she was lacking a little in concentration was true, but then she had plenty to disturb her concentration: Uncle Karl, Omi's strange remarks about breeding, the coming party, and, of course, and most disturbing of all, Fritz Kott.

And yet what was Fritz to her? Until a few weeks ago she had been scarcely aware of him except as a friendly and familiar face in class; but now, now she was very much aware of him—and he was very definitely aware of her; much to Erika's embarrassment sitting with her and Rosa at lunch, at the next desk in class, asking her out to the cinema and even, to Erika's amazement and, she suspected, his own, offering to help Paul with his homework—in the Nordern home, that is—an offer declined both by Erika and Paul, although Paul did corner Fritz in school and suggest to him that if he actually *did* the homework then he, Paul, would further his, Fritz's, courtship of Erika; Paul being shrewd enough to guess the motive behind Fritz's philanthropic gesture even though the square on the hypotenuse might remain a mystery to him.

Rosa gently teased Erika about the vestigial romance but was serious about the advice she gave, that Erika was not, repeat *not*, to get involved with a boy-friend, especially with the Indoor Championships drawing nearer, and with the Ministry of Sport keeping an eye on her.

It was advice Erika took seriously, distancing herself from Fritz as much as possible and adroitly using Rosa as a shield so that Fritz was forever baulked in his obscure desires.

But still, on the bus going to and from school, on her steady, daily runs in the park, swimming, weight-lifting, doing her exercises, and on those other rare occasions when she was alone and free from the demands of school, State, and family, Erika found herself thinking of Fritz, although what she thought she scarcely knew herself, except that she knew that she blushed when she did so. . . .

However, on the Wednesday, Erika's mind was freed from Fritz because her mother took her out.

'Meet me at the Centre after school,' she said, imperiously.

'I shan't be free until 7.00,' Erika said. 'I'll be in the gym.'

'That's all right,' Frau Nordern said.

'But what about supper—for Omi and Paul and Father?'

'They can look after themselves for once,' Frau Nordern said. 'Just meet me at 7.00.'

During the day, Erika wondered what her mother wanted her for, but after two hours in the gym she had given up wondering, and, indeed, had forgotten about it. In fact she was walking to the wrong bus-stop before she did recall it.

Getting to the Health Centre was a tedious business involving a bus and a clanking ride for a few stops on the underground and Erika was glad to find her way to it, jammed among the usual blocks of flats, although at that time of night they had rather a festive air with every window lighted.

Frau Nordern was free when Erika finally penetrated to her

room, sitting at her desk behind a mound of reports.

She shook her head at Erika. 'Some of these women,' she said. 'Forty years of socialism, education, propaganda, rewards and punishments, and still . . . It makes you despair at times. Let's go.'

Without explaining to where they were going she walked regally from the room swinging her brief-case which, unlike a great many brief-cases on the streets of Berlin, was filled with notes and papers and not stolen goods.

'One bus,' she said, as they stood on Lenin Allee. 'It should be here in a moment.' As if obeying her the bus did appear and ten minutes later she and Erika were at Frankfurter Allee, a roaring road choked with an army convoy: dozens of lorries, their contents masked by huge tarpaulins.

Frau Nordern did not give the lorries a second glance but dived down a side-street into a rather agreeable square. 'Here we are,' she said.

'Here' was the Buda, the restaurant where the great party was to be held, a long, low building, part of it pre-war, and with its outside liberally plastered with posters of a vastly hairy Karl Marx.

'I want to make sure that everything is in order,' Frau Nordern said, grimly, as they crossed the square. 'I remember Omi's birthday party.'

Erika remembered that, too. The restaurant had been double booked and when the two parties had met there had been a scene akin to the opening of World War Three until Frau Nordern, at her most imperious, and with the additional, strategic advantage that her husband was a state official and the opposition merely clerks from the Centrum store, cowed the manager and routed the clerks.

It seemed that the manager remembered it plainly, too, because as they entered the restaurant, he came from behind his desk like a bolted rabbit and, before Frau Nordern had time to speak, assured her that everything would be in order if only, his hands out wide, beseechingly, if only the gnädige Frau would give him a *date*.

The manager was a small Hungarian with the cosmopolitan air restaurateurs have the world over and full of a nervous, twitching charm. 'Just a little notice, gnädige Frau,' he begged. 'I shall have to get extra waiters, order the food, prepare the wine, get musicians—'

'We have our own musicians,' Frau Nordern said.

'Oh!' The manager's face fell as he saw that part of his commission disappear. 'But still, for the rest. . . .'

'You'll have plenty of notice,' Frau Nordern said. 'Now I want to see the room.'

'Ah, the room.' A subtle expression crossed the manager's face, almost a mocking smile. 'But you have seen the room.'

'Four years ago,' Frau Nordern said dryly, 'and it needed cleaning and painting then. The room!'

'The room.' The manager shrugged, as if defeated.

He led them down a small corridor, paused by a door, took out a huge bunch of keys, slowly, and deliberately, unlocked the door, and then, with a dramatic, indeed melodramatic, flourish, flung it open.

'*Voilà!*' he said.

There was a moment's stunned silence then, 'My word,' said Frau Nordern. 'My word! "*Voilà!*" indeed.'

And '*voilà*' was the word, Erika thought. Her memory of the room had been of a dingy, barrack-like hall with fine plaster swags, marred by the fact that chunks of them had been missing, and they, and the room, not improved by having been painted in a weird mixture of colour: purple, pink, green, ochre, rather like the bike belonging to the old man on the *S-Bahn*.

The manager leaned against the wall, arms folded, ankles crossed, in a typical hotelier's pose, and enjoyed his sensation. The plaster work had been restored and gilded so that it glittered against a dazzling white ceiling and against walls hung with crimson wallpaper. Echoing the ceiling, the woodwork was an immaculate white, picked out with crimson, and the floor had been sanded, showing a beautiful, if chipped, parquet.

'You like it?' the manager asked, as if the room had been especially redone for Frau Nordern's sake.

'I certainly do,' Frau Nordern answered, as if the room *had* been done for her.

'Come.' The manager crooked a finger and beckoned Frau

Nordern and Erika across the room. He jiggled with a formidable lock on a cupboard and opened it. 'See!'

The cupboard was stocked with linen, and of the finest quality. 'For the tables,' the manager said, somewhat unnecessarily, and, dropping his voice reverentially he murmured, 'Irish, the finest in the world.'

Frau Nordern fingered the linen with covetous hands. 'But how . . .?'

'Ah,' the manager smiled wholeheartedly. 'The combine did well last year—and it was my turn.'

'So that was it,' Erika thought. Like many businesses in the G.D.R. the Buda was part of a combine, leased from the State by the manager and also part of a co-operative. And, as was the rest of the country, reflecting a growing prosperity.

'But the linen,' Frau Nordern said.

'Ah!' The manager raised a finger and said, with pride in his voice, 'The Deputy Mayor gave a party here six months ago. A private party,' he gave a swift and completely Eastern European look around the room and, almost imperceptibly, lowered his voice; 'with some Friends.'

'Aha!' Erika thought. That was it. A prominent man, Friends—Russians in other words—and so skilled men, wallpaper, paint, gold leaf—and fine linen instantly available; she smiled as she wondered whether Bodo had had a hand in it. Quite likely he had.

'So,' the manager locked, and double locked the cupboard, led the way from the room, locked and double locked that door too, and took the Norderns into the restaurant bar. He pulled out two chairs from a table, brushed a table-cloth of distinctly inferior quality, insisted that Frau Nordern and Erika sit down, and, overriding their feeble protests, treated them to drinks, a large Bulgarian wine for Frau Nordern and a Club Cola for Erika.

'Sit,' the manager said, 'enjoy your drinks, think about your menu, but remember, gnädige Frau, *notice*, please.'

Rather more docile than when she had entered, Frau Nordern agreed that she would give notice, ample notice, more than enough notice to make sure that they had the room and raised her glass in salute as the manager beamed on Erika and then withdrew to welcome the first of his evening guests, stout, prosperous looking men in heavy dark suits: officials, with their wives.

'Well, well,' Frau Nordern sipped her wine. 'What a surprise. Nice, isn't it?'

It was, Erika agreed, much nicer than the Palast, as a matter of fact. She liked the Hungarian manager with his charm and evident desire to please, his pride in his dining-room and linen and his unabashed pleasure at their pleasure; so unlike the haughty anonymity of the Palast.

'So, the Deputy Mayor had a party in that very room!' Frau Nordern glanced at a menu, 'And the prices have hardly gone up at all.' She fished in her brief-case and, to Erika's amazement took out a packet of cigarettes. 'Oh yes,' she said, 'I do sometimes, especially after a day like I've had. No need to mention it to Father, though.'

Erika shook her head, hypnotised by the sight of her mother smoking.

'We really must find out when Karl is coming back,' Frau Nordern went on. 'I don't want to miss getting that room. We'll put flowers in it, bouquets . . . Omi will be so proud and happy.' She half-smiled. 'She still hankers after the Adlon.'

She tapped the ash off her cigarette and looked around the restaurant. More people had come in, well-dressed men and women, shedding vast overcoats, ordering wine, food, lighting cigars . . . a violinist, young, blonde, blue eyed, dressed improbably as a gipsy woman was playing a tzigane, accompanied by a pianist dressed even more improbably as a gipsy man.

'Ah,' Frau Nordern sighed, 'it will be nice when Hans gets his promotion. We'll be able to get out more, come to places like this. And get another flat, bigger, although you'll be away—no, Erika,' brushing aside any protest, 'Hans is sure you'll go, but another room will be so good. A room of my own, to have some privacy. . . .'

Privacy; Erika longed for it herself, often, but it occurred to her, for the first time, that her mother might long for it, too, might want it and, indeed, *need* it, and it dawned on her, also for the first time, that her mother had *never* had any privacy since the end of the War; that all her life since then she had

142

lived in small apartments, actually in one small room for long periods, and sharing even that room with others. . . .

Her mother was leaning back, her head tilted, a faint flush from the wine tinting her cheeks, the tilt of her head drawing the flesh from her chin and jaw, making her look young, younger than her years, and handsome, and, Erika suddenly realised, her eyes were of an exquisite forget-me-not blue.

Erika looked away, puzzled. Across the room a young man, eating on his own, was looking at her mother, and not innocently, either.

'Mother!' Erika whispered. 'That man, that man over there. He's staring at you.'

'Hmm?' It took a moment for Erika's words to sink in. Frau Nordern blew out a voluptuous stream of smoke and looked at the man who suddenly became extremely interested in his herring Bismarck.

'He's quite good-looking,' Frau Nordern said. The blue eyes turned on Erika like searchlights. 'Just an observation. An objective judgement.' She took a drink of her wine, and then, disconcertingly, asked, 'What's all this about a boy-friend?'

The blood rushed to Erika's face. 'What?' And then, with a flash of temper, 'Has Paul been telling stupid tales?'

Frau Nordern raised a shoulder. 'He didn't need to. You've been mooning about for a few weeks,' she chuckled, ruefully. 'I'm not blind, you know.'

'It's nothing,' Erika said. 'Anyway, I haven't got a boy-friend.'

'All right,' Frau Nordern said. 'Just don't go getting involved with some spotty adolescent. Not now at any rate, you've got too much at stake.' She gazed into her glass. 'I'm going to have another drink. It's so nice in here, not worrying about other people, or getting supper, or anything. And sitting with you. It's a long time since we did that.'

It had been more than a long time, Erika reflected. In fact she had never sat in a restaurant alone with her mother. They had taken an occasional coffee together after shopping, but this was a new experience. Totally new. And it was new seeing her mother leaning back with a drink and a cigarette, looking years younger than her age; and she herself felt different, older, suddenly, if older was the word she wanted. But how strange it was, the changes which the past two or three weeks had brought: not merely the changes of circumstances; her father and his hoped for promotion, herself going to the Stadium, Omi talking about herself, Fritz . . . but the whole relationship inside the family had altered, and she herself had changed, and it had begun with the arrival of Uncle Karl, as if he were a sorcerer, a wave of whose manicured hands could transform life, as alchemists thought they could transform base metal into gold or, with a certain sinister *frisson*, perhaps the other way around. But that was not a pleasant thought and Erika firmly pushed it away, thinking of movement from a lower to a higher stage of development, as Marx taught, and such as was taking place now, she and her mother sitting together, no longer like mother and daughter, teacher and child, but more like sisters.

Frau Nordern's drink came. She lighted another cigarette. 'Have a glass of wine,' she said. She waved away Erika's protest that she was in strict training.

'A glass of light wine won't kill you,' she said. 'Anyway, you'll have enough strict training where you're going.'

Sisterlike or not, Frau Nordern's word was enough and Erika found herself with a glass of light Hungarian wine and enjoying it, too.

Frau Nordern tapped ash from another cigarette into her ashtray. 'You're sure you want to go?'

'Go?' Erika blinked. 'We've just—' she gestured at the drinks.

'Go to the special sports school,' her mother said, a little testily. 'We are all excited about it, but you don't have to go if you don't want to. Remember that. I don't want you going just because you think that it will please us—Hans and me. It will mean giving up a lot, you know.'

'I thought that you wanted me to go,' Erika said.

'I do,' Frau Nordern toyed with her glass. 'But sometimes I wonder why. You know, most parents want their children to do things, do this, do that, make money, become famous, have a better house . . . car . . . although, actually, there are plenty who want the opposite—yes, that's true, some are jealous, full of hate—I see it at work—but you . . . I want you to go because *you* want to go. It will mean giving up a lot and—' she gave the ghost of a smile—'I know what that means. I missed a lot when I was your age.'

Yes, Erika knew that. Her mother had missed a lot; a refugee on that terrible trek with Omi, the bleak years in a ruined city in a ruined country, the children coming late, work again. . . .

'I'm sorry, Mother,' she said.

Frau Nordern waved smoke from her eyes, waved away the past. 'I'm not complaining,' she said. 'I was lucky. Your father was always good to me, and his uncle. Better than we deserved. What were we to them?' She veiled her eyes in a startling evocation of Omi. 'It wasn't what you might think. Women outnumbered men in those days, you know. The men were buried between here and . . .' she drew an invisible line with her fingers, as if sketching the road from Berlin to Stalingrad, Bonn to El Alamein, Stuttgart to Normandy. 'Yes, always good, to me and Omi, even in the rubble times. That's why I stayed—here I mean.'

Emboldened by her glass of wine, and by this new found intimacy, Erika asked, 'Mother, are you glad you stayed?'

'Glad?' Frau Nordern pushed her glass a little. 'What does that mean? If we had gone to the West, then what? I might have had a different man, a bigger apartment, a bigger car, travel that way instead of this. But things would have been much the same. They are really. People live their lives . . . somehow. . . .' She looked up, the blue searchlights glowing. 'I would have had different children. You and Paul might never have existed. That's a strange thought, isn't it? But here you are, and here I am, and I wouldn't have that different, *Liebchen*. But Omi . . . I don't know. I think that she might have gone. Does she ever speak about it to you?'

Erika shook her head. 'Never a word.'

'She wouldn't. She has honour. Give the old *Junker* that.'

Erika was shocked. 'Mother,' she said, 'the *Junker* put Hitler in power.'

'Yes, they did,' Frau Nordern agreed. 'Some of them. Some of them tried to blow him up, too. And they paid for it.'

That was true, Erika admitted: the July Plot in 1944 when a group of officers, aristocrats to a man, had tried to

145

assassinate Hitler and been caught and hanged with piano wire—and filmed being hanged—and the film shown at Hitler's headquarters as after dinner entertainment. . . .

'One of them was a relative of yours,' Frau Nordern said. 'You didn't know that, did you? A second cousin. And there were *Junker* and *Junker*. The Brombergs and the Ritters, they were always Christians, very devout, God-fearing. . . .'

'Were you one, a Christian?' In the warm intimacy of the café Erika felt emboldened to ask such a question.

'I was brought up as one,' Frau Nordern said, 'but after 1945 . . . a God who would allow that to happen . . . that's what I mean about Omi's honour. She gave her word to God when she was confirmed and she kept it. Just as she gave her word to Hans.'

'Gave her word?' Erika was intensely interested.

'Oh, not formally.' Frau Nordern toyed with her wine. 'No oath-taking on a Bible or anything like that, but there was an understanding.'

'An understanding?'

'Yes. You know your father. Working class, a socialist through thick and thin, and us. Two worlds, really. It could have been difficult. So the past was forgotten. Wiped out. Our past I mean. Even Father.'

For a moment Erika was at a loss as to whom her mother was talking about, then it dawned on her. 'You mean your father.'

'Who else? Of course I hardly knew him. I've forgotten him, actually.'

Yes, but Omi hadn't, Erika thought, she had not forgotten that handsome officer who had courted her all those inconceivable years ago.

'I'm a bit worried about Omi,' Frau Nordern said.

'Worried?'

'Yes, she seems, I don't know, a little withdrawn just now. Have you noticed?'

Erika put her chin on her hand. 'Yes,' she admitted. Omi had been rather silent, in the flat at any rate, although. . . . 'She talked when we went to church,' Erika said.

'Oh, what about?'

Erika shrugged. 'Family, breeding.'

Frau Nordern glanced at her watch but seemed in no hurry to move. 'I suppose that's because of Karl coming back. It must have stirred up some memories for her, days of wine and roses, eh? No matter how deep it's buried, the past, back it comes, like ghosts, really. This is a city of ghosts.'

Erika looked up, startled. What a strange remark that was, coming from her mother who always seemed so practical and matter-of-fact.

Frau Nordern did not miss Erika's surprise. She took another sip of wine and smiled crookedly. 'It is. Everyone here is haunted one way or another. The things that were done, the dead . . . strange isn't it, all those Germans killed by the Russians, Germans killed by Germans. Ach, it's best forgotten. It only leads to rows—like the other night.'

'But we can't forget everything, Mother.' Erika dutifully echoed the lessons of school. 'We have to learn from the past.'

'I suppose so.' Frau Nordern rose. 'Anyway,' she returned abruptly to the affairs of the practical world. 'We must find out when Karl is coming back so we can book the room. I don't want to miss that. Have you enjoyed it? Being out?'

Yes, Erika had enjoyed it, very much so; the proud little manager, looking at the other guests, the intimacy of the talk with her mother, and, knowing her mother's pride in her children, she had been touched by her concern about the special sports school. That thought in particular kept her warm as they left the restaurant for the bitter streets of the city.

Herr Nordern was a little grumpy when they got home. Steinmark was still absent and he, Nordern, was doing two men's work which annoyed him, particularly as he wanted to give the best possible impression of himself during the next few weeks.

He welcomed his wife and Erika briefly, said that as he had prepared the meal he was not going to wash up, and retreated into his bedroom. Frau Nordern and Erika ate, fussed over by Omi. Paul was dragged from his retreat to wash up, a little work was done, and then, as the family prepared for bed, the phone rang.

Frau Nordern threw her hands in the air. 'Always the same. You either sit down for a meal or get ready for bed and the phone goes.'

'I'll get it.' Erika picked up the phone and through a barrage of crackles heard a smooth voice. 'Uncle Karl,' she said, handing the receiver to her mother.

Frau Nordern snatched at it. 'Karl? Speak up, I can't hear you.'

The usual G.D.R. telephone conversation took place, as if two deaf people were talking to each other on a rowdy main road, but fragments of conversation filtered through as Frau Nordern repeated what Karl, presumably, was saying. 'Ah! . . . Good . . . yes, well . . . coming back! . . . What? . . . When? Yes . . . YES. . . .'

Frau Nordern beckoned Omi. 'He'll want to talk to you.'

Omi picked up the phone, said 'Karl' a couple of times, then frowned at Frau Nordern. 'I can't hear anything.'

Frau Nordern took the phone again, bellowed 'Karl!' several decibels louder than Omi, shook the phone as if it were a recalcitrant child, listened again, then put it down. 'Cut off,' she said. 'Never mind. It's all right. He's finished in Dresden and he's coming back tomorrow.'

Omi's eyes glowed but Frau Nordern raised a warning finger. 'He may not be able to get round immediately, but he'll let us know as soon as he can. So, now we can really get on with the party. Actually, I'll be glad to get it over with. It's so unsettling.'

The Norderns went to their beds. As ever, Erika peered through her window for a moment or two. The sky was clear and glittering with icy stars. A police car went past, the Dresden train, punctual to the minute, its klaxon, muted by distance, sounding a friendly, human signal. The owl hooted in the beech tree and, to Erika's deep delight, it was answered by another owl. Erika smiled, glad to know that her owl had company.

She gently turned Omi's pillow to stop her mild snoring and then drifted off into her own dreamless sleep.

Chapter 15

THE NEXT morning was bustle with Herr Nordern still a little grumpy. 'Didn't sleep well,' he said, mildly apologetic, snatching a bite of bread and cheese, gulping a cup of coffee, standing, before nodding curtly and dashing out into a freezing morning.

Herr Nordern's temper wasn't improved when, having caught the *S-Bahn*, he realised that he had left his book of tickets in his other jacket. He was strongly tempted to stay on the train and take his chance, but remembering the man he had seen the Railway Police arrest, he got off at Lichtenberg and bought a ticket at the machine.

He was cutting his journey fine and it was only by actually jogging from Friedrichstrasse, and feeling a fool for doing so, apart from almost breaking his neck by slipping on the icy pavement, that he arrived at his office before the ominous red line was drawn. Consequently he was in a ferocious temper when he got into his room and saw a mound of mail on his desk, half of which was addressed to Steinmark.

'Steinmark!' he exploded. 'Herr Nordern to attend to this—and this—and this—!' He scattered the letters across his desk. 'What the devil is he up to in Dresden? A few archives to look into! He's been there for weeks and I could have done the whole thing in a couple of days. I know what he's doing—' answering himself—'skiving off! And what's the matter with you?'

He looked sternly at Herr Müller who had an odd expression.

'You've not heard then?' Müller asked. 'About him?'

'About who?' Herr Nordern was testy.

'Steinmark,' Müller said. 'He's dead.'

'Dead?' Herr Nordern was astounded. 'Dead? That's impossible. He's as healthy as you or me.'

'Was,' Müller said. 'But he's dead all the same.'

Herr Nordern sat down heavily. 'It's . . . I mean . . . that's incredible. What happened?'

Müller shook his head. 'They say it was an accident. Someone said he was hit by a train.'

'A train!' Nordern stared at the mail, dumbfounded. 'How in God's name could that happen?'

Müller shrugged. 'I don't know. That's all I've heard.'

'But it's. . . .' Herr Nordern groped for words as he stared at the envelopes with Steinmark written across them. 'It's fantastic. I mean, how?'

'Your guess is as good as mine,' Müller said.

'Well,' Nordern fished out a cigar. 'I'll be honest, I never liked the man but—' he lit his cigar. 'I suppose that we'll get the details in time.'

'I hope we get a replacement,' Müller said heartlessly as they settled down to work.

At 10.30 Herr Nordern's phone rang. Herr Nagel, the Section Head, wished to see him.

'Come in, come in,' Nagel said as Nordern rapped on his door. 'Take a seat. You have heard of this business about Steinmark?'

'Yes,' Herr Nordern said. 'Terrible. Müller says he was hit by a train!'

Nagel was exasperated. 'I don't know how these things get around, but that's quite correct.' He flicked a finger against the palm of his hand. 'He was badly . . . well . . . mangled.'

'But how on earth can you get hit by a train?' Herr Nordern said. 'A child, yes, but a grown man! If it was a car . . . but a train!'

Nagel flicked his palm more vigorously then placed his hands on his desk. 'It seems. . . .' He hesitated for a moment and lowered his voice. . . . 'It seems that there are some, well, some low drinking dens on the other side of the tracks. It also seems that our Herr Steinmark had some . . . some degraded habits. He had been going there, to that area and . . . I don't need to spell it out for you but the assumption is that he was going back drunk and got hit. That information is for you only. Understood?'

'Of course,' Herr Nordern said.

'Yes.' Nagel nodded. 'I must say it makes you wonder what the Security Police are up to not knowing that—and Steinmark working with secret archives.' He stared bleakly over Herr Nordern's head. 'I dare say that there will be some questions asked.'

'I'll bet there will be,' Herr Nordern thought. There would be some uneasy heads lying on their pillows that night.

'Did you know anything about him?' Nagel asked.

'No.' Herr Nordern was emphatic. 'I never saw him outside work—apart from Union meetings.'

'I know,' Nagel agreed. 'These middle-aged bachelors . . . anyway, don't be surprised if Security want a word with you. But still, we have to think about our own work. I was hoping that Steinmark would be back on Monday but I'm afraid that you will have to carry on the best you can. I'll find a replacement as soon as possible. If there is anyone you would like to recommend let me know. And keep an eye on young Müller.'

'Müller is all right,' Nordern said, a little surprised at his own warmth.

'I'm sure he is, but these young men. . . . Anyway, carry on and let me know if there are any real difficulties. Sorry you are going to be burdened, but there it is. Now, about these figures for the meeting next week. . . .'

The talk drifted off into technicalities for a while, and then, those disposed of, Nagel told Herr Nordern that he could go.

'But keep this business about Steinmark under your hat,' he said. 'Oh, and perhaps as senior man you might like to arrange something for his funeral, a wreath, represent the Section, that sort of thing. If you would?'

Herr Nordern would, yes, although he would no more have refused than he would have tried to jump over the Wall. He went back to his office, made some sharp remarks to a surprised, and hurt, Müller about sloppy work, worked himself, then went to the canteen for his lunch.

The canteen, a gloomy area in the basement, was buzzing with talk about Steinmark. Herr Nordern was quizzed by the entire staff but stoically maintained that he knew no more than anyone else.

But as he attacked his potato salad Herr Nordern felt exultation. Not, of course, at Steinmark's death, but at how Nagel had confided in him and how, quite explicitly, responsibility for the sub-section had been handed to himself. Both were signs that he was, indeed, marked for promotion. It was hard luck on Steinmark, that went without saying, but if the man had been lurking in disreputable quarters and lurching home drunk, it was his own fault. All that now remained was to get the next couple of weeks over—have the party, get Karl away, see Erika settled, get the business of the accident cleared up and then, although he did not normally think in melodramatic terms—then the future!

He finished his lunch, went back to his office, gave a bemused Müller a stern warning about the standards expected from state officials, buckled into a solid afternoon's work and, when the working day was over, carried a bulging brief-case home.

He opened the familiar door, giving the aluminium plate a rub with his sleeve, but in the tiny vestibule he paused. A smell, rich, savoury, and unfamiliar was drifting from the flat. He raised his eyebrows and pushed into the sitting-room. There, with the rest of the family, drinking whisky, smooth, dapper, silver hair gleaming, face glowing, teeth shining, was Uncle Karl.

'My dear fellow!' As glossy as a fashion-plate, Karl jumped up, grasped Herr Nordern's hand, and beamed into his face. 'What a pleasure to see you again. I know that it has only been a couple of weeks but my word, it does seem longer, and so much has happened to you, hasn't it? I know because I called around early and took my sister out for tea. You don't mind, do you?'

'Of course not.' Herr Nordern was a trifle brusque, not only because he did mind Karl being in his flat at dinner-time, but also because he found his florid manners irritating.

'And,' Karl flourished a whisky bottle. 'May I tempt you?'

'Of course you may,' Frau Nordern said. 'Have a drink Hans—and can you smell that? Karl brought a saddle of venison.'

'Thank you.' Herr Nordern nodded to Karl, took the whisky, and then felt bound to be agreeable. 'How was Dresden? A successful trip?'

Karl smiled. 'Oh yes. Yes. I think that I can say it was.'

'I'm glad to hear it.' Herr Nordern slumped on a chair. 'Oddly enough, I had some news from Dresden today.' He looked across at Frau Nordern. 'Steinmark is dead.'

He told the details to an incredulous audience, although tactfully leaving out the part about Steinmark's base habits, merely suggesting that he had probably been taking a short cut across the line.

'Well,' Frau Nordern shook her head. 'People will do that. You see the children at the *S-Bahn* here. They just will not go over the bridge.' She frowned at Paul who affected an air of exaggerated innocence. 'But Steinmark! You never know, do you?'

'Still, it helps my promotion along,' Herr Nordern said. 'Are you all right?' He turned to Karl who had spluttered into his drink.

'Yes. Yes. Quite all right.' Karl dabbed his mouth with one of his beautiful handkerchiefs. 'Drink went down the wrong way.'

He poured himself more whisky, pressing Herr Nordern to have another, too, and saying that he was leading the Norderns into bad ways but that they must forgive him as it wasn't very often they saw him, ha! ha! and Herr Nordern, while not prepared to accept that he was led by anyone except the leaders of his country, took the whisky, thinking, what the devil, he had worked like a dog all day, and it was true, Karl would not be with them much longer and they would probably never see him again and, he had to confess, he wouldn't mind if he never saw him again as long as either of them lived. And it was excellent whisky.

'We've been working out the date for the party,' Frau Nordern said, producing an enormous desk diary. 'It will have to be a week on Saturday.'

'Why so late?' Herr Nordern asked. 'I would have thought Karl wants to get away before then.'

'Erika.' Frau Nordern said firmly. 'She can't be going off to a big party before the Championship. She has to go into *very* strict training for the week before, and a week on Saturday means we can have the party on the evening after the Championship.'

'That suit you Karl?' Herr Nordern said.

'Well,' Karl smiled, 'I would have preferred to go sooner but yes I can stay. A little more business, and maybe some sightseeing. It occurred to me that perhaps I could invite Erika and Paul out for lunch.'

'That is nice,' Frau Nordern said. 'And Erika might show you some sights.'

'Ah, sights.' Karl nodded. 'I have seen a few, you know, ha! ha! but yes, that would be excellent. A little sightseeing with a pretty girl—but you are sure it would not be inconvenient, Erika? It wouldn't interrupt your training?'

No, lunch and a little sightseeing would not interrupt Erika's training or, Paul eagerly assured everyone, his homework.

'It will be a great event, the party,' Karl said. 'A rare meeting, and you, dear sister,' he turned to Omi, 'will be at the head of the table with me!'

'Speaking of which,' Herr Nordern, while quite happy to lounge back with a good cigar and a glass of whisky, was also ready for his meal.

Reading his thought Frau Nordern stood up. 'All right, Hans. It should be ready now.'

The table was laid, the saddle of venison made its appearance, from his cornucopia Karl produced excellent wine, the venison was carved, toasts exchanged, and then there was a vigorous knock on the door.

'Now who can that be,' Frau Nordern said, exasperated. 'Go and see, Paul, and tell them that we're busy.'

Paul went, but the caller was not to be turned away. On the contrary he strode in, rubbing his hands and making it clear that he, too, would like a piece of venison, and he being Bodo it was not really possible to refuse him.

'Let me introduce you,' Herr Nordern said, resigned to his fate. 'My brother Bodo—Uncle Karl.'

Erika watched the meeting of the men with interest. Bodo, big in his brown overalls, holding out a large, square, calloused hand with broken finger-nails and taking Karl's white hand firmly but, Erika noticed, not squeezing hard. A surprisingly delicate gesture for such an apparently rough man.

'Well, I'm glad to meet you,' Bodo said. 'Of course, I've heard all about you.'

'And I have heard about you.' Karl flashed his charming smile. 'My dear sister was talking about you only today at tea. A builder! A splendid profession; to make homes for people, build new cities, really, a modern hero!'

He chattered on in his easy way to a somewhat sceptical family who were not accustomed to thinking of Bodo in this new and totally unexpected light. Bodo himself said little, tucking into the venison but, Erika noticed, he kept a sharp and shrewd eye on Karl.

Inevitably, over supper, the conversation turned on Karl. Bodo asked about the building trade in West Germany, Herr Nordern about economic planning, Frau Nordern was curious about the social welfare services, and Paul asked about rock and roll, about which Karl modestly denied all knowledge.

'*The Merry Widow* is more my taste, and my sister's, too. Is that not so?' Turning to Omi, skilfully bringing her into the conversation, and complimenting her on the way the venison had been cooked.

'But of course we know something about it, don't we?' He addressed himself to Bodo. 'Forgive me for saying so but in East Prussia—Poland, I should say!—we had our pick of game. Deer, wild boar, so we can claim to be connoisseurs. Although I must say it is difficult to find a butcher now who understands how to hang meat, dear me, yes. . . .'

The talk drifted away to food, shortages of in the G.D.R. stoutly denied by Herr Nordern, strange gluts of—equally stoutly defended by him, memorable meals of the past, the coming party, and, although Omi barely spoke a word, sitting silently, merely picking at her meal, Karl kept up a lively alert manner which belied his years.

Supper over, Paul, with astonishing docility, took the plates away and Karl produced brandy, the very best French cognac, and a little was sipped over coffee.

'I do hope that you don't mind, Bodo,' Karl said. 'This is

155

not in any way meant to be a slight on the excellent brandy one gets here.'

'It's about ten times better,' Bodo said bluntly and cheerfully, swigging his glassful and accepting another.

'Aha! I see that you are not afraid to speak your mind,' Karl said. 'I do like that in a man—openness and frankness. I've always found it paid, in the Army and in business. Tell the truth and shame the Devil, as they say, ha! ha!'

And that, Erika thought, was a curious remark for Karl to make, bearing in mind that he had lived a lie for many years but, glancing at her parents, and they not batting an eyelash, she kept quiet.

'Yes.' Bodo answered Karl, rolling a cigar in his blunt fingers and sounding profoundly sincere. 'That's what they say, right enough. By the way, Hans, did you hear any more from Ostkreuz?'

'Ostkreuz?' Herr Nordern blinked.

'Yes, the cops.'

'The Police?' Karl interrupted, his eyes bright and penetrating.

'Oh,' Herr Nordern was dismissive. 'Nothing, nothing at all. A case of mistaken identity.' He explained briefly what had happened and added, untruthfully, that the Police had been friendly, helpful, and understanding.

'It is odd though,' Frau Nordern said. 'Two accidents in just a few days.'

'I suppose so.' Herr Nordern told Bodo about Steinmark.

'And I was in Dresden only last night,' Karl said. 'A most unpleasant coincidence. I'm only—I won't say *glad*, no, that would be quite the wrong word, but, shall I say *relieved*, that it happened last night.'

'Why is that?' Bodo asked, casually.

'My dear chap!' Karl leaned forward and tapped Bodo on his knee. 'I might have been on the train that hit him! What a ghastly thought! Thank goodness that I came back this morning.'

'Right.' Bodo said. 'But I hope that there weren't any well-dressed men wandering around the railway line in Dresden last night.'

A little of Karl's immaculate poise slipped. He stared into

his brandy and then, rather sourly for such a charming man, said, 'I'm afraid that I don't quite follow you, Bodo.'

'I was thinking of Hans and the car accident,' Bodo said, quite unruffled. 'Some idiot might have seen a well-dressed elderly gent near the railway line and then you could have been questioned.'

'Oh, now I see!' The cloud lifted from Karl's face. 'Of course, I understand. Foul play suspected, mistaken identity, a wrongful arrest! My word, Bodo, I really think that you are in the wrong profession. You ought to be writing detective stories!' He laughed in his merry way. 'But I was tucked up in bed early—not difficult in Dresden you know, they don't have West German television down there—oh! Perhaps I should not have said that.'

'Why not,' Bodo said. 'Idiots' alley, we call it. Just because of that.'

'Do you indeed?' Karl was slightly disapproving. 'Forgive me, but as a guest of your Government I . . . well, I'm sure that you understand.' He glanced at his watch. 'But really, I ought to be tucked up in bed now. At my age . . . and I have ordered a taxi. . . .'

Karl was muffled up in his luxurious overcoat. He kissed Frau Nordern, Erika, and Omi, holding her firmly but gently, and staring into her old eyes, and saying, 'Do remember our little chat this afternoon, dear sister,' and she, her eyes moist, like a well refilling after a drought, promised that she would.

A peek through the window showed that the taxi had arrived, brief farewells were made to the men, and Karl left, promising to ring them the next day and making mock threats to Erika and Paul should they forget to meet him the following Sunday.

'As if you would,' Frau Nordern said to Paul as the door closed on Karl. 'But you would forget your homework. Do it now.'

'Homework,' Herr Nordern said with more sympathy than he would normally have allowed himself. 'I've plenty to do myself.'

'Understood.' Bodo was sympathetic. 'I'll be off in a minute.' He helped himself to another brandy and waved the bottle before Herr Nordern's eyes.

'Oh, very well,' Herr Nordern had a nip and, as Erika volunteered to wash up, Frau Nordern, not to be outdone, had one also, and, coaxed by the family, Omi had a thimbleful too.

'So,' Frau Nordern said. 'What do you think of Karl, Bodo. Isn't he a gentleman?'

'I suppose so,' Bodo said. 'I don't know the type so I can't tell. Don't mix with nobs much. Well-dressed though, and I wouldn't mind having his watch.'

Omi tutted censoriously but Frau Nordern was more open in her disapproval.

'Really Bodo, don't you think of anything but... but *things* and money.'

'No.' Bodo, gap-toothed, grinned. 'But I was thinking about Steinmark. Just shows, doesn't it?'

'Shows what?' Frau Nordern demanded.

'Oh, just that you can never tell. Put the right clothes on someone and everyone judges them by their appearance. Dark-blue suit, black hat, respectable official—like Hans—or Steinmark. Smart grey suit, business man; brown overalls—a thick head. All right! I'm joking. And I'm off.'

He stood up, shrugging his broad shoulders into a thick sheepskin jacket. 'So, good-night all. See you at the party if not before. Omi, you know how to cook venison.'

He edged around the sofa and banged on Paul's door. 'Keep up the homework,' he shouted. 'Get good marks and I'll give you a terrific record. Erika—' calling through the plastic ivy. 'Don't forget, I'm taking you to the Stadt Berlin. See me out Hans.'

Herr Nordern followed Bodo into the vestibule and on to the landing.

'Close the door,' Bodo muttered.

'What?'

'The door.' Bodo put out a large hand and pulled the door to. 'Come down to the bar with me,' he said.

'The bar?' Herr Nordern could not believe his ears. 'At this time of night?'

'There's one by the *S-Bahn*,' Bodo said. 'Come on. I mean it.'

'Bodo!' Herr Nordern sighed hugely.

'I want to talk to you,' Bodo said.

'What about?' Herr Nordern was incredulous.

'I can't tell you here,' Bodo muttered, with more than a touch of impatience. 'It's important. But if you don't want to hear it . . .' he made as if to go but Herr Nordern took him by the elbow.

'Is it really important?'

'It's why I came round,' Bodo said.

'But . . .' Herr Nordern stared for a moment into Bodo's steady brown eyes. 'All right,' he said. 'Just a minute.'

He went back into the flat, grabbed his coat, told an astonished Frau Nordern that he was going out for a moment and, without waiting for any protests, dashed out and joined Bodo at the foot of the stairs.

The bar was crowded with men coming off shift from the electronics factory all arguing heatedly about a disputed penalty in a soccer match being shown on a T.V. set above the counter, the fact that the match had taken place two months before in no way diminishing the fervour of the argument.

Bodo and Herr Nordern found a table in a back room. Ignoring his brother's plea that he didn't want any, Bodo ordered beer.

'Well?' Herr Nordern demanded.

Bodo held up a warning finger. 'Wait for the beer,' he said, and while they waited exchanged jovial insults with the men at the counter.

'You know the men in here, too, do you?' Herr Nordern asked.

'Some of them.' Bodo pointed to a seedy-looking character. 'He got you those spark plugs.' He chortled as Herr Nordern shuddered, and laughed again as the waitress, a stout fifty year old, brought the beer and refused his offer to take her for a sensuous holiday in Siberia.

'I thought that you said this was an important matter,' Herr Nordern snapped. 'I didn't come here for a boozy evening.'

Bodo took a long mouthful of beer. 'It is,' he said. 'It is important. Believe me.'

'Well?'

Bodo lowered his glass. 'Have you heard any more from the cops, about that accident?'

Herr Nordern felt a flicker of alarm. 'No,' he said. 'Not at all. Why, have you heard anything?'

'Well. . . .' Bodo waved his hand and ordered more beer. 'Speak normally,' he said. 'Don't shout, but don't whisper, either.'

Herr Nordern was aghast. 'You mean someone might be listening!'

'You never know.' Bodo asked the waitress if she would take the romantic lead in a film he claimed to be making and when she had gone, said, 'I don't think so, but you never know, do you? It's one of the advantages of a bar, they can't bug them all. Still. . . .' he paused and lit a cigarette. He waved out the match, gazed at it thoughtfully for a moment, dropped it into the ashtray and then looked at Herr Nordern. It was a hard, uncompromising look, like a prize-fighter weighing up an opponent.

'Listen, Hans,' he said. 'You've not done anything wrong, have you?'

'Wrong? Me?' Herr Nordern's voice quivered with indignation. 'What wrong could I have done?'

'Dunno,' Bodo said. He suddenly stood up. 'Back in a minute.' He strode to the counter and began talking earnestly with a burly man dressed in white house-painter's overalls.

Herr Nordern gulped his beer and drummed his fingers on the table. He was sweating, and not just because of the stuffiness of the room. He fished out a cigar and lighted it with fingers which were trembling. Despite everything he had drunk already that night he badly wanted a brandy—and a large one at that. And as Bodo made his way back to him he ordered two from the stout waitress who didn't stop and joke with *him*.

'Sorry,' Bodo said, lowering his bulk next to his brother. 'I had to see that man. What's this?' he asked as the waitress brought the brandies. 'You don't want to hit that stuff too hard,' knocking his back without a qualm.

'Never mind that,' Herr Nordern gulped his brandy. 'What's this about something being wrong?'

'Well,' Bodo looked cheerful and unconcerned, but his

160

voice was serious. 'I've been asking around, about Werner—you know, the cop at Ostkreuz.'

'I know,' Herr Nordern said. 'Get to the point can't you.'

'I'm getting there,' Bodo said. 'But listen, Hans, come on now, we are brothers.'

'Of course we're brothers.' Herr Nordern clenched his fist. 'For Christ's sake, I brought you up!'

'All right, all right,' Bodo said. 'I know that. But Hans, tell me, have you been mixed up in any rackets?'

Herr Nordern almost dropped his glass. 'Me! In a racket?'

'*Keep your voice down*,' Bodo said.

Herr Nordern made a huge effort and controlled himself. 'Of course I haven't been in any rackets. You're the one for that,' he added bitterly.

Bodo did not deny the charge. 'But I'm serious. You've not got mixed up in any fiddles?'

'What fiddles could I be in?' Herr Nordern said.

'I don't know.' Bodo shrugged. 'Some racket in your Department. Currency, maybe. Something to do with Karl.'

'Karl!' Herr Nordern was astounded. 'You mean Uncle Karl?'

'Sure. Why not? He's a crook,' Bodo said flatly.

Herr Nordern could not believe his ears. 'How can you say such a thing? How can you? You only met him tonight.'

'He's a con man,' Bodo said. 'I can spot them a mile off.'

'I think that is a wicked thing to say,' Herr Nordern said. 'Truly wicked.'

Bodo was genuinely surprised. 'What's wicked about it? I don't mind. Good luck to him if he can get away with it.'

'I don't mean that,' Herr Nordern said, 'and you know it. I mean it's wicked even to say it. Karl is a guest of the Government!'

Serious or not, whatever the business Bodo had to talk about with his brother, to Herr Nordern's dismay he burst out laughing. He patted Herr Nordern on the shoulder and shook his head. 'All right, Hans,' he said. 'All right.'

He was still laughing as two policemen came into the bar, but, despite himself, and despite his certain knowledge of his complete innocence, Herr Nordern's heart sank as they made their way towards his table.

'Oh the devil,' he whispered, but Bodo was quite unperturbed. 'Hello Heini, Joachim.' He jabbed a thumb at Hans. 'My brother.'

Hands were shaken, drinks offered, regretfully refused by the policemen. Heini leaned forward and murmured into Bodo's ear.

'No problem,' Bodo said. 'A hen-house. You've got the timber?'

The policeman whispered something and Bodo grinned. 'Should be good stuff then. O.K. Some time next week? Fine.'

Heini nodded thanks and left the room, followed by his colleague, both giving piercing, policemen's glances around the bar as they left.

'Sorry,' Bodo said. 'Got to keep in with them, though.' He looked sideways at Herr Nordern. 'What was that you were saying about guests of the Government?' he added dryly.

Herr Nordern shook his head. 'Do you know everyone in Berlin? But I can't stay here much longer—' he groaned as the waitress came with two beers and two gins. 'From the cops,' the waitress said.

'Got to keep drinking,' Bodo said. 'Look normal.' He filched one of Herr Nordern's cigars. 'But all right. Business.'

'At last.'

'Right.' Bodo took a deep breath. 'I've been asking around about Werner, who interviewed you about the accident. Well listen, Hans, there isn't a Werner at Ostkreuz cop-shop.'

Against his better judgement Herr Nordern gulped some beer and then mopped his face with his handkerchief. 'What are you saying?'

Bodo shrugged. 'I don't know, but there was a Werner at Schwerin in '81.'

'So?' Herr Nordern's voice rose.

'He was in the Border Police then,' Bodo said.

'The Border Police? But what's he doing dealing with a traffic accident?' The room seemed to spin a little and Herr Nordern grabbed the table. 'It doesn't mean a thing,' he said. 'Werner—it's not an uncommon name—no?' he asked, as Bodo shook his head.

'I think it's the same man,' Bodo said.

'I don't understand.'

'I don't either,' Bodo said.

Both men were silent for a moment then, clutching at a straw, Herr Nordern said, 'It must be something to do with you. You're the one up to your neck in rackets. My God, do you realise what could happen if there was any scandal? I'm up for promotion, and there's Erika. . . .'

'I've thought about that,' Bodo was serious. 'But I don't think so. In fact I'm sure of it. They wouldn't bring in the heavy mob for me, I'm not important enough. Besides, I've done too much for the big pots. They wouldn't want any scandal, either. But this business of the car crash, it sounds phony to me.'

'But why in hell should the police make up a story about an accident?' Herr Nordern demanded. 'Why? Where's the sense in it?'

'Search me. But if you've done nothing wrong then you've got nothing to worry about—' although Bodo rather spoiled this optimistic remark by adding, 'I hope.'

'So what should I do?'

Bodo shook his head. 'I still wouldn't do anything.'

'But—'

'No buts,' Bodo said. 'If you don't do anything then you've got no worries, see? Start doing something and it looks as if you *have* got worries.'

'But I am worried,' Herr Nordern said.

'I know, I know. But appear not to be. Just carry on as normal, right? I'll do the poking around. So. Let's go.'

They left the bar, Bodo exchanging farewells as if he had not a care in the world. Herr Nordern staggered as the night air hit him and Bodo held his elbow as they lurched back to the flats.

'O.K.' Bodo climbed into his pick-up. 'I'll be in touch. Just—' he hesitated for a moment and Herr Nordern leaned forward eagerly.

'Just what?'

'Just keep a low profile,' Bodo said, as he started the engine and roared away.

Herr Nordern went up the stairs, into a dark flat and a discontented bedroom.

'Where have you been?' Frau Nordern hissed.

'Only with Bodo,' Herr Nordern swore as he pulled his shirt off and it became entangled with his vest.

'Only with Bodo!' Disapproval seeped from Frau Nordern. 'What were the two of you up to?'

'Having a drink.' Herr Nordern sat down heavily, making the bed lurch. 'Go to sleep.'

'I was asleep,' Frau Nordern said. 'Where are you going now?'

'Bathroom.' Herr Nordern wove unsteadily across the living-room into the bathroom and plunged his face into cold water. 'Stupid,' he thought, looking at his flushed, dripping face in the mirror. 'Utterly stupid. Drunk and stupid.' He began to clean his teeth, jabbing at his mouth, then dropped the toothbrush on to the floor. He picked it up, banging his head on the bowl. He drank some water and felt worse, then groped his way back to the bedroom.

He climbed into bed and lay on his side, not moving and scarcely breathing. There was silence for a moment or two and then, like the voice of doom, Frau Nordern spoke again.

'What did Bodo want?'

Nordern groaned. 'I'll tell you tomorrow,' he said. 'To-morrow.'

Another silence. Herr Nordern breathed a little easier, then:

'Now.'

Herr Nordern pressed his hot face against his pillow. 'You know Bodo.' He had a flash of inspiration. 'He wanted to borrow some money. To build a hen-house.'

It sounded utterly preposterous but it led to a longer silence. Frau Nordern's breathing became deeper and more regular. Herr Nordern relaxed a trifle.

'Did you? Lend him the money?'

'No! No. No. Now go to sleep. I've got work to do tomorrow.'

'You won't do it drinking with Bodo till all hours,' Frau Nordern said, but it was a Parthian shot as she did, then, go to sleep.

Herr Nordern lay awake, listening to his wife blowing little bubbling breaths. He did not feel well. In fact he was not far from being sick. What was the matter with him? he thought.

164

He was drinking like a fish, and had been for weeks. And now he was lurching about his flat with innocent children asleep in their beds, and he had lied to Helga. He had never done that before in all their life together. Just the thought of it made him feel unclean. For a moment he was tempted to wake her up and confess but thought better of it. 'But I will tell her tomorrow,' he promised. 'Some of it, anyway.' Then he, too, slipped off into an uneasy sleep, and strange, vivid dreams, in which Lieutenant Werner chased him down endless, war-torn and shattered streets, for ever.

Chapter 16

HERR NORDERN did not feel better the next morning, in fact he felt considerably worse. As he shaved his reflection seemed to be the face of a low criminal—or like one of Bodo's associates—and when he went into the sitting-room his wife bore more than a passing resemblance to an exceptionally severe judge about to condemn that criminal to hard labour for life.

Herr Nordern gave her a ghastly, feeble grin, as if asking for remission, but Frau Nordern turned a cold face away, showing only an upright back and stiff neck which in their rigidity seemed to symbolise the rectitude of all the generations of the Houses of von Bromberg and von Ritter.

Gulping coffee, Herr Nordern stared at that unyielding back and felt his heart sink. As he went into the bedroom for his brief-case he shook his head. 'I can't do it,' he thought. 'I really can't go through the day feeling like this.'

He looked through the window. It had snowed during the night but not heavily. He took a deep breath and opened the door.

'Er . . . Helga. . . .' he said.

Frau Nordern did not hear him or at least seemed not to.

Herr Nordern cleared his throat. 'Helga?'

This time Frau Nordern deigned him a glance, but only that. 'Your brief-case is on the dressing-table,' she said before turning back to her coffee.

'Ahem, ahem.' Needlessly Herr Nordern cleared his throat again, frowning at Paul who was goggling at him while stuffing himself with cheese and cold ham. 'It's not that. Could you spare me a moment?' He shook his head and beckoned at the same time, feeling an unutterable fool for doing so.

Frau Nordern gazed at him for an icy moment then stalked into the bedroom.

'Well?' she demanded.

Herr Nordern closed the door. As he did so his wife raised her eyebrows as if at some freakish aberration.

'What on earth are you doing that for?' she asked.

Herr Nordern held out his hand. 'Helga,' he said, 'listen, I want to talk to you.'

'Talk to me?' Frau Nordern was, or sounded as if she was, utterly amazed. 'Now?'

'Well, not now. Not just this minute.' Despite himself Herr Nordern was irascible. 'Look, I'll get the car out and drive you to work and tell you as we go.'

'Get the car out? Tell me as we go? Tell me what?'

Beneath his new submissiveness Herr Nordern felt another flicker of exasperation, the more so because he *was* being submissive. 'I'll tell you in the car,' he said. 'If you want to come.' He looked at his watch. 'But we'll have to go now.'

Frau Nordern gave him a calculating look then nodded. 'All right,' she said. '*If* the car works.'

For an anguished three minutes Herr Nordern thought that the Lada would not work but, in company with a neighbour's antiquated Volkswagen, after a bout of racking, early morning, heavy smoker's coughing, it came to a sort of half-life as, quite unnecessarily, because the Lada's engine could be heard half-way across Berlin, Herr Nordern tooted its feeble horn.

In the flat Frau Nordern drained the last of her coffee, snatched her brief-case, kissed Omi, and swept to the door.

Still munching cheese, Paul made a dive for his coat only to be halted by his mother's withering glare.

'Aren't we coming?' Paul demanded indignantly.

'Coming where?'

'In the car.'

'The car?' Frau Nordern gave Paul a cold, blue stare. 'Just you make sure that you don't miss your bus—and bring your homework back.'

The door slammed behind her as Paul looked dolefully at Erika.

'What's the matter with them?' he demanded.

'Nothing.' Erika was firm. 'And—' to an approving nod from Omi she added, 'don't say *them* about Mother and Father. It isn't polite.'

'It's them who aren't being polite,' Paul muttered, *sotto voce*.

And in fact Frau Nordern was not being polite as Herr Nordern drove the Lada in a wobbly course down Klara-Lettkin-Strasse.

'I hope that you have something worth saying,' she said.

'Well,' Herr Nordern struggled with the gears as a gigantic lorry with a huge sign saying 'Workers of All Countries Unite' painted on it cut across him, its horn blaring. 'Helga—' he cursed as another lorry swung across his bonnet.

Clutching her brief-case, Frau Nordern jerked her chin. 'If all you can do is swear—'

'For Christ's sake!' A motor-cyclist slithered towards the car. 'Just a minute.' Herr Nordern heaved on the steering-wheel and swung the Lada into the relative safety of a narrow street shadowed by the bulk of a church where he pulled up, although wisely keeping the engine running.

Frau Nordern raised her head as if appealing to the Deity presiding over the church. '*What* are we doing *here*?' she asked, as if, by some miracle, they had arrived in Lapland.

'Just a moment. One moment.' Herr Nordern pulled out a cigar. 'Can't talk in that traffic. I'm sorry.'

He lighted his cigar, puffed furiously, sank back in his seat, as far as it would allow him to, and stared fixedly through the windscreen, already lightly furred with snow. 'Look, Helga, it's about last night. When I got back.'

Frau Nordern turned a marmoreal face, and when she spoke her voice was as cold as her face. 'You were drunk.'

'Er....' Herr Nordern fidgeted with his cigar. 'Not actually drunk, Helga.'

'You were!' Frau Nordern was contemptuous. 'Lurching about the flat. I heard you.'

'Well, all right. I was—a bit. But that's not it.'

'Not what?' Frau Nordern turned her face away.

168

'Don't do that, Helga,' Herr Nordern said. 'Look at me, please. Thank you. I was worried—let me finish— Bodo—'

'Bodo!' Frau Nordern was withering. 'I thought that he'd have something to do with it.'

'No, it's not what you think—'

'You don't know what I think.' Frau Nordern struggled with her window. Smoke billowed out and a few snowflakes fluttered into the car. 'You did lend him the money, didn't you?'

'Lend him money?' Herr Nordern said blankly.

'Forgotten already.' Frau Nordern jerked her chin. 'I said that you were drunk.'

'All right!' Herr Nordern threw his cigar out of the window. 'I was. I was drunk. Drunk! Don't keep going on about it. I'm trying to talk to you.'

There was an ominous minute's silence and then, even more ominously, Frau Nordern spoke.

'He's in trouble, isn't he? Serious trouble.'

Herr Nordern tapped the steering-wheel. 'No. No, he isn't in trouble. But he told me something. It . . . it was about Werner.'

'Werner?'

'Yes. The policeman. The one who interviewed me about the accident.'

'What about him?'

Herr Nordern tugged at his collar. 'Bodo said—' he repeated what Bodo had told him.

Frau Nordern listened intently. When Herr Nordern had finished some of her iciness had melted. 'What does it mean?' she asked.

'I don't know.' Herr Nordern shook his head. 'But that's why I was worried and drank too much.'

'So it wasn't about lending money to Bodo at all?'

'No.' Herr Nordern stared at his hands. 'I'm sorry, Helga, lying to you.'

'That's all right.' Frau Nordern forced her window up. 'I didn't believe you anyway.'

'You didn't?' Herr Nordern was rather offended.

'No.' Frau Nordern half-smiled. 'You're not a good liar,

Hans. Not enough practice.' She paused. 'And Bodo said don't do anything?'

'Yes.'

'I see.' Frau Nordern looked at her watch. 'We'd better get going, I'm late already.'

Twenty minutes later, after a silent, worried drive, Herr Nordern dropped off his wife at the Welfare Centre.

'I'll pick you up tonight if you like,' he said.

Frau Nordern hesitated then shook her head. 'I may have to go to a meeting. I'll see you back home.' She nodded curtly at a respectful errant mother then stooped to the car window. 'Don't worry your head about Werner. It can't be anything.'

She raised her hand as a dubious Herr Nordern forced the car into almost the right gear and drove off with a curious jerking motion, then turned and went into the Centre with a look on her face which boded ill for anyone who crossed her path that day.

The brief Berlin day faded away. Errant mothers wished that they weren't or, given that they were, had a different case officer from Frau Nordern. In his office an anxious Herr Nordern gouged out a few marks from unenthusiastic colleagues for a wreath for Steinmark's funeral. It stopped snowing but grew colder as the East breathed an icy wind across the city, and in the Egon Schultz school the music of Johann Sebastian Bach echoed through the corridors.

The music came from members of the school orchestra who, with Erika on the flute, were rehearsing the 'Musical Offering' by Bach, an unusual piece as it was Bach's only work written for five instruments. Erika was surprised to find that she was beginning to like Bach. As short a time as a few weeks previously she had been, when not bored, repelled by his music. It had seemed, the great choral works excepted, mere mathematics, endless, tedious variations on simple themes, clever, of course, but no more than that. But now she was being drawn, as it were unwillingly, into his world which although intellectual—abstract, even—was, she was discovering, informed by deep, profound passion.

It was an excellent rehearsal and the music teacher, Frau Fegel, was delighted.

'Very good,' she said. 'Really good. The balance was correct, and the technical quality. But we must concentrate on drawing out the *feeling*.' She looked at the clock. 'We could run through it once more.'

'I'm sorry, Frau Fegel,' Erika said. 'I have to go to the gym.'

'Ah, athletics.' Frau Fegel was less than enthusiastic. 'If you must.'

Must was the word and Erika left the music room, Frau Fegel taking her place; the sound of the music followed Erika as she went down the corridor to the gym.

And there, after her warming-up exercises, she leaped like a gazelle, undisturbed by the fact that she was being filmed on video by two pupils and barely noticing that during the session a small group of people tiptoed on to the gallery, and she did her last jump to applause.

Showered and changed, she went back into the gym and found Fräulein Silber standing modestly in the background while, very much in the foreground were Herr Wolf, from the National Stadium, and Fräulein Carow.

Herr Wolf shook Erika's hand. 'Excellent jumping,' he said. 'You remember Fräulein Carow, of course. You see we haven't forgotten you, Erika. Not that we came just to see you. Even promising young athletes don't bring us out on a winter's day; we do have little tours of inspection, occasionally.' He smiled his pleasant, open smile. 'We have been to other schools. I must say that the standard of high jumping is very good this year. So, congratulations, Erika. I notice that you have got your left leg sorted out. Well done Fräulein Silber. We'll see you at the next coaches' meeting.'

To cordial goodbyes they left, leaving Erika and Fräulein Silber alone in the huge gym.

'Good,' Fräulein Silber said. 'Really good, Erika.'

'It's thanks to you, Fräulein,' Erika said.

Fräulein Silber waved the thanks aside but Erika persisted. 'I mean it. If it hadn't been for you, after my fall. . . .'

'You did that yourself, recovering,' Fräulein Silber said. 'All the coaches in the world wouldn't have been of any use if you hadn't had courage. And now—' she made a typical high-jumpers' gesture, that which marks them out from all other

171

athletes, raising her arms and stretching her torso, as if taking off to challenge that dappled crossbar.

'You noticed what Herr Wolf said?' she continued. 'They'd been to other schools and the standard is high? Yes, and there is one girl in particular, in Pankow, Karen Bloxen. She's only just moved to Berlin so I don't know much about her—these provincials . . .' Fräulein Silber gave a wintry smile, 'and her coach is keeping her heights dark, but I know that she is keeping the bar up. However, we'll see about that—it's one thing jumping well in your own gym, but it's another one altogether doing it in a stadium—in a championship—with thousands of people looking at you. That's when people crack. That's when courage counts—and nerve.'

'You won a championship,' Erika said.

'Yes.' Fräulein Silber smiled a little crookedly. 'The Pomeranian Zonal Championship.' She subsided gracefully on to a mat and motioned Erika to join her. 'Area Junior Champion, but that was my limit. I went to a special sports school—not Leipzig,' she added hastily, to a nod from Erika who knew very well what Leipzig meant in the athletic world of the G.D.R., the absolute, superlative top—'but I was a second rater there. Oh yes,' she raised a finger as Erika tried to protest. 'I was. But I had a fine training, the best in the world. Better even than the Americans. And now I have a good job, one I like. And I was with them, with the Greats. Do you know that I once beat Ulrike Meyfarth!' She laughed. 'Yes—two years later she won the Gold Medal in the Olympics. But I saw them, I saw them face to face. And one day I will say that I saw Erika Nordern, say that I coached her. That will be something.'

'Fräulein!' Her face crimson, Erika protested.

'It's true.' Fräulein Silber turned her green eyes on Erika. 'I mean it, you have the real stuff. So.'

She stood up. 'One week to go. A week of *real* concentration, and then. . . .'

Erika stood up, too, and gave a rueful shrug. 'Concentration.'

Fräulein Silber was suddenly sharp. 'What about it?'

'Oh,' Erika sighed. 'It's just that we are having a party—after the competition,' she added hastily. 'It's for my great-uncle. People are coming from all over the place, and the flat. . . .' she held out her arms.

Fräulein Silber clicked her teeth in exasperation. 'That won't do. It won't do at all.'

'But—' Erika began, only to be cut off.

'No buts about it.' Fräulein Silber's voice had the snap of authority.

Erika shook her head, for once letting authority go unheeded. 'We can't put the party off, Fräulein. All the arrangements have been made.'

'Of course,' Fräulein Silber said. 'I'm not suggesting that. But I've been thinking about next week. You are crowded at home?'

Erika hardly bothered to say 'yes'. For a family in the position of hers it would have been like saying one needed air to breathe. But Fräulein Silber was in a different position.

'My flat is small,' she said, 'but there's room for two, and it's quiet. It would be a good idea if you came and stayed with me. Not if you don't want to, of course. Would you mind?'

Erika blinked. 'No, I don't think so.'

'And your parents?'

Erika thought for a moment—a brief moment. 'I'm sure that they wouldn't,' she said, although wondering what her mother would say.

'Ask them anyway. But the main thing is yourself.' The green eyes peered at Erika. 'It's an important week and if you would be happier at home. . . .'

Erika did not need that last qualification. To have a week away, and with Fräulein Silber . . . even the thought of Omi faded as she thought of it; after all, it would only be for *one* week, pushing away the traitorous thought that one week for herself was quite different from a week in Omi's life, and, treachery giving way to treason, she did have her own life to lead; and so she said, firmly, 'It will be all right, Fräulein. And thank you. Good-night.'

She walked away across the polished floor, then halted and turned. Fräulein Silber was standing by the high jump, one hand resting on the bar.

'Thank you so much, Fräulein,' Erika called. 'For everything.' And then, overcome by her own emotion, she ran from the gym, and the school.

Outside the door she paused, breathing the chill and chilling air. From the school came more music, the school choir rehearsing for Christmas. She could see the choir through the windows of the Hall: a hundred pupils, rapt, or, at any rate *looking* rapt, under the vast banner of the G.D.R. They were singing a folk-song, simple but moving, and Erika came close to tears. Perhaps she *was* destined for glory. Perhaps, one day, the pupils singing would say—boast!—that they had known Erika Nordern. She remembered what her father had said that day in the Stadium; the German Democratic Republic was a good country, a great country, a miracle. The choir sang:

'*Ah! Wald und Berg. . . .*
Ah, forest and mountain,
River and lake
My love for you will never fade. . . .'

And then a tentative voice called from the darkness.
'Erika?'

Erika broke away from her reverie and peered into the gloom. 'Who's there?' she said. 'Who's that?'

'It's me.' Preceded by a cloud of vaporised breath, a figure shuffled into the light spilling from the Hall.

'Fritz!' Erika raised her hand. 'What are you doing here?'

Fritz Kott gave a hangdog grin. 'I was just passing.'

'Just passing?' Erika was amazed. 'You live miles away.' She had a sudden insight, at once alarming and ludicrous. 'You haven't been waiting here since school ended, have you? I mean waiting for me?'

Fritz gave an even more ghastly grin. 'Er . . . no. No. I was just passing.'

'You have been waiting!' Erika stamped her foot in vexation. 'Tell the truth. Are you crazy? Standing around in this weather for ages.'

'It's not cold.' Fritz shuddered as he spoke.

'Of course it's cold. It's freezing!' A devastating thought

struck Erika. 'I hope that no one has seen you hanging about round here.'

'No, no one. Honest.' Fritz spoke with fawning eagerness.

Erika flushed. 'So you *have* been waiting. What are you thinking of? You'll have the whole school talking.'

'No, really.' Fritz took a step nearer. 'Honestly, Erika, no one has seen me. I just wanted to see you, that's all.'

'But you see me every day,' Erika snapped. 'You saw me today.'

'Yes.' Fritz stared at his shoes. 'But it's . . . you know . . . it's not the same.'

'Not the same as what?' Erika demanded.

'Not the same as . . . as . . . you know. . . .' Fritz's voice tailed dismally away. He rolled his eyes and tugged at his collar and blew on his finger-nails; and then Erika felt a sensation she had never known before; one that in all her life of order, regimentation, structures, and of love and caring, too, it had never occurred to her that she might have. She felt a sense of power: power utter and complete over another human being, and in the black and bitter night, she used it.

'Know what?' she asked, knowing that Fritz was there to be toyed with.

Fritz gave her an earnest look which was, if anything, even more ghastly and idiotic than his grin. 'The . . . the disco,' he said, huskily, as if lowering his voice would give that humble word a significance beyond all words.

'The disco?' Erika frowned and tilted her head as if trying to remember and then, cruelly, said, 'Oh yes, where I danced with that interesting lad, and with Herman Guttenbruk.'

'Erika!' Fritz was outraged. 'You know what I mean.'

'I haven't the faintest idea what you mean.' Erika had her mother's iciness. 'And please don't tell me what I know or don't know.'

'No! No, of course not. Sorry.' Fritz made a strange gargling noise. 'I just meant, I mean, er . . . would you like to come for a coffee. The Kiev isn't far.'

'The Kiev!' Erika, who rather liked the Kiev, was disdainful. 'I certainly wouldn't go there.'

'All right.' Fritz took another step forward and almost fell over his feet. 'Listen, we could go to the Baltic—' naming a horribly expensive café and one far beyond his means—'it's only a few stops on the bus—'

But the little game was over for Erika. Her fingers and toes were chilling and slowly and almost imperceptibly the mist settling on her fur collar was turning a frosty white.

'I think that you're crazy,' she said. 'You really are. Anyway, I should be home by now. Don't hang around school waiting for me ever again. Good-night.'

But the good-night was not as definite as it sounded and Fritz, cowed though he was, knew it and walked with Erika to her bus-stop and waited with her in the cold until the bus did trundle along, and even then he made an attempt to get on it with her, a ploy which, with a deft use of her elbow, Erika foiled, leaving him standing at the bus-stop; a lonely rejected youth, bowed as with the sorrows of all the world—and yet irresistibly comic.

'He's in love with me!' Erika thought, and burst out laughing.

But comical though he was, and although Erika laughed, yet her heart was touched, and as the bus juddered through the deserted streets, all the way home she looked into the window, seeing not the flats, factories, and dark parks, but, wonderingly, her own reflection.

As ever, Omi was in, sitting patiently at the table, writing one of the many letters with which she kept the tattered network of Brombergs and Ritters precariously bound together. She smiled as Erika entered the room although her smile had that new wistfulness about it.

Erika kissed Omi's old cheek, and then made hot chocolate. 'Have you had a good day, Omi?' she asked, sitting with her grandmother.

'Ach! Such a day.' Omi shook her head. 'The telephone. On, on, on! I've written down the messages.'

She made to rise but Erika forestalled her and got the telephone pad.

'I couldn't hear what they were saying most of the time,' Omi said, as Erika ran her eye down the list of calls written in Omi's shaky, old-fashioned script. 'The line was so bad, clickings and buzzings, and I'm not quick. . . .'

'It's all right.' Erika was cheerful. 'They'll call again, anyway. Bet your boots on it.'

Omi chuckled. 'Ah, *Liebchen*, you do my heart good.' She peered over her spectacles. 'And how pretty you look. Such a complexion. Like the English girls. I had a cousin, Heinrich von Ströbel. He fell in love with an English girl just because of her cheeks. . . .'

Erika felt the blood flow into *her* cheeks. She lowered her cup. 'Omi,' she was about to tiptoe into that mysterious realm summed up by the word *love* when, maddeningly, the phone rang.

'Another!' Omi said as Erika, mildly—internally—cursing, reached and took the receiver.

'Erika?' Through a barrage of clicks and crackles, Frau Nordern's voice reached Klara-Lettkin-Strasse sounding oddly ghostly. 'Erika? It's your mother. *Your mother!*'

'Yes, I can hear you,' Erika said.

'What?'

'I know,' Erika shouted across the bedlam on the line.

'Know what? Is that you Erika?'

The interference mysteriously stopped and through a clear line Frau Nordern's voice boomed with all its usual authority, as if the ghost had miraculously become embodied with all the solidity of human flesh.

Erika held the phone away from her ear for a moment then spoke into it quietly. 'Yes, it's me, and I can hear you.'

'Good. Who is there?'

'Omi and I.'

'Where's Paul?'

'At the F.G.Y.'

'Hm.' There was a brief pause, then, 'Are you sure?'

Erika sighed. 'Yes, it's Friday night.'

There was a suspicious assent. 'And Father isn't there?'

'No.'

'Well listen, Erika—are you listening?'

'Of course I am.'

'Good. I may be a little late so don't wait supper for me. Do you understand that?'

For a moment Erika was strongly tempted to say that she didn't but instead she meekly said, 'Yes, Mother.'

'All right.' Suddenly the cacophony broke out again on the line. Erika heard something vague and peremptory from her mother and then, as the line went dead, the front door rattled, Herr Nordern came in, and Erika shrugged and dropped the phone back on to its holder.

At the other end of the line Frau Nordern did much the same, then stood up and stuffed her brief-case with various documents. She locked her desk and her office, and moved majestically out of the Centre.

She caught her usual bus, but instead of getting off at Frankfurter Allee and catching the *S-Bahn* to Biesdorf, she stayed on it, all the way to Ostkreuz where, like Herr Nordern once before her, she made her way to Ostkreuz Police Station.

Chapter 17

HERR NORDERN would have recognised the scene inside the Station as if it were a replay of a film, or a remake, rather: the shady characters and the drunks, and the *badinage* reflecting a curious *bonhomie* between the Duty Officer and the offenders, although the cast was different and, it being later, the Station was busier; the offenders looking more offensive and the policemen more policeman-like, bigger, harder, and, in all senses of the word, more arresting—although, big and hard though they were, two of them, bundling out an unfortunate to a police van, gave way respectfully to Frau Nordern as she stalked towards the desk.

The Duty Officer, elderly and paunchy, raised a lumpy face from a crime sheet, or a sports paper, both of which were on his desk, looked again, and stood up.

'Frau?'

'Lieutenant Werner,' Frau Nordern said.

The Duty Officer leaned forward. 'Who?'

'Werner,' Frau Nordern said. 'Lieutenant Werner. And I haven't got all night.'

The lumpy face creased into a puzzled frown. 'Werner?'

Frau Nordern heaved up her brief-case and let it fall on to the desk with a satisfying, rather official thud. 'That's four times we've said the name.'

'Werner.' The Duty Officer made it a fifth time, glanced, not without anxiety at the brief-case, momentarily at Frau Nordern, then with relief, over her shoulder, and jerked his lumps and bumps.

'Frau.' A striped sleeve rested on the desk. 'Can I help you?'

Frau Nordern turned. A sergeant with a face which looked

as if its owner was more used to giving lumps than receiving them was standing next to her. With an air of hugely controlled patience she said, 'I want to see Lieutenant Werner.'

'Why is that, Frau?'

Frau Nordern gave an ominous drum-roll on the desk with her fingers. 'That is for me to tell the Lieutenant.'

The Sergeant waited for the drum-roll to die away, and for a drunk, shouting incoherently, to be dragged through a grim looking door. 'We're busy tonight,' he said reasonably, 'Frau . . . ?'

'Nordern!' Frau Nordern snapped. 'And I'm busy all the time. Now get me the Lieutenant.'

'I'm afraid that he's not here, Frau,' the Sergeant said in a blank, bureaucratic voice.

'Then get me whoever *is* in charge,' Frau Nordern said, in an equally bureaucratic voice.

The Sergeant hesitated for a moment. 'And I'm to say?'

'Say I'm from the Ministry of Justice.'

The boozy gabble of the offenders was suddenly silenced, although whether it was the tone of Frau Nordern's voice or the word 'ministry' which stilled it, it would be hard to say.

In the uncanny silence the Sergeant looked again at Frau Nordern, and at the brief-case. 'Very well,' he said. 'Er, would the Frau like a seat?' He gestured at the row of chairs where the offenders lolled. Frau Nordern gave them a contemptuous glance and the Sergeant coughed. 'No, perhaps not. If the Frau would wait just one moment then.'

'*One* moment,' Frau Nordern said, placing a well aimed dart between the Sergeant's broad, grey-clad shoulders as he went into an inner office.

The moment stretched into one, two, three, a minute, another. The hands on the big wall clock jerked around with the enthusiasm of a convict doing forced labour, the offenders stared at their battered and scuffed shoes in awed silence with the exception of a drunk who had missed the dreaded word MINISTRY and who openly admired Frau Nordern's figure but who, with the solidarity of the criminal underworld, was instantly hushed into silence by the other offenders. His sports paper having mysteriously disappeared, the Duty

Officer scratched furiously at a vast form, a flush, as ominous as a gathering storm began to show on Frau Nordern's neck, and then the door of the office opened, the Sergeant came out, and behind him a stocky man in plain clothes, smoking a cigar, and blinking through bloodshot eyes, waved Frau Nordern forward.

As Frau Nordern went into the office a babble of voices rose behind her, still audible, although muted, as the door was closed by the man with the cigar. He waved Frau Nordern to a seat and took one himself.

'Marx,' he said. 'Otto Marx. No relation. And you are Frau Nordern?'

'Yes,' Frau Nordern sat bolt upright and gave Marx her commanding glare which, however, did not have quite the same effect on him as it had done on the Duty Officer.

'So you want to see Lieutenant Werner?' Marx said.

'Yes.' Frau Nordern waved at the cigar smoke but, unperturbed, Marx puffed vigorously away.

'He's not here,' he said.

'Well, when will he be here?' Frau Nordern demanded.

Marx blinked his bloodshot eyes. 'Couldn't say.'

Frau Nordern frowned as Marx stubbed out his cigar and promptly took out another one. 'What rank are you?' she asked.

'Sergeant.' Marx struck a match. 'Detective Sergeant.'

'And are you in charge of this station?'

'No.' Marx lighted his cigar.

'Then who is in charge?'

'Inspector Grün, but he's not here either, so in a manner of speaking I suppose I *am* in charge just now.'

From behind the frosted-glass door there were bangs and scuffles and a wild drunken bellow. Marx blinked at what could be seen of the office ceiling through the hanging cloud of his cigar smoke. 'Business improving,' he observed. 'Friday night. Is this a Ministry affair, Frau?'

Frau Nordern hesitated. 'No, not exactly.'

Marx peered at Frau Nordern. 'You said you were from the Ministry.'

'I work there,' Frau Nordern said.

'Not quite the same thing,' Marx said, mildly and without rancour, as if half-truths and no-truths were part of his life, which they were. 'Still, if there's anything you want to talk about you'll have to talk to me or no one.'

Frau Nordern bit her lip in vexation. 'When can I see Lieutenant Werner?'

'Couldn't say.' Marx shrugged.

'Inspector Grün then?'

Marx shook his head. 'Difficult. Very difficult.' He picked a shred of tobacco off his lip. 'Especially if you won't say what you want to see him about.'

Frau Nordern gave an exasperated 'tut'. 'Does Lieutenant Werner work here?' she demanded.

Marx's manner altered abruptly. He gave Frau Nordern a hard stare. 'You ought to know better than to ask that. Who works here is a State Secret.'

'Yes—of course. Sorry.' Frau Nordern, uncharacteristically meek, was forced on to the defensive. Even asking about State Secrets was a serious crime, and both she and Marx knew it. 'You're quite right.'

Marx nodded grimly. 'All right, Frau, we'll forget it. Now what do you want?' He leaned forward confidingly. 'One policeman is the same as another.'

'Very well.' Frau Nordern coughed in what for her was a diffident manner. 'It's about my husband. He was called in here a few days ago, about an accident.'

'Yes?'

'What do you mean, yes?' Frau Nordern allowed herself a note of exasperation.

Marx blinked his bloodshot eyes. 'I mean yes. What accident was it?'

'Oh.' Frau Nordern nodded. 'It was a motor-cyclist, he was knocked down and the driver didn't stop.'

'So?' Cigar ash spilled down Marx's jacket.

'So we want to know what's happening.'

Marx pawed at his jacket, rubbing the ash in rather than dusting it off. 'Why?'

Frau Nordern had a flash of temper. 'Why do you think? My husband's worried about it.'

'Oh?' Marx sounded mildly surprised. 'Just a minute.' He

stood up and went to a battered grey filing cabinet, rummaged through it, and grunted. When he turned around he was leafing through a file.

'Yes, Nordern . . . accident . . . number . . . statement taken . . . .' He leaned against the cabinet forcing Frau Nordern to turn awkwardly in order to see him. 'What's he worried about, your husband? He says he had nothing to do with it.'

'He certainly hadn't,' Frau Nordern snapped.

'So?'

Frau Nordern flushed. 'So I want to know how the investigation is getting on. We have a *right* to know. Do you realise what it's like having something like this hanging over your head?'

Marx re-lit his cigar. 'No, I don't,' he said blandly.

'Well you ought to,' Frau Nordern flashed, then, realising the oddity of the remark, retracted. 'Of course I don't mean that you should. . . .'

She paused, at a loss for words, but Marx wasn't.

'I hope that you don't,' he said in a tough, menacing voice.

'Yes.' Frau Nordern was taken aback by the toughness and the menace. 'But I just want to know what's happening, that's all.'

Marx yawned, showing blackened teeth. 'Enquiries proceeding.'

Frau Nordern made another foray. 'Who is the case officer?'

Marx dropped the file back in the cabinet and slammed the drawer shut. 'State Secret, too.'

He went to the door and opened it. There was a babble of voices, astonishingly cheerful under the circumstances. Marx rolled his cigar from one side of his mouth to the other. 'They're not worrying,' he said. 'And they *are* guilty. Good-night, Frau.'

Frau Nordern snapped a good-night back and stormed out of the Station, and such was the mood showing on her face that on the *S-Bahn* a railway policeman checking tickets did not ask for hers but wisely changed carriages at Lichtenberg station and looked for other prey.

The family had finished their supper when she got home,

but her temper was soothed by her reception: Herr Nordern coming from the bedroom to greet her, Omi fussing, Erika getting her meal, even Paul helping her off with her coat, although he rather spoiled his effect by then chucking it over the back of a chair instead of hanging it up.

She finished her supper of pork and sauerkraut then, as she had a coffee, Herr Nordern joined her and the family and had coffee himself. Feeling rather guilty, Frau Nordern listened as he described the arrangements for Steinmark's funeral.

'It seems to be taking a long time,' Omi observed.

'It's the inquest,' Herr Nordern said, 'and they're having the devil of a job finding a relative to make any arrangements.'

'Has he no family?' Omi asked.

Herr Nordern shook his head. 'Seems not. All wiped out in the War and he was brought up in an orphanage. He was a lonely, miserable wretch. The Police opened his flat, hardly any furniture, just a pile of dirty magazines.'

There was a moment's silence and, as Omi murmured a prayer for Steinmark, Frau Nordern looked around at her family and felt her throat tighten. 'My God,' she thought. A lonely, miserable wretch, living a furtive life in a shabby room somewhere, uncared for, unmourned, and it could have happened to her husband, to herself, Omi . . . the War could have done that, its implacable hand wiping out all human ties. As she looked again at the faces of her family she was ready to burst into tears and almost did so but Erika, moving lightly into the kitchen, said:

'Fräulein Silber thinks that I should stay with her next week.'

Lobbed through the plastic ivy it was a minor bombshell. Steinmark was forgotten, and even Werner and the accident slipped from Frau Nordern's mind as the family clucked over this news.

'A week away from home? Before the Championships?' Frau Nordern shook her head. 'You should be here, sleeping in your own bed and eating good food.'

Omi, too, shook her head, in sadness rather than disagreement, but, as usual, Herr Nordern was bluntly common-sensical.

'What's the fuss? Erika has been away plenty of times, and

if Fräulein Silber thinks that it is the right thing to do then it *is* the right thing. She's the expert, but it's up to you, *Liebchen*.'

As Erika had already made up her mind, that effectively ended the debate. The television was switched on, Omi started a new piece of crochet-work, Herr Nordern abandoned his statistics, Frau Nordern her reports, and Paul, boldly and half-truthfully announcing that he had finished his homework, joined Erika on the sofa to watch a good thriller on West German television. It began to snow again and the dark streets of Berlin had a new, immaculate blanket, hiding the grime and grease of the day.

The film ended most satisfactorily, vice punished and virtue rewarded, the villain caught and the heroine finding true love with the detective. As Herr Nordern said, it might easily have been made in the G.D.R., yawning as he spoke, that being a signal the whole family understood.

A few minutes later, Erika sat by Omi. 'It was a good film, wasn't it?' she said, smoothing Omi's pillows.

'Yes.' Omi took her Watchword. 'So you will leave.' She raised her hand, stilling Erika's voice. 'Of course that is right. You must have peace and quiet before such an event. Here—' she smiled—'it will be like a railway station, people coming and going—staying, too. No, you must go, rest, relax, and then win your vaulting.'

'Jumping,' Erika said.

The familiar gurgle came from the bathroom. 'My turn.' Erika took her dressing-gown and slipped out, deftly avoiding her mother who was going to her room.

'Good-night, Mother,' Erika said.

'Good-night.' Frau Nordern paused for a moment then waved her hand. 'Ah, go to Fräulein Silber. It's the sensible thing to do.'

Erika disappeared into the bathroom, Frau Nordern into the bedroom where Herr Nordern was sitting at his desk, looking absently at the wall.

'You're not thinking of starting work, are you?' Frau Nordern asked in a tone of voice which strongly suggested that if he was then he could go and do it somewhere else.

'Eh?' Herr Nordern blinked. 'No, no. I was just thinking.'

'Yes?'

'Oh, about Steinmark, and us. How lucky we are, a family together, and how lucky I am.'

'How lucky *I* am.' Frau Nordern said. 'And my mother.'

'No.' Herr Nordern shook his head. 'You would have been all right in the end. But men . . . they go downhill so quickly.'

'Oh, Hans.' It was rare for Frau Nordern to kiss her husband affectionately but she did so now, kissing him on the cheek and ruffling his hair.

Herr Nordern smiled. 'Thank you, my Dear.' He gazed at Frau Nordern as she squeezed past the desk and sat on the bed. 'I'm so glad I told you the truth this morning. I would have felt bad all day otherwise.'

He stood up, stretched his arms, took two paces to the window, and peered, with some difficulty, through a hedge of cacti. 'Still snowing,' he said. 'Ah, honesty is the best policy. It really is.'

Frau Nordern looked at her husband's broad back. 'Honest Hans,' she thought. 'Solid, thorough, plodding, even,' (that had been said of him by a Bromberg once to Frau Nordern— but once only) 'but kind in his shy way and decent to the very core.' She thought again of Steinmark and his lonely miserable life, and of the single women, and there were many in Berlin, living their lonely lives in bare rooms across the city. . . .

She bit her lip, took a deep breath, and spoke. 'Hans, I went there today.'

'Hmm?' Herr Nordern half-turned. 'Where?'

For a moment Frau Nordern was tempted to lie, to say that she had been to a meeting, or a mother. 'After all,' she thought, 'why say something which might upset Hans?' Some things were best left unsaid, after all, some bones best left unrattled, some secrets left buried. But it wasn't the time for secrets, or the place.

'I went to Ostkreuz,' she said. 'To the Police Station.'

It took a moment for the truth to sink in, but when it did Herr Nordern jumped. 'What!' He turned, caught his hand on a cactus spike, swore, and gaped. 'Ostkreuz?'

Frau Nordern moved uneasily on the bed. 'Yes.'

'But . . . .' Herr Nordern shook his head. 'But why? I mean . . . did they send for you?'

'No,' Frau Nordern shook *her* head. 'I just went.'

Herr Nordern sat down heavily at his desk. 'Just went? I don't understand.'

'I wanted to see this Werner man.' Frau Nordern raised her chin pugnaciously. 'I wanted to know what is going on.'

'But Bodo—'

'Don't Bodo me,' Frau Nordern snapped, but immediately raised her hand in apology. 'Sorry Hans. I didn't mean to speak sharply. I know what Bodo said about letting the matter lie, but I don't agree with him. We have a right to know what is going on, so I went to find out.'

Herr Nordern sucked his thumb for a moment, biting at the cactus spike. 'And what did you find out?'

'Well,' Frau Nordern tugged at the collar of her dressing-gown. 'Not much.'

Herr Nordern bit impatiently at his thumb. 'Did you see Werner?'

'No, I saw a sergeant called Marx.'

'Marx?'

'Yes.' Despite herself Frau Nordern laughed. 'A stubby man, chain-smoking cigars.'

Herr Nordern grunted. 'I think he was there when I saw Werner. Bloodshot eyes?'

'Yes.'

'And what did he say?'

'He said enquiries were proceeding.'

'That's all?'

'Yes.'

'So it's still hanging over us.' Herr Nordern frowned. 'Did you find out anything about Werner?'

'No.' Frau Nordern shook her head. 'They said any information like that is a State Secret.'

'Of course it is.' Herr Nordern was sharp. 'You ought to know that.' He rapped the desk. 'I wish you hadn't gone. I really do. Bodo was quite right.'

Frau Nordern agreed that he probably had been.

'And what did you find out? Nothing, nothing at all.'

'I know.' Frau Nordern was meek.

'All you've done is make us look suspicious.'

Frau Nordern demurred. 'I don't see that. There's nothing wrong in asking about an accident.'

'No,' Herr Nordern said. 'But there is in asking about Werner.'

There was a glum silence for a moment or two then Frau Nordern climbed into bed. 'Put the light out will you?'

Herr Nordern switched off the light but went back to his desk. There was the sputter of a match as he lighted a cigar.

'Aren't you coming to bed?' Frau Nordern asked.

'In a minute.'

Frau Nordern joggled her side of the bolster. 'I'm sorry,' she said.

'It's all right,' Herr Nordern said. 'You meant well. Go to sleep. I'll be in bed soon.'

But ten minutes later, as Frau Nordern was drifting off into an uneasy slumber, Herr Nordern was still at his desk, staring into the darkness, the end of his cigar glowing like a red warning signal as the snow drifted down on to Berlin, and his family, and the city, slept.

Chapter 18

FRAU NORDERN woke to a clear cold light and, to her amazement, Herr Nordern looming over her with a coffee.

'I didn't sleep very well,' he said, almost apologetically. 'I thought that you would like a coffee in bed for a change. You're not going to work are you?'

Frau Nordern took the coffee and blinked sleepily. 'No. Saturday isn't it?'

'All day.' Herr Nordern turned to the door. 'Sorry if I was sharp last night, about you going to the Police. It just took me aback.'

'It's all right.' Frau Nordern sipped her coffee. 'It was stupid of me.'

'No. Why shouldn't we ask. Anyway, I'm going to the office. *The office*,' he repeated. 'No more secrets, eh?' He smiled shyly. 'Be back by 1.00—I hope. 'Bye.'

Leaving behind an amused wife he went into the living-room where Erika, dressed in a track suit, was having her breakfast.

'*Liebchen*,' Herr Nordern heaved on his overcoat. 'Going running?'

Erika wagged a finger. 'Been,' she said. 'Five kilometres.'

Herr Nordern waved a goodbye and walked along the familiar road to the *S-Bahn* station. 'My God.' He shook his head. 'Five kilometres and it's barely light. 'I couldn't run five metres.' As the train rattled into the station he felt a glow of pride. 'What a girl—and my daughter. I just hope that there is nothing to this Werner business. My God, I hope not.'

Behind him, in the flat on Klara-Lettkin-Strasse, there was a cheerful atmosphere. Touched by her husband's bringing her coffee Frau Nordern was in a good humour, dismissing her own worries about the accident as mere alarmism stoked by Bodo, and tempering her authoritarian ways by letting Paul stay in bed for an extra fifteen minutes instead of, as usual, rousing him in the manner of a sergeant in charge of a penal battalion. The arrival of the mail helped, too: a mound of letters from the relatives who were, or, if they were to be given free accommodation, thought that they were, coming to Uncle Karl's party.

'I think that Fräulein Silber was right,' she said, reading a letter from an obscure, elderly maiden cousin who lived in an even more obscure district of the country. 'Hetta's coming. My God, Mecken, what a place to live!'

Erika laughed and Omi smiled, breaking her wan mood.

'Yes,' she said. 'That awful bog-land. When we were children we were told that we would be sent there if we were naughty. Poor Hetta. Still, it will be good to see her.'

Erika, who had never set eyes on Hetta in her life, stoutly agreed, and even Paul, making a dishevelled appearance, said with his new courtliness that he would like to meet her, causing Frau Nordern to raise a sceptical eyebrow and warn him not to be sarcastic at that time of the morning.

'So.' Erika stood up. 'I'm going to the gym. I can tell Fräulein Silber that I'll be staying with her next week then?'

'Yes,' Frau Nordern looked at her mail and added, ruefully, 'I wouldn't mind staying with her myself.'

The sun had broken through as Erika went to the bus-stop and by the time she had reached school it was quite warm, this pleasing Erika who feared that really severe weather would cause Uncle Karl to cancel the tour of Berlin the next day. In the gym, though, in front of the school video team, Fräulein Silber was at her most severe, even criticising Erika's warm-up exercises and clapping her hands with exasperation at Erika's run-up, that curved and crucial approach to the bar.

But after an hour of steady jumping, Fräulein Silber's mood changed abruptly. With an approving clap of her hands she ended the session, smiled, and said, 'Excellent. Very good.' She dismissed the video crew with the threat of terrible penalties if the video tape was not perfect, waved Erika down on the mat, and joined her.

She leaned forward, her face serious. 'Erika, you jumped really well there at the end. First-class technique—you'll see for yourself on the video tape. But—'

Erika's face fell, 'But.' Life seemed full of them. Her father would take her sailing on the Wannsee next summer—*but*! They might move into a bigger flat—*but*! She was jumping A.I—*but*!

'Cheer up.' Fräulein Silber's somewhat chilly face splintered into a smile. 'What I'm saying is this. Until a few weeks ago you were jumping with passion. Yes, with real feeling. With—' she searched for the right word. 'With *dynamism*. That's it. You were dynamic. Watching you jump was . . . well, it was like seeing a firework going off, a sky-rocket. You just shot up, whizzing all over the place, erratic but really zooming, and that partly compensated for any lack of technique. Now your technique is good, not perfect by any means, but good. But the fire has gone. Wait.' She raised her hand, stilling Erika's instinctive protest. 'Don't worry. It always happens. People start spontaneously in sport. It's a natural activity; running, jumping, kicking footballs. Having fun, really. But then to be good at a sport, really good I mean, you have to learn how to do what you are doing naturally in the best way possible. And that means technique. But, and it does happen, learning the technique dampens the fire—and then we have to stoke it up again.'

Fräulein Silber paused and looked steadily at Erika. 'In fact you have to forget the technique. It's there now. It's built into you. What was unnatural has become natural, you don't have to think about it, your body will do the right thing in the right way, like breathing. Strange, isn't it? You spend years learning something only to forget what you've learned. Like riding a bicycle.'

'Or playing Bach,' Erika said.

'Bach?'

'Oh,' Erika stretched her legs. 'Frau Fegel was saying the other day when we were playing Bach that our technique was good but that we had to learn to put feeling into our playing.'

'Just so!' Fräulein Silber smacked her muscular thigh.

'Exactly, and remember, art and sport have this in common, they are both means of self-expression. But they are more than just that. A child screaming is expressing itself, or like those artists who daub things in the West—they say they are expressing themselves.' It was clear from Fräulein Silber's face that she did not think highly of modern art. 'But with discipline, art and sport are ways of *developing* one's personality. And it can be done at any level. Even a paraplegic can be a sportsman. That is why we encourage mass sport in the G.D.R. And—' adding a little hastily—'mass part-icipation in all forms of human activity, art, crafts, and—' somewhat improbably—'philosophy, Marxism-Leninism. But—'

She rose with the fluent movement of the athlete. 'Enough of that. So, you will be staying with me next week?'

Yes, Erika would.

'Good. I'll call for you in my car tomorrow. Next week we put the fire back into you. Goodbye—and don't forget your exercises this afternoon.'

They parted and Erika caught her bus, wondering about the relationship between technique and feeling. It was an interesting thought, to learn something in order to forget it; as Fräulein Silber had said, like learning how to ride a bike, but like many other things, too, learning to play a musical instrument for instance. And this business of self-express-ion—she thought of Bunte with her striped hair. 'I really must think about the whole question,' she thought, as she went up the stairs to the flat.

Her mother and Omi and Paul were in, going through the arrangements for the party and wondering where the various guests could be put up—for free. Erika joined them, scanning the mail, and Bodo bustled in, ruddy from the cold, rubbing his calloused hands together, taking a glass of plum brandy, and filling the flat with an air of cheerful, rough, vigorous outdoor life.

'Just called to see you about the musicians for the party,' he said. 'How many? Six? Eight? Ten?'

'Three,' Frau Nordern said promptly. 'Piano, drums, and a what-do-you-call-them? An accordian.'

Bodo shook his head. 'They'll only play with four. That includes a violinist.'

'How much?' Frau Nordern asked—and blenched when she heard the figure. 'I'm certainly not paying that,' she said indignantly. 'Half would be too much.'

'Come on Helga.' Bodo swigged his brandy. 'It's a good price and—' he winked slyly at Erika— 'and for another twenty marks they'll wear gipsy dress.'

'Gipsy—' Frau Nordern began, but stopped as Erika burst out laughing.

'Oh, a joke. Very funny. But I'm not paying that much if they dress up as ... as .... ' She searched for words, and was still searching for them as the front door opened and Herr Nordern came in.

At once Frau Nordern went on to the attack. 'Hans, the money Bodo wants for his musicians!'

'Not *my* musicians,' Bodo said. 'I won't make anything out of them.'

Frau Nordern gave him a disbelieving stare. 'Anyway,' she said. 'You tell him Hans—and we only want three.'

Herr Nordern hesitated, then nodded. 'Yes. Er, come into the bedroom, Bodo.'

Bodo blinked. 'A secret session.' He guffawed. 'It's about a musician not a disarmament conference.'

'Yes, yes. But come anyway.' Herr Nordern brusquely waved Bodo into the bedroom and closed the door behind them.

'What the—' Bodo began, then saw the expression on his brother's face. 'Oh. Serious.'

'Maybe, perhaps, I don't know.' Herr Nordern rummaged in his desk, brought out a half-bottle of schnapps, two glasses, and poured drinks. 'Sit down,' he said. 'It's this Werner business, Bodo. Helga went to Ostkreuz last night.'

Bodo whistled. 'Not wise, Hans. Not wise.'

'I know that.' Herr Nordern gulped his drink. 'But she didn't tell me she was going.'

Bodo downed his drink and held his glass out for more. 'So what happened?'

Herr Nordern told him, barking savagely at an innocent Paul who poked his head around the door to ask what time they wanted lunch.

'Asking about Werner .... ' Bodo shook his head.

'Yes. But what's the harm in it—I mean what?' Herr Nordern said, then held out his hand. 'I know. I know. Anyway, she saw this man Marx. What do you know about him?'

But Bodo did not get round to answering that question because, to another curse from Herr Nordern, the door opened again—only this time the frame was blocked by Frau Nordern, her pale face paler than usual, her hand at her throat, and her eyes wide and staring.

'It's for you,' she said to her husband. 'It's that man from Ostkreuz. It's Sergeant Marx.'

There was a stunned silence, broken finally by Herr Nordern. 'What?' he said. 'Marx? Here?'

'At the door,' Frau Nordern said. 'He's waiting.'

'I can't believe . . . . ' Some of the blood drained from Herr Nordern's face. 'What does he want?'

'He wants you,' Frau Nordern said.

The rest of the blood seeped away from Herr Nordern's face, leaving it as white as his wife's. He licked his lips and looked at Bodo who, grim-faced, shrugged.

'Have to see him,' Bodo said. 'He isn't going to go away.'

'No.' Herr Nordern stood up rather stiffly and squared his shoulders. 'He won't.' Automatically he smoothed his hair and adjusted his tie.

'Well, it can't be anything—' and again, passionately, 'it can't be! You'll come, Bodo?'

'Sure.' Bodo stood up, as solid as a brick wall. 'All the way.'

'Right, then.' Herr Nordern went through the sitting-room to the front door. Marx was there, leaning on the door-frame, a hat rammed on the back of his head, a cigar jammed in the corner of his mouth, blinking his bloodshot eyes.

'You want to see me?' Herr Nordern said.

Marx nodded and gave a chesty cough.

'What about?' Herr Nordern tried to sound firm and innocent although, as he was desperately aware, sounding feeble—and guilty.

Marx coughed again. 'Perhaps we ought to go inside.'

'Inside? Oh, of course. Yes.'

As if they were doing a bizarre dance, followed by Marx,

194

Herr Nordern backed through the tiny vestibule, into the sitting-room, and a silent, apprehensive circle of Norderns.

'You've met my wife, I think,' Herr Nordern said. 'This is my mother-in-law, my children, and my brother.'

Omi and the children got perfunctory nods from Marx but he peered intently at Bodo who, massive arms folded, was leaning against the wall.

'I know you,' he said.

'And I know you,' Bodo answered in a tough, unyielding voice. 'And you've got your hat on.'

Herr Nordern's heart jumped, but Marx merely raised his eyebrows. 'So I have,' he said, and removed it. ''Scuse me.' He addressed Frau Nordern. 'Where I spend my time people don't bother.'

Herr Nordern gave a placatory smile and was about to say, completely untruthfully, that he—they—understood, when, to his horror, Bodo butted in again.

'Well we do here,' he said in his toughest voice.

Herr Nordern held his breath but Marx nodded. 'I suppose you do.'

There was a long moment's silence. The Norderns looked at Marx who stood before them as if he was quite happy to stand there in silence all day.

Finally Herr Nordern spoke. He tried to sound jocular but realised that he sounded almost pleading.

'And what can I do for you, Sergeant? It is Sergeant, isn't it?'

'Yes. Detective Sergeant.' Marx looked around for an ashtray, found one, and deliberately ground out his cigar-end. 'It's about the accident. You remember that, I suppose?'

Again Herr Nordern was going to speak, knowing as he did so that he would sound feeble, when again Bodo stepped in and said, in a distinctly non-feeble voice, which sounded like a cement-mixer, 'Of course he remembers. Get on with it.'

Herr Nordern's pounding heart stopped momentarily. 'Oh my God,' he thought. 'Oh Bodo, please keep your mouth shut. Don't provoke the Police. Don't make matters worse.'

But Marx, in an equally tough voice, merely said, 'O.K. Let's do just that,' put his hand in his breast pocket, slowly pulled out a horribly official-looking envelope, and slowly and carefully took from that an even more horribly official-looking form, folded once, in what to Herr Nordern seemed an indescribably sinister manner from top to bottom instead of side to side.

Marx unfolded the form and spoke to Herr Nordern. 'Perhaps you'd like to sit down.'

'Yes. Yes, if you say so. Thank you.' Herr Nordern sank on to the sofa and, astonishingly, found himself holding his wife's hand, and feeling hers firmly gripping his.

Frau Nordern turned her head. 'Erika, Paul, go to your room. Omi?'

But as Erika and Paul obediently, docilely, left the room—not without a backward glance from Paul—Omi shook her head.

'I will stay here if I may,' she said, looking at Marx as if he were an unpleasant insect.

Not that the look bothered Marx. He blinked at Herr Nordern, then peered at the document and began to read aloud, in a hoarse voice:

'"By Order of the Minister of Justice, I, the Chief of Police of the City of Berlin . . ."'

In Omi's room, the door opened a crack: herself frightened, Erika peeked into the sitting-room and hushed an even more frightened Paul into silence as he whispered, 'What is it? What's going on?'

'Nothing,' Erika whispered back. 'It's all right,' although, as she looked through the crack it did not seem all right at all; in fact it seemed all wrong. Her father and mother were sitting tensely on the sofa, Omi at the table, upright, disdain on her fine features, Bodo, huge against the wall, and all of them staring at the stubby, shabby, ash-stained figure of Marx, blinking through his red eyes at the document and reading aloud in an artificially solemn voice, practised in legal jargon and with which he, no doubt, had read out a hundred, a thousand, such documents.

'" . . .of the City of Berlin . . . you, Herr Nordern, official, of 13 Klara-Lettkin-Strasse, Biesdorf, in the jurisdiction of the City of Berlin, are hereby given official notification that—"'

'Oh,' Erika placed her hand over her mouth. 'Please,' she

thought, 'please, please.' And then, summoning up all her courage, listened to Marx continue.

'"That the accident at the corner of . . . resolved . . . culprit apprehended . . . said Herr Nordern cleared of all suspicion . . . and etc., and etc., and etc." And that's that,' Marx said unemotionally as he folded the form and slid it back into the envelope.

Herr Nordern felt his hand tremble. With an effort of will he tried to stop it but it carried on trembling. 'Cleared?' he said. 'Cleared? You mean . . . you mean I'm cleared?'

'That's right.' Marx stuck the envelope into his pocket. 'Actually, I shouldn't be telling you yet, but as your wife came to the station saying how worried you were I thought I'd call in and tell you. You don't mind, I hope?'

'Mind!' Herr Nordern jumped from the sofa, exultant. 'My God, thank you. Thank you, Sergeant. Cleared! Do you hear that, Helga? Bodo? Ah! A drink. We must have a drink on it. Erika, Paul, come in, come in. Get some glasses, Erika. Ha! ha! Sergeant, you'll have a drink with us? Of course you will.' He opened a bottle of brandy, his hands trembling and his face no longer white but red. 'Here Sergeant.' He handed a brimming glass to the imperturbable Marx. 'And thank you. Thank you very much. *Very much.*'

Marx downed his glass in one gulp and absent-mindedly held it out for more. 'That's all right,' he said as Herr Nordern eagerly refilled it. 'You would have heard officially on Monday but I thought why not tell you now and save you a week-end's worry. I was passing anyway.'

'Passing!' Herr Nordern laughed. 'I'm glad that you were, Sergeant. Hey, Helga? Bodo?' He filled glasses and took one himself. 'But the other man, the culprit?'

'Oh,' Marx was dismissive. 'We got him. It's like I said, the witness got the licence number garbled.'

Herr Nordern gave a huge sigh of relief. 'You did say that, Sergeant. Yes, you said that when I saw you at the station, ha! ha!'

'And the victim?' Omi whispered from her seat behind the table.

'Oh, him. He seems to be pulling round,' Marx said.

'Thank God,' Omi said, a sentiment shared cordially by all the family.

'And thank you again, Sergeant,' Herr Nordern said, as Marx stood up, spilling cigar ash over himself and the carpet. Herr Nordern shook hands with him, escorted him to the door, and saw him down the stairs as an excited buzz broke out among the family.

'I can't say how glad I am,' Frau Nordern said. 'Over! That nightmare.'

'That's the word.' Herr Nordern came back, rubbing his hands. 'Nightmare. I can't believe that it *is* over. You were right, Bodo, saying to leave the matter alone— although you gave me a turn when you were so . . . so abrupt with the Sergeant.'

Bodo sat down, making the chair creak. 'You don't want to let the cops walk all over you,' he growled. 'Anyway, I knew it was nothing when he came in.'

'You did?' Herr Nordern said.

'Sure. They come in twos when they're out for trouble. Anyway, you were innocent all along.'

'Ach!' Frau Nordern waved her arms. 'What does it matter. It's over, that's the thing.'

'And it's past lunch-time,' Herr Nordern said, adding hastily, 'not that I'm bothered, but the children, and Omi . . . .'

Lunch was ready, Bodo, pressed to stay, was persuaded, two bottles of wine were opened, a good, warming goulash brought in, and then, as Herr Nordern rather ceremoniously raised his glass to offer a toast, the telephone rang.

The whole family groaned, then burst out laughing. 'Leave it,' Herr Nordern said as Erika moved to take the call, but, as usual, the phone was hard to resist and, pulling a face, Herr Nordern took the call himself.

The line was surprisingly good, free from the usual squawks and clicks, and coming through, smooth, bland, was the voice of Uncle Karl.

'Hans? My dear fellow. Karl here. How are you, and the family?'

'Well. We're all well,' Herr Nordern bellowed from force of habit. 'In fact we're very well indeed.'

'Really?' Karl sounded intrigued. 'Hans, you sound . . .

exhilarated. Have you heard some good news?'

'Yes, yes!' Herr Nordern was triumphant as he told Karl of Marx's visit.

'Ahh,' Karl purred with satisfaction. 'Splendid. Simply splendid. Of course I never doubted that your excellent police force would catch the real culprit, but it must have cleared your mind. Most unpleasant having something like that hanging over your head. No—' in answer to Herr Nordern's promptings—'I'm truly sorry but I can't join you today. Actually I was calling to confirm my little trip with Erika tomorrow.'

The phone was handed over to Erika, who confirmed the trip and then gave the phone to her mother, who exchanged a few banalities and then handed it to Omi, who cooed and clucked and finally returned it to Herr Nordern who said, briefly, that they all looked forward very much to seeing Karl again and firmly replaced the receiver before anyone else could claim it.

'Eat,' he said, in a voice which meant, undeniably, *now*.

Eat it was, the goulash excellent, good black bread, and the wine very passable. Herr Nordern looked around the table, exuberant, dizzy with happiness, and then, remembering the toast he had been about to make, raised his glass.

'To us,' he said proudly. 'To all of us, but especially to you, Erika. The week of your life ahead of you!'

Frau Nordern and Omi beamed on Erika, Bodo banged the table with his fist, making the plates bounce alarmingly, Erika blushed, and, for reasons known only to himself, Paul went a fiery red, too.

'And what did Karl want with you?' Frau Nordern asked when the hubbub had died down.

'Oh,' Erika said. 'It was about tomorrow. *Tomorrow*,' she repeated after getting a blank stare from her mother. 'I'm meeting him, to go on a trip round the city. That's if the weather is good.'

'Of course, I'd quite forgotten,' Frau Nordern said. She spooned goulash down her handsome throat. 'Where will you take him?'

'The zoo,' Paul butted in, only to be butted out by his mother.

'The zoo!' She was blistering. 'You might as well say take him on the swings in the park. What would you say, Omi?'

Omi half-smiled. 'It isn't the weather for sightseeing, but he might care to look at the old Adlon hotel.'

Herr Nordern, pouring out more wine, shook his head. 'Do you think so, Omi, really? Not much to see there and it's a bit near the Bun—' he chopped his sentence short. 'Sorry.' He coughed. 'Shouldn't have mentioned it, but you know what I mean.'

They did—even Paul. Herr Nordern had been about to say 'the bunker,' the stretch of waste land behind Friedrichstrasse where, in his concrete tomb, as the Russians had battered their way into the city in 1945, Hitler had lived his final appalling fantasy; commanding armies which did not exist, so condemning thousands, hundreds of thousands of civilians to death in those final lunatic days. Under docks and willow-herb, the Bunker was still there, sealed but poisoned and poisonous, in a haunted city the spectres of an evil past still emanating from it, not least the ghosts of the six children of the Goebbels, killed by their own parents as a final insane act of homage to Der Führer.

For a moment the ghosts hovered around Klara-Lettkin-Strasse until Bodo exorcised them.

'Take him on a tourist bus,' he said. 'They're still running. Whizz round the sights and then if you've got any sense get back inside the Palast.'

Although the idea of the Palast appealed to Frau Nordern she was not too sure of the propriety of Karl's being whizzed around anywhere, especially on a tourist bus.

Bodo grinned. 'Well . . . what about you Paul? Any more ideas?'

Paul had plenty but as, owing to a fixed and completely unbreakable appointment with the F.G.Y., he was not going on the tour, his ideas were of no consequence.

'But you're coming to lunch,' Erika said, consoling him.

Paul perked up at that and, in any case, Herr Nordern shifted the topic. 'Wait until tomorrow before you decide,' he said to Erika. 'The weather might be too bad, anyway.'

That prospect looked increasingly likely as the day wore

out its brief existence. The clouds were lifting and breaking and at dusk, as Erika padded home from her run in the park, the temperature was falling.

It grew colder still as the night fell, a crackling frost under a sickle moon, but the coldness did not reach into the Norderns' flat and it would not have done so even had the central heating broken down, the joy and relief of the family generating enough warmth to melt the polar ice-cap if necessary. 'I can't say how I feel,' Herr Nordern said for the twentieth time. 'I really can't. It's all over. Done with. Finished. Now all we have to do is our duty to the State and it's full steam ahead for the Norderns.'

Frau Nordern agreed, although not without adding a rider of her own: 'I always did think that Bodo was being alarmist.' But she said that almost as if it were expected of her rather than with conviction—and the family knew it.

Paul, in fact, moved to Bodo's defence. 'Uncle Bodo is all right,' he said, only to be crushed by his mother.

'And who said he wasn't?' she demanded, and, pulverising as well as crushing, added, 'Go and tidy your room or you won't watch television tonight.'

Paul, whose remark had been the opening move in a carefully planned campaign to enhance Bodo's image so that his plan to leave school and work with him would not meet resistance, meekly accepted the rebuke and the order, especially as the television *he* wanted to watch was a rock concert.

Frau Nordern sternly watched Paul's retreating back then, dotingly, smiled at Erika. 'You ought to get ready,' she said.

Erika, rubbing her hair after her shower said, 'Get ready for what?'

'For tomorrow,' her mother said. 'You're going to Fräulein Silber's.'

Erika laughed. 'There's ages of time.'

'No.' Frau Nordern was sharp. 'You'll be busy tomorrow and besides, I like things done with plenty of time to spare.'

Erika following her, she bustled into Omi's room and began rummaging in the dressing-table pulling out garments to a running commentary of, 'Are these clean? Is this? This one isn't. I'll lend you my suitcase, yours isn't fit to be seen . . . . '

Erika sat on her bed smiling and when, after a few vigorous minutes, her mother announced that all was ready, she burst out laughing.

'And just what is so funny?' her mother demanded.

'Nothing really,' Erika said. 'It's just that I might as well have stayed in the sitting-room, that's all.'

She laughed again and, after a suspicious moment, Frau Nordern laughed too, a rich, throaty chuckle.

'I suppose so,' she said. She shook her head. 'I can't get used to the idea that you're growing up and can look after yourself. And I shouldn't go through your things. I know I hated it when Omi did it to me when I was your age.'

'It's all right, Mother.' Erika smiled, an enchanting open smile which illuminated her entire being and the entire room. 'Look away. All open for inspection. No secrets.'

Frau Nordern looked at Erika for a long, long moment. 'No secrets,' she said. 'Bless you, child.'

In the next room, Herr Nordern, reading the evening paper, heard the laughter, and the warm voices, and felt again profound happiness and contentment in his heart. He lowered his paper, lighted a cigar, and looked across at Omi.

'We live in a good country,' he said.

'Mmm?' Omi raised her head from her crochet-work. 'If you say so.'

'I *do* say so.' Herr Nordern was vigorously affirmative, combative even, but he was taken aback by Omi's response.

'You didn't think that the other day,' she said.

'I beg your pardon?' Herr Nordern was indignant.

Omi hooked a thread around her crochet-hook. 'When you were complaining about the Police,' she said.

Herr Nordern raised his hand in protest but let it fall again. 'Ah,' he thought, 'why argue? She's just an old woman living in the past, and if I never have another one this evening is going to be a good one.'

And good it was: good wine, good food, and a good film on the television, even Paul's request for the rock concert being allowed—for ten minutes.

Omi sat quietly crocheting, Erika conscientiously worked

on her sightseeing list for the next morning, writing out appropriate comments from the official guide to the city, Herr Nordern, guilt-free, smoked and drank brandy and Frau Nordern sat by him, having a drink, too, wondering whether she might have a cigarette—but deciding not to, preferring to keep that secret to herself. And then, good-night, and good-night, and the Nordern family went to bed.

As ever, Erika sat with Omi for a while, holding her hand.

'You are packed already?' Omi said.

'Yes.' Erika looked at the splendid silver plastic suitcase on her bed.

'Mother did it.' She laughed again, but Omi did not join in. Erika looked at her thoughtfully. 'Omi,' she said, 'you're not sad, are you? I'm only going to be away for a few days.'

'I know.' Omi patted Erika's hand. 'Only a week, and you must have a good week. And you must have a good morning tomorrow with Karl.'

Erika had a sudden thought. 'Why not come with me?' she asked.

A half-smile played on Omi's lips. 'I think not,' she said. 'Not in this weather, but thank you for the thought, my dear one. Thank you.'

The flat fell quiet. Erika slipped into the bathroom and met her father coming out.

'Good-night, *Liebchen*,' he said. 'Oh, just one thing. 'Tomorrow . . . .'

'Yes?' Erika said.

'Show Karl Bebel-Platz,' Herr Nordern said. 'Make sure he doesn't miss it.' And on that enigmatic note he kissed her cheek and went to bed.

When Erika tiptoed back into the bedroom Omi was asleep. Erika took the Watchwords from her hands, flicked out the bedside lamp, and stood by the window: a silent street. No one moving, not a man nor a woman, not a car or a motor bike, not even a dog barking under the sickle moon which shone in an opalescent sky surrounded by a diadem of stars.

In the beech tree, over the boulder, the owl called, for all the bitter frost warm in his golden feathers, and soon Erika was in her fleece of down, sleeping the sleep of the young and the innocent and the pure of heart.

Chapter 19

No snow fell during the night and at 10.00, after Erika had run her five kilometres under a dazzling blue sky, Karl rang and said that he thought, he rather did, that a brief tour of Berlin would be possible and that he would be waiting in the lounge of the Palast at 11.00; adding that Paul should meet them at the Television Tower at 1.00.

Waiting he was in the gold and brown of the Palast, himself immaculate, pink, flashing his smile as he complimented Erika on her appearance and, in her leather coat and with her fur hat at a rakish angle, and her face glowing with health, Erika deserved the compliment.

'The streets aren't icy?' he asked, and, reassured that they were not—not in the city centre, anyway—he suggested that they might take a short stroll, just a short one, if that suited Erika.

'Of course,' Erika said. She took out her list. 'I thought that we would go up the Television Tower and see the view, then go to the museums, especially the Pergamon, then the Palace of the Republic, then . . . . '

Her voice died away as Karl benignly shook his head. 'A most interesting programme, my Dear, but perhaps a little *too* much. I have seen a great many sights, you know. My hosts have taken me around, and I thought that we would have lunch in the Television Tower—in fact I have reserved a table. No, I thought that perhaps a stroll down Unter den Linden—such memories for me there—and then I have another idea. A surprise, ha! ha!'

A little crestfallen, Erika put her list away and dutifully said that of course she would be happy to do whatever Uncle Karl wished to do.

'So.' Karl waved a hand, a brown-uniformed attendant gave them a respectful salute, and they sauntered out.

Karl tucked Erika's arm under his as they crossed the bridge over the green, splintered ice of the Spree which formed a chill moat around the great museums, by the great dome of the Protestant Cathedral, and on to the broad stretch of Unter den Linden.

'Ah,' Karl shook his head as he looked down the avenue. 'It has changed, the bombing, the battle, but . . . some has survived, shops, libraries, the Embassies . . . . '

Erika took out her notes. '"A great deal of damage was done during the anti-fascist struggle but the German Democratic Republic is restoring these monuments to art and culture."'

'Admirable.' Karl took a pace or two forwards. 'My hosts have driven me down the avenue and given me the figures. Most admirable. And to see that—'

With surprising agility Karl darted across the road to where, on a bronze plinth, brazen himself, a mighty figure rode a horse. Erika followed Karl with a few lithe strides.

'Frederick the Great,' she said, unreeling her lesson learned by rote. 'King of Prussia.' She pointed to the frieze under the formidable warrior-king: 'General Yorck, General Blücher, General Scharnhorst, principal generals of the War of Liberation in which the German people freed themselves from French occupation in 1813. Although representatives of the Prussian ruling class they played a necessary role in the development of the national aspirations of the people which was to lead to our new Germany . . . . '

But Karl was not listening. He placed his hand on the plinth as one might lay a hand upon a sacred object so that its virtue might flow from it to oneself. But when he turned, his face was as bland as ever.

'Yes indeed,' he said. 'Frederick and the generals, Prussian generals, ha! ha!' he laughed meaninglessly. 'Shall we saunter on?'

With less alacrity he allowed himself to be guided across the other lane of the avenue, on to the safety of the pavement, and to an oddly impressive square, framed by the Catholic Cathedral, the Opera House, and the old Royal Library.

'The State restored the Cathedral,' Erika said. 'It was badly damaged by shelling in 1945.'

'Most meritorious,' Karl murmured. 'I do know the square—rather well.'

'It is called August-Bebel-Platz now,' Erika said. 'And Father thought that you ought to see this. It is new since your time.'

She walked across the cobbles and pointed to a plaque set in the wall of the Library.

'Another interesting sight.' Karl gave a vulpine smile as, in her clear voice, Erika read aloud:

'"On this spot, on the tenth of May, 1933, under the evil spirit of Fascism, the gangsters of the Nazi party burned the noblest works of German and World Literature.

'"Let the burning of these books remind us to be everlastingly on our guard against Imperialism and War."'

The plaque, and the *Platz*, always moved Erika. And the scene of the burning of the books, seen on film by her many times, was as vivid as an actual memory: Hitler's jack-booted thugs in their brown shirts, swastikas on their arms, heaving the books from the Library and heaping the heritage of the world on to a pyre, dancing and gloating as the flames consumed book after book, volume after volume: Heine, Schiller, Brecht, Thomas Mann, Einstein, Freud, Marx: history, poetry, novels, science, the works of philosophers, psychologists—men and women who had dedicated their lives for the betterment of the brutes who burned their books; brutes living in utter ignorance, leading lives as dull and limited as the beasts of the fields, inspired only by resentment, vile prejudice, and blind hatred of what they could not understand, and, it was true, victims themselves of poverty and ignorance seeking victims in their turn—and finding them. And not only in their books.

Erika knew the words of a Protestant pastor, himself tortured and executed by the Gestapo:

'First they came for the Jews—and we said nothing. Then they came for the Communists—and we said nothing. Then they came for the Socialists—and we said nothing. Then they came for the Trades Unionists—and we said nothing. And then they came for us, and there was no one left to defend us.'

'Yes.' Standing in the *Platz* in her elegant coat and furs Erika was on the verge of tears: first the books were thrown on to the flames and then, in a terrible and inevitable sequence, human beings were put into the incinerators. And it was an *inevitable* sequence. The books were the products of minds, and the minds were the products of brains and bodies, so what more natural than to burn the bodies which produced the minds which produced the books? And all the rest of humanity which offended you, too: Jews, gipsies, the mentally handicapped, Poles, Russians—the *Untermensch*— the subhuman, subhuman because they did not have blue eyes and blond hair, white skin or, that vaguest, and because most vague, most potent of myths, the right *blood*. As if humanity distinguished between the blood of a Jew, or a Pole, or an African, or an Indian—or a German.

Erika, born after the smoke of the death camps had stopped drifting across Europe, wanted deeply to try and say this to dapper Uncle Karl, born before the smoke fouled the skies. She turned to speak to him, but he was not there.

'Uncle?' She ran past the Library to the corner of Unter den Linden and saw Karl, notable in his elegant overcoat, sauntering down the street.

'Oh dear,' Erika snapped her fingers and caught up with Karl.

'Uncle, I thought that you would like to see the very spot where they burned the books,' she said.

'Yes, yes.' Karl nodded. 'Terrible. Awful. But I was getting a trifle chilled—just a trifle, you know, and on this beautiful day—' he waved a gloved hand at the brilliant sky and the buildings, dazzling in a chiaroscuro of stone and snow, the snow making the grey stone look black, the stone making the snow blindingly pure. 'Yes, such a day, and to stroll along as I did so many times in the old days. How gay it was in spring, under the linden trees: people sauntering, the cafés full, everyone enjoying themselves, and to walk it now with—' he smiled again, an elderly uncle's smile, recalling long lost days, when the linden trees bloomed along the avenue— 'with a pretty girl. Ah . . . what memories among these buildings . . . . '

'Yes.' Erika's assent was less than whole-hearted, for, although she was proud of the care the State was lavishing on the old buildings, and although, in fact, she preferred this part of the city, she felt it a duty to defend the crude and blatant concrete of the post-war Berlin.

'Nowadays most people go to Alexanderplatz,' she said. 'To the new city.'

'Of course, of course.' Karl clutched Erika as they negotiated a rather icy patch of pavement. 'But this *is* new.'

'Oh,' Erika paused with Karl. 'The Embassy.'

'*The* Embassy.' Karl, as it were, added the italics as he cast a speculative eye over a huge grey building which loomed over the avenue like a battleship over a flotilla of cargo boats and from which, in the still, clear air, hung a vast flag, red, with a golden hammer and sickle emblazoned on it.

Karl looked across the street to where, among the cargo boats, the French and British Embassies hung out *their* flags, then looked again at the battleship. 'It is large, isn't it.'

Erika had to agree. There was no denying that the Soviet Embassy was large, enormous, one might say, making lilliputian a convoy of Russian lorries parked outside from which, mysteriously, soldiers in olive green and red were taking canteens of food.

'Yes,' Erika said, feeling oddly defensive. 'But of course, the Soviet Union is our best friend.'

'So I understand.' Holding Erika, Karl sauntered past a G.D.R. policeman and looked sideways at the Russian troops. 'Do you know,' he said, 'in all my stay here I have hardly ever seen a Russian soldier.'

'No,' Erika said. 'The Friends are usually in the country-side. They go to dances and, of course, they join in exercises with our People's Army.'

'How comradely,' Karl said. 'How pleasant, too, dancing with the country girls. So . . . *unaffected*. No wonder you call them Friends. The official title is it not? Yes, I rather like that. And this.'

He halted at the corner of Unter den Linden and Grotewohlstrasse. Across the street, beyond a wide stretch of frost-laced gravel, there was a huge triumphal arch on which were four horses driven by a goddess of peace, over whom, in turn, hung two flags, both enormous as if vying with each other and both striped red, orange and black, the far one with those stripes alone, but the near one bearing the wreath, hammer and dividers of the German Democratic Republic, and under it all, cutting the avenue in half, halting it with the abruptness of Finis at the end of a book, and behind a fragile metal fence, snow on its top giving it an odd, festive look, there was a drab grey wall made of concrete blocks.

Karl gazed across the street, looking at the arch, and the horses and goddess, and the flags of the two Germanys. 'The Brandenburger Tor,' he said.

'We call it the Gate of Peace now,' Erika said.

'The Gate of Peace.' Karl pressed his hand to his mouth and coughed. 'What a charming name. But the . . . the concrete?'

'The Anti-Fascist barrier,' Erika said dutifully. 'It was built to prevent Fascist agents from the West entering the G.D.R. and committing acts of terrorism.'

'A most wise precaution,' Karl said. 'The Anti-Fascist Barrier. And to think that in the West they merely call it the Wall. But I see that we can go a little nearer.'

Looking carefully both ways, he led Erika across the road, on to the gravel plaza, and peered through the metal fence. 'The Anti-Fascist Barrier. How insignificant it looks, but what a bold conception. Really, quite a stroke of genius. But, Erika,' he lowered his voice a little. 'These people—' he gestured to a group of men and women, posing in three lines, the front row kneeling, the tallest at the back, all beaming as a photographer stepped back in order to get their picture with The Wall in a clear focus. 'Who are they?'

Not for the first time that morning Erika felt slightly uncomfortable.

'They are tourists,' she said.

'Tourists?' Karl raised his eyebrows.

'Friends,' Erika said. 'Russians.'

'And so they are! So they are!' Unnervingly Karl burst

into a high-pitched hyena-like laugh. His shoulders shook underneath his beautiful overcoat. 'Ha! ha! ha! hee! hee! hee! Oh dear! Oh dear me!' He dabbed his eyes with his immaculate handkerchief. 'Forgive me.' He exploded with laughter again. 'Hee! hee! hee! How Adolf would have relished this.'

'Adolf?' Erika turned and stared at Karl's face, crimson with laughter, horror dawning in her violet eyes.

Karl stopped laughing as suddenly as he had begun, his face grave and concerned and kindly. 'Excuse me, my Dear, laughing so. Most undignified in an old man.' He poked his head forward, like a tortoise coming out from its shell. 'You look quite shocked, Erika.'

Instinctively Erika recoiled. 'Adolf,' she whispered.

'Ah!' Understanding dawned on Karl's face. 'I think I understand. But I was thinking, looking at them—' he gestured towards the tourists— 'seeing them in a group, it reminded me of a time in cadet school. We had a group photograph with a long time-exposure and a friend of mine, a dear friend, ran from one end of the back line to the other and had his picture twice on the same photograph. He was called Adolf. Adolf von Seydlitz.'

Relief flooded through Erika, and showed in her face.

'But of course!' Karl slapped his side. 'Of course, of course! Adolf means only one person to you. But remember, before that terrible man Adolf was an honoured name in Germany.'

'Yes, Uncle Karl.' Erika was contrite.

'There, there.' Karl patted her arm, making Erika feel that she was deeply in the wrong but was being forgiven. 'A little mistake on your part, but we will forget it. These misunderstandings do take place, the generation gap, as they say over there.' He gestured to where the flag of the other Germany hung over the old *Tiergarten*.

Erika smiled, pleased that the little cloud had passed over. 'I'm sorry.' And, receiving another encouraging nod from Karl pulled out her list. 'So, where would you like to go now? Omi thought that you might like to see the old Adlon. It isn't far—'

Karl shook his head. 'Just between ourselves, I have been

there!' His eyes twinkled. 'Just for old times' sake I went, not that there is much to see! But I rather thought, you know, if you wouldn't mind, we might go to Treptower Park.'

'Treptow?' Erika was startled. 'You mean the Pleasure Park?'

'No.' Karl shook his head, amused. 'I'm a little too old for pleasure parks. I thought we might go to the War Memorial.'

'The Soviet War Memorial?'

'Yes,' Karl said. 'I've heard about it but it is one of the sights my hosts haven't shown me. Shall we go?'

'If you want.' Erika agreed but was somewhat dubious. 'It's rather a long way, though. We would have to go to Alexanderplatz and get the *S-Bahn* . . . . '

'That won't be necessary,' Karl said. 'I have a car!' He glanced at the watch Bodo admired so much. 'And if the man is punctual he should be here—now! And so he is.'

He pointed across the street to where a long, black, polished car had pulled up.

'Good German efficiency,' Karl said, as they crossed the street and climbed into the back of the car.

Karl leaned forward and spoke to the driver. 'You have the map?'

'Yes,' The driver flourished a street plan, with a route marked in red.

'Good.' Karl settled back. 'Go.'

With what to Erika, used to the erratic behaviour of the old Lada, was miraculous smoothness, the driver let in the gears and drove down Grotewohlstrasse but instead of turning left at Leipziger Strasse, carried on into a warren of tiny streets. Determined to be her Uncle's guide Erika said, 'I think that we are going the wrong way, Uncle. There are only factories down here.'

'I know, my Dear,' lolling back in the car Karl nodded lazily. 'But you must remember that I *am* an industrialist and, really, factories are as interesting to me as museums, ha! ha!'

The car zigzagged through the streets. Karl, his head turned steadily to his right, peered intently at the run-down flats and battered buildings and factories lining small side-streets, each and every one of which ended in that apparently insignificant, almost unobtrusive wall of grey concrete blocks.

As they crossed the broad reach of the Spree at Elsen-strasse, where tugs were crunching through the ice, Erika pointed out what sights there were to see but Karl merely gave a perfunctory nod and returned to his absorbed stare through his window.

They drove past the big Siemens factory, plastered with huge portraits of Marx and Lenin, on to the broad, tree-lined avenue of Am Treptower Park, swung into a car-park, and stopped.

'Treptow,' the driver grunted.

Erika and Karl got out of the warmth of the car into a crystalline coldness, walked up an avenue lined with bare trees and came to an enclosed garden. In its middle was a statue of a weeping woman holding her slain son.

'The Motherland mourning her dead,' Erika murmured.

'The Motherland?' Karl queried.

For a moment Erika was puzzled by the query, then she understood. Karl would still think of Germany as the Fatherland. 'It means the *Soviet* Motherland. Of course there is a memorial to the German victims of Fascism and militarism. It is on Unter den Linden and—'

'I've seen it.' Karl almost jerked the words out. He turned his head and walked towards a flight of shallow steps above which jutted two triangles of red granite.

'Red flags dipped in mourning,' Erika said.

Karl nodded and began to walk slowly up the steps, Erika by his side, moving at a funeral pace. Step by step they climbed, and as they ascended, black against the dazzling blue sky and glazed under a shroud of ice, a vast figure began to loom: a helmeted head, a flowing cape, a sword in one hand and a child in the other, and beneath its booted feet, visible as Erika and Karl reached the top of the stairs, a broken swastika, and bearing the whole gigantic figure, a grassy mound.

Between Erika and Karl, standing at the top of the steps, and the statue there was a sunken garden, its sides punctuated by slabs of concrete. It was quiet, hushed almost. No one else was in the garden and dense rows of leafless poplars damped the grinding roar of the lorries on Am Treptower Park.

'And this is it?' Karl said.

'Yes.' Erika pointed to the looming statue. 'That is a Soviet infantryman of the Red Army.'

Karl peered bleakly forward. The corners of his mouth were dragged down and his plump cheeks looked shrunken, like withered apples. He looked very old. 'I know the shape,' he said.

'Of course,' Erika thought. Having spent years fighting them, Karl would recognise a Russian soldier. 'How tactless of me,' she said to herself, and to cover up the awkwardness she felt she pointed at the statue. 'The soldier is carrying a German child rescued from Fascism,' she said, 'and the swastika....' But that hardly needed explaining. 'Would you like to go down and look at the inscriptions on the slabs?'

For a long, long moment Karl hesitated then, with a curious shrug of his shoulders, he said, 'Yes. By all means let us see the inscriptions.'

They went down the steps and walked slowly around the garden. The inscriptions in German and Russian were cut into the concrete blocks, each of which carried a bold, crude, but appropriate carving.

'These represent the glorious struggle of the Soviet Union in the fight against Fascism,' Erika said.

'So I observe.' Karl paused at the first block and then started back, looking truly astonished. 'These words are by Stalin! Josef Stalin!' He cackled mirthlessly. 'My God in His Heaven! Josef Stalin!' He shook his head in wonderment. 'This must be the last place on earth where his words are public—except Albania.'

For a reason not quite clear to her, Erika felt embarrassed, as if there were an irony in Karl's words, especially the reference to Albania, which she felt she was not clever enough to understand. 'I can't really say about that,' she said, 'but—' launching into a text learned by heart—'although guilty of many deviations from Marxism-Leninism and Socialist legality, Stalin did lead the heroic resistance of the Soviet peoples in the anti-Fascist war.'

They sauntered on, Erika conscientiously describing each slab as they reached it: 'Tribute to the glorious soldiers of the Red Army ....Tribute to the glorious airmen of the Red Air

213

Force . . . . Tribute to the glorious peasants of the Soviet Union . . . . ' her voice clear in the silent garden as the enormous statue loomed over them.

At the foot of the mound they halted and peered up at the statue, eerie under its glaze of ice, which stared sightlessly far above their heads. A flight of steps led up the mound to the base of the figure.

'We could go up,' Erika said. 'There is a room inside.'

'And what is inside the room?' Karl asked.

'Well . . . nothing really,' Erika confessed. 'It is a dome. With mosaics.'

'Mosaics. How very Eastern,' Karl said.

'This mound is a mausoleum,' Erika said. '5,000 soldiers of the Red Army are buried under it. Killed in the Battle for Berlin.'

'5,000?' Karl pursed his lips. 'They lost more than that, 100,000, more like. Berlin did not fall so easily.' There was an edge to his voice, of defiance, almost.

'I suppose so,' Erika said, a little lamely. 'There are other cemeteries.'

'Yes.' Karl turned and walked back along the other side of the garden, although this time Erika did not draw his attention to the words of Josef Stalin paying tribute to glorious workers, doctors, nurses, and so on. They re-climbed the steps to the granite flags and there Karl turned and looked again at the statue, his face still sunken and sour.

Rather timidly, and feeling that somehow she had let her uncle down, Erika touched Karl's arm. 'Don't you like it?' she asked.

'Like it?' Something which might—or might not—have been a smile, touched Karl's lips. 'Let me put it this way, child. It is . . . inspiring.'

'Really?' Erika glowed with pleasure.

'Yes, really. That is exactly the right word. This—' he waved his hand—'this has given me true inspiration. Now, come.'

They took a pace or two and then, suddenly, Karl turned back and spat a couple of words.

'I beg your pardon?' Erika, a pace ahead, turned, too.

'Nothing. Nothing at all.' Karl said sharply and then, with

something of a return to his jolly, Uncle Karl manner, he said, thoughtfully, 'Have you noticed, there are no birds here. None at all.'

Chapter 20

An hour later they were in Alexanderplatz having taken the same route back, although on the return journey Karl had sat on the left-hand side of the car and peered as eagerly at the side-streets as he had done when going to Treptow.

Paul, freed from the F.G.Y meeting, was waiting for them at the entrance to the Television Tower, excited and looking a little ill at ease in his best and most sober clothes.

The tourist season was long over but there was a steady trickle of visitors going into the Tower: East Europeans, a few Africans and Asians, late birds from the West, the usual crowd of citizens in from the countryside and Turks from West Berlin.

Karl, Erika, and Paul were carried smoothly in the lift to the viewing platform, its windows lined with viewers, which was a floor beneath the revolving restaurant. There was a queue for that but Karl slid to the front, whispered something to the formidable girl attendant, a document flashed, and they were waved upstairs, Erika and Paul feeling vastly privileged and important.

'You must have been here before,' Karl said to Erika and Paul, who certainly had not, as they took a seat by the window. He scanned the menu and urged Erika and Paul to look at theirs. 'First the food and *then* the view,' he said. 'Choose anything, anything at all. Your Uncle's treat—and all tax-deductible, ha! ha!'

He laughed in his agreeable, jolly uncle's way, gave the order, chose wine, and leaned back, scarcely casting a glance at the view, which in fact was not inspiring as their table was, as it were, at ten to twelve and below them stretched the jumble of flats which made up most of the north of the city.

The wine came and was tasted and approved. Erika took a small splash of it and Paul was given a Club Cola. 'Now Paul,' Karl said. 'Tell me all about yourself.'

Paul mumbled a tale hardly recognisable as having anything to do with his actual existence, but Karl appeared absorbed and nodded sympathetically, as a good uncle should.

'Excellent,' he said, as though Paul had announced he had won high academic honours. 'And you, Erika?'

Erika modestly disclaimed that there was anything interesting in her life but over consommé, which Paul privately thought was so thin that the restaurant must be watering it, Karl waved her modesty aside.

'No, no. You are an athlete with a great future. I know all about it! My sister told me when we had tea in the Café Köpenick.' He raised his glass and drank as the view shifted six more degrees to twelve o'clock. 'My dear sister,' Karl sighed. 'We had such a long talk. Did she mention that to you?'

Yes, Omi had mentioned it to the family, Erika agreed.

'You are very close, aren't you?' Karl said, pushing his soup plate aside. 'How enchanting that is, grandmother and granddaughter so friendly. Did she tell you what we talked about?'

Erika shook her head. 'Just old times.'

'Yes, old times.' Karl glanced through the window, still showing the flats of North Berlin, and turned again to Erika. 'She was a little worried about this police business, but that has all been cleared up, I gather?'

'It has,' Erika was fervent. 'Father was so worried.'

'I'm sure he must have been,' Karl said. 'Anything to do with the Police . . . so tiresome. Officers calling round, checking on one, asking questions, talking to the neighbours. . . . '

'Oh there was nothing like that,' Erika said.

'No?' Karl smiled, a slow satisfied smile, as the soup plates were removed. 'And my sister, she has seemed well and happy?'

Erika frowned a little as the waitress brought *Bœuf Bourguignon*. 'She has seemed a bit . . . a bit wistful. Mother thinks that is because you are going away. Family means a lot to her, you know. *All* her family, Norderns as well as Brombergs,' she added loyally if not quite truthfully. 'But otherwise she's fine.'

'Good.' Karl beamed and took a mouthful of his beef as the restaurant crept on its slow revolution, the flat and vast white horizons of the north slowly giving way to the belching factories of Hain.

'Quite palatable,' Karl said, toying with his food. 'But Erika! I'm in danger of forgetting!' He raised his glass. 'A toast to you and your success. It is next week isn't it, your championship?'

It was and the toast was drunk, the waitress beaming over them as she gave Paul a second helping of beef. As she did so, Karl produced a map of Berlin—rather a good detailed one, Erika noticed, and one such as she had never seen before, as it showed both Berlins. And Karl noticed her noticing, as it were.

'Ha! ha!' he said, urging Paul to eat as much as he wished, and waved for another bottle of wine. 'One should not only see the sights, but know which sights one is seeing, hey?'

He looked through the window. Hain was sliding away and the glinting Spree was appearing, busy with barges and toy-like tugs, and lined with factories and warehouses, and beyond them was that thin grey line; shabby, shoddy even, and which could have been a cheap backyard wall—looking completely natural among the factories; really nothing much at all. The most moderate of pole vaulters could have cleared it with ease, except that had one done so he would have landed on an odd swathe of cleared land, 450 metres wide, lined with pylons carrying enormous floodlights, and flanked to the west by another grey wall.

It was curiously like a running-track, but one which ran for mile after mile, and one on which the runners would have to take part in a lunatic obstacle-race as it was festooned with barbed wire and sown with land-mines. And it was a track on which the only runners were ferocious guard dogs.

Karl, looking at the Wall—and at his map—raised his

head, caught Erika's eye, and beamed. 'It is interesting you know,' he said. 'And your admirable father told me of the many advantages which the . . . the Anti-Fascist Barrier has brought to your country. As I said at the Brandenburger Tor—I should say the Gate of Peace—quite a stroke of genius. Yes.'

He offered Paul more beef which Paul, in response to a sharp kick under the table by Erika, politely declined, and ordered a pudding, apricots and cream, and brandy for himself. And as they ate the apricots, beyond the Wall, West Berlin edged into sight, glittering towers of chrome and steel and glass beyond the grey wall, dazzling in the crystal light, flaunting neon signs, and drawing Paul's attention as surely as the North Pole attracts a compass needle.

Karl sucked an apricot and let the rind fall on to his plate. 'You haven't been, Paul? No, of course not. But would you like to?'

'Not much!' Paul almost knocked over his Club Cola. 'And if I don't go soon I shan't be able to go until I'm ninety.'

'Paul!' Erika spoke in her most Frau Nordern-like admonitory tone, but Karl was pacific.

'I understand, Paul. What is it? Between sixteen and sixty your Government prefers you to stay here, in your fine new state and work for the good of your society. It is quite understandable, laudable—as I said to your father, Erika. But Paul, you are still young enough to go.'

He turned to Erika, smiling, reassuring. 'I mean for a holiday, of course.' He looked at Paul and said, 'Why not come and stay with me?'

This time Paul did knock over his Club Cola. 'Stay with you?' he demanded incredulously. 'Really stay? Are you kidding me?'

No, Karl wasn't kidding, but Paul's face fell. 'I've got no money anyway,' he said.

Karl chuckled over his brandy. 'I don't think that will be a problem. Let me mention it to your parents.'

'Really?' Paul asked. 'Really?'

'Yes, really,' Karl said, and ordered coffee and another brandy.

Slowly the restaurant revolved, West Berlin's brazen towers

moved away, Pankow crept into view and then, looking again at the limitless East, Karl called for the bill, paid it, was helped into his overcoat, and Erika into hers by a clearly admiring under-manager—although Paul was left to his own devices—and they went to the stairs. And there an unfortunate incident took place.

Coming up the stairs was a young Turk accompanied by a German girl. He was obviously one of the multitude who lived in West Berlin, who had turned large areas of it into a Turkish city and who, often with Berlin girl-friends, crossed the border at week-ends to take advantage of the cheap food, cigarettes, and even cheaper alcohol, which the capital of the G.D.R. offered, bringing with them precious western currency in exchange.

Possibly the Turk had already taken advantage of the cheap drink but he was by no means drunk. However, he did stumble and brush against Karl. It was the slightest of touches, a fleeting contact such as one might experience a hundred times a day in any city and, although the Turk was young and large and muscular, and Karl none of those things, the touch was not enough to disturb Karl's progress for one second; but the effect on him was astonishing.

'*Verdammte Schweine!*' 'Damned swine!' He spat the words out, his pink face beetroot-red with rage.

The Turk, who clearly was unaware that he had even touched Karl, was amazed. 'Huh? What do I?' he asked in bad German and held out his hand in what was obviously a conciliatory gesture. But Karl struck it aside viciously.

'Don't touch me!'

The girl with the Turk took his arm. 'Come away, Esmet,' she said.

'Yes, get away—both of you.' Karl filled the words with loathing. 'You and your harlot.'

The Turk may not have had much German but he understood that. 'You watch out,' he said, and took a menacing step forward.

But already the under-manager had interposed a shoulder between the two men, and the manager made a portentous appearance, asking what the trouble was—asking Karl, that is, not the Turk—and being told in clipped Prussian tones

that the Turk had rudely elbowed him—Karl von Bromberg
—and that he did not expect to be pushed and threatened by
louts in a good restaurant, especially in the capital of the
German Democratic Republic.

The Turk began to protest, hotly, but the manager took
one look at Karl in his exquisite clothes, his pink, distinguished face poised commandingly on a ramrod back—and
one look at the Turk, clad in a shoddy purple jacket, tight
jeans, tieless, his hair thick with oil.

'Out,' he snapped. He bent, deferentially, to Karl. 'My
profound apologies,' he began, but the Turk thrust forward.

'Why me out?' he demanded. 'I have nothing wronged.
Nothing!' He flung out his arms in an expressive gesture,
unfortunately hitting the under-manager.

The manager scowled. 'Out!' he repeated. *'Schnell.'*
'Quick.'

The girl tugged at the Turk's elbow but he shrugged her off.
'What I do? Fräulein—' he appealed to Erika. 'Do I harm
anyone?'

Erika was ready to answer the appeal, to say that what had
happened was a mere unfortunate misunderstanding, but the
manager said to his assistant one word. 'Police.'

'Ah.' The Turk nodded. 'Police. I know,' he said in the
bitter voice of one who had known from infancy what that
word meant—when applied to him. 'We go. We go.' He
made a mock bow to Karl, 'Thank you, sir,' and, his girl
tagging behind him, went down the stairs, affecting a swagger
but his back showing a defeat, and showing it was used to
many.

There were profuse apologies from the manager, references
to undesirables crossing the border, an offer of a drink on the
house, and a discreet suggestion that Karl might care to be
accompanied out, which he rejected with bristling scorn.

'To be protected? From that type? I know how to deal with
them.'

In the event no escort was needed. They did not see the
Turk or his girl again, but in the lift down Erika stood in a
thoughtful silence, not unnoticed by Karl because on the
ground floor he raised the subject himself.

'You think I was harsh, Erika. I can see that in your face.

But you don't understand, my Dear. That Turk, he was trying to pick my pocket. Yes! You didn't notice that, but when you have had my experience of the world . . . but there.' He gave her a reassuring pat. 'Don't let it upset you, or you either,' he said to an undisturbed Paul. 'But so.' He clapped his hands. 'I must thank you for the morning: such interesting sights, fascinating history, a charming lunch and,' his eyes twinkled, 'for being envied for being with such a pretty girl!' And to Erika's intense embarrassment he tweaked her cheek.

'Ha! ha!' Karl laughed his jolly laugh. 'And Paul, I'm sorry that you could not join us this morning, but work before pleasure. That is the way, it is indeed. The good old German way, the way which made us great. Keep it up. But now, I must rest a little as I have other people to meet this evening, business, you know. I will try and see you in your championship, Erika, and most certainly we shall meet at the party. My best regards to your parents—and my dear, dear sister.'

He led the way out into the bustle of Alexanderplatz, made a formal farewell and proceeded gingerly to the Palast.

Paul rolled his eyes idiotically. 'Who has he been with?' he asked.

'Been with?' Erika raised an eyebrow. 'What do you mean?'

'That pretty girl, the one he's been with this morning.'

'Very funny. Come on.' Erika stepped out towards the huge hulk of Alexanderplatz railway station.

'Are you going home?' Paul asked.

'No, but you are,' Erika said firmly, noticing Paul's eyes roving around the square.

They dodged the workmen laying out the equipment for the Christmas Fair, and the touts selling watches, and went into the station, Paul grumbling about being escorted.

'You're not my gaoler,' he complained.

'No, I'm not,' Erika said, 'and don't think I like having to keep you in order, but I promised Mother that you would go straight home—and you promised, too—so I'm being good to you, helping you to keep your word.'

This logic defeated Paul, and his protest that there was no need for Erika to pay ten pfennig to see him on to the platform, and the *S-Bahn*, was feeble, although, as his train pulled away, he stuck his tongue out at her—and Erika stuck hers out at him.

The small, childish exchange cheered her and she walked back down the station steps laughing at herself, but in the gloomy cavern of the underground line where the skulls of the posters stared at her through hollow eyes, her cheerfulness ebbed away and it was in a thoughtful, almost sombre mood that she made her journey to Pankow and went up the stairs to Rosa's flat.

Rosa's mother, Frau Halton, opened the door. 'My word, Erika,' she said, 'you do look smart. Come in. Rosa has gone to pick up some tickets for the concert tonight but she should be back in a minute. Have some coffee.'

She chattered amiably on as the coffee heated. 'We haven't seen much of you these past weeks. Rosa says that you have been training hard—and your uncle coming! That must have been exciting. How is your family? My husband has been swept off his feet at work, the Poles not delivering on time, and the Hungarians aren't much better. . . . '

She rattled on until Rosa came in, pleased that she had got her tickets, and pleased, too, at seeing Erika. Rosa took Erika into her bedroom, larger than Omi's and Paul's put together, but, in the nature of rooms, seeming just as cluttered, with books, clothes, old toys, posters. . . .

Rosa waved Erika on to a battered armchair and stretched out on the bed.

'So,' she said. 'Out with Uncle Karl again! Living high. But you don't look very pleased about it. I wish a rich uncle of mine would turn up and take me out.'

Erika shook her head. 'It's just that . . . well . . . there are a couple of things but—it's nothing.'

But Rosa was not one to be shaken off easily. She sat upright. 'What sort of couple of things?'

Erika was reluctant to say, mainly because she was not sure that there *was* anything to say. After all, what had happened? One or two odd actions by Karl which might not have been odd at all, and this affair with the Turk; and if Karl had been right and the Turk had been a pickpocket, he was lucky not to have been handed over to the Police. But still she was disturbed, as she had been three weeks previously when the man on the *U-Bahn* had shouted about the posters and the mirror wall. It was as if in her world of steady normality a door had opened a crack giving her a glimpse into another world; one bizarre and twisted and deformed, and into which she did *not* want to look but which she now knew was there just the same, a sort of Fourth Dimension of horror.

But still the impulse to tell was there and tell she did. Not that Rosa was bothered about what she heard.

'Well, who does want to see those old plaques,' she said. 'We have to go because they make us at school but he must know all about them anyway. And standing about in the cold, brrrr! And he's not young, is he?'

Erika admitted it. 'But the way he laughed at the Gate of Peace. It was creepy. And when he said Adolf!'

But Rosa was equal to that, too. 'He explained didn't he? About the boy running around the group to have his photo taken twice—whatever that means. And *millions* of people were called Adolf. Anyway, you'd have to be really dotty to laugh at the Anti-Fascist Barrier, wouldn't you? And he's not is he? Dotty?'

Erika agreed that Uncle Karl showed no obvious signs of dottiness. 'But the Turk,' she said.

'Oh that!' Rosa casually lay back and bicycled her legs in the air. 'He probably was a pickpocket.'

'I don't know.' Erika was dubious. 'It was just that . . . well . . . there seemed more to it than that. Honestly, it was as if Uncle Karl hated the man just for *being* a Turk.'

Rosa stopped her cycling, leaned forward and touched her toes. 'Well he's not alone in that,' she said casually.

'Rosa!' Erika was deeply shocked. 'That's racial prejudice.'

'That's what they call it,' Rosa agreed. 'But you've been around Friedrichstrasse Station when they come over at week-ends, haven't you?'

Erika admitted that she had, and also that she had undergone one or two unpleasant experiences there. 'But,' she said, 'the Turks are just exploited peasants imported by the capitalists of the West to provide cheap labour but presenting new contradictions in their economy.'

'I heard that lesson, too,' Rosa said dryly, 'but it doesn't

make much difference if one is being a nuisance, does it?'
Despite herself Erika had to agree with that. It was a point
where theory and practice did not coincide, and it was true
that for all the exhortations of the State there was still plenty
of racial prejudice in the G.D.R.

'So,' obviously a little bored with the topic of Uncle Karl's
quirks, Rosa led the conversation away from him to more
alluring topics: the coming championship, the intriguing
prospect of Erika's spending a whole week with Fräulein
Silber—and Fritz Kott.

Erika said, firmly, that she did not want to talk about *him*,
but not firmly enough, and a fascinating hour passed as the
two girls discussed Fritz in particular and boys in general:
their horrid, gawking manner, their idiotic sheep-like stares,
their pathetic boasting and, in short, their peculiar fascination.

The sun went down in a bloody sky. Erika had coffee and
cakes with Rosa and her mother, accepted warmest good-
wishes for the championship and then, as light, feathery
snowflakes began to drift down, made her way home on the
S-Bahn and to her delight saw the old man with the bicycle;
and she was even more enchanted when from some mysterious pocket he produced a handful of confetti and scattered
it over the passengers, announcing that he was getting
married the next day—for the sixth time—although, bowing
gallantly at Erika, he said that he was prepared to jilt his bride
and marry the Fräulein instead.

The whole family was in when she got home and, as she
had expected, Paul had already told the story of the Turk,
without it raising any great sensation. 'They're always drunk,
anyway,' was Frau Nordern's comment. But Erika was
eagerly questioned about the morning trip, the private car
being much admired.

Not wishing to spoil the evening, Erika did not mention the
little incidents which had made her uneasy. However, her
father did raise his eyebrows when he heard that Karl had
asked to see the Soviet War Memorial, but he made little of it,
merely saying that it must have been a strange sight for Karl.

'Although I must say it is for me, too,' he admitted. 'A
statue of a Soviet soldier in Berlin. I would never have
believed it possible. But there it is.'

Supper was a rather ceremonial meal, and with Erika firmly excluded from its preparation. Delicacies such as smoked salmon were dished up and a good wine with which Herr Nordern formally toasted Erika.

'The home will seem dark without you,' he said, adding, with an uncharacteristic rhetorical flourish, 'but your light will burn brighter when you return.'

Frau Nordern and Omi clapped genteelly, Paul looked completely baffled, and Erika blushed furiously, as if a lamp were burning inside her.

Frau Nordern dabbed her mouth with her napkin. 'What time did you say Fräulein Silber was coming?'

'Soon,' Erika said.

'Ah!' Frau Nordern stood up. 'I must get ready.'

Herr Nordern looked at her quizzically. 'Ready for what?'

'For going with Erika,' Frau Nordern said.

'Mother!' Erika could not believe her ears. 'You can't!'

'Can't?' Frau Nordern raised her head like a lioness.

'Yes, you can't,' Erika said, mixing her language in the heat of the moment. 'It's . . . it's ridiculous.'

Frau Nordern could flush, too, and did so. 'Did I hear you say ridiculous?' she demanded in her most awesome voice.

Unawed, Erika retorted that her mother certainly had heard her say it and that her mother was not, most definitely and decidedly not, going to Fräulein Silber's. There would be no point, she was needed at home, there would be no room and—but she stopped there because her mother burst out laughing.

'Of course I don't mean to stay for the week. I just want to see you settled in, goose.'

'Oh!' The cloud of discontent lifted from Erika's face but settled on Herr Nordern's.

'And just how do you propose getting back?' he asked.

'With you, of course,' Frau Nordern said.

'*Not* with me,' Herr Nordern said, 'because I'm not going. I've hardly any petrol left, but besides that, how do you think Fräulein Silber will feel, you going there and snooping over her flat.'

'I would certainly not go snooping.' Frau Nordern was indignant.

'Then what would you be doing?' Herr Nordern asked.

Frau Nordern was silent for a moment then said, a little uneasily, 'Seeing that Erika will be comfortable.'

Herr Nordern smiled. 'Helga, everywhere else that *is* called snooping.'

Frau Nordern frowned. 'I could come back on the bus. . . .' She looked at Erika. 'Don't you want me to come?'

'No!' Erika snapped.

'Not just to. . . .'

'No!'

'Well . . .' Frau Nordern accepted the situation with reasonable grace. 'I suppose not then, although it just seems motherly to me. Anyway, let's clear the table.'

Herr Nordern and Paul began washing up, Frau Nordern went into the bathroom 'to freshen up' and Erika went into her room to get her suitcase. She heaved it from under the bed and turned to see Omi standing by the closed door.

'Omi.' Erika took her grandmother's hand, its skin as dry and brittle as old paper. 'I'm only going for a week.'

'I know, *Liebchen*.' Omi nodded. 'You must be tranquil so that you jump well on Saturday. I shall be so proud of you. Yes. But here—' she pressed an envelope on Erika. 'It is only a few marks. I couldn't get out to buy you anything but buy yourself a little present—some perfume—no—' she waved away Erika's protest. 'Please, I want you to have it.'

'Omi.' Erika embraced her, strong young arms around shoulders as fragile as a bird.

Omi stood erect and held Erika at arm's length. 'Remember one thing, my dear child. For me.'

'Of course,' Erika said. 'Anything. Anything at all.'

'Just one thing.' Omi gazed at Erika, her eyes behind her spectacles dark, almost purple. 'I would never do anything to hurt you. Never. Ever.'

'Hurt me?' The thought was so preposterous that Erika laughed, but her laughter died as she realised that Omi was in deadly earnest. 'But you would never hurt me, Omi. Never.'

'Yes.' Omi raised her hand as if giving a benediction—and then the doorbell rang. Fräulein Silber had arrived.

Arrived and ready to go, there and then, refusing even a coffee and, much to Herr Nordern's amusement, giving his

wife a lesson in formidable authority by making it quite clear
that Frau Nordern would not be welcome at her flat at any
time during the next week.

'If you wish to send any messages give them to Paul,' she
said, skewering him with a glance which made it clear that
she knew all about him. 'And now we must go.'

Erika was ready but Herr Nordern stepped forward and
exerted *his* authority.

'One moment, please,' he said, and raised his forefinger.
'Paul.'

'Yes?' Paul gaped at his father.

Herr Nordern sighed with exasperation. 'The—' he jerked
his head.

'Oh!' Paul grinned and shambled into the bedroom and,
after what was, for Erika at least, an intensely embarrassing
moment, shambled back swinging a bouquet of violets.

'From us,' Herr Nordern said. 'From all of us,' and handed
the bouquet to Fräulein Silber with a bow. 'With our deepest
thanks.'

Fräulein Silber denied that there was any need for thanks,
or presents, but she took the bouquet with a glow of pleasure.
'But now,' she said.

Now it was: last farewells, hugs, kisses, surreptitious tears,
the family crowding on to the staircase to wave more
goodbyes then hurrying back inside to see through the
window Fräulein Silber's car start, which it did, and to wave
again as Erika left to prepare for her date with destiny.

Chapter 21

FRÄULEIN SILBER lived in Marzahn, in the top storey of an old house on Chaussee Alt. It was not a long journey but one done in silence because Fräulein Silber made it clear that she did not talk when she was driving because it distracted her. Not that there was much to be distracted from in the empty, snow-clad streets. But they carried on mutely as the odour of the violets mingled with the reek of cheap petrol and oil fumes.

After twenty minutes, Fräulein Silber pulled sharply into a driveway.

'Here,' she gave Erika two keys. 'That's the front door. Go straight up the stairs. The other key is for my flat. Go in. I have to wrap the engine with blankets. Take the flowers, I'll bring your case.'

Erika climbed out of the car, opened the front door, went up the stairs, opened the second door, entered Fräulein Silber's sitting-room, and gasped.

A polished pine floor with a deep green rug, a divan, green too, green curtains, a mahogany table with a surface like a mirror, and the rest of the room, ceiling, walls, woodwork, painted silver-white. It was the most elegant room Erika had ever been in and although, if anything, it was smaller than the living-room in Klara-Lettkin-Strasse, it seemed oceanic in its space and, after the bamboo and ivy, dazzling in its simplicity.

There were footsteps on the stairs and Fräulein Silber came in. 'My place.' She waved her hand. 'Silver-white. People smile at me because my name means silver but it's only because I like the colour. You know they say white contains all the colours? I like that thought. I would have painted it like this if my name had been Black. It's not a popular colour, though.'

Erika could understand that. In the icy winters of Central Europe most people liked to get home to rooms which at least looked warm.

'So.' Fräulein Silber was brisk. 'I'll put these flowers in a vase and show you round.'

She opened the door which led into a tiny room as big as a telephone box. 'The kitchen. And this is your room.' A narrow cell, a divan with a blue duvet, photographs, books. 'Bathroom downstairs,' Fräulein Silber said. 'I share with an old couple on the ground floor. They get up late and go to bed early so you won't see much of them. Unpack and I'll make some coffee, then we'll get down to work.'

'But Fräulein,' Erika had been counting the doors. 'Where is your room?'

'I'll sleep in the sitting-room,' Fräulein Silber said. 'No protests. It's very comfortable. I used to share this flat and slept there all the time.'

Erika unpacked and put her bear on a tiny dressing-table then went into the sitting-room. Fräulein Silber was arranging the violets in a vase.

'Pour the coffee would you?' she asked, 'While I. . . . '

From underneath the table she slid out a television set. It was a very good set, too; a twenty-four inch screen in a black metal frame. Compared to it the Norderns' set seemed prehistoric which, electronically speaking, it was.

'Not mine,' Fräulein Silber said. 'Borrowed from the Athletic Association. It plays video tapes.' She nodded at Erika. 'Count your blessings. Are you comfortable? Good. Sit, watch, and learn.'

She flicked a switch, took her coffee, and sat down next to Erika. The screen glowed into life and numbers flickered across it: 10. 9. 8. 7 . . . down to zero—then a title: *State Athletic Archive. Women's High Jump. European Games. Zagreb. August 1981.*

There was a shot of a stadium and a smooth woman's voice said. 'Reichstein, German Democratic Republic. Third jump at 1 metre 86.'

The cameras closed up on Reichstein in the black and white of the G.D.R., taking the nervous little steps high jumpers always take before starting their run, rocking backwards and forwards, beating time with her arms, index fingers extended, taking the last deep, profound breath, a curving, elegant run, an explosive take-off—and the bar tumbling down.

'Watch.' Fräulein Silber clicked the remote control. Reichstein rose into the air, the bar bounced rather comically back into place, Reichstein ran backwards, and the sequence started again in slow motion only this time, as she pressed off her left foot for take-off, the film stopped.

'Wait,' Fräulein Silber said. The camera angle changed and Reichstein ran again, and again the film stopped at take-off.

'Too close to the bar,' Fräulein Silber said and was confirmed in her opinion by the commentator who said that Reichstein was indeed too close to the bar and had been forced into arching her back too abruptly, so not gaining the necessary height.

Fräulein Silber flicked the film off. 'A question of millimetres,' she said. 'She lost her concentration and wasn't looking at the bar. Look.'

Reichstein ran again, doomed to bring the bar down for all eternity; and others did so, too. Jumpers centimetres too close to the bar, centimetres too far from it; arms too high, too low, heads tilted fractionally the wrong way, left or right, hips and shoulders not swinging; disqualifications for a mere finger crossing under the bar. . . .

For two hours Erika watched the Greats of her world bring down the bar in a long sequence of disasters—including one jumper who, losing her approach, actually knocked the bar down with her head, that bringing a smile even to Fräulein Silber's chilly face.

Finally Fräulein Silber flicked the set off. 'Bedtime,' she said. 'Early nights from now on. I'll give you some hot milk and show you the bathroom—but, perhaps, just one more jump.'

One more, and there was Rosemarie Ackermann, sixteen years old, in a vast, packed, incredulous stadium, defying gravity, breaking the leaden bonds of earth, jumping, soaring rather, over 2 metres, clearing the bar with ease and free-falling back.

There was silence for a moment then Fräulein Silber said, 'That's how it's done. Yes. That's it.'

She showed the way to the bathroom, said good-night, and left Erika alone. Showered and changed, Erika went to the window of her room and, sipping her milk, peered out: snow glimmering in the night, silence, in the far distance the lights of a remote factory.

She listened for her owl, but no owls were calling and then, quite unconsciously she turned to take away the Watchword from Omi's hands.

She lay in bed, looking at her friendly old bear, missing the familiar bumps and gurgles of home, and missing, deeply, Omi's thin breathing.

She put off the little bed-side light and pulled the duvet over her ears. 'How stupid,' she whispered into her pillow as her tears dampened it. 'How silly. I'm only twenty minutes from home.'

But still, as she cried herself to sleep, she knew that she was farther away than that.

But the tears had gone the next morning, and if they had not gone then the following days would have wiped them away, for when Fräulein Silber said that they were going to concentrate she meant exactly that, and there was no time for sentimental repining. All Erika's lessons were dropped except for the sacrosanct Marxism-Leninism, and music, since even Fräulein Silber recognised that she had to have some relaxation.

But for the rest it was an iron routine: running in the morning, exercises, swimming, weight training, rest, exercises, rest, jumping, rest, swimming, exercises . . . and in the evening, in the green and silver room, watching tapes although, as the week passed, they were subtly modulated. The shock treatment of film of failed jumps was replaced, little by little, with film of successes but these, too, were subtly paced; some were crude amateurish shots of school-girls in minor competitions, grainy, badly filmed, not always focused properly, but all stopping at some crucial moment: start of run, length of stride, the leap. And all the film was shot from different angles so that there was always a fresh view of technique. Then there was the *real* film, expertly made, of the Greats in the great events: European Championships, World Championships, the Olympics. And, artfully, there was film of Erika herself, shown to the accompaniment of Fräulein Silber's sharp, sometimes corrosive commentary. And then there were the entrants for the competition. Usually athletes knew each other, but, because of her long absence, Erika had lost touch with her contemporaries. Fräulein Silber hadn't though, and together they poured over recorded heights, Fräulein Silber remarking on the girls: 'She won't get far. She could be a danger. I've seen her and her technique won't stand up to pressure . . . ' but always ending with one name on her lips, 'Karen Bloxen'.

Karen Bloxen: the name was beginning to invade Erika's mind, and the girl behind the name was assuming mythical proportions. But it was the images of the Greats which Erika took to bed with her.

Of course, Erika saw people at school: Rosa, full of cheerful optimism, Fritz, stammering with a moonstruck grin, Herman Guttenbruk, fawning with an equally ludicrous embarrassment, and, of course, Paul, with news from home daily, questioning notes from her mother demanding to know details of the food she was getting, the bed in which she was sleeping, the clothes she was wearing . . . .

'And I'll tell you, Erika,' Paul said, handing over the daily note, 'you're lucky you're away. It's more like a lunatic asylum at home than anything. Relatives coming and going, the phone ringing all day, and Mother having fits.'

'And what about Omi?' Erika asked.

'Oh,' Paul shrugged. 'She's all right. Actually she spends most of her time in her room, out of the racket.'

'In her room?' Erika felt a pang of remorse at the thought of her Omi spending long, lonely hours in the tiny room. 'Alone?'

'Well . . . .' Paul stared at his boots. 'Numlone,' he mumbled.

'What?' Erika frowned. 'Speak up can't you.'

Paul wriggled and, showing a Bromberg trait, blushed. 'Not alone,' he said.

233

'But who is with her?' Erika demanded. 'Mother?'

Paul shook his head. 'No.'

'Then who?'

'Me.'

Erika could not believe her ears. 'You!'

Paul made a hideous gargling noise which Erika took for agreement.

'You? What do you do?'

'Talk,' Paul said.

Erika was even more incredulous. 'You sit and talk to Omi? What about?'

'Lots of things,' Paul said. 'The old days, when Omi was young in Bromberg.'

'Is this true?'

''Course it's true.' Paul sounded hurt.

Erika peered closely at him. 'This hasn't got anything to do with that crazy plan of yours to get Omi's room, has it?'

'No it hasn't!' Paul was indignant. 'We're going to get a bigger flat anyway when Father gets his promotion.'

'Hmm.' Erika still did not totally trust Paul. 'You never bothered talking to her before, did you?'

It was Paul's turn to be aggressive, even though mildly. 'I never had a chance did I? It was always you who were with her.'

And there was truth in that, Erika realised. It had always been herself and Omi; naturally enough, they were the same sex and shared the same room—and had the same tastes, come to that—whereas Paul, a boy, and a rather rebellious one . . . it occurred to Erika that her mother didn't have much to say to him and that when she did speak it was usually a reproof, and their father was too absorbed in his affairs to spend much time with Paul. She made a mental note to speak to her parents about it.

'Well,' she said, 'that's really kind of·you, Paul.'

Paul gave an embarrassed shrug. 'It's interesting. I never knew what it was really like then. All those servants and horses and all that.'

'Now then,' Erika warned. 'Remember, those were the bad old days.' But her rebuke was mechanical, a mere echo of the incessant propaganda to which she had been subjected since infancy and she knew it—and so did Paul.

'Oh, that,' he said, vaguely. 'Yes, but she's a nice old lady,' speaking as though he were referring to a neighbour.

Erika laughed. 'So she is. And you're a nice boy. Now give them all my love and—'

She was about to say that Paul should tell her mother to stop sending her notes but a bell rang, summoning Paul to his lesson with Herr Schmidt, forgiver of forged grades, and Paul shambled off down the corridor looking as though he had confessed to some heinous crime, rather than the simple, decent action he had described.

Erika watched him go, smiled, shook her head in amazement, and went down to the gym. And there she found Fräulein Silber and another woman.

'Frau Milch.' Erika was introduced to the woman, who did have a rather sour-milk face but who, as Fräulein Silber explained to Erika in the changing room, was a good coach.

'A very good coach,' Fräulein Silber said. 'A specialist in high jump. She is a severe critic but don't be put off. Jump your best. Remember that she is doing us a great favour coming here.'

A little nervously, Erika went back into the gym, did her warm-up exercises, and then, the preliminaries over, she began to jump.

Up and up crept the bar, occasionally falling on to the landing bed, although that was inevitable in a prolonged sequence, until after an hour, and with the bar at 1 metre 71, too far below Erika's best for comfort, it fell three times.

'Enough.' It was Frau Milch who spoke.

Erika looked at Fräulein Silber who nodded her assent. She showered, changed, and went back into the gym for the verdict.

'Not bad,' Frau Milch said. 'I wouldn't say it was bad. I would make your approach a little wider.' She drew a bold chalk-mark on the floor. 'Like this rather than that.' She drew another curve inside the first one. 'That's your present run. Come out a little and you will get more momentum. It might be too late to alter your stride now, but try it, anyway. Also you are dipping your right shoulder when you take off. Keep it up. Really work on that. I have seen more foul jumps because of that than any other single fault. So, not too bad, but,' she clicked her teeth in a rather discouraging way. 'In a competition that depends on the opposition, doesn't it? And from what one hears. . . . '

'What does one hear, Frau Milch?' Erika asked respect-fully.

'Oh, at Rosa Luxemburg School, Pankow, they think that they have a real star.'

'Karen Bloxen,' Erika said.

'You've heard of her? Well, they're keeping her heights dark, or I should say that they are giving out ridiculously low heights, but things do slip out.' Frau Milch looked sourly at Erika as if *she* were responsible for giving out the false information. Then, surprisingly, she said, 'She's been talking about you.'

'Karen Bloxen? Talking about me?' Erika was sur-prised.

'Yes.'

'But how can she know about me?'

'How do you know about her?'

Erika felt a little foolish. 'I've just heard her name, that's all. But what is she saying? I mean, I've never met her and she's never met me. . . . '

Frau Milch sniffed. 'She says that she is going to make a fool of you at the Championships.'

Erika was genuinely staggered. 'But that's not a very nice thing to say.'

'No,' Frau Milch said. 'But I hear that she isn't a very nice girl. Oh, I'm told that she says that this school is no good. Just for backward pupils.'

A flush, and a hot one, blazed on Erika's cheeks, and her eyes darkened. 'She does, does she?'

'So I hear.' Frau Milch sniffed again and dabbed her nose. 'This school is no good and she is going to make you look a dummy on Saturday.'

'We'll see about that,' Erika said. 'We'll just see—on Saturday.'

The red danger signals were still glowing on her cheeks as she strode down the school corridor where, purely by chance, of course, dawdling by the notice-board, absorbed in an appeal to all students to join the German-Soviet Friendship Society, signed by Herman Guttenbruk, Fritz Kott saw the danger signals and wisely decided that he would not try to speak to Erika *that* evening, although he certainly would the next day, and contented himself with what he fondly imagined to be a romantic smile but which an objective observer might have taken to be merely a hideous, fawning, adolescent leer.

But in Fräulein Silber's silvery flat, watching the video tapes and concentrating as she never had before, Erika's danger signals slowly faded as she watched the Immortals: Simeoni of Italy, Bykova of the Soviet Union, Yolanda Balas of Romania, Rosie Ackermann, gods not coming to earth but leaving it, and she went to bed happy, feeling that, like them, she too could defy Newton and his Law of Gravity, or, if not *quite* that, then certainly Karen Bloxen.

She was happy, too, as, snuggled in her duvet, she read a letter from Omi saying that all was well, and that Paul was being very kind, a true gentleman—and, typical of Omi's thoughtfulness, saying that the owl called every night as if asking where was its friend from Klara-Lettkin-Strasse.

And as she put out the light, far from weeping, Erika smiled at the thought of Paul listening, goggle-eyed, to Omi's reminiscences, and she laughed at the memory of Fritz in the corridor, and she felt, as she drifted off to sleep, that she could beat all the Karen Bloxens of the world rolled up into one.

She woke to a grey and sullen Friday and one day to go, but as Fräulein Silber said over breakfast, a day of rest. Not total, but easy exercises, a little running, mild weight training. . . .

'Just to keep you supple,' Fräulein Silber said. 'But relax. Enjoy yourself. Talk to your friends and make good music.'

All of which Erika did, quite excelling herself in the Bach piece, and finding time after her balletic exercises to have a long talk with Rosa, she having skipped a lesson on the New Czechoslovakia in order to sit with Erika in the empty canteen.

A long dreamy talk in which Fritz Kott figured prominently but who, it now appeared, had also been gazing on Rosa with a doting air, other boys, plans for a night out and, of course, the Championship.

'Will you be there?' Erika asked tentatively.

'But of course!' Rosa was astonished that the question should be put. 'Lots of us are going. We'll be cheering you on, don't worry about that. And give that Karen Bloxen a hiding. Everyone wants you to win. Everyone!'

True words, too, for as Erika wandered about the school she was touched by the good wishes she received, even from the loutish element. To her own surprise, Erika discovered that she was rather a popular girl and that the good wishes were the more heartfelt because Karen Bloxen's scathing comment about Egon Schultz School had mysteriously spread and had succeeded in doing what all the exhortations of Herr Lettner, his staff, and the F.G.Y. had never done—united the pupils.

Erika saw Fritz, too, and, somewhat in the manner of a film star, deigned to give him a brief interview in which, remembering Rosa, she was at first icy but, thinking that, after all, she did not want to lose him to her best friend, thawing a little, nodding graciously when he said that he would be at the stadium and going so far as not refusing outright when he asked her if she would go to a dance with him the following week, although he almost ruined his chances by telling her that she would need *lots* of relaxation.

'Will I?' Erika asked in her most Brombergian, freezing manner. '*I* will decide that.'

'Of course!' Sweat burst out on Fritz's forehead. 'I didn't mean . . . er . . .um . . . excuse me . . . sorry. . . .' He gabbled on in a wretched, panicky way until he was regally dismissed. 'And that,' Erika thought, 'will teach you to make eyes at Rosa.'

Later in the day Erika met Paul. All was well at home, the family sent their love and best wishes and would be at the stadium the next day.

'Is that all?' Erika asked.

Paul scratched his head. 'Karl's been.'

'Oh?' Erika said.

'Yeah, well he came and talked about the party with Mother, and he took Omi out to a café.'

Although pleased by that, as she went to the gym Erika felt mildly disappointed. Quite why she did not know. After all, what more could her family do than send their good wishes? But still, as she did a few laps of the track, rounding the corner where the man had sat on that sinister night four weeks ago, the disappointment stayed with her, nagging away in a remote corner of her mind.

At 3.30 Fräulein Silber called a halt, but after Erika had showered and changed, instead of the usual walk to the car, Fräulein Silber led her up the stairs to the staff-room.

'Just wait a moment,' Fräulein Silber said, and went into the staff-room leaving Erika waiting.

The moment stretched out, rather; in fact it turned into minutes. The school began to empty, Erika got more good wishes from late leavers, the cleaners began to rattle their buckets, and Erika began to frown.

'What is this?' she thought. 'Being left hanging about like . . . well, like a *delinquent* instead of a—' she realised that she had been about to say 'a star'! But she pushed that unworthy thought away. 'Mustn't get a swollen head,' she said to herself. 'You're behaving as if you were *some-one.*'

And then, at last, the staff-room door opened, but instead of Fräulein Silber coming out, Erika was beckoned in—and then she felt rather as if she *were* someone.

The whole staff was assembled, standing, with Herr Lettner to the fore—and, in his full regalia of the F.G.Y., but very much in the background, Herman Guttenbruk.

'Ah, Erika!' Herr Lettner boomed. 'Come in, come in.' He coughed portentously. 'Erika, on behalf of all the comrades here, and of the whole school, I wish to offer you our best wishes for tomorrow. We have no doubt that you will distinguish yourself and bring honour to the Egon Schultz School and to Fräulein Silber.'

He paused and pulled out a piece of paper. 'As Article eighteen of the constitution of our beloved country says—' he peered at the paper, '"Sport is an element of socialist culture and serves the harmonious physical and intellectual development of the individual."' He stuffed the paper away. 'But you will also bear in mind, Erika, that outstanding individuals reflect the *mass* basis in all fields of human endeavour which has been established by the foundation of a democratic, socialist state in Germany.'

To enthusiastic applause he beckoned Herman forward. 'A word from the leader of the school F.G.Y.'

Herman wormed his way through the teachers and stood with one hand behind his back. 'Comrade Nordern,' he began in his nasal, sanctimonious whine, 'on behalf of your comrades in the F.G.Y., and the pupils of the whole school, I wish you success tomorrow.'

He paused and looked as if *he* were going to pull a speech out, but a growling cough from Herr Lettner made him change his mind. Instead he said, 'But our Principal has said whatever I can say, and far, far better. So I merely present you with this token of our esteem.'

To another round of polite applause he took his hand from behind his back and presented Erika with a bouquet of the inevitable violets.

Erika blushed from her forehead to her toes and rather wished that she were somewhere else. 'Thank you,' she said, 'thank you all, er, Herr Principal, honoured teachers, and you, Herman Guttenbruk . . . and . . . and the F.G.Y . . . and the pupils.' She glanced at Fräulein Silber who nodded vigorously, meaning 'more'.

Erika peered into the violets, searching for inspiration. 'I will do my best,' she stammered, feeling, as she was now undergoing the torture of expressing herself, a pang of remorse at the way she had treated Fritz— 'and I will remember the words of our Principal.'

That seemed to be sufficient. Certainly it was for Herr Lettner, and consequently for the rest of the staff, not to mention Herman who whined that he would certainly be at the stadium, although Herr Lettner made it quite clear that important business would prevent *him* from going, ushering Erika, Herman, and Fräulein Silber to the door as the rest of the staff collected their coats and week-end marking.

In the corridor Herman gazed amorously at Erika and was about to speak but Fräulein Silber withered him with a glance and swept Erika off. 'Something about that youth I can't abide,' she said, as they got into the car. 'But he'll probably end up a senator.'

They reached the silvery flat, had a light meal, washed up, and returned to the sitting-room, but the T.V. stayed blank.

'No more athletics,' Fräulein Silber said. 'What you don't know now you won't learn tonight. There's a film on later. You can watch that if you like.'

She looked at the bouquet. 'Sorry to spring that on you, Erika. But they meant it, you know, the staff, even Guttenbruk. They wanted it to be a surprise.'

Erika gave a rueful grin. 'I felt a fool, I couldn't think of anything to say.'

'You did very well. Kept it short and sweet.' In her turn Fräulein Silber smiled. 'Speeches—the curse of this country. I seem to have spent half my life listening to them. They seem to get longer, too, or maybe it's just that I'm getting older—or perhaps because life has got a bit easier people think that they *can* make their speeches longer. Mark you, they certainly went on in the old days. I remember in the F.G.Y. . . .'

She slipped away in reminiscence, and as she spoke it occurred to Erika for the first time that Fräulein Silber was rather a lonely person: unmarried—although in a country short of men that was not unusual—and glad to have a receptive ear to talk to. And Erika was glad to listen as Fräulein Silber talked about her life: born in the grim and grinding 'fifties, 'And grim and grinding they were,' Fräulein Silber said. 'Everything short, food, clothes, heat—and that was in the countryside. Goodness knows what people in the cities went through. At least we had potatoes and kept a pig and a few chickens. And the bitterness. . . .' Fräulein Silber sighed. 'Terrible. People falling over to inform on each other. You know, so and so had been a Nazi, someone else had been in the S.S. She had been a Block Leader. And they came for them, the *Volkspolizei*. Yes, and some of them never came back. Not that my parents ever shed any tears over them.

They'd done it too. The Gestapo, coming for people in the night, whole families crammed into the back of a lorry and none of those came back. The camps, you know. . . .'

Yes, Erika did know and at times the knowledge was a torment to her: that human beings could have behaved like that in the camps where people by the million had been killed: gassed, shot, beaten to death, tortured, starved, flogged, experimented on. Millions. Millions upon millions upon millions. At Buchenwald, where every East German child was taken at least once in their school life, Erika had seen a film: an S.S. documentary, filmed by another human being, who had actually stood behind a camera and made the film which was of children, a line of children, some of them smiling, being led by a Father Christmas, a jovial Father Christmas, laughing through his whiskers as he led the children past a line of jovially laughing S.S. guards—into the gas ovens. It was hard to believe, but it was true.

'Forget it,' Fräulein Silber read the sadness on Erika's face. 'It's over. Over and done with. Have a shower, watch the film, hot milk and an early bed. Tomorrow you are jumping for the future.'

Erika had her shower, worried, as she always was, that its stupendous gurgling would awaken the old couple—whom she still hadn't seen—darted back up the chilly stairs, and watched the film, a rather good historical drama about landlords and coal-miners in Silesia in 1896, then Fräulein Silber made her a glass of hot milk.

'Drink this,' she said. 'And, oh, take this if you want.' She opened her hand and showed a white tablet. 'It's just a sleeping-pill,' she said as Erika recoiled. 'Merely a sedative. No need to take it.'

Erika shook her head. 'I'll sleep.'

'Good.' Fräulein Silber pocketed the tablet. 'But if you can't sleep don't hesitate to waken me. Good-night, Erika.'

'Good-night, Fräulein,' Erika said, 'and—'

Fräulein Silber held up her hand, 'No more thanks. Go to bed now. Sleep well. And remember, tomorrow you will be jumping for the future.'

'Jumping for the future.' Erika thought of the phrase as she lay in bed in the darkness. Perhaps it was true. Perhaps tomorrow she would be jumping for the future, leaping for better days—and years, and helping to exorcise the ghosts from Germany's terrible, haunted, past.

Thinking that, and without the help of sleeping-tablets, she fell asleep and, unstirring, slept until she woke on her day of destiny.

Chapter 22

A BELL rang, far away it seemed. Erika awoke and stared into the darkness. For a moment, and, oddly, for the first time that week, she wondered what she was doing in a strange bed. Then Fräulein Silber's alarm clock stopped its tinny ring, and Erika knew, that today was *the day*. 'Oh dear,' she said, and felt her stomach turn.

With some relief she heard the sitting-room door open and Fräulein Silber moving. She got out of bed, put on her dressing-gown, and poked her head into the tiny kitchen where Fräulein Silber was making coffee.

'Erika,' she said. 'Sleep well? Good. Go into the sitting-room. I'll bring the coffee.'

The coffee was brought, poured, heaped with sugar. 'Take it,' Fräulein Silber said. 'Energy.'

Erika leaned back on the divan, sipping the sweet coffee. The sky streaked red, the frost on the window melted just a fraction, Fräulein Silber made breakfast. A tremendous one: Polish smoked ham, eggs, cheese, salami, yoghurt.

'Eat it all,' Fräulein Silber commanded. 'You'll need it.' She nodded vigorously. 'Here.' She passed a programme across the table and attacked her own breakfast.

Erika pored over the programme. To her intense disappointment, although the name of the Deputy Mayor of Berlin, who was going to be present, was printed prominently, none of the competitors were named.

The rest of the programme was merely a list of the events and their approximate time, the High Jump beginning at 2.30 p.m. And that tiny disappointment reminded her of her chagrin of the previous day when Paul had brought only casual greetings from home.

She tried to shake off the thought as, at Fräulein Silber's urging, she spread jam thickly over rye bread, had more coffee, listened to the radio, and then the door-bell rang.

Fräulein Silber raised her eyebrows. 'Who can that be?' she said. 'It's too early for the post.'

She went downstairs, came back, and placed a large parcel on the table. 'It's for you. A man brought it. Wouldn't say who he was.'

It was a very large parcel and a tough one, as Erika discovered when she attacked it, and attack was the right word. It might have contained the deepest secrets of the Kremlin; tied with string, stapled, stuck with yards of heavy-duty Sellotape. Erika tore and scratched and bit. She took a knife and hacked at it, mined it, sapped it, and finally broke its defences down and then, as Fräulein Silber laughed out loud, she found, inside the defences, another parcel—and inside that another, and another and another, until, at last, she found a mass, a stack of cards, letters, telegrams, from Norderns and Brombergs across the G.D.R. wishing her luck.

Fräulein Silber laughed and Erika laughed with her, all disappointments gone, but even as she laughed tears came into her eyes as she opened an envelope and found three messages, the first two of which read: 'To our dear daughter who honours us. With love. Father and Mother.' 'Erika, I'll bet you bash them to bits, Paul.' And, bringing more tears, the third note, in a familiar shaky hand, which said, '*Liebchen*, I pray for you day and night. May God give you all you wish. Omi.' But the tears were staunched when Fräulein Silber handed over a note in a bold, crude hand, which said: '*Don't* go in for any more competitions. It means me getting up early to deliver parcels.'

'So that's who it was,' Erika said. 'Bodo!' She looked across at Fräulein Silber who was looking abstractedly at the ceiling. 'You knew!' she said and laughed again.

9 o'clock; Fräulein Silber collected the dishes. 'I'll wash up,' she said. 'You pack.'

Erika packed her suitcase and her track bag and, the bear

under one arm, went back to the sitting-room, and announced that she was ready.

'Have you checked your bag?' Fräulein Silber asked.

'Oh yes.' Erika was airy.

'Check it again.'

'But I. . . .' Erika's mild protest faded under Silber's stern gaze. She heaved her suitcase on to the settee.

'Not that one.' Fräulein Silber pointed to the other bag—the important bag—the athlete's bag.

Erika nodded. 'I see.' And see she did. Her suitcase contained a great deal which was important to her, but her sport bag held more. She went through it: vest, shorts, jumping shoes, track shoes, plasters, embrocation, tissues, scissors . . . two of every kind, like the animals in Noah's Ark.

'Good,' Fräulein Silber said. 'That's your tool-bag. *Always* double check it. I once went to a track with only one pair of shoes. They tore and that was that. So. Are you ready?'

Erika took a deep breath. 'Ready,' she said.

Fräulein Silber took a long look at Erika, green eyes gazing into violet. 'I think that perhaps you are,' she said. 'I'll start the car. No!' She lifted a commanding hand as Erika reached for her luggage. 'I'll take your bags. No lifting for you—or waiting in the cold.'

She went downstairs leaving Erika in the elegant sitting-room. 'Well, well,' Erika thought. So this was what it was like, star treatment. Bags carried, no standing in the cold, cars waiting. What would it be like to be a real star, she wondered? She tried to shake the thought off, but as Fräulein Silber called her and she went down the stairs, her heart was beating a little faster, just the same, and it beat faster still as Fräulein Silber drove with brusque efficiency through the streets of the city, buses and lorries seeming to hastily make way for her at the crash of her gears as they made their way to the snow-clad Dynamo Club.

The Dynamo Club did not have the grandeur of the National Stadium, but it seemed grand enough to Erika as she was driven to a forbidding gate which bore a large sign saying, 'Officials and Competitors only'.

Beneath a huge, obligatory poster showing Marx, Engels,

and Lenin, a young man in a track suit and an anorak looked at their passes and waved them through. 'You know the way?' he asked.

'Yes,' Fräulein Silber knew it like the back of her hand: an arched doorway, concrete steps tumbling into the basement, and the changing rooms, cavernous, festooned with grimy heating pipes and lined with scarred and battered green lockers which banged and screeched as competitors tried to get them open—or shut—and the whole damp cavern reeking with old sweat and embrocation.

'Glamour.' Fräulein Silber smiled ironically.

'Yes,' Erika smiled back. She dumped her bag by the nearest open locker but Fräulein Silber shook her head.

'Follow me,' she said.

Obediently, Erika followed her as she walked the length of the basement, past other girls and their coaches, exchanging brief greetings here and there, until they came to a pair of doors marked, 'To the Arena'.

'This will do.' Fräulein Silber pointed to a vacant locker. 'Nearer the arena. Less walking.' She gave a deprecatory shrug. 'It's a small point but World Championships have been won and lost on smaller ones. Learn to think that way. Be . . . be meticulous.'

Erika changed, pulled on her track suit and tried to close her locker door.

Fräulein Silber shook her head. 'I don't know why it is but wherever you go the lockers never close properly.'

'Like our car doors,' Erika said, and raised her foot to kick the door shut.

'No!' Fräulein Silber paled. 'Not your foot! Goodness, you could twist your ankle.'

Erika paled, too. 'Yes,' she thought, 'and that would be that!' 'Sorry,' she said. But determined not to be beaten by the locker door, she gave it a terrific slam with her hand and had the satisfaction of hearing it screech shut, the explosive release of energy easing her tension.

'That's the spirit,' Fräulein Silber said. 'Now, let's go.'

They went through the double door, up more steps, through another door, along an interminable corridor, and

Erika began to see the force of Fräulein Silber's remark about 'small points'. Another door, another corridor, yet another door—and then they were in the arena.

The indoor arena was vast and superbly equipped, as it needed to be for the long winter months; racked tiers of seats, a raked oval running-track, a full 200 metres of it, and the arena itself, long enough for a javelin throw and stretching away so that at the far end mist hung under the girdered roof.

By the entrance, at a row of tables, officials were sitting, business-like, efficient, but friendly, sparing a half-smile as they asked Erika for her identification, checking form against form, looking at her photograph and sharply at her, and then, satisfied that the Erika before them was indeed the Erika Nordern of the Egon Schultz School, handing over a square of blue plastic on which was printed boldly in white, 'Erika Nordern, Competitor'.

'Good luck, Fräulein,' they said.

'Thank you,' Erika said, but her response was a little mechanical because she was looking at her badge. Competitor! It was silly, childish, even, but as she pinned the badge on to her tracksuit she felt taller, stronger, more important—and more competitive.

The arena was already filling with other competitors, stretching, bending, running, jumping, watched by hawk-like coaches. Fräulein Silber took Erika by the arm and led her to a vacant corner.

'Just relax,' Fräulein Silber said. 'Take your time. Get the atmosphere. Slow routine. Off you go.'

Still in her track suit Erika moved into her warm-up exercises, swinging her trunk, touching not just her toes but the floor—with her hands flat—squatting, doing press-ups, high kicks—and all with the grace and slow elegance of a Javanese dancer.

Fräulein Silber leaned back in a chair watching her, seeming casual and relaxed and the relaxation oozing on to Erika. After twenty minutes or so Fräulein Silber called a halt. 'Feel all right?' she asked. 'No stiffness, strains? No? Good. Go for a run—two laps easy, two laps circuit.'

Erika walked to the track which slanted in a rather dramatic and exciting way. The inner lanes were already monopolised by the sprinters so, like a pedestrian waiting to cross a busy main road, Erika prudently waited her moment before darting across to the outside lanes where, in a comparatively sedate manner, the distance runners were loping along with their long, fluent strides. Erika dropped in among them, did her two laps, then two laps of circuit running—an easy pace interspersed with explosive bursts of fifty metre sprints.

Four laps and the blood was warm in Erika's veins as she dropped off the track and rejoined Fräulein Silber.

'Put your track suit on,' Fräulein Silber said. 'Take a break. Here.' She took out a thermos flask. 'Glucose. Energy. Drink.'

Erika sat down, sipping the drink and watching the other athletes, secretly amused at the way in which in spite of all the exhortations of State and School, the girls had separated from the boys and pre-empted a half of the arena for their own use; for limbering up, that is, as no equipment was allowed during the morning session.

Erika finished her drink, then, at a nod from Fräulein Silber, wandered around the girls' reservation. Some of the girls she knew and greeted with the friendly camaraderie of athletes, but she was looking for name tags—especially one with Karen Bloxen on it.

But there was no Karen Bloxen to be seen and Erika was called back by Fräulein Silber, put through more exercises, more laps of the track, and then it was time for lunch, taken in the canteen, light: soup, a little ham, fruit, milk sweetened with glucose.

As Erika ate, Fräulein Silber commented on the other competitors. 'Treat them with respect,' she said, 'but don't be frightened of them. They must all be fairly good or they wouldn't be here, at least they've all made the qualifying height. You might get one or two false jumps but don't let that fool you. They'll all go through the first rounds. It's when the bar starts to get high that they'll fail.' She paused and looked thoughtful. 'Actually, I have wondered whether you might pass the first rounds. . . .'

'Hmm,' Erika was equally thoughtful. It was a ploy that could be used: a high jumper could enter the competition at any height, putting pressure on her opponents by assuming an air of superiority, but it could work against one.

'What do you think?' Fräulein Silber asked.

Erika shook her head. 'I'll take every jump.'

'Perhaps that's as well,' Fräulein Silber agreed. 'It will get your run-up right. But don't be alarmed if any of the other girls pass.'

'I shan't,' Erika sounded more confident than she felt.

'Good.' Fräulein Silber looked at her watch. 'Time for a rest.'

They went down to the changing room. Fräulein Silber found a vacant bench. 'Stretch out,' she said. 'Relax.'

Erika stretched her long frame on the bench and stared at the water-pipes. She breathed steadily, evenly, deeply, and the racket of the room, chatter, calls, occasional shouts, the banging of locker doors, merged into a queer cacophony of noise, swirling around her, seeming sometimes near, sometimes far, merging into a strange half-dream, half-reverie, in which she thought that she was in the village where she had spent a holiday with the F.G.Y: a distant tractor, cows lowing, a farm dog barking. Clouds drifted silently across a bright blue sky and, oddly, Omi was there crocheting with baling wire and, even odder, so was her father, jumping over a fence and shouting, 'That's the way to do it! And don't let your left leg trail!'

And then she opened her eyes, saw the grimy water-pipes, heard the babble of voices, and saw Fräulein Silber leaning over her.

Erika started and, a little panicky, began to rise, but Fräulein Silber placed a hand on her shoulder.

'All right,' she said. 'Take your time. You've been dozing.'

The hand was withdrawn and Erika sat upright. 'Good,' Fräulein Silber said. 'A pleasant nap. The really experienced athletes can fall asleep whenever they feel like it. With novices it's sometimes just nervous fatigue, but not with you. Go and freshen up.'

Erika went to the showers, splashed her face with cold water and rubbed herself vigorously. When she had finished and returned to Fräulein Silber a warning bell was ringing and officials were gesticulating. It was 2 o'clock and time to go.

Back through the double door, along the corridors, and into the arena, but a vastly different one: music swirled about the raftered roof, the spectators' seats were in darkness although from them rose an excited buzz of conversation, and spotlights played on a rostrum draped with the flags of the G.D.R. and the city of Berlin.

The athletes lined up before the rostrum. As a fanfare sounded, a group of men and women entered the hall to a burst of applause. They mounted the rostrum and, with a tremendous clatter of tip-up seats, the stadium stood to the National Anthem, and when it was over, sat down in a respectful hush as Herr Wolf introduced the Deputy Mayor of Berlin—he to whom the Norderns owed the redecoration of the room in the Budapest Restaurant.

The Deputy Mayor expressed his delight at opening the Berlin Indoor Championships, admired the arena, wished that he had been born in a time when such facilities were available to all and had he been, who knows, but that he himself might have been an Olympic Champion—pause to indicate that this was a joke—how proud he and the nation were of the splendid young people standing before him and he trusted that they understood the debt they owed to the nation led by the Communist Party, and also that they would compete in a comradely spirit of good will, and he was sure that all present would remember the debt they owed to the selfless work of schools, coaches, the F.G.Y., the Ministry of Sport, workers by hand and brain, the Government, all guarded by the *Volkspolizei* and the People's Army and, so—not wishing to delay matters further, and on behalf of the German Democratic Republic and the citizens of Berlin, he was happy—proud—to declare that the competition could now begin.

Applause; the audience and the athletes applauding the Deputy Mayor, the Deputy Mayor applauding the audience, and then, like amiable sheep-dogs, the officials surrounded the competitors and chivvied them into order, Erika and the other girl high-jumpers being sent to the far end of the arena, away from the starting line of the runners, and there, as the lights came on, she saw a solid block of pupils from the Egon Schultz School, Fritz, Herman and Rosa prominent, but in front of them, sitting firmly in the front row, beaming and waving, her father, mother, Omi, Paul, and, a massive fist raised in salute, Bodo.

Rather shyly, Erika waved back then turned and saw, a few metres away, a girl, tall, cool, long-limbed, haughtily good-looking, formidably athletic, seeming as if she could, there and then, saunter into the National Team, and wearing on her track suit a badge saying, Karen Bloxen.

The two girls' eyes met and Erika half nodded, but Bloxen merely gave a cold, horribly self-possessed stare, and turned away to her coach.

'So,' Erika thought, 'that *is* the way she is, arrogant and disdainful.' Just the sort of girl who would make unpleasant remarks about other girls, and other schools. 'Well,' she murmured, 'just you wait, Fräulein Bloxen. Just you wait and see.'

And wait they had to as the High Jump was not due to start until 2.30. Not that the half-hour was idle. With their coaches fussing around them the girls took their practice jumps, getting the feel of the floor, the all important pacing of the run-up exactly right, marking their steps, weighing up the opposition, and trying to jump off any nervous tension.

And that was not easy, Erika found. It was a long time since she had jumped competitively, and jumping in the gym at school was nothing like jumping in the arena. The noise alone was disturbing as feet pounded on the track, the crowd applauded, and whistles shrilled as judges called athletes to order. The presence of her own supporters was an additional pressure, people moving behind the bar were disconcerting, and above all there was the looming presence of Karen Bloxen.

She was disconcerting, too. She had an air of supreme, arrogant confidence as she practised, having the bar set first at 1 metre 60, and then at 1.65—15 centimetres above the opening height of the competition—and clearing with effort-less grace, and Erika had an uneasy feeling that if the stadium had burst into flames she would have carried on jumping, and clearing, without turning a hair. To make matters worse, unlike any of the other girls her practice was faultless: her run-up perfect from her first jump and her technique seeming effortlessly efficient. And to make matters worse still, on her own last practice jump, Erika, who had twice fouled on her run-up, lost her stride completely and, at a very easy 1.55, brought the bar down.

Disconsolate and embarrassed, Erika walked back to her seat although, to her surprise, Fräulein Silber was unconcerned. 'Don't worry about it,' she said. 'It's what practising is for. You'll be all right when the competition starts.'

Reassuring words, but Erika was not totally reassured. 'What a fool I am,' she thought as she pulled her track suit on and, looking covertly at Karen Bloxen, sitting perfectly relaxed with her coach, her heart sank.

The last girl took her last jump and then, coaches clustered around, the draw for the order of the jumps was made. The numbers were solemnly taken from a bag and given to the girls. And it was odd, although, in fact, the order could make no real difference to the girls' performance, there was real anxiety amongst them. For one thing nobody wanted to go first, and nobody wanted to go last, and Erika very much did not want Karen Bloxen in front of her—but she was. Out of the eight girls competing, Bloxen was six, nicely placed in the middle, and Erika was last.

The crossbar was raised to the minimum height of 1 metre 50 and scrupulously measured by a woman with a giant ruler, the landing bed was tested, two judges sat at either side of the bar, the coaches left the arena, for this was a competition in which no coaching was allowed, girls against girls without advice or assistance, and then, satisfied at last, the senior judge, who turned out to be Frau Milch, raised a placard bearing a bold number one, the first girl stepped forward, and the competition had begun.

Chapter 23

THE RULES of the competition were simple. Each girl had three attempts at the same height. Three failures at any height spelled O. U. T. but one clearance in any of the three attempts meant that the girl could go through to the next round. If the competition was a tie, that is if more than one girl went through to the final height and all failed, then the girl with the least failures overall was the winner, which meant, of course, that first, or even second time clearances could be of crucial importance.

The starting jump, at 1 metre 50 centimetres, was a relatively easy height for a goodish competition and the first girl to jump, stocky and small for a high-jumper, cleared the bar easily, as was to be expected, and so did all the others except Karen Bloxen, who chose not to jump.

So, Erika thought, it was as Fräulein Silber and herself had discussed earlier: pass a jump and put a little psychological pressure on the other competitors. For a moment she was tempted to pass herself but, she reasoned, if she did jump then the pressure would be reversed. If it came to a tie then her jump would count in her favour and Bloxen's pass would count against *her*. She wished that Fräulein Silber was there to give her advice, but as she was not, it was up to herself. Play safe, she thought, be prudent, and walked to her mark, acutely aware of the audience, the judges, the other girls, and even more aware that she had exactly ninety seconds in which to prepare herself.

She took a deep breath, rocked forward on to her left foot and raised her hands, nodding her head as she counted her run-up, visualising the jump. Seven metres away the crossbar set its challenge, on the track behind it runners poured past, somewhere a starting-pistol cracked. . . .

'Oh dear,' Erika murmured and, forgetting everything that she had ever learned, dashed forward like a startled pony— and brought the bar down.

Sweat glistening on her face, Erika draped her track suit around her shoulders as the judges rearranged the bar. 'That was nothing,' she told herself, 'nothing at all. Just a nervous start,' and she had two more jumps to go anyway.

Not daring to look across the track at her family, or anyone else, she waited as the bar was replaced, measured, and her number held up again.

The bar, which on her first jump had looked almost contemptibly low, now looked as high as the Television Tower; impossible for her to jump over, utterly and com- pletely impossible, hardly worth the effort of trying, al- though, of course, she had to.

'Concentrate,' she said. 'Concentrate and take your time,' and doing neither she ran, missed her approach, almost took off on the wrong foot and launched herself too soon and despairingly upward. She did not turn properly and her shoulder brushed the bar. She arched her back despairingly, kicked her heels high, and bounced on the landing bed as the bar actually trembled above her. Trembled but stayed where it was.

Erika rolled off the bed unable to believe her eyes when she saw the bar still on its uprights. She was still looking at it over her shoulder as she walked back to her chair. The stocky girl grinned sympathetically, a gawky girl gave her a friendly nod, one or two of the other girls came up to her with soothing remarks and friendly advice, but Karen Bloxen turned her contemptuous head away.

Her track suit on, Erika slumped in her chair feeling that she deserved the contempt. A failure and a near failure at 1.50. A height she could jump with a sack of potatoes on her back. It was incredible, quite incredible. She stared at her toes, utterly dejected. 'I'll never make it,' she thought, 'never. And what will my family think? And the school and Fräulein Silber? I shall be a laughing-stock. And Herr Wolf, what will it mean to him? Nothing. A shrug of his shoulders and another girl who could not make it under pressure written off. . . .'

The second round was about to begin. The bar was edged up three centimetres and the stocky girl took her mark. With an audible grunt she cleared the bar, as did all the others except Bloxen who passed again, showing her intention with a dismissive wave of her hand.

Then Erika's number was held up. To murmurs of 'good luck' she went to her mark, made a bold effort to look confident, took her time, ran, jumped, and failed.

Unable to believe what was happening to her she trudged back to her chair, her eyes downcast. 'But I *can* do it,' she muttered as the bar was replaced. 'I can!' Although she felt in her heart that she couldn't—and she didn't, catching the bar with her heel as she turned over it.

No cheers from the Norderns, no rowdy applause from the Egon Schultz School, and an embarrassed silence from the other competitors as the bar was replaced for the second time and Erika was called for her jump.

'It is those wasted months,' she thought, as she tried to compose herself. 'All that time missed, a lack of competition.' But neither of those reasons helped her as she looked at the bar and realised that this was her last chance. If she failed now then she was out. She rocked and raised her hands, trying to allow those drilled, automatic movements to calm her. And then she ran in and in her first two strides thought of Frau Milch's comment that her run might be too narrow, tried to widen it, missed all her marks, and came into the jump with her shoulder down and her head tilted, but despite that she cleared—just.

Just, but as she walked back to her chair to a little muted applause from her supporters, and as she wiped the sweat from her face, at the back of her mind a tiny, tentative whisper murmured, 'You are still in, Erika, still in. You did everything wrong that a high-jumper could conceivably do but you cleared the bar—and you are still in.'

But as the third round began, out of eight girls who had started, eight girls were still in, and only Erika had failed any jump, and she had failed three times, a dismal thought to mull over as the bar went up three centimetres to 1.56. Not a sensational height by any means but tough enough to be testing, and Erika hoped fervently that it would test her opponents more than it would test herself.

It certainly tested the stocky girl, who failed, and another, spotty girl, but also Erika who, realising on her last stride that she was too near the bar tried to pull away but was judged to have let her hand cross under the bar and so was penalised.

The stocky girl joined Erika as she sat down. 'Cheer up,' she said.

Erika adjusted her headband. 'Not much to be cheerful about, failing at these heights.'

'It's just nerves,' the stocky girl said. 'Anyone can see that you're a good jumper. Try and relax.'

'Relax!' Erika looked curiously at the girl. 'Aren't you depressed?'

'No.' The girl grinned. 'Actually, if I clear this height I'll have broken my own record.'

'What!' Erika was amazed. '1.56?'

'That's right.' The girl borrowed Erika's towel and rubbed her head vigorously.

'I'm not a high-jumper at all. Actually I'm a pentathlete— and this is my worst event! They only stuck me in because all our high-jumpers have the flu. Still, give it a go, hey?'

Yes, Erika liked that thought. Give it a go. Give it all you've got so that you could at least walk out of the arena with your head held high. That was the way to do it. 'Good luck,' she said. And she meant it.

And luck—and spirit—were with the girl as she ran in, her short legs pumping away, driving forward and clearing the bar and bouncing off the landing bed with an ecstatic grin, and waving at *her* family who waved back and cheered as though she had won an Olympic Gold Medal.

But there was no luck for the spotty girl who fouled and walked back biting her lip as Erika took her mark, and cheered by the stocky girl's success, and thinking, 'If she can do it, I can,' did do it, and did it quite well she thought, as the spotty girl failed for the third time and walked off crying, her hands over her face, the first casualty of the competition. And for the first time that afternoon it occurred to Erika that other girls had their own honour to consider, and their own ambitions, and that, in his spacious office, over coffee, Herr Wolf might well have spoken to other girls as he had to her, smiling his frank, open smile, and suggesting all sorts of glorious prospects, if only. . . .

The arc lamps shone down on an apparently endless stream of runners charging around the track, shouts and bellows echoed across the stadium, screams of excitement arose as something extraordinary happened in the Boys' Long Jump; but none of that mattered to the seven girls watching the bar being raised to 1.59 as the fourth round began.

The stocky girl failed on her first jump, as did the next girl. A platinum blonde girl went over the bar without too much trouble, so did the rather gawky girl, but number five failed . . . and then Karen Bloxen stood up and joined the competition.

Was it her imagination, Erika wondered, or had the arena hushed as Bloxen, tall, elegant and aloof, walked to her mark? Certainly, and almost ludicrously, she herself held her breath for a moment as Bloxen stood poised, one elegant hand held forward, the gesture itself seeming enough to hush the world if need be, and her slender white neck preordained to bear a gold medal.

'The winner,' Erika thought. 'The winner. Destined for victory. Destined for the laurel wreath.' And despite herself, but with the true, selfless admiration of one athlete for another, she felt a prickle of admiring envy as, with impeccable timing, and truly beautiful movement, Bloxen ran to the bar and jumped—floated—over it.

And that was that, Erika thought. Yes, that was that. The winner had jumped. All that remained was a battle for a place. But, still thinking too of the stocky girl's remark, she said to herself, 'Well, give it a go,' and took her mark, ran, jumped and cleared with a fine supple leap, her first really good jump. The stocky girl failed again, the other girls succeeded. The stocky girl failed for the third time but bounced away with a broad smile and a cheery wave of her hand and getting warm applause for it.

Six girls left from eight, sweating as the bar went up to 1.62. The judge raised a card, number two, and number two went to her mark, ran, jumped and failed, and failed badly. It was clear that the height was a little too much for her, and, although the platinum blonde and the gawky girl cleared, number five failed, too. With her air of supreme confidence, as if her mind were on other, and more important, affairs, Bloxen made light of her jump, and Erika, although making heavy weather of it, scraped over; another first time clearance for her, and she sat a little straighter in her chair as number two and number five tried twice more, and failed twice more, and walked off into the dark tunnel which led to the locker-room, and athletic oblivion.

And now there were only four girls left and, as the bar went up to 1 metre 65, Erika changed her socks and drank glucose and reflected on the height and the other girls. 1.65 was a reasonable challenge but not one which would have frightened her in the gym and, although she was jumping badly, unbelievably so, really, it was a height she could jump; the question was, could the other girls do it, too? No doubt they could, that was why they were in the competition, but if she could pull herself together anything might happen. She might make third place—perhaps —and then, if not Leipzig, she could probably get a place at another sports school, and she would be happy enough with that.

And so Erika tried to relax as the Blonde jumped and failed. The Gawk cleared, although not without effort. Bloxen was smoothly successful but Erika lost her rhythm, although as she swerved from the bar she managed to avoid fouling. But the false try disturbed her a little and she failed on her retry. The Blonde failed again but, gritting her teeth, Erika scraped over and sat down with a prickle of excitement. If the Blonde failed again then, whatever happened, she herself was in the last three, and even if she did go out then it would not be with ignominy. But she did not think that she would go out. High-jumpers tended to get worse as a competition went on: they tired and lost their rhythm and concentration. That had happened to the girls who had been knocked out. But she felt that she was improving, not that she could possibly have got worse, and her last jump had not been that bad. She had, at last, hit all her marks accurately and she had gained real speed as she reached her take-off, and that was very important indeed.

'It's all a matter of confidence,' she muttered. 'Confidence.' Although hers was a little dented as the Blonde succeeded on her third jump.

The judges went into their ritual and Erika looked along the row of chairs with their four vacant places. At the end, Bloxen was deep in conversation with the Blonde, gesticulating and swinging her torso. Erika frowned. Clearly Bloxen was giving advice and encouragement, and of course—Erika clicked her fingers—there were only four girls left and Bloxen was trying to make sure that the Blonde was amongst the last three, thus cutting out Erika Nordern of the Egon Schultz School.

So, Erika nodded. That was the way it was going to be. Very well, she would show them. They were in for a fight such as they had never been in before, and would probably never be in again, come to that.

And then the Blonde was called for the first jump in the seventh round with the bar at 1.68.

Whatever advice Bloxen had given the Blonde it was ineffective and, Erika thought, if the world champion herself had been advising her it would not have made any difference. The Blonde had reached her limit in the previous round and she was not going to exceed it. And then the Gawk jumped and she failed too, and although Bloxen cleared, watching her like a hawk Erika wondered if she had not been forced to stretch just a little.

With renewed hope, and with her jaw set in a very Nordernish way, Erika went to her mark. For the first time that afternoon the bar looked accessible to a human being instead of a kangaroo. 'So, clear first time,' she told herself. 'Go over and put the pressure on the Blonde and the Gawk. *Do it.*'

She went through *her* ritual, gave herself every second of her ninety, made a good approach run, took off well, and clipped the bar with her heel.

As she rolled off the landing bed she groaned with frustration, but back on her chair she did not feel the despondency of the previous failures. Almost unknown to her the competition had hardened her, the blows of failure hammering out any weakness of will she might have had, as the blows of the smith drive out the impurities of iron. *Now* she could think that one jump failed meant two jumps left, and she had only barely clipped the bar with her heel. In fact she had done everything right, and felt that she had plenty of strength left, and the level of her leg could be dealt with.

She drank glucose as the blonde girl jumped again, and failed again. The Gawk jumped and cleared and Erika jumped and cleared, too, and, she thought, stylishly, and so, trying to look unconcerned, she leaned back in her chair as the Blonde took her mark.

Sweat streaming down her face, her vest clinging damply to her, the Blonde went through her ritual, as aware as Erika and everyone else that she was jumping for survival, ran in too slowly, hit the bar with her shoulder, and was out.

Holding her head high, she collected her bag and walked off, getting a friendly pat on the shoulder from Bloxen who caught Erika's eye, looked at her coldly, and sat by the gawky girl who, almost unnoticed, had become a major threat.

Erika flushed, the menacing Brombergian red. The look from Bloxen had been a flagrant declaration of war, the row of empty seats was a no man's land, and the talk between Bloxen and the Gawk an obvious hatching of a plot between two allies against a common enemy.

'Very well,' Erika thought. 'Plot away but I'll jump until I die. If I burst my heart I'll beat you both. Yes.'

The judges altered the bar and Erika drank glucose and wiped her face. 'You are at least third,' she thought. 'Whatever happens you have made it into the last three.' And that was something. After her first two jumps she would have cheerfully settled for that. But now it was not enough. Now, after battling her way this far she wanted to go further. She wanted to win.

'*Achtung!*' The judges called for the eighth round at a height of 1.71. Three girls left and the seats by the High Jump were filling as the word spread that a really cracking competition was developing.

The Gawk prepared for her jump. She looked strong, there was no doubt about that, long and sinewy with hard, thin muscles which might have been specially made for endurance. She rocked, leaned back, ran in, seeming all elbows and awkwardness, and cleared, jumping off the landing bed with a triumphant punch in the air and walking back with her high-stepping action to a loud 'well done!' from Bloxen.

But, Erika pondered, for all the Gawk's obvious strength and assurance, her technique was not good. Her approach varied wildly, almost eccentrically, and she was taking off for her jump almost at random. But mere lunging strength alone could not keep her clearing the bar for ever, that was certain. It was a minor miracle that she had come so far and she would be found out. Erika had no doubt about that, but for the moment her eyes were on Bloxen whose technique seemed well nigh perfect and whose nerve appeared to be unbreakable.

Bloxen stood at her mark, icily cool, a marble statue brought to life, and ran, and even Erika had to admit that it was not the best moment to go. Although the High Jump was tucked away from the runners' starting line, a sprint relay was taking place. The third leg of the race was at an angle to the bar but visible from the corner of one's eye, and as Bloxen went into her run the sprinters came hurtling down the track. To a terrific racket of shouts, batons were exchanged, a runner fell, the crowd roared, and Bloxen brought down the bar.

She walked back, her cold features for once almost showing emotion, and passed Erika who gave her a look as haughty as those she had herself received. Bloxen turned her head away but Erika did not mind that. 'Look away as much as you like,' she thought, 'but you failed, you . . . you iceberg!'

Erika poised herself and took a long, long look at the bar. 1.71 was a good height there was no doubt about that, after all it was as high as a fairly tall woman. But she had done it in the gym, and often, and she could do it now, and with Bloxen having failed at last now was the time to do it again. For the first time in the competition she was in a position to put the screw on Bloxen, and a good clearance, a really good one, would make Bloxen as edgy as she herself had been for the past ninety minutes, and then maybe that icy composure would crack, and then, maybe, that technique might not be as flawless as it appeared. And a really good jump would give the Gawk something to think about too.

With those thoughts in her mind, Erika went for the bar, *attacked* it as Fräulein Silber would have said, hit her marks perfectly, rose, turned, arched her back, cleared the bar with her head, her shoulders, her seat, her thighs and calves, and clipped it with her endlessly trailing heel and brought it down.

For a moment, for one devastating moment, as she lay on the landing bed, Erika was tempted to walk out of the arena. With all the odds in her favour she had failed to beat Bloxen on a jump and now, she felt it in her bones, she would walk out of the competition a third, and a poor third at that; and, as insidious as a virus, the thought came to her that she could pretend that she was hurt. Nothing could be easier. She could limp back to her chair pretending that her old injury was back, retire with honour, and be greeted, not with disdain or ridicule, but with sympathy and understanding.

She came near to doing that. As she began what seemed to be a mile long trudge back to her chair she almost let her left leg buckle, but, from the spectators came a huge, a gigantic, hoarse, and true Berlin worker's bellow. 'You can do it, Erika!'

Bodo's voice; only he could have one that big and raucous. Erika peered into the darkness across the track. She could, or thought she could, vaguely make out her family. Certainly she could see Bodo because he was on his feet, a fist in the air, as if he were at a football match. Next to him would be her father and mother, Paul, and all her other supporters: Fritz, Rosa, Fräulein Silber, pupils from school, and, most important of all, Omi. And as, dripping with sweat, Erika reached her chair, she remembered what her mother had said that surprising night in the café: Omi had *honour*.

Yes, that was a word to conjure with, honour, and Erika knew that if she cheated now she would never be able to look her grandmother in the face again, nor anyone else, either, and so she walked firmly to her chair, wiped herself, sat down, and watched Bloxen take her second jump and clear, and, racing to the bar, cleared it also.

'And now,' she thought, as the bar went up again to 1.74, 'the battle is really on.'

And the Gawk failed, misjudging her run and trying to turn away at the last moment. But the judges declared that her whirling arm had crossed underneath the bar and so was a fault. And Bloxen failed, too, running immaculately but clipping the bar and bringing it down. But Erika, Bodo's bellow ringing in her ears, cleared. So she could sit back and watch the others sweat it out.

She could also do a little thinking about the next rounds. One thing was certain: if it did come to a tie, if she, Bloxen and the Gawk failed three times at the same height, then she would be in a dull third place. She had lost count of her failures but she knew that she had more, and a lot more, than either of the other two girls. The only way she was going to win was to win outright, to out-jump both her opponents, and that, she was beginning to realise, was to be partly a psychological battle; if, now, she showed nervousness or loss of confidence, that would make the others feel stronger and more confident. No, the thing to do was what Bloxen had done from the first round, stamp her authority on the competition and make the other two girls feel inferior, losers at these really challenging heights.

'So,' Erika said to herself. 'Now we'll try it the other way round.' And as the Gawk went for her second jump, Erika leaned back in her chair, her hands behind her head, affecting, though not feeling, mild boredom, as if now the result was preordained, with herself as the inevitable winner.

But it did not quite work out like that. In her clumsy way the Gawk cleared, and in her fluent way so did Bloxen, and the bar went up three more centimetres; and from the corner of her eye Erika saw that Herr Wolf and Fräulein Carow had come across the arena and were sitting a few metres away from the bar.

For a moment or two Erika did not take in the significance of that, assuming that as the High Jump had turned into a good tussle they were interested as any athlete would be in a good event. It was only when the board was held up with 1 metre 77 on it that she realised what was happening: they were now going into really good, first-class heights, and records were beckoning, and everyone was interested in those—particularly the masters of sport in the G.D.R. In 1983 the sixteen to seventeen-year-old girls' group at the Junior Spartakiad had been won by a jump of 1.79. That had been an exceptionally poor height, of course, the fifteen-year-old group had been won at 1.86. But still the bar called for a good leap.

The presence of Herr Wolf and Fräulein Carow was an added pressure but Erika tried to maintain her new pose of disinterest as the Gawk jumped the new height, and failed, and Bloxen went, and failed, and she went, and failed also.

But waiting for the Gawk to jump again, Erika was curiously undisturbed at her own failure. The bar was as much a psychological barrier as a physical one, and better jumpers than she could ever hope to be had failed at this height at her age only to go on triumphantly to world records. And besides, she felt that her jump had been good so that, despite her growing fatigue, her technique was holding up under pressure. It remained to be seen whether the other girls would react in the same way.

But, disconcertingly, they did. The Gawk cleared the bar but only just, and Bloxen, although Erika did not miss the look of relief on that iceberg's face as she made her way back to her chair; but Erika hoped that it changed to a look of dismay as she too cleared.

Round eleven; heat, sweat, the sickly smell of talcum powder, and the bar going up to 1 metre 80 and Erika, knowing that she had cleared that height before in the gym, with Herr Wolf watching, waited her turn and wondered whether the Gawk and Bloxen had. Bloxen still looked dangerous and the Gawk seemed as if she could jump over the moon if she had a fit of inspiration; and she had one on her first jump, making a gigantic leap which brought a gasp from the crowd, and landing in a strange tangle of limbs. But she was clear, unlike Bloxen who failed and, unfortunately for herself, Erika, who took off too soon and caught the bar with her wrist. Bloxen cleared on her second jump, although it seemed to Erika a leap without inspiration, and Erika cleared, too.

The judges huddled around the bar, the giant ruler was brought out, the landing bed inspected, and, as Erika sat alone, Bloxen and the Gawk sat together, deep in conversation.

But her isolation did not bother Erika. Since the stocky girl had gone out she had not exchanged a word with anyone. But she was still in the competition and, she hoped, looking as though the next height, in the twelfth round, to be attempted after nearly two hours, was not one to terrify *her*; the trouble being that it did not look as if it was terrifying the others, either. But then, she thought, perhaps they were bluffing too, or—disturbing idea—perhaps *they* were not!

In any case she was about to find out as the Gawk took up her ungainly stance, ran, and in a blur of elbows and knees, failed, returning with a disconsolate air as if she knew that she was facing an impossible task. Then Bloxen went forward, took her time, ran in her beautifully collected way, but brought the bar down just the same.

And Erika brought down the bar, too, but as she walked back she was warm inside as well as outside; despite the heat, tiredness, nervous strain, competition against real opposition, and hostility, she knew that her jump had been good. If anything, and she was aware that in view of the fact that she had failed it seemed odd, her jump had been *too* good in the sense that it had been, as it were, mechanically correct, but that was not a bad thing at all. It showed that her technique was still holding up under pressure. And she was level still with the other girls in this round—and she was sure that the Gawk was going out, which would leave her one of two jumpers left; a change from that round—a lifetime ago it seemed—when she had actually considered faking an injury.

But, she reminded herself severely, she was anticipating

since the Gawk had not yet taken her second jump, and neither had the imposing Bloxen, and neither had she herself.

'Don't count your chickens before they are hatched,' she said, but the Gawk did fail again, really crashing into the bar, and Bloxen, missing her run-up, was adjudged to have fouled, the judge tapping her hand to show that as the girl had veered away her hand had crossed under the bar, and that, Erika knew, was a genuine sign of cracking nerve—and cracking technique.

Bloxen came back to her chair, shaking her head, and went into an earnest discussion with the Gawk as Erika's number was shown—and once again she went to her mark.

She stood stock-still, beathing deeply and evenly, trying to block out every distraction and concentrating on the black and white bar.

'You've done it,' she said to herself. 'You've done this height. Herr Wolf said so in the gym. So do it now!'

And she did, hitting her marks perfectly, sprinting in to the bar, taking off perfectly, and knowing even as her head soared above the bar that she would clear it.

Although she doubted if there was much space between her and the bar, that did not disturb her as she walked triumphantly back to her chair. She had done it. She was over, and at her best ever competitive height, and now the Gawk and Bloxen had to face the bar again—and it was a last chance for both of them—and, although she felt slightly ashamed of herself for doing so, she willed that both of them would fail.

And it *was* the last chance for the Gawk. Although Bloxen walked to the mark with her, and gave her an encouraging clap on the shoulder, and although it was clear that she was concentrating as she had never, perhaps, done before, her eyes half-closed, her hands clenched, biting her lip, and although she bounced forward as though she were wearing spring-heeled shoes, the height was too much for her and she was out, a not ignoble third.

Or, perhaps, equal second, since Bloxen had to jump again, but whatever hopes she might have had in that direction were dashed as Bloxen cleared leaving, at last, herself and Erika head-on.

Head-on but hardly face to face for, as the judges fussed with the bar, the two girls sat at opposite ends of the row of chairs, and although Erika stared defiantly at Bloxen, Bloxen merely turned her head away; that gesture, as Erika, to whom contempt did not come easily, felt, being more effective than her own childish stare.

She sipped her glucose, trying to relax, breathing deeply as she had been taught, wishing that she could change her vest, wishing that she could have a shower, wishing that the competition was over—with herself as winner, of course —and then it occurred to her that a rather long delay was taking place.

She looked up. The judges were in an earnest huddle. One of them left the group with the odd half-run officials always seem to effect and returned with a man in a red blazer and white slacks, obviously a very senior official, quite probably the Field Referee himself. The man bowed his head, listened, waved Herr Wolf forward, listened to him, and then nodded, obviously in agreement; the group broke up, and a judge, trim in white, her face grave, walked towards the two girls.

Erika's heart sank. With absolute certainty, she knew that she was going to be disqualified for some obscure infringement of the rules, a copy of which the judge held in her hand, and each and every one of which she knew that she had breached.

A few feet from the competitors' chairs the woman paused, her eyebrows raised in surprise at the distance between Erika and Bloxen and being, as it were, at the apex of a triangle, the corners of which were the two girls, she was uncertain which of them to approach. However, being an official, she solved the problem in an official manner by beckoning them to her.

Erika nervously, Bloxen with her ingrained coolness, walked forward and stood before the judge who looked at them severely.

'I am sorry,' she said, and Erika's heart, already in her shoes, sank into the floor. The judge's brown eyes moved from Erika to Bloxen, and back again. 'I—we—are sorry for this delay. But you know what the next jump is?'

The next jump? Erika began counting on her fingers—the tenth, eleventh, twelfth?—but arithmetic was not needed because, maddeningly, Bloxen knew.

'The junior record,' she said.

'Yes. Good.' The judge nodded approval. 'The junior record. We are going to announce it on the public address system. It won't take more than a minute or so. Please don't let it disturb your rhythm. Just sit and relax. Thank you.'

Erika's heart returned from the locker-room and resumed its normal place as the judge looked curiously at the two girls, made as if to speak, then merely nodded. 'Good luck,' she said. 'To both of you.'

She walked away holding up her hand and a muted but penetrating gong boomed across the arena three times, followed by a soft, woman's voice.

'*Meine Damen und Herren*—Ladies and Gentlemen. The final of the 4 by 400 metres Relay Race will be delayed as in the Girl's Junior High Jump Championship, the competitors, Comrades Karen Bloxen and Erika Nordern, will be attempting to equal the national junior record for this event. Thank you.'

Applause, not, perhaps, echoed by the relay runners, reverberated around the arena. Number six was held aloft, Karen Bloxen pulled off her track suit and walked to her mark. For a moment or two she stood perfectly motionless, one leg a little extended, as coldly beautiful and composed as a Greek statue, and then, the statue coming to life, she moved, rocking, heel and toe, forearms extended, then ran forward with her smooth, powerful, high-legged run, hit the ground with her left foot, rose—and hit the bar.

An eerie muted murmur filled the arena as she rolled off the landing bed, walked to her chair, and pulled on her track suit, expressionless, almost, one might have said, indifferent.

Then eight was held up, a muted voice behind her called, 'Good luck,' and Erika walked to her mark, almost symbolically, it occurred to her, opposite from Bloxen's, Bloxen being a left-footed jumper and approaching the bar the other way round.

Without the pounding of feet on the track, the shouts of other athletes, the shrilling whistles, bells ringing, the calling of the crowd, the arena was hushed and expectant, and collecting herself at her mark, Erika wished that it wasn't. After jumping in the cheerful racket of the competitions all afternoon the silence, the watching eyes, and above all the sense of being the complete centre of attention brought its own, new pressure, and Erika remembered what Fräulein Silber had said: 'It's all very well jumping in a gym—but in a stadium, with 50,000 people watching—that's what sorts out the champions from the rest.' And although there were not 50,000 people in the stadium, 5,000 at the most, Erika understood the force of the remark. But there they were, those watching thousands, and here, willy-nilly, was she, and there was nothing she could do about it other than walking off—and there, gleaming black and white, at an impossible, ludicrous height, was the bar.

Erika blew out her breath and drew it back, right down to the bottom of her rib-cage. 'Concentrate,' she said. 'Concentrate, concentrate, concentrate,' and ran, bouncing off her right foot, driving upwards, the arena swivelling as she twisted backwards, the lights spinning dizzily, her back arching, legs high, and she was over—and clear.

Barely aware of the applause and cheers, she knelt on the landing bed and raised her hands. 'I've done it!' she said. 'Done it, done it, done it! Equalled the record!'

Equalled it! She jumped to the floor, shaking her head, and ran across the arena to her parents, they on their feet, shouting and clapping, but a white-suited arm barred her way.

'Fräulein!' A judge waved her back. 'You must wait. Wait.' She pointed. 'The other competitor has to jump.'

'Ah, of course. Excuse me.' Erika tried to collect herself. She walked, bounced, back to her chair, jubilation in her heart and jubilation on her face, and not deigning to hide it from Bloxen who, as she approached, was pulling off her track suit.

'Now,' Erika thought. 'Now, Bloxen. *You* sweat it out.'

The arena quietened as Bloxen went for her second jump, still poised, cool and calm, her run fluid and her jump fluent, but not fluent enough as, to a groan from the crowd, she failed again.

She came back to her seat but did not put on her track suit, rubbing her legs vigorously with a towel. She took a mouthful of glucose from her flask and then, without a glance at Erika, went for her third jump.

For all Erika's antagonism towards Bloxen, she felt a flicker of admiration for her poise as she took her mark, and Bloxen needed all the poise she possessed as, in a dead hush, she stood, a solitary figure, knowing, as Erika very well knew also, that three centimetres, the width of two fingers, and those alone, stood between her and defeat. Two finger-widths, but that was enough although, as Erika leaped to her feet, her arm raised in a victor's salute, Bloxen rolled off the landing bed, to the bouncing of the bar, as composed as she had been when the competition had begun.

'And now I have done it,' Erika said, 'I *have*,' speaking aloud although applause drowned her words as, ignoring Bloxen, both arms high in salutation, she ran to the track and embraced Fräulein Silber.

'Erika!' Fräulein Silber hugged her. 'Well done. Oh well done. What a triumph!'

'Thank you.' Tears spilled down Erika's cheeks.

'Thank *you*,' Fräulein Silber said. 'Now, are you ready?'

'Ready?' Erika was only half paying attention as she peered over Fräulein Silber's shoulder, looking for her family. 'Ready for what?'

'Why,' Fräulein Silber held Erika at arm's length. 'For your next jump.'

'What?' Erika stared at Fräulein Silber incredulously. 'Another jump? But I've won!'

Fräulein Silber smiled. 'Of course you have. But now to *break* the record.'

'Aah!' Erika understood. The winner of a championship was always given the chance to go on and try to break the record. 'Should I try?'

'Of course you must.' Fräulein Silber was not amused. 'It is expected of you. But now sit down, relax. I'll be allowed to sit with you. I'll be with you in a minute.'

She strode towards the judges who were gathered in a

271

conclave, scrupulously checking their mark-sheets and Erika went back to her seat. As she got there Bloxen stood up.

'Congratulations,' she said and offered her hand.

Erika took the hand, touched it, rather. 'Thank you,' she said in a frigid voice and half turned away but, manners overriding distaste, and feeling a little more was needed, especially from the winner to the loser, added, 'hard luck.'

'Are you going again?' Bloxen asked.

'Yes.'

'Well, the best of luck,' Bloxen said. 'Break the record. I hope you do.'

'Do you?' Erika was incredulous.

'Of course I do.' Bloxen frowned, the first sign of naked emotion she had shown all afternoon. 'What's the matter with you, anyway?'

'With me?' Erika's temper, bottled up for the past long hours, flared. 'You mean what's the matter with you.'

Bloxen's frown deepened, and she looked formidable, too. 'With me?'

'You. Yes.' Erika gave an emphatic nod. She glanced over her shoulder. The judges were still conferring, Fräulein Silber and Herr Wolf with them. 'Don't think that I don't know. You were going to make a fool of me. Oh, I heard about that—and what you said about my school. And this afternoon, never a word to me but advising the other girls. *And*—' but she stopped abruptly. 'This is ridiculous,' she thought. 'I've just won the Championship, I'm about to jump for the G.D.R. record, and here I am wrangling like a spoiled child.' Not for the first time that afternoon, she was surprised at herself, but she was even more surprised at what Bloxen said.

'I don't know what you're talking about.' Bloxen was unmistakably sincere.

'But—' Erika frowned in her turn. 'But I was told—'

'I don't care what you were told,' Bloxen said. 'All I've ever said about you is that you had courage coming back from an injury and I was looking forward to meeting you. And I did—want to meet you. But what happened? You turned your back on me. You didn't even answer when I said "good luck".'

'You shouted that? Oh dear.' Erika sat down with a bump. 'I thought that it was Fräulein Carow.' She looked up, crimson with embarrassment. 'I don't know what to say. I mean . . . I do really. I'm sorry. Really and truly sorry. But I was told. . . .'

Bloxen smiled, the smile transforming her cold features. 'You were psyched.'

'Psyched?'

'Yes. Your coach gave you an enemy. Someone to go against. And it worked.'

Erika shook her head. 'But that isn't fair.'

'Never mind. It didn't affect me, did it? You won because you were better on the day. Now go and break the record. We'll meet again, as friends.'

The conclave of judges was breaking up and Fräulein Silber and Herr Wolf were coming towards the girls. Bloxen gave Erika a clap on the shoulder. 'Do it. And my name is Karen.'

The gong boomed mellifluously as Fräulein Silber and Herr Wolf stood over Erika.

'*Meine Damen und Herren*. . . .'

'Well done, Erika,' Herr Wolf said. 'And the best of luck.'

Fräulein Silber vigorously massaged Erika's legs as the public address system announced that Comrade Nordern was going to attempt to beat the Junior Indoor Record.

'Now, Erika,' Fräulein Silber turned her muscular attention to Erika's arms. 'I'll be with you for this round. You have three attempts so don't worry if you fail the first time. *Drive* as you jump. *Drive!*'

Silence as Erika walked to her mark, another race delayed and the entire arena, from the Deputy Mayor himself down to the children acting as helpers, hushed and watching; the Nordern family not in their seats but on the edge of them; Herr Nordern clutching Frau Nordern's hand, Omi's old hand in Paul's young one, Bodo's massive fists clenched, Fritz Kott gnawing a knuckle in the approved melodramatic way, Rosa peeping through her fingers, Herman Guttenbruk solemnly holding a copy of the rules of the F.G.Y. as if its talismanic influence could impel Erika over the bar.

And, the centre of attention, standing at her mark and feeling as lonely as Robinson Crusoe, stood Erika, in that place where all the good will and good wishes in the world could not help her, looking at the distant bar over which only her own skill and courage and strength could take her.

And on her first jump they were not enough. The bar came down at the merest brush of Erika's heel, and they were not enough on the second jump, either, as she made a bad turn and caught the bar with her hip.

Erika sat with Fräulein Silber as the bar was replaced, drained and spent, not so much physically, although she was that, as mentally, feeling that one more sight of the bar would make her be sick.

'I can't do it,' she said.

'You *can*.' Fräulein Silber poured glucose down Erika's throat and kneaded her legs and arms. 'You can do it. One centimetre. Just one, and you have the record. One more jump. Just one. It's in your mind, Erika. *Will* yourself to clear.'

'I'll try,' Erika said, as her number was held up. 'I really will try.'

She walked to the mark with leaden legs and leaden arms, for all the glucose her mouth dry although the rest of her was sopping wet, and looked at the bar and thought of the mocking, tantalising centimetre which stood between her and the record book.

'I *can* do it,' she whispered as she launched herself forward, running, as she felt, in slow motion, the bar appearing to come to her rather than she to it, willing herself to clear it, pulling out every one of her last ebbing resources, snatching a last breath as she took off, head, shoulders, hips, rising above the bar, thighs, calves clearing as she fell backwards, but, to a huge, collective groan, her heel catching the bar and, as she fell, it falling with her.

Erika lay on her back, staring at the lights and the rafters to sympathetic applause, and for the first time in her life she swore. '*Verdammt!*' she said. 'Damn it! Damn it! Lost by a millimetre. *Verdammt!*'

But she was given little time to repine. As whistles blew and starting-pistols cracked, and the cheerful row of the competitions restarted, Fräulein Silber hustled her out of the arena and down into the locker-room.

'Celebrations afterwards,' she said, 'when you get your medal. Have a hot shower and change. Quickly, before you get cold and stiffen up.'

The locker door proved to be as hard to open as it had been to close, but eventually, glowing from the shower and in clean clothes, Erika sat on the bench again.

'Here,' Fräulein Silber handed over a flask of hot, milky, very sweet coffee, and a bar of chocolate. 'Get these down you. No need to watch your diet for a while.'

Erika obediently drank and ate, Fräulein Silber watching her intently.

'How do you feel?' she asked.

'Drained,' Erika said.

'That's natural.' Fräulein Silber pressed more chocolate on Erika. 'A long tough competition. It always seems an anticlimax afterwards—even when you've won.'

'I suppose so.' Sullenness was foreign to Erika's nature, but she sounded sullen as she spoke.

A little wrinkle appeared between Fräulein Silber's eyebrows. 'What's the matter? You're not fretting about the record, are you? Don't worry about that. To equal it was a tremendous achievement. Really tremendous.'

Erika looked down the shabby locker-room with its battered lockers and grimy pipes. 'It isn't that,' she said.

'No? Then what is it?'

Erika took a deep breath. 'It's about Bloxen. Frau Milch should not have said what she did. Karen didn't say anything about me, or the school.'

'Oh.' Fräulein Silber looked grave. 'She told you then?'

'Yes.'

'And?'

Erika raised her head. 'I don't think it was right. It was cheating.'

'Cheating!' Fräulein Silber looked decidedly cross.

'Yes.' Erika stared defiantly at Fräulein Silber. 'We're supposed to regard our opponents with respect, aren't we? Respect and in a spirit of comradely fairness. That's what the books say, isn't it? But it wasn't fair or comradely to send me out despising a nice girl. Was it?'

Fräulein Silber looked away, a trace of sadness on her face. 'No, perhaps it wasn't.'

'Perhaps.' Erika was little short of contemptuous.

'There's really no need for that tone of voice,' Fräulein Silber was sharp. She glanced at her watch and obviously decided they had a little time to spare. 'Erika, I'm sorry, but I was worried about you. I knew that you had everything, courage, stamina, technique, but I didn't think that you had . . . had the killer instinct. So I thought . . . well. . . .'

'Well?' Erika deliberately turned the phrase round. 'It wasn't well. Not well at all. And as for that other thing—the *killer* instinct—I don't want to have it.'

'It worked though,' Fräulein Silber said. 'You won.'

'I might have won anyway,' Erika said. 'I don't want to win by tricks. I want to do it on my own merits.'

'But you did win,' Fräulein Silber pressed her point.

'Winning isn't everything,' Erika said. 'And if I had been friendly to Karen she might have helped me. She was helping the others. I might have broken the record then.'

'Yes, you might have done,' Fräulein Silber admitted ruefully. 'But you have to be hardened, you know. When, and I mean when, when you go into international competitions, when you meet athletes from the capitalist world, then you'll have to go through the fire.'

'I don't want to hear about the capitalist world.' Erika gestured impatiently. 'For all I know they're as nice as Karen. I'd sooner lose in a socialist way than win like that.'

Fräulein Silber sighed. 'All right. All right. But promise me one thing.'

An hour ago Erika would have promised unhesitatingly and without qualification but now she said, 'What?'

Fräulein Silber noticed that, and clearly didn't like it. But still she spoke in a quiet, reasonable tone. 'Don't say this to anyone else until you've thought about it and spoken to me again.'

Erika thought for a moment. It wasn't an unreasonable request and she did want to think the matter over, and, clinching her argument, Fräulein Silber said, 'You don't want to spoil your family's day, do you?'

No, Erika certainly didn't want to do that and so, as the public address called the winners of the Girls' High Jump to the rostrum, she agreed.

'Thank you.' Fräulein Silber stood up. 'Time to go, but I'll tell you one thing Erika. You'll feel differently when you go on to the rostrum.'

As Erika entered the arena to applause and walked to the victors' rostrum, followed by Karen and the Gawk, she did feel rather different. The halo of stardom was on her head and it felt comfortable and when, on the rostrum, she dipped her head and the Deputy Mayor slipped a medal around her neck and kissed her cheek, and when Karen and the Gawk warmly shook hands and said, 'Well done, you won fair and square,' she was beginning to feel that Fräulein Silber had not been far wrong, after all; and when, freed from officialdom, but still glowing from the congratulations of Herr Wolf and Fräulein Carow, she went to her rapturous family, she was beginning to think that she been too hasty by half in judging her coach.

Rapturous her family was, too. Her mother embraced her in a bear-like hug and her father, standing back in his shy way, had moist eyes behind his thick spectacles. Omi, on Paul's arm, perhaps slightly bewildered but upright and proud. Bodo, his chipped and battered face split in a huge grin, Fritz, behind, gazing on Erika as though she had come from the moon trailing its beams with her, Rosa, clasping her hands over her head, Herman, undoubtedly seeing Erika's victory as a triumph for Marxism-Leninism, other friends, pupils, other athletes, relatives, until, bearing her laurels and surrounded by admirers, Erika was ushered out—and by the time she had been handed into the car, what remained of her scruples had quite gone; for the time being, at any rate.

Chapter 24

THE LADA banged and boomed its way back home where, to Erika's inexpressible delight, as she wriggled from the back of the car, the owl called from the beech tree.

'Inside,' Frau Nordern said. 'It's too cold to stand about.'

Erika turned to take Omi's arm but found it was being firmly held by Paul.

'Go on,' Paul said. 'We're all right.'

Smiling wryly, and feeling just a little rejected, Erika went up the stairs and was taken aback to find on each floor the neighbours waiting to congratulate her and, over the door of number thirteen a large, jolly picture of a girl high-jumping and written across it, 'Welcome home, Erika. Our Champion.'

Herr Nordern opened the door with a flourish. Erika blinked. The flat was full of people, more than it seemed possible for it to hold, and as Erika entered they burst into cheers.

'Thank you,' Erika said, her voice completely inaudible. 'Thank you very much.'

Behind her, aided and abetted by Bodo, Herr Nordern bellowed for silence.

'No speeches now,' he said. 'This is just to say how proud we are of our daughter. Now, Helga, Omi, Paul—where's Bodo?'

The Nordern family lined up against the wall, beaming; Bodo unceremoniously shoved the guests out of the way and photographed them, having to go all the way into the kitchen to get a focus.

'Good,' Bodo shouted, pulling down chunks of ivy. 'Another snap! Smile! The medal? Where's the medal?'

The medal was produced, universally admired, photographed, flash-bulbs flared as the friends and neighbours took out *their* cameras. Erika was much in demand and smiled and held up her medal, her hand was shaken, her back slapped, the more vigorously as the glasses were filled and refilled, and then she mouthed at her mother, 'Must change.'

Frau Nordern nodded meaningfully and took up a guardian's position at the door as Erika backed into her room.

'Phew!' Erika gave a little sigh of relief at the relative quietness, sank on to her bed, and patted it as if it were an old family pet. Home again, *her* room, for all its smallness, friendly, although lacking the bear which she placed on her little table, growling at it as it growled at her.

She smiled at her own childishness. It was good to be home again and yet, after the austere, silvery elegance of Fräulein Silber's flat the Norderns' sitting-room looked garish, cheap even, and she wondered whether, when they moved to a new flat, she could have a talk with her mother about the decorations. She would have liked to have another shower but she was a little shy, with the flat so crowded, and there were probably guests in the bathroom anyway. She contented herself with rubbing herself vigorously with a rough towel, took her best dress from the cupboard, and was brushing her hair when the door opened and Omi entered.

'*Liebchen, Liebchen,*' Omi took Erika's hand. 'How good it is to see you back.' She sat on her hard and upright chair. 'How splendid you looked on the rostrum when you got your medal. You were like a goddess.'

'No!' Erika dismissed that, laughing as she did so. 'I felt more like a scarecrow.'

Omi shook her head. 'You were splendid. And the way you jumped, hour after hour. Aren't you tired?'

'Not now. I was,' Erika confessed. 'After the last jump I felt as though I couldn't even walk. But now I'm fine. Really. Are you going to change for the party?'

'No,' Omi shook her head. 'One change a day is enough at my age, but my feet. . . .'

'Ah!' Erika knelt and took Omi's shoes off.

Omi sighed with relief. 'The pleasures of age. Having your shoes taken off!'

'How have you managed, Omi?'

'Well enough, child. Come, don't kneel. Sit with me for a moment. Everyone has been good. And Paul!' She chuckled. 'He has been as good as gold, sitting with me for hours.'

'He told me.' Erika laughed, too. 'He was embarrassed about it.'

'I can imagine,' Omi said. 'Boys that age are very strange. Ashamed of being kind.'

'And the way they walk,' Erika said, not without thinking of Fritz. 'Shuffling about. . . . '

'Yes.' Omi was amused. 'They did when I was young. So. I think that I will rest for a little while. No—' waving her hand in denial as Erika said that she would stay—'no, no. Go, enjoy yourself. You are the star.'

'Well,' Erika helped Omi on to the bed. 'I suppose I have to show myself. I'll get them to be quiet though.'

'Not at all.' Omi was firm. 'It's a night for celebrations. Really, I shall enjoy listening.'

'No problem there,' Erika said, as she went into the sitting-room. There was no problem, either. More people had crammed into the flat, voices were raised as the wine went down, and Paul, under the illusion that this was to be a western-type party, had brought out his record-player and was playing ancient rock records to a circle of elderly and bemused cousins.

Frau Nordern, a little flushed with wine, took Erika's arm. 'How pretty you look. Doesn't she?' Rounding on a circle of ogling guests who chorused that she did, indeed she did, holding out their glasses as though this unexceptional tribute had earned them another drink.

'And Fräulein Silber,' Frau Nordern said. 'Now she came in a moment ago. Where is she?'

She peered around but Erika had already seen her coach. She wriggled through the crowd and into the kitchenette where, behind the rehabilitated ivy, Fräulein Silber was sipping a small glass of wine with Herr Nordern and Bodo, who were drinking large glasses.

Herr Nordern smiled at Erika and raised his glass. Bodo raised his, too.

'Told you, didn't I?' he said in his gravelly voice. He winked. 'It's the Nordern blood. When that starts to run hot—' he bunched his fist and made a mock punch.

'It's Fräulein Silber we have to thank,' Herr Nordern said. 'That patient encouragement after Erika's fall . . . and we do thank you, Fräulein.' He raised his glass. 'And you are welcome to come to the party—' he turned to Erika. 'I'm trying to persuade Fräulein Silber to come along.'

'No,' Fräulein Silber said. 'It is kind of you but it's a family party. Perhaps . . . perhaps you would come and have supper at my place next week. We could look at the tapes of Erika.'

'It was filmed?' Herr Nordern was startled.

'Oh yes. Now it goes into the State Athletic Archive.' Fräulein Silber half-smiled and gazed at Erika, and Erika gazed back, knowing very well what was behind that remark, and knowing, too, that her own pang of conscience about Karen Bloxen was rapidly easing.

'But I must go,' Fräulein Silber said. 'Thank you for inviting me.'

'You've been more than welcome, Fräulein.' Herr Nordern stood also. 'And thinking of going . . .are you ready, Erika?'

Erika was ready and went to make sure Omi was. When they came out of the bedroom the flat was emptying, an exodus aided by Bodo using techniques learned in many a bar.

The neighbours and friends made their reluctant farewells, Fräulein Silber was thanked again and pressed to stay, refused again, but promised to call in at the party after the meal.

'Now.' Herr Nordern stood in the centre of the sitting-room surveying the half dozen or so relatives who were going to the party. 'We have to get to the restaurant. Most of the others are going there directly, but we want to be there in good time to get things organised. So, we—' indicating his own family—'we'll go in our car. Bodo can get three in his truck, you—' pointing to a cousin—'you could take four, yes? And—'

'And that's everyone.' Frau Nordern took over. She looked at the littered room. 'We'll wash up when—'

'When we're ready,' Herr Nordern said. 'Now we go. *Now.*'

They went, clattering cheerfully down the stairs with one last minute alarm about whether Erika had brought the medal. Outside they crammed into their old bangers, wisely waiting to make sure that each others' cars had started before, with the usual ferocious grinding of gears and snorting of exhausts, they set off in convoy to the Buda.

The manager was waiting for them, dapper, welcoming, and delighted—or seeming to be delighted—by the news of Erika's victory.

'And now the room,' Frau Nordern said.

'Ah yes, the room.' The manager led them down the corridor and threw open the door, smiling as Frau Nordern gasped—but not with horror.

'Nice?' The manager asked.

'Yes. Yes. Very nice indeed,' Frau Nordern said. And it was: the best linen on the tables, gleaming plates, sparkling cutlery, and bouquets of flowers.

The manager raised a conciliatory hand as Frau Nordern peered at the bouquets. 'The flowers are paid for. Herr Bromberg ordered them.' He led the family further into the room and pointed to the tables which were laid out in a hollow square. 'I think that this arrangement is best, yes? No one has their back to anyone else, the guests of honour here. . . .'

'The food,' Frau Nordern said, getting her priorities right.

'All prepared,' the manager said hastily. 'All good. The best available. And you wish to greet your guests where?'

'In the bar,' Frau Nordern said.

The manager coughed a little anxiously. 'The bar. Yes. Of course it could get a little crowded, and tonight. . . .'

'Understood,' Herr Nordern said. Obviously on a Saturday night the restaurant would be busy and the manager would not want his bar crowded when there was a room available. 'We'll stay in here.'

'Thank you.' The manager gave his quick, eager smile. 'I have laid out a small bar over there in the corner. If you like I could have a waitress in to. . . .' He made a delicate gesture.

'To sell the drinks,' Frau Nordern said undelicately. 'A

good idea. All drinks before dinner to be paid for.'

'Excellent. I'll send the waitress in.' The manager withdrew and Bodo volunteered to wait in the outside bar to guide the guests into the dining-room.

Frau Nordern wandered around the room. 'It's beautiful,' she said. 'We're going to have a good party. I can feel it in my bones. We'll sit here—oh, and we mustn't let the two families divide, either. But we should be by the door to greet the guests. Omi, you sit down.'

Not ungratefully, Omi sank into a chair which Paul gallantly brought forward although, consumed with his gallantry, he didn't bring it forward enough and only prompt action by Erika saved her grandmother from falling on to the floor.

A waitress, as formidable as a traffic policeman, came in and stood behind the bar, the guests from the flat entered, crying ecstatically at the gleaming room; the other guests began to arrive: tough Norderns, aristocratic Brombergs, prosperous Norderns and faded Brombergs, relatives Erika knew well; Aunt Bertha and her railway husband from Eisenhüttenstadt, remote cousins from remote places, even more remote than Cousin Hetta's lair in Swabia.

Herr Nordern and his wife stood behind Omi who sat in queenly dignity receiving the guests as they came in, it was explained that Karl would arrive at 8.00, the bar, to which Frau Nordern firmly pointed, did a good trade. Bodo, his face split with a grin, ushered in his musicians who, to Frau Nordern's intense, although suppressed, annoyance, were improbably dressed as gipsies after all—that is, they wore blouses and had red spotted handkerchiefs wrapped around their heads.

The band began sawing at a foxtrot, more guests came in, there were cries of recognition, blank stares of non-recognition, and despite all Frau Nordern's efforts the party gradually and insidiously divided into Brombergs and Norderns—and they in turn divided into male and female groups. But as the clock moved towards 8.00, the chatter and the babble of reminiscence and gossip began to die away and, as in a church before a service, an expectant hush fell on the guests, all eyes turned towards the door, and, at 8.00 exactly, it opened, Bodo stood there, took one look at the room and, not without sly humour, bellowed, 'Herr Karl Bromberg!'

It was a ceremonial entrance. One might have expected a fanfare from the band which, however, stopped playing in an uncertain discord, as Bodo stood aside and revealed, beaming, in yet another superb suit, and, although wearing no jewellery, giving an air of golden opulence, Uncle Karl himself.

In dead silence Karl, unperturbed, walked into the room with his prancing step, through the guests who craned to see him with a natural curiosity not unmixed with ghoulishness —he had after all come back from the dead—and, Erika thought, a certain gloating over his manifest affluence.

Smiling and bowing to his right and left, like a king or a high Party official, Karl moved forward to little cries and murmurs from the Brombergs: 'It's him! *Gott im Himmel*! It's Karl!' But he did not stop until he had reached Omi. He bowed formally, with that faint suggestion of a click of the heels, kissed Omi's hands, Frau Nordern's too, shook hands with Herr Nordern, bowed to Erika, murmuring, 'I congratulate you,' then turned and bowed to the guests and, amazingly, they applauded him, heartily clapping—at least the Brombergs, who then burst into the vigorous German salutation: '*Hoch hoch hoch! Dreimal hoch*!'

Karl inclined his head graciously as, prompted by Frau Nordern, Herr Nordern stepped forward. He cleared his throat with a gruff cough and, looking at his feet rather than the guests, mumbled, '*Damen, Herren*, family . . .er, um . . . no speeches now . . . later . . . but all most welcome . . . um, er, thank you.'

He halted in his uncertain address but, urged on by Frau Nordern, added, 'Food in thirty minutes.'

Instantly Karl was surrounded by a horde of Brombergs whom, rather like the Pied Piper of Hamelin, he led to the bar, insisting, against the slightest of opposition, that he would, he must, he insisted on buying the drinks, including the Norderns in his munificence, although they were noticeably less eager to have drinks on Karl.

The band struck up again, a medley of old songs, Karl moved smoothly among the guests, a circle of old ladies gathered around Omi, and the guests subdivided, officials talking to officials, manual workers to manual workers, the young or, rather, the relatively young, talking to their own age group, and the old, to the old until the manager unobtrusively appeared at Herr Nordern's elbow and suggested that the meal might start. Herr Nordern thought that it might, the guests were persuaded to sit, although, despite his plea, a row of Brombergs faced a row of Norderns, as the manager clicked his fingers and waitresses entered with soup.

Spoons rattled against plates as the guests attacked the soup, wineglasses chinked, and conversation started again as the wine went down.

At the head table Karl dabbed his lips with a napkin in his characteristic, rather old-maidish way. 'How charming. What a wonderful sight. All the family—the families, I should say, ha! ha! So many faces I remember. And my dear Erika—' he raised his glass to her—'I'm so sorry that I could not see you this afternoon, but a splendid achievement. The Bromberg inheritance, dare I say. We were always a sporting family.'

He chattered on in his easy, practised, rather facile way as the soup was finished, the plates cleared, the waitresses clumped in with fish, carp from the Harz Mountains, more wine. Toying with the fish, Karl turned his full charm on Omi and Frau Nordern. Erika smiled at her father who was solidly chomping away. He looked up and smiled back.

'Happy, *Liebchen*?'

'Very happy,' Erika said. 'And you?'

'Ah! How could I not be?' Herr Nordern laid down his fork. 'This is the greatest day of my life.'

'Now, now.' Erika waved a warning finger. 'Remember the day you got married.'

'Oh!' Herr Nordern clapped his hand to his mouth. 'Don't tell Mother I said that.'

'It depends how good you are to me,' Erika warned. 'And what about when I was born?'

'Right.' Herr Nordern shook his head. '3.30 in the morning! It couldn't have been a worse time—or a worse night, come to that. A real blizzard. And then there was Paul. A difficult birth. Your mother went through it.... But anyway, I've never been prouder than today. Let me toast you.'

He raised his glass and drank. 'And there's something else; but that's a secret. No! I won't tell you now—you'll find out later.'

The fish course finished, and apart from Karl's plate none were left unscraped; the guests clearly feeling that if they were paying for the meal then they were going to eat it—proceeding to do that to the *Wiener Schnitzel* which followed the fish—and, appetites unblunted, to do the same to the pudding, a very good Hungarian dish with blackberries and ice cream laced with kirsch.

Mellowed and relaxed the guests leaned back, smoking large cigars donated by Karl, and looking appreciatively at a very good wine, also Karl's gift, which was brought in. Given a meaningful look by his wife, Herr Nordern rose to his feet.

He stood peering through his spectacles, a heavy figure in his best blue suit. Before him, in a haze of smoke, the gabble went on unabated. He coughed, and coughed again. Erika bit her lip with vexation and poked him in the ribs.

'Speak up,' she said. 'Tell them to be quiet.'

But the advice was not needed for Bodo stood up, too, and in his best building-site bellow roared, 'Silence!' adding as an afterthought, and in what passed for him as a normal tone of voice—'Please.'

There was instant and total silence. Bodo gave a satisfied nod and sat down, winking at Erika.

'Thank you, er, Bodo. Ladies and gentlemen, friends, family.' Herr Nordern fumbled in a pocket, then in another, finally fished out a piece of paper and held it up to his eyes.

'Honoured guests,' he said. 'Today is a great day for all of us, Brombergs and Norderns alike.'

There was a mumbled assent and some brave soul rapped his glass with a spoon.

'Yes,' Herr Nordern cleared his throat. 'A great day. To our, um—' he looked again at the paper, 'um, amazement and joy, Karl has returned to us after many years.'

To bolder applause he bowed at Karl. 'Karl, I know that I speak for all of us, those here and those who have not been able to come, when I say what deep pleasure it gives us, and myself personally, to see you er . . . reunited, yes, reunited with your family.'

There was more clapping led vigorously by Bodo. Erika

clapped too and looked at her father. She knew how he hated standing and speaking in public and yet, for all his stammerings and hesitations, his little speech had dignity, warmth, and sincerity. Erika felt rather proud of him then.

The clapping died away and Herr Nordern continued. 'May we see you again many times, Karl, and be assured that there will always be a warm welcome here, in Berlin, in the German Democratic Republic, and among your family. And now—'

He gestured, wine was poured, and, with all standing, he said, 'A toast to our relative and friend, Karl.'

The toast was enthusiastically quaffed, the more so perhaps as the wine was free.

'Yes, good.' Herr Nordern had not finished. 'But we have another reason to be proud and happy tonight. As you might know, my—er—our daughter Erika—today, after a long struggle against an injured tendon—today she won the Berlin Indoor Girls' Junior High Jump Championship!'

Said like that there seemed to be rather too many qualifying adjectives but, having become accustomed to it, the guests applauded even more vigorously, their faces beaming through the tobacco haze at a furiously blushing Erika.

'And,' Herr Nordern raised a hand for silence. 'And she equalled the all-time G.D.R. junior record, and here is her medal.'

Among vigorous Nordernian cheers, and more muted Brombergian applause, Herr Nordern held up the medal and the guests gazed at it with suitable veneration.

Herr Nordern gazed upon the medal himself then, despite a hissed 'no' from Erika, he hung it around her neck.

He turned again to the guests. 'But that's enough from me. I must now—'

'Not yet!' Frau Nordern leaned across Omi. 'Tell them.'

The mystified party watched as Herr Nordern shook his head and Frau Nordern vigorously wagged hers.

'Tell them now,' she said in an audible whisper. '*Or I will!*'

Herr Nordern gave a long resigned sigh. 'All right,' he said. He looked down at the table, mumbled, 'Justtosaygotmypromotiontodaythankyouverymuch', sat down abruptly and planted his elbows on the table in a manner which clearly meant he was not going to stand up again.

There was a baffled stir among the guests. People looked at each other, eyebrows raised, asking, 'What was that? What did he say? Prom what?'

But Bodo put their minds at rest by booming that his brother had heard that very morning that he was to be promoted, jumping two grades, and being specially selected for re-training.

Beaming, Bodo shook Herr Nordern's hand as the guests, many of them still not clear what the fuss was about, clapped heartily. In fact they were now in a mood to applaud anything and Erika suspected that if the manager had announced that the restaurant's cat had caught a mouse, they would have cheered that, too.

But, kissed by his wife and Erika, Herr Nordern was forced to his feet again. He waited for silence then said, 'Honour to invite Karl to speak.'

In silence, Karl rose. He stood, poised and immaculate, glowing with health, affluence radiating from him, his benign smile revealing his gleaming teeth; the very picture of the father of his clan, leader of the Brombergs, and benevolent friend to the Norderns.

'Dear family and friends,' he began. 'My honoured nephew-in-law has said better than I can what a joyous occasion this is for all of us. For me, I am sure for you, for dear Erika who has brought honour on us all, for my dear, dear sister—' he flashed his smile at Omi—'and of course we must all congratulate Hans on his well deserved promotion.'

He talked on smoothly, effortlessly, without notes, serious and humorous by turns, skating lightly over his missing years and the horrors of the past and yet managing to suggest his own courage and bravery in enduring them; talking of his delight in finding his family, and himself, for, having been a stranger for so long he felt a stranger no longer, rippling on and on. But while admiring his eloquence, Erika felt again a prickle of dislike for him. He seemed too smooth, too poised, too fluent, and too well-dressed, making the rest of the party, even though they were dressed in their very best clothing, seem dowdy and poor, underprivileged, badly fed, and unhealthy. And there was something patronising about Karl. The way he had said that her father could express things better than he himself was obviously untrue, and his saying it did not seem like a normal courtesy but more like a malicious, private joke. That was inconceivable, of course, but still . . . she tried to catch her father's eye but he was staring resolutely at his hands.

Karl spoke on, praising the new Germany and its achievements, the harmony and unity of its people and noting—was there malice there, too?—that before the dreadful war it would have been inconceivable for the Norderns to be dining with the Brombergs, *von* Brombergs, then, of course, and adding, manifestly untruthfully, that now they could do so without any unease whatever, ha! ha! And what a good thing that was. Indeed, it seemed that Karl could talk on for ever if he wished but, after complimenting everyone and everybody, he neatly drew his speech to a close by proposing a series of toasts: to the Brombergs, the Norderns, Erika, Paul, Bodo, and then he said:

'And now, if you will, one moment's delay.'

He snapped his fingers and the waitresses tramped in bearing champagne—French champagne—and tulip glasses.

Karl beamed around. 'Is everyone served? So. You will forgive the champagne. A little extravagance but, speaking for myself, I regard it as a rather special drink—' and this time, Erika was sure, there could be no mistaking the unpleasant irony, because not only did she believe that for Karl champagne was an everyday drink, but also, in a subtle way, he had stressed the 'I' when it was obvious that no one else in the room saw French champagne more than once in a blue moon, if then.

Karl paused for a long moment. 'I now wish to propose another toast; the last but, being the last, the most important. All of us here over a certain age have seen enormous changes and lived through shattering events. But there is one here who has seen greater change, than any of us and who has carried into the new Germany the values of the old one, and who enshrines in her person and in her very being the true, the old, the proud, and the immortal German virtues. Having said that I know that to say a name is redundant. But, will you stand.'

He gestured with his manicured hand and, as obedient as puppets to their strings, or dogs to their master, the guests stood up.

With surpassing elegance, and manners from an old school, Karl turned, bowed, clicked his heels sharply, and said, 'Gertrude Ute Reglindis von Bromberg.'

The toast was repeated in a reverential whisper and Omi bowed regally in her chair, murmured a 'thank you', and offered a cheek for Karl to kiss.

'So.' Karl, who had now taken over the role of host, smiled at the guests. 'That ends the formal part of the evening. Now the tables are to be cleared and we can relax, talk.'

As the guests hastily swigged the remaining champagne the manager waved a magician's wand, plates and glasses vanished, the tables were moved, chairs placed around the sides of the room, the bar was reopened and the band struck up a waltz.

Upright, Karl with his pattering steps, Omi stiff, they waltzed once ceremonially around the floor, although one circuit was enough for Omi who then sat down, with Karl, and held court to the Brombergs who crowded around them, eagerly questioning Karl about his past experiences and, perhaps more to the point, his future prospects.

The Norderns danced, sedate foxtrots and more daring quicksteps. Herr Nordern danced with Frau Nordern. Paul was claimed by Aunt Bertha and did a despairing shuffle around the room, although he positively refused to dance with Erika who was then claimed by her father.

'Ah,' Erika said, as light on her feet as her father was heavy, 'Promotion! Keeping secrets hey?' She tutted. 'What way is that to behave?'

'I *meant* it to be a secret for you,' Herr Nordern said, beaming. 'But it worked out wrong.'

'Serves you right,' Erika said with mock severity as Bodo took over from Herr Nordern.

'Enjoying it kid?' Bodo asked, showing surprising nimbleness as he steered Erika into an intricate double *chassé*.

Erika would not have taken the 'kid' from anyone else but it was natural and friendly coming from Bodo. 'Enjoying it?' she said. 'I should say so—well, most of it.'

'Most?' Bodo held Erika away and looked at her thoughtfully. 'I saw you when Karl spoke. Didn't like it, hey? Can't say I was overkeen myself. Oily and . . . ' he neatly avoided two lumbering Brombergs . . . 'and, what's the word, jibing. A bit mocking. Still, the hell with him. Listen, just wait there and don't let anyone take you away.'

He went to the band-leader who nodded vigorously and led his musicians into a tango.

'There we go.' Bodo reclaimed Erika from under the nose of a lurking Nordern. 'The tango, baby,' he said out of the side of his mouth like a gangster. 'Degenerate music. It's a good job Cuba is an ally or they wouldn't let us dance it.' He grinned. 'Terrible band isn't it?'

Erika laughed, both because it was a terrible band and because it was typical of Bodo to say so, especially as he had provided it. 'Mother is furious about them being dressed as gipsies,' she said.

Bodo chortled. 'I know. Gipsies! The pianist is a bricklayer. Just listen to him. And those handkerchiefs on their heads!'

The bricklayer and his cohort banged and sawed away, the waltz was much in demand, and Erika, after a dance or two, found herself with Karl, who could certainly waltz but who poured fulsome flattery on her in a manner she found odious.

But the party was turning into a real success. Aided by drink, the early inhibitions broke down and Norderns and Brombergs mixed, danced, chatted together. Erika danced with this person and that, and so did Paul, obviously determined to be polite. Fräulein Silber kept her word and appeared, and was promptly monopolised by Bodo.

'Something up, there,' Aunt Bertha said to Erika during a brief respite, adding that it was about time Bodo settled down.

'You never said a truer word,' Frau Nordern, sitting next to Bertha and holding a large vodka, agreed vehemently. 'He'll bring disgrace to us all one of these days. And this band! One of his jokes. Why, once—' she was about to elaborate but was stopped in her tracks by a warning look from Erika.

'Of course, he's Erika's favourite uncle and he does have a good side to him.' Frau Nordern was pacifying but, as Erika was led away to dance by an aged relative, she was unable to refrain from saying—'Somewhere, I dare say.'

The aged relative was a Bromberg from Schwedt near the Polish border.

'You remember me, of course,' he said, as he shuffled arthritically in a spare corner.

'Of course,' Erika said, although to the best of her recollection, she had never set eyes on the man in her life.

'Amazing to see Karl,' the man said. 'Quite amazing.'

'Yes,' Erika had heard enough of this to last her the rest of her life but, conscientiously, she agreed.

'Done well for himself, too. Very well. Of course, in the West. . . .' He sighed, breathing a mixture of smoke, peppermint, and schnapps. 'But a Bromberg would do well anywhere. Breeding will tell. Don't you agree?'

But Erika's sympathetic patience did not stretch that far. 'No,' she said, 'I don't.'

'Really?' The man blinked at Erika through faded, watery blue eyes, his mouth gaping a little showing false teeth which looked as if they had been made by a half-witted stonemason, his neck scrawny, sticking up from a cheap shirt, an ill-fitting suit. 'But to be bred to command, you know, natural leaders, born not made. It's in the blood, you know.'

'Well, as you say.' Erika felt a pang of pity for the old man, and what was the point in arguing? Let him, and all the others, live in their dreams and their fantasies of blood and breeding, as if people were like dogs or horses. 'Yes,' she said, as they made a last, tottering round of the floor before the old man, almost symbolically, collapsed on to a chair.

Other guests were subsiding, too. Although the band played on with undiminished proletarian vigour, elderly knees, no matter what breeding they possessed, were succumbing to the weight of years. The younger element were happy enough, and indeed there was a rumour that for a consideration the band would play disco music, but closing eyelids—closed in some cases—were signalling that the party was coming to an end.

And if those somnolent signals were not enough, the appearance of the manager, smiling, friendly, genuinely pleased that the party had been a good one, and whispering in

Herr Nordern's ear that he was quite ready to keep the restaurant open, but that, of course, would mean additional expense, was enough to persuade Frau Nordern that the time had come to end the festivities.

It was time, too. Omi was clearly exhausted and, when approached, Karl was not displeased.

'Yes.' He glanced at his magnificent watch and permitted himself the slightest suggestion of a yawn, hidden in the most gentlemanly way by a pink hand. 'A pity to bring such a wonderful evening to an end but. . . .'

So the great party ended. Farewells were made, addresses exchanged, Karl extended invitations to all and sundry to visit him in his land of milk and honey, the National Anthem was sung, Herr Nordern's baritone booming out, and then the guests shuffled out into whatever awaited them, shaking hands with Karl who stood at the door like a baronial lord bidding his peasants good-night after a farm dinner.

And then Karl left, climbing into his private car, assuring the Norderns that he would, he most certainly would, try to see them again before he left. 'Tomorrow afternoon? At 5.00? Good. Er,' he paused. 'Hans, my dear fellow, could you spare a moment?'

Herr Nordern bent, listened, stood up, and rubbed his chin thoughtfully as the car drove off through the snowy streets.

'What was that?' Frau Nordern demanded.

'Nothing,' Herr Nordern pulled up his overcoat collar. 'He just said that we weren't to be concerned if we had a little surprise.'

'And what does that mean?' Frau Nordern asked.

'Don't know.' Herr Nordern shrugged. 'A present I guess. Anyway, let's get home.'

Bodo waited until the Lada started and waved them good-night as they went, leaving the delights of the Buda for the darkness of the familiar streets, circling the Strausberger Platz where the accident had taken place which had given such fear for over two weeks, and perhaps mindful of that Herr Nordern drove slowly, crept, one might say, to the beech tree, the hidden boulder, the owl, and the flat on Klara-Lettkin-Strasse.

Chapter 25

THERE WAS a crack in the ceiling. It ran from the light bulb to the corner of the ceiling. In the middle it zigzagged and if you looked hard enough it was like the face of Herr Lettner.

Erika stared at the crack. There were none in the ceiling at Fräulein Silber's and there were none at home, either. For a moment she thought that she was dreaming then she sat up with a start. The crack in the ceiling was new but the rest of the room was its old self: books, posters, and Omi blinking into wakefulness.

But still Erika felt strange, as if she had awoken into another world, and then she remembered. Of course, and how amazing that she should have forgotten it—if only momentarily: she had won the Championship and there to prove it was her medal, propped up against the old bear whose stubby arms were thrust forward as if to protect it.

'*Liebchen?*'

Erika turned. Omi was awake, her hand extended. Erika got out of bed, slipped on her dressing-gown, and sat by Omi, holding her hand.

Omi smiled. 'It is good to waken and see you.'

'And you.' Erika smiled back. 'Have coffee. Have breakfast in bed. A treat for a special day.'

'A special day?' Omi's eyes clouded. 'What do you mean?'

'Why—' Erika hesitated. 'I . . . I don't know, really. But it's—'

'But it's because you are a champion.' Frau Nordern was at the door, a tray in her hands. 'Coffee for both of you. Just this once. Don't think that it's going to happen every day.'

She put the tray down. 'Breakfast as it comes. We're going to have an easy morning.' She sat down on the other side of Omi's bed, making it lurch alarmingly. 'Did you sleep well?' She yawned. 'I slept like the dead myself.' She shook her head. 'And like a fool I promised Cousin Hetta I'd see her off at the station. She's afraid of getting on the wrong train. I'm taking Paul, too,' she added ruefully. 'It was quite a day though, but I wouldn't care to go through it too often.'

'I'd watch Erika win a medal every day of the year.' Herr Nordern stood at the bedroom door. 'Excuse me Omi, Erika.'

Erika giggled. 'Come in, come in. Come one come all.'

Herr Nordern raised his hand. 'I'll get myself some coffee. No—' as Erika jumped up— 'I'll do it. And well done, *Liebchen.*'

'And well done to you,' Erika said.

Herr Nordern ducked his head in a deprecatory way. 'Strange, really, when you think of it. It occurred to me last night, driving back. If that accident hadn't happened the Director might never have seen my file, and if Steinmark hadn't been . . . been killed, who knows? I might never have had a chance of promotion. Funny old world, isn't it? You never know what's going to happen next.'

He ambled off to loyal proclamations from Frau Nordern and Erika that he most certainly would have got promotion anyway.

Frau Nordern sipped her coffee. 'I didn't mean that I couldn't watch you win medals, you know. It was the party, I meant.'

'Of course, Mother.' Erika looked through the window. Someone had built a splendid snowman by the beech tree, a couple were pulling a sledge with a muffled infant on it, children from the flats across the street were snowballing each other: a charming, Sunday morning scene, the sort that made winter almost worthwhile.

Erika smiled down on the street, gave Omi more coffee and went to shower and the morning began, homely, warm, and unusually relaxed. Even Paul was not scolded when he eventually showed himself.

'Did you enjoy yourself, Paul?' Herr Nordern asked.

Paul had, although with reservations about the band. 'They

looked like puddings with those handkerchiefs on their heads.'

'The band?' Frau Nordern came from her bedroom. 'Wait until I see Bodo. And they didn't play one gipsy tune.'

'Now, now,' Herr Nordern said. 'It wasn't bad. And you, Omi, a great occasion, hey?'

'Yes,' Omi said. 'It was. To see so many of the family again. Some of us will never meet again.'

'Omi!' Frau Nordern sat at the table. 'You mustn't talk like that.'

'It's true though.' Omi nodded confirmation of her remark. 'We're growing old, old.'

'Maybe,' Herr Nordern said. 'But there's lots of life in you, Omi, and the others, of course,' he added hastily. 'You're a long-lived family. Look at Karl, he was as fresh as a daisy last night.'

'He was.' A fugitive smile crossed Omi's lips. 'Indeed he was.'

'So there.' Frau Nordern spoke as if that settled it and that Karl was going to live for another century. 'More coffee?'

Yes, more coffee. The family sat around the table, united in the warmth, and doting on the medal which had been brought from the bedroom and propped on the milk-jug.

'We can have it mounted,' Frau Nordern said. 'In one of those cases with words underneath.'

'A good idea!' Herr Nordern was pleased. 'I dare say Bodo will know someone who—er—I mean I'm sure that we can find a man to do it. Erika Nordern. Champion. Yes. What an afternoon you had *Liebchen*.'

'Phew.' Erika waved her hand. 'It was a nightmare. I just couldn't get started. All those failures! Even at the end I wasn't jumping well.'

'That doesn't matter,' Herr Nordern said. 'Other things count in competitions. Fräulein Silber told me that,' he added hastily as Frau Nordern stared at him as if to ask what he knew about high-jumping. 'It's courage, stamina, nerve.'

Erika modestly disclaimed possessing any of these attributes, and to turn attention from herself said, 'And what about you? Your promotion?'

'Ah!' Herr Nordern lighted a cigar. 'It's all fixed. I go on the re-training course and if I pass—whoa!' He stopped the united protest of the whole family that of course he would pass. 'Now then, don't count your chickens before they're hatched. It's a tough course, the maths alone, and all this stuff about robotics . . . mm . . . you'll have to help me out there Paul! But anyway, if I do pass—all right!' He held up his hands in surrender. '*When* I pass, I go up two whole grades. Actually on to a different level altogether, executive instead of administrative.'

'What's those?' Paul asked.

'*Are those. Are.*' Herr Nordern shook his head. 'Don't you know your grammar? Well, the executive make decisions, the administrative grades carry them out.'

'And you'll be doing that,' Erika asked. 'Making decisions?'

'Yes,' Herr Nordern said with profound satisfaction. 'Only at a low level to begin with, of course, but still, making them. Shaping the future of the country. That will be something.'

'And better pay,' Frau Nordern said. 'Longer holidays, a bigger flat, a real car. . . .'

'Yes, yes, those too.' Herr Nordern was a little impatient. 'But to create! To plan for the future, your future, Erika and Paul, and all like you. Yes.' He peered through his cigar smoke and beyond, into some imagined future.

Erika was deeply moved. 'I'm so glad, Father. So happy for you.'

'Eh?' Herr Nordern came back to the present. 'Sorry, got carried away, silly of me. All that's a long way ahead—but I know what I'm going to do now.' He stood up. 'I'm going to the bar with Bodo!'

'What!' Frau Nordern gave an indignant squawk.

'No, no!' Herr Nordern held up his hands in mock surrender. 'A joke, Helga, a little joke. Just wait a minute.'

He went into the bedroom. Frau Nordern raised her eyebrows in her characteristic, mildly outraged expression but Erika looked through her parents' door to where her father was rummaging under the bed. 'He's changed,' she thought. 'In the space of a couple of days he's altered.' It was as if the news of his promotion had peeled away layers of repression and shyness revealing a playful and happy man who had been hidden all these years.

'Here.' Herr Nordern came back and put a bottle of champagne on the table. 'It was left over from last night and Karl said we should have it.'

'And just what do you think you're going to do with it?' Frau Nordern said.

'Drink it,' Herr Nordern said. 'Get five glasses, Paul.'

'But it's only 11 o'clock,' Frau Nordern said.

Herr Nordern unscrewed the wire and let the cork fly out with a satisfying 'pop'. 'I don't care what time it is. We're going to have a little celebration. *Our* celebration.'

He poured the champagne, a splash for Erika and Paul, a large one for Omi and himself, and, without more than a token protest from her, a large one for Frau Nordern, too.

'So!' He raised his glass. 'To us. To all of us here, and to our future.'

The glasses were raised and downed. Herr Nordern smacked his lips appreciatively. 'I could get a taste for this. Here.' He refilled his wife's glass and leaned over to pour more into Omi's but paused, looking at her, slightly concerned. 'Are you all right, Omi?'

'Yes. Yes, thank you.' Omi clasped her hands and bowed her head for a moment then sat upright. 'I have something to tell you.'

'Good! Excellent! Another toast.' Herr Nordern made to raise his glass but halted as Omi shook her head. 'No?'

'No,' Omi said. She looked around the circle of concerned faces and took a deep breath. 'I'm going away.'

'Going away?' Frau Nordern blinked. 'What do you mean? You're going to stay with someone? Ah! Someone you met at the party.'

'No,' Omi said quietly. 'I'm going to the West.'

There was a stunned, shocked silence. Frau Nordern spread her hands, knocking over her glass and sending the champagne trickling unheeded on to the floor. 'The West? You mean. . . .'

'I mean West Germany,' Omi said.

'You're going with Karl.'

'Yes.'

'But. . . .' Frau Nordern mopped aimlessly at the spilt champagne. 'But . . . it's incredible. Have you thought about it? I mean really thought?'

'Yes, I've really thought.' Omi unclasped her hands. 'I'm sorry.'

There was another pause. A long one which seemed as though it might stretch to eternity, then Herr Nordern cleared his throat.

'No need to apologise,' he said. 'The West, with Karl. Most interesting. I would like to go myself. In fact I might one day, officials do go, you know. And there is nothing to stop elderly people going, nothing at all. You just go to Friedrichstrasse . . .' His voice died away and he dropped the dead end of his cigar into his saucer. 'Er, when were you thinking of going, Omi?'

'Tomorrow,' Omi said.

'Tomorrow!' Frau Nordern screamed. 'Tomorrow! That's impossible. You can't go then. You can't. Tell her Hans, tell her she can't go.'

Herr Nordern had relighted his cigar and was puffing at it furiously. 'Well,' he coughed, 'tell her . . . can't . . . er . . . um . . . mark you, it's only, well obviously, twenty-four hours. . . .' He poured himself more champagne, and plenty of it. 'Twenty-four hours. Yes. Er, Omi, when did you decide?'

'A week ago,' Omi said.

Frau Nordern seized her husband's glass and gulped the champagne down. 'A week! My God! Why didn't you tell us sooner?'

'I . . . I didn't want to upset things.' There was the faintest quaver in Omi's voice. 'Erika was having her competition and I didn't want to upset her, and Karl said it would be better if I said nothing. . . .'

Her voice quivered again, trembled, broke, and Erika took her hands. 'It's all right, Omi,' she said. 'Really. Isn't it?' she appealed to her father.

'All right?' Herr Nordern took off his spectacles and rubbed them. 'Oh, yes, yes,' he said in an unnaturally hearty voice. 'Of course it is. Why shouldn't it be? You want to stay with Karl, what could be more natural? It is a little short notice, but the best of motives, the very best. Hey, Helga?'

Frau Nordern came back to earth. 'What?'

'I said Omi had the best of motives—for not telling us earlier.'

'But of course.' Frau Nordern bridled as though her husband had impugned Omi's honour. 'Of course she had the best of motives. Who said that she hadn't?'

'No one,' Herr Nordern sighed. 'That's the point.'

'Very well.' That point, obscure as it was, settled, Frau Nordern sat bolt upright. 'But Omi, can't you postpone it? At least think about it for a week or so.'

But Omi shook her head and old as she was and frail as she was, she was resolute. 'I have thought about it,' she said. 'Day and night, and prayed for guidance. I love you all, but I do so want to stay with Karl for a while, just a few weeks. Just to talk of . . . of the old days. When we were young.'

Her eyes filled with tears. At once she was overwhelmed by solicitude, her hands, shoulders, arms patted and stroked.

'It's all right, Omi,' Herr Nordern said gruffly. 'Really, go, of course.'

'Yes.' In a determined attempt to be cheerful Frau Nordern said, 'And you'll be back soon. Why, it's as if you were going to stay with Aunt Tina, or someone. Ah!' She raised her hands as if a gigantic spider had just crawled across the table. 'Your clothes! They'll need washing and ironing. No?'

'No.' Omi half-smiled through her tears. 'I did them all during the week.'

'But,' Herr Nordern leaned forward, frowning. 'Omi, if you are going tomorrow—your papers.'

'All done, too,' Omi managed a full smile. 'I went to the Police with Karl. Everything is in order.'

'All in order. Yes. Well, why shouldn't it be?' Herr Nordern shook his head and the champagne bottle, the latter of which was empty. 'I'm going to have a real drink.' He brought a bottle of schnapps from the kitchen and filled his glass. 'And arrangements?' he asked. 'When is Karl calling for you?'

'He's not,' Omi said.

'Not?'

'No,' Omi shook her head. 'He has to go tonight, by car.'

Herr Nordern looked thoughtfully at his glass. 'Then why not go with him? A couple of hours won't make much difference and he can look after you.'

'Business,' Omi said. 'Karl has to spend the night with business associates. I'm going by train tomorrow and he'll meet me at Hanover.'

'I see,' Herr Nordern said, in a voice which suggested that he didn't see at all. 'I must say, it seems a bit odd to me, but if you are happy.'

'I am,' Omi said.

And that was that. A stunned family broke away from the table. Looking rather upset, Paul went to his room to change and Frau Nordern thought that she ought to get ready, also, although she was reluctant to go.

'I don't think that I should,' she said. 'See Hetta off, I mean. Paul could go. I should stay here.'

'No, no.' Omi was insistent. 'You must go. Hetta will be distressed if you aren't there.'

'You should go, Helga,' Herr Nordern said. 'You won't be all day, will you?'

No, Frau Nordern didn't think that she would be and so, still reluctant, she left with Paul, having been assured by Herr Nordern that under no circumstances would Karl leave before saying goodbye to her.

'Of course he won't,' Herr Nordern said. 'Anyway, he's not calling before 5.00.'

Frau Nordern and Paul having left, Omi thought that she would go to her room for a while.

'Just to rest,' she said, as Erika took her arm for the few steps into the bedroom and eased her on to the bed. 'You don't mind, *Liebchen?*' she whispered. 'My going?'

'Of course not.' Erika leaned forward and kissed Omi on the forehead. 'I mean I *am* sorry, and I will miss you, and I wish I was going with you—to look after you, I mean, not because of—' she stopped, embarrassed.

'Not because of the excitement of the West. Of course not. I know that, child. But Karl—my only brother. I do want to be with him, and he says that we can go south, to Italy!'

'Italy!' Erika's eyes widened.

'Yes. I didn't mention it because Hans and Helga might

have thought that it was too far for me to go. But Karl said a spell in the sunshine. . . . Ah, he is so kind.'

'I should say so!' Erika whistled. 'Italy!'

'Yes.' Omi's eyes were faraway. 'I went there before the War, you know. What beauty and culture, the olive groves and the cypress trees. Florence, Rome, such harmony.'

'Now I *do* wish I was going with you,' Erika said. 'But are you sure that you have everything?'

'Oh yes,' Omi said. 'I'm only taking the one case.'

'Hmm.' Erika pursed her lips. 'That old thing.' She leaned under the bed and pulled out Omi's battered old suitcase. 'Goodness,' she said, in an unconscious imitation of her mother. 'It's worse than mine. It looks like a refugee's case. Wait.'

She darted across to her parents' room. Herr Nordern was lying on the bed.

'Yes?' he asked, drowsily.

'Nothing.' Erika took her mother's silver suitcase. 'Have a drink! Sleep.'

She marched back to her room and put the suitcase on her own bed. 'I'll repack for you,' she told Omi in a voice which brooked no refusal. 'Just lie still. So, hoop-la!'

She deftly turned Omi's suitcase upside-down placing its contents on her bed in reverse order. The last item to fall out was a stout type of Jiffy bag. It had been torn in one corner and plastic bobbles were spilling out.

Erika tutted. 'This is torn, Omi.'

Omi turned her head. 'Oh dear, yes. It got caught on the lock.'

'Never mind,' Erika said. 'I'll get a new one. Father has millions of them.'

She went back to her parents' room. 'Envelopes,' she said, opened a drawer, and took out the biggest envelope she could find.

'Don't bother asking,' her father said.

'I don't need to,' Erika said. 'It's an executive decision!' And left her father chuckling.

Erika had taken the largest envelope she could find but in the nature of envelopes the one would not fit inside the other.

'Grrr!' Erika growled as she wrestled with them. 'Here,

Omi,' she said. 'Take out your papers and put them in the new one.'

She handed Omi the two envelopes but Omi was oddly reluctant to take them. 'It's all right,' she said. 'Really, don't bother.'

'Not at all.' Erika's stubborn streak showed itself. 'You can't go carrying your papers in a torn envelope. That's not correct. Besides, you'll have these bobble things all over your case.'

Again Omi hesitated. 'I don't like to,' she said.

'Don't like to?' Erika was puzzled. 'But Omi, joking apart, you don't want your documents in a torn envelope. They might get damaged.'

Omi looked at the envelope for a long, long minute. Then she said, 'It isn't mine.'

'Not yours?' Erika said. 'Then whose is it?'

There was another long silence. Omi plucked nervously at the sleeve of her blouse as Erika stared at her, bewildered.

'Well,' Erika said, 'of course, Omi, if you don't want to tell me. . . . In fact I shouldn't have asked. I'm sorry. There now. I know, I'll seal it with Sellotape and it will be fine.'

She started to rise but Omi shook her head. 'No, *Liebchen*,' she said. 'You're quite right. But you see they're not my papers, they're Karl's.'

'Karl's?' A tiny prickle went down Erika's spine. 'Uncle Karl's? But why do you have them?'

'They're family papers,' Omi said. 'Karl wanted me to have them.'

'Family papers!' The prickle left Erika. 'But that's marvellous, Omi!' Her face glowed. 'And we thought that we'd lost them all! How wonderful. They'll be about the Brombergs, of course. Are there photographs? Is there one of you as a girl? I would love to see that, and photos of Mother's grandfather and grandmother?'

'I don't know,' Omi said.

'Don't know?' Erika was bemused. 'But how can't you know?'

'Because . . .' Omi hesitated. 'Because I haven't seen them.'

'But,' Erika tapped the envelope, 'but how couldn't you have seen them?'

Omi rolled her head on her pillow, almost in distress. 'Karl didn't want me to see them.'

'But they're your family papers,' Erika said. 'Why shouldn't you see them, and why. . . .' she looked at the envelope with deep suspicion. 'Why do you have them and not him? Why hasn't he got them?'

'Leave it, child, leave it.' Now there was real distress in Omi's voice. 'Karl wants me to have them because women should keep the family papers, and he didn't want me to look at them because he said we should go through them together, when we had plenty of time, just the two of us, the last of the family. . . .'

But Erika was not listening. Her eyes were fixed on the inoffensive, commonplace envelope, spilling out the rather playful bobbles, but her mind was on Uncle Karl, and on something he had said once, at the Gate of Peace.

'You are taking it for him,' she said. 'Omi, you are taking that for *him*, across the border.'

As she spoke, the hairs on the nape of her neck stirred as the skin contracted, and something else stirred, too, at the back of her mind; something terrible, unthinkable, like the worst nightmare imaginable, or the thought of the worst possible thing conceivable, such as hearing that one's entire family had been killed in an accident, something so atrocious that the mind mercifully blotted it out—except that this was not a dream or a fear, but an actuality, and one not masked by symbols, but there, in the prosaic envelope clutched in Omi's hand.

'Omi,' she whispered. 'Do you know what is in there? Tell me, please, have you seen it? Seen it with your own eyes?'

'Family papers,' Omi groaned. 'Family papers.'

Erika leaned over her grandmother, her fresh violet eyes staring into faded violet eyes. 'But have you seen them? You must tell me, Omi. You have to.'

Omi gave a despairing sigh. 'No,' she said. 'No. I haven't.'

'No.' Erika nodded. 'No, of course you haven't. He made you promise. And you are honourable. Give me the envelope, Omi.'

'No.' Omi shook her head, but Erika held out her hand and

304

took the envelope. Omi tried to hold on but it slid from her old and bent fingers.

Erika put her thumb in the rip. She was breathing deeply, her rib-cage expanding and contracting as if she were preparing for the most testing jump of her life. Slowly she tore the rip wider. More bobbles spilled out, bouncing on the bed, and she had a memory. Someone else had done this, someone long ago, and then as she looked at the bobbles she remembered. It was Pandora in the Greek myth. She had opened a forbidden box and all the evils which cursed the earth had flown out of it. How odd that she remembered that now—and in such detail; she had been told it in junior school by her teacher, Fräulein Olden, and she could remember the class-room with its paintings and maps and pressed flowers, and the mural the class had made from coloured paper, and the pet rabbit, Willy, and the girl who had shared her desk, Irmgard Lutter, and the boy she had fought with in the playground, and soundly beaten—Franz Teller; and as the rip grew wider and the bobbles fell out she remembered, too, that after all the evils had flown from Pandora's box, after greed and envy and hate and lust and selfishness had been let loose into the world, still there was something left inside the box and that flew out and it was hope.

But as Omi moaned, 'No, no,' and the bobbles bounced and she ripped the envelope open, she had a terrible, piercing intuition that whatever was inside it was not hope. And then she pulled out the papers from the envelope and looked at them.

Chapter 26

'OMI!' ERIKA could hardly bring herself to speak. She looked
again at the documents, willing them to change; but they
stayed unchanged and as Erika's hand shook uncontrollably,
the documents shook with it, and, stamped across the top of
them, the black, crooked cross shook too.

'Omi,' Erika forced the words out, 'these are . . . are. . . .'

'Family papers.' Omi struggled upright. 'Private papers.
Give them back, child.'

She held out her hand but Erika backed away, shaking her
head, as much to deny what she was holding as to refuse Omi.
'It can't be true,' she whispered. 'It can't be.'

But it was. Demons were stalking Klara-Lettkin-Strasse,
conjured up by the documents she held in her hand, which
were stamped with the swastika and the letters S.S. and which
bore a grinning skull.

With a cry of horror Erika turned and plunged blindly
across the living-room and in to her father.

'What, again?' Herr Nordern was irate. 'What do you want
now, Erika?'

But his manner changed as he saw Erika's face. 'What is it?'
He fumbled for his spectacles. 'What's the matter? Is Omi ill?'

Erika shook her head and, dumbly, held out the documents.

'All right.' Herr Nordern put on his spectacles. 'Just calm
down. Now, what are these?' He put a calming hand on
Erika's shoulder and looked at the documents—and then *his*
hand shook.

'My God!' he cried. 'What?' He stared incredulously at the
documents as he riffled through them. 'What are these? This

can't be true. It can't be. Erika, where did you get . . .get these . . .?'

'Omi had them,' Erika stammered.

'Omi? Omi!'

'She doesn't know what they are,' Erika cried. 'I opened the envelope by accident and . . . .'

'Omi had them?' Herr Nordern's face was crimson with rage. His head down like a bull he made for the door but Erika stood her ground.

'She didn't know, Father, she didn't. Karl gave them—'

'Karl!' Herr Nordern's face contorted with rage. He took hold of Erika's shoulder and flung her from the door but Erika struggled back.

'Jesus Christ!' Herr Nordern stared at Erika as if she were a stranger. 'Get away from the door.'

'No! Don't go like that.' Tears streamed down Erika's face. 'Please, Father.'

Herr Nordern loomed over Erika, breath rasping in his throat. 'O God,' Erika thought, 'let this be a bad dream. Let me wake up. Please.'

Herr Nordern's breath slowed a little and he said, thickly, but with more control, 'Move, Erika. I shan't hurt Omi. You know that. But I have to talk to her.'

'Yes. Yes, of course.' Erika moved slowly from the door. 'But gently. Please.'

'Gently,' Herr Nordern said.

Erika stood clear and followed her father into Omi's room. Omi was up, erect in her chair, her head held high. She stared at Herr Nordern and said, icily, 'I'm not aware that I have invited you into my room.'

Herr Nordern clenched his fists until his knuckles whitened. 'We've no time for that. Omi, these.'

Omi turned her head away. 'Those are private family papers,' she said. 'Erika had no right to give them to you and you have no right to look at them. Please return them to me.'

Herr Nordern bit the corner of his lip until blood came. 'Omi, do you know what these papers are?'

'I have told you,' Omi said.

'Have you seen them. Seen them for yourself?'

'Certainly not.'

'Then please,' Herr Nordern offered the papers. 'Please, look at them.'

'No!' Omi said. 'How dare you suggest such a thing? And how dare *you* look at them?'

Herr Nordern fought to keep his voice under control. 'You *must* look at them.'

'*Must*?' Omi turned her face and stared at Herr Nordern. '*Must*? You give me orders? You?'

Herr Nordern raised a fist in the air but Erika slipped under his arm and stood by Omi.

'You should look at them,' she said, gulping back the tears. 'Please do as Father asks.'

'No!' Omi was adamant. 'Do you think I will break my word? And you, child. What have you done?'

'I was trying to help you, Omi. Just helping you.' Erika burst into tears, sobbing, her face in her hands.

'Be quiet Erika,' Although Herr Nordern's voice was controlled there was a thick, animal-like quality in it. 'All right, Omi. If you won't look you will listen.'

He held up one of the documents. 'Listen, Omi. Listen for the love of God.' He took a deep breath. '"From *Obergruppenführer* Eicke." *Eicke*, Omi, a war criminal. "To *Obersturmbannführer* Karl August von Bromberg, S.S. *Totenkopfdivision*," dear God, Omi, the S.S. "Absolutely private and confidential. Your request to command an *Einsatzgruppe* is hereby granted." An *Einsatzgruppe*, Omi. A death squad. A murder squad, and he asked to be in command. And this, Omi, *listen*: ". . . am instructed to give you the *Reichsführer* —"' Himmler, Omi— "the *Reichsführer's* commendation for your work in Byelorussia—"' that means—' Herr Nordern literally struggled for breath— 'that means murdering Jews, Omi. And this—O sweet Jesus—1941, September. Orders to go to Kiev. Kiev, Omi. 35,000 Jews were butchered there. And this: orders to go to Warsaw, April 1943. 1943. That is when they slaughtered the Jews, Omi. 50,000. 50,000.'

His face ashen and his shoulders slumped, Herr Nordern turned to another document. 'Omi, orders to go to France. "Recommend you to contact Klaus Barbie." Barbie, the torturer.'

'Lies,' Omi said. 'All lies.'

Herr Nordern ignored her. With stunned amazement he was looking at the documents. 'There are names here,' he said. 'God in Heaven above. These people are still alive, industrialists, politicians . . . this one is Dutch! And this, a Frenchman, and these, Germans. . . .'

'More lies.' Omi's voice rang out harshly. 'Lies and slanders.'

'No.' Herr Nordern's voice was a croak. 'He—Karl—he was a murderer, a mass murderer. A war criminal. Do you realise—'

'Forgeries,' Omi said. 'Lies and forgeries. Slanders.'

'No.' Herr Nordern threw the documents on Erika's bed. 'No. They're real. Real.'

'Real,' Erika thought. 'Real. Real. Real.' As the flat filled with horrors scarcely conceivable: the dead arose from the charnel house of Europe; gassed, burned, tortured, frozen, bludgeoned, stabbed, hanged, torn alive by dogs; dead of typhus, dysentery, cholera, starvation; old men and women, young men and women, children, infants, babes in arms, shuffling through the cosy flat and the ivy and the bamboo; the dead who would not stay buried, the murdered whom all the weight of history could not keep in their graves. The endless resurrection of the vile, unspeakable deeds of Nazism. And on her bed, pinned to a document, smirking at her, was a picture of Karl; an identification card; kind Uncle Karl in a black uniform and peaked cap. Very smart, very striking, with the zigzag insignia of the S.S. on his collar and the skull of the death's head division on his cap.

Looking at it Erika felt her gorge rise and she stepped forward and swept the papers off her bed, as if their very presence there would foul it.

'Tell her, Erika,' Herr Nordern said. 'You tell her.'

'Omi,' Erika could hardly speak. 'These papers, they are about,' she tried to say Karl but the word stuck in her throat like a bone. 'They are about . . . him. Truly they are.'

'No.' Omi's head was shaking. 'Not my Karl. Not my brother. No Bromberg would ever . . . ever. . . .'

And then Herr Nordern spoke again and, strangely, his voice was calm and quiet. 'Of course, of course. But Omi, Karl did give you these, didn't he?'

Even more strangely, Omi's head stopped its convulsive shaking, as if the matter-of-fact question was calming. 'Yes.'

'And,' Herr Nordern picked his words. 'And Omi, could you tell me when Karl gave them to you, please?'

'Of course.' Omi spoke with frigid politeness and frowned in concentration. 'It was when Karl took me out to tea.'

'To tea!' Herr Nordern left the room, one hand out-stretched like a blind man.

As he left, Omi looked at Erika. 'They are not about Karl, you know,' she spoke in a calm, rational way. 'He was in the Brandenburg Regiment. How could anyone think that he would be associated with those unspeakable scum of the S.S.? Karl, a von Bromberg!' Her voice strengthened as if other ghosts, other spirits, raised from a different and more noble past, were at her shoulder and giving her comfort with their ancestral voices.

'But Omi. *Those*—' Erika gestured at the documents and broke into wracking sobs. And, had it been possible by doing so to obliterate them and what they represented, she would gladly have given her young life, yes, laid it down with all its promise and hope, and counted the sacrifice worthwhile.

She looked up. Her father, haggard and seeming to have aged twenty years, was in the doorway.

'When you went to tea with him,' he said. 'Do you know what date that was? I've looked it up in my diary.' He stumbled into the room. 'That was the day we heard Steinmark had been killed in Dresden, and *he* was in Dresden, too, and Steinmark was working in the State Archives. . . .'

He swung his head slowly, like a caged bear, a creature trapped in a strange and horrifyingly new universe. 'I don't know what to do. It's a . . . a. . . .' He pawed the air as if searching for a solution to the insoluble. 'What *can* I do?'

It was a rhetorical question, but Erika, her world in ruins, still found an answer. 'Get Uncle Bodo,' she said.

'Bodo!' Herr Nordern raised his head like a bear scenting freedom. 'Yes! What time is it?' He looked at his watch. 'He might be in watching the football.'

He lunged into the sitting-room and grabbed the telephone. Erika crossed her fingers. 'Let him be in,' she willed. 'Let him be in. Let someone else come and share the burden.'

Herr Nordern spoke. 'Bodo? Thank Christ I've got you. Get here at once. No! Now! *Scheiss* on the football. Yes! A real emergency.'

The phone clacked down and Herr Nordern came back into the bedroom, a drink in his hand. 'He's coming,' he said. 'I can't believe this is happening. I just can't.' His voice rose to a bellow. 'What have we done to deserve this? Christ Almighty!'

There was no answer to that and so they sat in silence, waiting, as snow drifted from an ominous sky, and the death's head grinned malevolently at them.

Five, ten minutes passed, interminably, and then the front door opened. Herr Nordern and Erika went back into the sitting-room as Bodo, big, tough, and annoyed, barged in. ''Lo, Erika,' he said. 'All right, Hans, what's the panic?'

Herr Nordern lurched forward. 'Thank God you're here.'

'O.K.' Bodo shrugged. 'What's going on?'

'A moment.' Herr Nordern gave Bodo a huge glass of schnapps. 'Sit down and have a drink.'

Bodo looked thoughtfully at his brother for a moment. 'Right,' he said. 'Sit down, drink.' He did both and lighted a cigarette. 'Now what?'

'Now this.' Herr Nordern handed over the documents.

Bodo put down his glass, placed his cigarette carefully on an ashtray. 'Not another accident is it?' he asked, and then he looked at the documents and his face changed. 'Holy Jesus,' he said. 'Holy suffering Jesus! Where did these come from?'

'Karl.' Herr Nordern poured himself another drink. 'He gave them to Omi and Erika found them, just now.'

Bodo was staring at the documents, transfixed. 'I don't get it,' he said. 'This stuff—it's dynamite. These other names . . . why the hell did he give them to Omi?'

'Oh, you don't know.' Herr Nordern wiped sweat from his face. 'She's going across, tomorrow.'

'To the West?'

'Yes. He gave her an envelope and said they were family papers. You know, they never really bother with old people, so she'd take them out and he'd pick them up over there.'

'Right.' Bodo's face darkened. 'Where's Omi now?'

'In her room.'

'Huh.' Bodo grunted. 'Erika, better go and sit with her.'

Erika left the room obediently and as the bedroom door closed behind her Bodo exploded with rage.

'The bastard. The dirty, filthy, stinking bastard.' He breathed through his mouth, his chest heaving, and his face like granite.

'But that's not all,' Herr Nordern said.

'No?'

'No.' Herr Nordern filled Bodo's glass, and his own. 'I think I know where he got these.'

'Yeah?'

'Yes.' Herr Nordern leaned forward. 'You remember Steinmark? The man from my office. He was killed in Dresden.'

'You mentioned him,' Bodo said. 'Hit by a train wasn't he?'

'Well,' Herr Nordern hesitated as if what he was about to say was so preposterous it would be unbelievable. 'Steinmark was working in the State Archive. There's tons of stuff there that no one has ever looked at.'

'I'm with you.' Bodo dragged savagely on his cigarette. 'He nicked the documents, gave them to Karl, then Karl bumped him off.'

'Yes,' Herr Nordern said. 'But what do we do? For Christ's sake what do we do?'

Bodo was silent for a moment. 'Who knows about this stuff?' he asked.

'Just us,' Herr Nordern said. 'And Karl of course.'

'No one else? The authorities?'

Herr Nordern jumped. 'I don't see how they can know. Steinmark must have come across the stuff by accident.'

Bodo lighted another cigarette. 'How did Steinmark and Karl get in touch?'

'I've thought about that,' Herr Nordern said. 'Steinmark was at the Archive last spring, then he went to Bonn on a trade mission. He must have met Karl, or some other Nazi, then.'

'Sounds likely,' Bodo said. 'So, there's just us and Karl—and he isn't going to squawk. O.K. We burn them.'

312

'Burn them!' Herr Nordern was horrified. 'Bodo, they're State documents.'

Bodo gave his brother a profoundly sceptical look. 'Hans,' he said, patiently, 'if the State gets its hands on these, what do you think will happen?'

Herr Nordern shook his head. 'I don't follow you.'

Bodo sighed. 'I thought that you had more sense. Listen, you'd be finished. Think about it, your mother-in-law hiding State documents, colluding with a war criminal, Karl wandering about the country bumping people off, and doing Christ knows what else—'

'But that's nothing to do with me,' Herr Nordern cried. 'I've done nothing at all. You can see that.'

'Keep your voice down,' Bodo said. 'Listen, I know you're innocent, and you know you're innocent, but that's not how the cops will look at it and it will be the Secret Police—yes,' he emphasised the point as Herr Nordern groaned. 'At the least you'll be under suspicion for the rest of your life. You'll be kicked out of the Ministry, Jesus, you'll be lucky to get a job sweeping the roads. And then there's Erika.'

'Erika!'

'Yes, sorry. But no sports school for her. And Helga—' Bodo jerked his thumb.

Like a burst balloon Herr Nordern seemed to shrink internally. 'What a disaster. God above, what a disaster.'

'Pull yourself together,' Bodo said. 'We can work something out.'

'Can we?' Herr Nordern clutched at the straw.

'Sure.' Bodo was reassuring in his hard, matter-of-fact way. 'Nobody's going to tell, are they? We won't, Omi won't, that bleeder Karl won't, and Erika's got her head screwed on, right?'

'She has.' Herr Nordern agreed. 'But then there's Helga.'

Bodo nodded. 'She'll have to know. It's a pity but there it is.'

'And Paul—'

'No.' Bodo was absolutely firm. 'You've got to keep him out of it. He's too young to keep his mouth shut.' He paused. 'Where are they anyway?'

'Seeing Cousin Hetta off.'

'And what time will they be back?'

'About 5.00.'

'Paul too?'

'Yes.'

'Well don't worry about that. I'll get rid of him. What time is Karl coming?'

'He said early evening. He's crossing over tonight.'

'He's taking a chance,' Bodo said. 'Leaving those behind.'

'Not leaving them with Omi,' Herr Nordern said.

'I suppose you're right.' Bodo leaned back and drank. 'Take it easy Hans. We'll get it sorted out.'

'We will?' Herr Nordern snatched at the assurance, and at the bottle.

'Absolutely. But leave that bottle alone, you're going to need a clear head.'

'Quite right,' Herr Nordern muttered. 'Thank God you're here, Bodo.'

'Nothing to it,' Bodo said. 'You're my brother, aren't you? We'll see it through.' He managed a chipped grin. 'I might even get a good mark with Helga.'

Herr Nordern tried to grin, too, but failed miserably. 'Are you going to burn the papers now?'

'No.' Bodo shook his head. 'I'm going to wait until Karl gets here and stuff them down the bastard's throat.'

'I'd like to kill him,' Herr Nordern said. 'I'd like to tear him apart with my bare hands. I'd like to—'

But whatever else Herr Nordern would have liked to have done to Karl was never said because the telephone rang.

Herr Nordern stared at the phone as if it were a venomous snake, as it rang, and rang again, and again. He reached out a trembling hand but Bodo held him back.

'I'll take it,' he said, a tightness in his voice showing that beneath his tough, casual manner he was as tense as his brother. But when he picked up the phone he sounded as calm as ever.

'Nordern,' he said.

There was silence, a sinister silence, as if, at the other end of the line, someone was considering very carefully whether or not to speak. But then Karl's voice came through.

'Hans? Is that Hans Nordern?'

'No. Is that Karl?' Bodo sounded cheery. 'It's Bodo here. Hans is in bed—sleeping it off.' He laughed. 'After last night you know. Do you want me to get him?'

There was another long, guarded pause and then Karl said, 'No, that isn't necessary. I'm just ringing to confirm about my calling round. Is Helga there?'

'She's out,' Bodo said. 'But she'll be back by 5.00.'

'I see.' There was another pause, then, 'Bodo, is my sister there?'

'Yes,' Bodo said. 'But she's sleeping, too. She's a bit worn out after yesterday.' Amazingly, he laughed convincingly. 'Everyone's a bit hung-over you know.'

Karl laughed back, a knowing man-to-man laugh. 'I understand. But Bodo—' his voice was concerned. 'She's all right I hope, my sister?'

'Oh fine.' Bodo was easy and unconcerned. 'She was saying how much she enjoyed the do.'

'Excellent.' There was another long pause and then Karl said, 'Er, Bodo, my dear fellow, perhaps you can tell me. Has my sister said anything about a journey?'

'A journey?' Bodo sounded a little puzzled for a moment, then he clicked his tongue. 'Oh, about going to the West and staying with you? Yes, she told us at lunch.'

'I see.' Karl's voice became confidential. 'Bodo, I trust that you won't mind my asking this but . . . but how have the family taken it?'

'No problem,' Bodo said heartily. ''Course it was a bit of a shock and Helga was taken aback—you know how she is. But when Omi explained about it everything was fine. It's a good idea. I think so anyway.' He laughed again. 'I wouldn't mind going with her.'

'And how nice that would be.' Karl was suave.

'Too true,' Bodo said with feeling. 'Do you want me to get her?'

'No. No, don't disturb her.' Karl sounded quite different, brisker, as if the scent of danger had drifted away. 'I'll see her later. Will you be there?'

'No, sorry,' Bodo said. 'I've got to go. A little deal to fix up—you understand.'

'I do indeed.' Karl chuckled. 'Business before pleasure hey? I thought the moment I saw you that you were a business man. So, just tell the family that I shall call and say goodbye, my dear fellow. A pleasure meeting you and I trust that we shall meet again—and perhaps do a little business, hey?'

'My language,' Bodo said. 'And a pleasure meeting you, Karl. We'll meet again some day. *Auf Wiedersehen*. Good luck.'

He put the receiver down and turned to Herr Nordern. 'Got the bastard,' he said.

Chapter 27

IN THE bedroom Erika had been listening to the men's voices, but most of what they had said had been in a mumble. Whether Omi had heard, or understood, it was impossible to tell. She sat in her chair, rigid, and staring into what vistas only she could say.

Erika had tried to speak to Omi but she might as well have spoken to a waxwork dummy and so she sat on her bed, her face tight with the stains of tears, and round and round her mind went the thought that not only was Karl a mass murderer but that he had come into the flat, shared their food and drink, laughed and joked with them, and all merely to use them for his own vicious purposes.

The minutes ticked by, each seeming an hour, the men mumbled, the telephone rang and then, to her unutterable relief, Bodo called her.

'I shan't be a minute, Omi,' she whispered. 'I'll only be next door. You just sit there and. . . .' She patted Omi's unyielding back, raised a helpless hand, and went into the sitting-room.

Bodo was sitting drinking schnapps and her father, white faced and dishevelled, was slumped in his chair, smoking furiously.

'How is she?' Herr Nordern asked.

'I don't know,' Erika said. 'She's just sitting there. She won't talk or . . . or anything.'

The tears welled up in her eyes again and her father put his arms around her. 'Don't cry, *Liebchen*. Everything is going to be all right, isn't it, Bodo?'

'Sure it is,' Bodo drawled in his deep voice. 'And don't worry about Omi. It's shock, people react like that. Hans, make some coffee. Erika, you wash your face, you'll feel a lot better, then come and sit with me, I want to talk to you.'

Herr Nordern clattered clumsily in the kitchen as Erika went to the bathroom and washed, and it was true, she did feel refreshed.

'That's better, kid,' Bodo said. 'You look more like yourself.' He winked, and the wink, too, made Erika feel better.

'Now listen,' Bodo leaned forward and took Erika's slender hands in his scarred fists. 'Just look at me and listen. Good, that's the way. Now this is bad-news day, all right, but we can cope. Don't worry about that. But you have to keep your mouth shut. Never a word to anyone as long as you live. *Never.* Got that? Your mother will have to know, but Paul must *never, never,* hear about it—or anyone else. Got that?'

'Yes,' Erika nodded, reassured by Bodo's massive presence. 'But Omi . . . ?'

'Yeah, Omi.' Bodo lowered his voice to a gravelly whisper. 'She won't be going on her trip. You understand that?'

'Yes,' Erika whispered back. 'Of course.'

'And Erika,' Bodo's voice grew more urgent. 'You and Omi, you've always been close. Now, a lot's going to depend on you. She's going to need help and plenty of it, and you're the one she's going to turn to. Yes, she is, believe me. Right now she's shattered, but she'll need propping up and you'll be the prop. And you've got to help make sure she doesn't talk about this, otherwise we're all up the spout. Can you do that?'

Bodo's grip tightened and Erika nodded. 'I'll try,' she said.

'I know you will, kid. You can do it.' Bodo relaxed his grip as Herr Nordern brought in the coffee.

'Take one to Omi,' Bodo said to Erika. 'Plenty of sugar.'

'Yes.' Erika hesitated. 'But what about the documents?'

'We're going to burn them,' Bodo said.

'And Karl?'

Bodo spread his hands. 'He goes.'

'You mean he goes free?'

'Yes. Free as a bird.'

'But he's a war criminal.'

'Right,' Bodo said.

'A murderer.'

'A murderer. Yes.'

'He gassed people. He gassed children.'

'He did.'

'And tortured people.'

'I guess so.'

'And you say that he's to go. . . to go free?'

'Yes.'

'No!'

'Hey.' Bodo frowned. 'Now Erika—'

'No!' Erika shook her head violently. 'He can't go free. He can't.'

Bodo heaved himself up and took Erika by the shoulder. 'Erika, I'd like to chuck him off the T.V. Tower, but there's nothing we can do. What do you think would happen if we turned him in?'

'He'd get the punishment he deserves,' Erika said.

'Sure.' Bodo's voice was bleak. 'And do you think they'd give us medals?' He stared at Erika's stubborn face. 'We'd be in the clink in ten minutes, all of us. And what would happen to Omi? Think about that. A 'von'—an old *Junker*. What would the cops make of that? Tell her, Hans.'

'It's true.' Herr Nordern sounded like a broken man. 'We just have to settle for—'

'For getting out of this with our hides still on,' Bodo said.

'So,' Erika spoke slowly. 'So the innocent suffer and the guilty go free.'

'That's the way it is, Erika,' Bodo said. 'It's a cruel world at times.'

'Cruel,' Erika said. 'I see.'

'I know,' Bodo said. 'It's hard to take but that's it. Now take Omi some coffee, hey.'

Omi would not touch the coffee. 'Please,' Erika begged. 'Take it, you must have something. For me.'

Omi, her head still averted, took the cup and had a token sip, but no more.

'Omi,' Erika went on her knees. 'Omi, you said, not long ago you said that you would never do anything to harm me. You *said* it.'

Omi stared down, her face a cold mask. 'I did.'

'But can't you see!' Erika gripped Omi's skirt. 'Can't you see what you've done?'

'I have done nothing,' Omi said. 'Nothing at all. Now leave me. Go.'

Of all the blows she had endured that day, the cold dismissal hurt Erika most of all and she took her hidden wound into the sitting-room where, with Bodo and her father, she sat, like them, in silence; each locked inside their horrified thoughts until, as darkness crept in, there was a scuffle at the door.

Bodo jumped up. 'I'll get it. I put the latch on. You stay put.'

He opened the front door where Frau Nordern was fumbling with the key. 'Bodo!' Frau Nordern was mildly exasperated. 'Who left the latch down? And what are you doing here?'

'Just visiting.' Bodo stood aside to let her in but blocked Paul off. 'Paul,' he jerked his head and with a jog of his shoulder brushed Paul on to the landing, closing the door behind himself.

'Listen Paul,' he said, confidentially. 'Will you do me a favour?'

'Sure!' Paul was ready to do Bodo a million favours.

'O.K.' Bodo pulled out his keys. 'I know this is a lot to ask but will you go to my flat?'

'Course,' Paul said. 'What do you want?'

Bodo beckoned Paul to the head of the stairs, away from the doors of the flats. 'It's like this.' He looked over his shoulder melodramatically. 'I've got a business deal on, see.'

'A deal, right.' Paul rather tactlessly left out the 'business'.

'Yes,' Bodo said. 'Now a man is going to call round at my place. He's called Teller, Johann Teller. Got that?'

'Teller,' Paul nodded vigorously.

'O.K. Well you go to my flat and when Teller comes tell him to ring me here. You'll do that?'

'Sure, I'll do that Uncle Bodo. Trust me. Keller.'

'*Teller*,' Bodo said.

'Yes, Teller.' Paul made to get around Bodo's bulk.

'Where are you going?' Bodo asked.

'In there!' Paul pointed to the flat.

320

Bodo shook his head. 'No, no. I want you to get to my place right away.'

'But I've only just got here,' Paul protested. 'And I want to see Uncle Karl.'

'I know that.' Bodo sounded reasonable. 'But that's the problem. I've got to see him too.' He bent down and whispered in Paul's ear. 'It's part of the deal, see?' He rubbed his fingers suggestively and Paul's eyes widened. 'Me, Karl, and Teller.'

'Wow!' Paul was excited. 'Uncle Karl!'

'That's right,' Bodo whispered. 'But it's a secret. So you get off and I'll fix up with Karl to meet you in the Palast before he leaves.' He looked at his watch. 'But you'll have to go now.'

'Well. . . .' Paul hesitated.

'Go on.' Bodo gave Paul a gentle push. 'Here—' he shoved a wad of money in Paul's hand. 'Get yourself some Cola. Help yourself to anything in the flat.' He steadily ushered Paul down the stairs. 'And don't forget, the man's called Teller and don't tell anyone else where I am. No one.'

'No one,' Paul said as he leaped down the stairs, a landing at a time.

'I'll pick you up later,' Bodo called as he watched Paul off the premises. Then he went back into the flat.

One glance told him what he had to know. Frau Nordern was sitting on the settee, distraught, clutching the documents.

'Sorry Helga,' Bodo said.

Frau Nordern stared at him with eyes dilated by shock. 'Sorry?' she said. 'Sorry? Is that what you have to say with . . . with these in the flat?'

Her voice had begun to rise unnervingly and Herr Nordern, himself looking shell-shocked, moved next to her and took her hand.

'It will be all right, Helga. We're going to fix things, aren't we Bodo?'

'Sure,' Bodo said, hoping his voice would carry enough conviction to calm Frau Nordern down. 'It will all be over in an hour.'

'That can't be true,' Frau Nordern said tonelessly. 'It will never be over.'

'Yes it will.' Herr Nordern put his arm around his wife's

321

shoulders as Bodo made a covert gesture to Erika who took the hint and went back into her bedroom.

'Where is she going?' Frau Nordern asked.

'Just in the bedroom,' Herr Nordern said. 'Now don't fret yourself. We'll burn these papers and then it will be done.'

'Done?' Frau Nordern said in the same toneless voice. 'Burn the past. Can you do that?'

Herr Nordern moved uneasily. 'No. No, Helga, we can't do that. But we've got to think of *now*, and the future.'

'We have no future,' Frau Nordern said.

''Course you have, Helga.' Bodo leaned against the wall. 'And plenty of it.'

'No,' Frau Nordern stared blankly at the bamboos. 'Whatever happens it's ruined. I'll never be able to trust anyone again as long as I live.'

'You mustn't think like that, Helga,' Herr Nordern said. 'Must she?' He appealed to Bodo.

'No, 'course not,' said Bodo, but without conviction since he hardly trusted anyone, anyway.

'There, you see.' Herr Nordern patted his wife. 'There—' as the doorbell rang.

Herr Nordern held his breath and looked at Bodo who nodded. 'I'll get it,' Bodo said with an air of deep satisfaction. 'Just sit tight.'

He went into the tiny vestibule. The Norderns heard the front door open and Bodo say, easily, 'Hello Karl. Yeah, I managed to stay after all. Come in.'

The front door clicked shut and then Bodo said, 'Yes, come in you ill-gotten git.' There was a thud and, in his immaculate overcoat and gloves, and clutching a bouquet, Uncle Karl came flying into the room, crashed against the table and, his dazzling teeth spewing from his mouth, sprawled on the floor, his pink, plump face, without teeth, transformed. Shrunken and mummified.

Sitting in a frozen silence with Omi, Erika heard the crash. She opened her door. Bodo, looking genuinely terrifying, was standing in the middle of the room while at his feet, on all fours, like a toothless dog, was Karl.

Like a dog, too, Uncle Karl shook his head. 'So,' he mumbled. 'You know.'

322

'Know? You bastard.' Bodo rasped the words out and took a step forward, his fist raised.

'Bodo!' Herr Nordern jumped up and held his brother. 'Don't. You'll kill him.'

'Not kill him,' Bodo said. 'But I'm going to beat the living daylights out of him.'

On his hands and knees, Karl backed away, cramming his teeth back into his mouth and baring them in a snarl, his eyes no longer twinkling but set in a baleful glare. It was an eerie change; like a man turning into a werewolf, the façade of humanity cracking and revealing the beast within.

'I wouldn't advise that,' he said, and his voice had changed too. It was not the jolly voice which suggested that life was a good-natured affair with a joke around every corner. It was contemptuous. The voice of a superior talking to a despised and despicable underling. The voice of the Superman talking to the *Untermenschen*, the sub-humans: the authentic voice of the death camp.

'No.' Karl climbed to his feet. 'No more violence. I have a driver with me.'

'I'll drive you into the ground,' Bodo said.

Karl spared him a reptilian glance. 'I think not,' he said. 'It wouldn't be wise.' With hideous composure he brushed his sleeve and took out his gold cigar case. 'This is most unfortunate,' he said.

'Unfor—' Herr Nordern said in a strangled voice. 'Is that how you put it?'

'Why yes,' Karl selected a cigar with care. 'It really is a pity—I see those—' he gestured at the documents. 'If you hadn't found them . . . ' he raised his eyebrows as if to suggest that an unpleasant but minor incident would have been avoided. 'However, as they have been found, I suggest—'

But he was cut off by Frau Nordern who stepped towards him. 'You,' she said. 'You unspeakable . . . how could you? You came here smirking and grinning and *fouled* us. Us, your own family. And those—' she pointed to the documents. 'What you did.' She suddenly gagged, clapped her hand to her mouth and staggered to the bathroom.

'Mother!' Erika darted after her and found her on her knees, vomiting into the lavatory.

Erika took a flannel and mopped her mother's face. 'It's all right, Mother,' she said, although she knew that it was not all right at all.

In the sitting-room the sound of Frau Nordern being sick could be clearly heard. 'You hear that?' Herr Nordern said. 'You hear my wife?' He cracked Karl across the face open-handed.

Karl took the blow, his face a mask of hatred, and moved behind the settee. 'I would not do that,' he said. 'One more blow and—'

'And what?' Herr Nordern's voice was thick with rage. 'And what, you scum?'

Karl held a hand to his cheek. 'Bruises might be difficult to explain at the check-point, might they not?'

Herr Nordern, his hand raised for another blow, hesitated and Karl nodded. 'Your excellent brother will agree with me. Will you not?' He addressed Bodo.

'Yes.' Bodo dragged the word out. 'Come here, Hans.' He pulled his brother back.

'Very sensible,' Karl said. 'I always thought that you were a level-headed chap, Bodo. Of course, it's obvious that you don't have any silly ideas about informing the Police. No. I admit that if you did the consequences would be most unpleasant for me, but then they would be unpleasant for you, too, would they not?'

'What makes you think that?' Bodo said. It was a bluff and Karl knew. He merely smiled thinly and waved his hand as if the point were not worth discussing.

Frau Nordern and Erika came from the bathroom. Her face wet, Frau Nordern sat on the settee. Karl looked at her dispassionately. 'I would give her brandy,' he said. 'Most restorative.'

He sat down, too, leaned back, crossed his legs, swinging a gleaming shoe, and lighted his cigar, looking as if he were the absolute master of the situation, which indeed he was. And, maddeningly, Herr Nordern knew that the advice was sensible and that he ought to act on it, and he did. He poured out a brandy for Frau Nordern, and himself, and for Bodo.

'And I'll have one,' Karl said.

'You get nothing in this house,' Herr Nordern said.

'Oh, I think I shall. I really do.' Perfectly composed Karl blew a smoke ring and watched it float to the ceiling. 'Shan't I, Bodo?'

Bodo took a huge breath. 'Give him one, Hans.'

Herr Nordern poured out a brandy. 'I wish it was poison,' he said.

'No doubt.' Karl sipped his drink, rolling it around his tongue as he savoured it. 'But, melodrama apart, we have a little dilemma, do we not?'

'No dilemma,' Bodo said. 'None at all.' He jabbed his blunt forefinger at the documents. 'Those are being burned and you're clearing out tonight. Oh, and Omi isn't going over. Get that through your head.'

'Is she not?' Karl sounded politely regretful. 'Where is she now, by the way?'

'In her bedroom,' Herr Nordern said. 'But you're not going to see her.'

'A pity.' Karl did not seem unduly concerned. 'By the way, how did you find my papers?'

No one answered and Karl said, 'It's really quite important, how many people know, I mean.'

It was a statement that demanded an answer and, trapped by it, Herr Nordern said, 'Erika.'

'Ah!' Karl gazed at Erika, a long and frightening gaze. 'Well,' he said, 'I'm sure that Erika can keep our secret. Can't you?'

Disregarding the question, Erika stared back at Karl with a horrified fascination. He was, recognisably, the same Uncle Karl who had come into their lives a month ago, recognisably a human being. But how could he have done what he had done? All her life Erika had been taught about the extermination camps, and the S.S. death squads who ran them—but, in the end, they had only been abstracts: unreal figures on old film, names in books. Now she was seeing a war criminal face to face; sitting in her father's chair, smoking a cigar, drinking brandy, for all the world an elderly, kindly, retired and prosperous gentleman, and yet he had strutted in his dramatic uniform with its silver insignia and skull . . . she turned her head aside as Karl repeated the question.

'You can keep our secret, can't you, Erika?'

'Don't speak to her.' Frau Nordern, her face and voice full

of hatred broke the silence. 'Don't dare speak to her, you filth.'

Karl shifted his appalling gaze from Erika to Frau Nordern. 'Very well. But where is Paul? I sincerely hope that he isn't aware of our little problem.'

There was blatant, venomous irony in his voice, but Bodo chose to ignore it. 'He doesn't know,' he said. 'Now get moving.'

'I should like to,' Karl said. 'Believe me there is nothing that I should like more. Just to leave this ghastly country will give me the deepest satisfaction. But I'm afraid that it isn't quite that simple.'

'And why not?' Bodo asked.

Karl peered into his glass, refilled it, swilled the brandy around and then looked up. 'I really must have the documents.'

'Well you're not getting them,' Bodo said. 'That's final.'

'Hmmm,' Karl peered into his glass. 'It can't be. You see, if I arrive in the West without them there will be the most undesirable consequences—for me,' he added, as if the rider would evoke sympathy.

'Good,' Herr Nordern rasped. 'Undesirable consequences. I hope that they set dogs on you.'

'I'm sure you do,' Karl said. 'But you will understand that I don't share your point of view. I'm not a young man but I think that I would prefer to continue living. And in comfort.'

Bodo frowned. 'I don't get it. What's the difference to you?'

'All the world.' Karl sighed. 'The truth is, Bodo, there are people, associates of mine in . . . in various parts of the world, who are simply going to *insist* on having those documents. It's why I was sent here. Really.'

'Well they're not going to get them,' Bodo said. 'No matter what the consequences.'

'Ah,' Karl said. 'I have to disappoint you there. You see, if I don't go back with the documents then I'm not going back at all.'

'I don't understand.' Pallid, unshaven, Herr Nordern leaned forward. 'What is he talking about?'

'Tell him, Bodo,' Karl said, contempt in his voice.

'It's like this, Hans,' Bodo said, quietly. 'If we don't let him have the documents he's going to the cops—here. He reckons that if he goes over without them he'll get bumped off anyway. So he'll drag us down with him.'

'Admirably succinct, Bodo!' Karl sounded genuinely complimentary. 'My word, you have a flair for language. Indeed you do. You ought to think of taking up writing. And of course, it will be very bad for Hans if I do go to your admirable Police.'

'Me? Why me—in particular?' Herr Nordern said.

Karl smiled, a vicious, sadistic twist of his lips. 'Well, Hans, you have worked in the Dresden Archive, haven't you?'

'Yes, but . . . but. . . .'

'He means he'll say you got the documents for him,' Bodo said.

Herr Nordern fumbled with his spectacles. 'But Steinmark got those.' He paused and blinked, comprehension dawning on his face. 'He would lie. Yes, of course. I understand. Unspeakable. Really.'

'Well, unspeakable. . . .' Karl demurred. 'But all our little difficulties can be overcome with a little reason.'

'Reason?' Frau Nordern re-emerged from her stupor. She leaned forward and looked at Karl with a strange penetrating stare. 'Why did you do it?'

Karl sighed. 'Really, I don't think that I need explain more.'

'I don't mean that,' Frau Nordern said. 'I don't mean whatever dirty business you're involved in. I mean what you did. What those documents say. No!' She held up her hand as Karl shrugged. 'I *need* to know. You're a Bromberg, my mother's brother, my uncle. We're from the same family. That's why I need to know. Is it genetic? Can it be inherited? I mean, are we tainted, the Brombergs?'

Karl stared at her coldly. 'Tainted? You don't understand.'

'No I don't,' Frau Nordern said. 'But I need to. For my children's sake.'

Karl gave her his dehumanized, baleful glare. 'You talk of genetics. So. We were *purifying* genetics. Cleansing the gutters of Europe of filth, of human ordure. Germany before the War, it was infested, like a noble creature with lice: Slavs, gipsies and Jews, you saw them at every street corner. Here in

Berlin, in the capital of the Reich, they were everywhere, in the Stock Exchange, in business, in the slums—'

'In the universities,' Herr Nordern said. 'In the hospitals, in the concert halls. Great thinkers, musicians, artists.'

'Yes, yes.' Karl snapped like a dog. 'Einstein, and the rest of the scum. All Jews, traitors to the Reich and German blood. We were well rid of them. All of them.'

'And you helped to get rid of them,' Frau Nordern said.

'Yes!' Karl tilted his chin. 'What a work that was. Do you realise what it cost me, a von Bromberg, to mix with that human filth? Only a great belief could have made me undergo it. A great belief and a great leader.'

'You mean Hitler,' Bodo said.

'Yes.' Karl's eyes glowed as if the fires of hell were burning behind them. 'The *Führer*. The greatest genius mankind has ever known. The saviour of Germany.'

'Saviour?' Bodo spoke, but not vehemently, rather as if he were querying some minor point. 'Didn't we lose millions of dead?'

'A worthy sacrifice,' Karl said. 'What is life for if not to lay it down at the foot of a hero?'

'I see. But wasn't there the little matter of the cities?' Bodo said in the same reasonable way. 'Every one destroyed.'

'What are cities?' Karl said. 'Sticks and stones. Nothing.'

'Nothing,' Bodo said. 'And the people under the sticks and stones, the women and children. The civilians.'

'There are no civilians,' Karl said.

'And the socialists?'

'Traitors. Jews, all of them.'

'And the communists?'

'All Jews.'

'And the mentally ill?'

'Unfit to live.'

'And the trades unionists?'

'Enemies of the State.'

'And the clergy?'

'Weaklings.' Karl was contemptuous. 'Prattling about mercy and humility and their slave religion.'

Bodo folded his arms. 'I understand. And all murdered.'

'Executed,' Karl insisted. 'The purification of the race, wiping out a plague.'

'Hmmm,' Bodo was thoughtful. 'All that and we lost the War.'

'We were betrayed!' Karl's voice rose. 'Betrayed by Jews and communists. The great international conspiracy of Jews. Churchill and Roosevelt and Stalin.'

'I didn't know that they were Jews,' Bodo said.

'Pawns in the conspiracy,' Karl said. 'Manipulated by Jewish finance, by Jews whose dream was to destroy German purity. But the cause lives on.'

'Not here, it doesn't,' Bodo said.

Erika looked at Bodo with surprise. They were the first words she had ever heard him say which sounded remotely like support for the G.D.R., but one glance at his rock-hard face showed that he meant it.

'I said not here it doesn't, ' Bodo repeated. 'Whatever else is wrong, here we stamped out vermin like you.'

'Did you?' Karl smiled a vicious, self-satisfied smile. 'I would look at the background of some of your leaders, Bodo. But as you wish. However—' he looked at his watch. 'Fascinating as this conversation is I'm afraid that I must leave you.'

'Get out,' Frau Nordern spat.

'Yes, get out,' Herr Nordern said.

'Unanimous.' Bodo handed the documents to Karl but, astonishingly, Karl shook his head.

'No, no,' he said. 'I'm afraid that my original plan is still operative.'

Bodo cocked his head. 'What plan is that?'

'I mean,' Karl spoke slowly and distinctly. 'I mean that my dear sister will be taking the papers with her tomorrow.'

There was an incredulous silence, so profound that the tick of Bodo's watch was audible, then Herr Nordern said, 'Do you really think that we will let Omi. . . .'

'Oh yes.' Karl was unnervingly sure of himself. 'It is essential.'

Frau Nordern suddenly laughed, although it didn't sound like a laugh. 'You're insane,' she said. 'A lunatic.'

'We shall have to agree to differ about that,' Karl said.

'But you think—' Bodo pulled up a chair and sat close to Karl, peering into his face, as if searching for the answer to a riddle. 'You *believe* that we will let Omi take those papers out for you?'

'I do,' Karl said. 'I really do. You see, Bodo, there is the matter of the check-point. It's true that I'm a guest of the Government and it is unlikely that I shall be searched, but one never knows. And if those documents were found on me it would have the most painful consequences for *us*, all of us—but I have explained that. My sister, however, well, who will give her a second glance? An old woman, all her papers in order, a perfectly legitimate reason for crossing, her son-in-law a respected official. And at Friedrichstrasse—all those old people, dozens of them, going over every day. It will be perfectly all right, I do assure you.'

He sat back, swinging his polished shoe, exuding confidence and prosperity.

'Insane,' Frau Nordern whispered. 'Do you really think that Omi will take them?'

'I'm quite sure that she will,' Karl said.

'What makes you so sure?' Herr Nordern said, wonderingly.

'Because she is my sister,' Karl said. 'Because she is a von Bromberg, and she has given her word.'

'I don't care who she is,' Herr Nordern said. 'She isn't going anywhere.'

But Karl was not looking at him, he had risen to his feet and was bowing to Omi who had come from her room.

'Sister,' Karl said.

'Brother.' Omi bowed her head.

'They say that you won't join me,' Karl said.

'They?' Omi looked around the room, her mouth set and, Erika suddenly realised, looking very like Karl. 'Then they are wrong.'

'No!' Frau Nordern held up her hands but Omi ignored her.

'I am going,' she said. 'And I will.'

'But he wants you to take the documents!' Frau Nordern cried.

'I *am* taking them,' Omi said.

'No!' Frau Nordern covered her face with her hands as if to blot out what was happening.

Herr Nordern took up the plea. 'Omi', he said. 'I *beg* you to listen. The documents—they prove that he . . . ' he was unable to bring himself to say Karl's name, 'he—'

'Family documents,' Omi said in her frozen voice.

'For Christ's sake!' Herr Nordern shouted. 'Look at them. Use your eyes!'

'Do not take the name of the Lord in vain,' Omi said. 'And I do not need to look at the papers. They are what my brother has said they are. Do you think he would lie to me?'

Herr Nordern groaned from the bottom of his heart. 'Bodo.' He appealed to his brother.

Bodo shrugged helplessly but tried. 'Omi—' he began.

'Frau von Ritter,' Omi said.

Bodo raised his head and looked at the ceiling and his lips moved in a silent curse, but when he spoke again he was quiet and respectful. 'Of course, *gnädige* Frau.' He used the honorific prefix. 'Gnädige Frau, those . . . those family papers. It is illegal to take them out. They are the property of the State.'

'The State!' Omi was contemptuous.

'It's our State,' Herr Nordern said.

'Yours. Not mine,' Omi said.

'All right.' Herr Nordern struggled to keep his self-control. 'But at least it's your home.'

'Is it?' Omi swung her fine head around. '*Your* State gave *my* home away. The home we were brought up in, generations of us. And now what is it— full of Poles.'

'Jews,' Karl ejected his venom into the sitting-room.

'All gone,' Omi said. 'All we had, all we owned. And here we are in this.' She waved contemptuously. 'Serfs. Spied upon, unable to travel unless our masters allow us, and the Wall—that obscenity!'

'Hitler built that Wall,' Herr Nordern said.

'The Russians built it,' Omi said. 'The scum of the earth.'

'You mustn't say that,' Herr Nordern said. 'The Russians are our allies, helping us to build a new future.'

'Future?' Karl gave his hyena-like laugh.

'Yes!' Herr Nordern rounded on Karl, his face contorted with rage. 'A decent future for ordinary human beings. But scum like you wouldn't understand that.'

'Scum!' Omi stepped forward. 'You dare call a Bromberg scum? You! A clerk! You call the Brombergs scum and the Russians Friends?'

Too late Herr Nordern tried to take his words back. 'I didn't mean it that way, Omi. Really I didn't.'

'Did you not?' Omi's face was flushed and her unnatural, icy control was visibly disintegrating. 'The Russians—' Horribly, little bubbles of spittle appeared at the corners of her mouth. 'What did the Russians do to us?'

'It was the War,' Herr Nordern cried. 'The War, Omi. Hitler's war.'

'And the peace?' The spittle flew into Herr Nordern's face. 'What happened then? After the War, when they came into East Prussia, those animals, beasts, pigs—'

'Omi,' Erika tried to take her grandmother's arm but was shaken off.

'Pigs! swine!' Omi rocked to and fro. 'Do you know what they did? Do you know what they did to the women? Do you know what they did to me?'

Chapter 28

HERR NORDERN lurched backwards as if struck, Frau Nordern clapped her hands on her ears and rocked sideways in a kind of agony, and Erika closed her eyes.

'Dear God,' she thought. Another horror in a day of horrors, and one to make the others seem almost negligible.

'No! No! No!' Frau Nordern wailed. 'It isn't true. It can't be. Say it isn't so.'

Omi stared at her daughter as if she were a stranger. 'Why do you think that you were left untouched?' she said.

'So.' Omi looked at Karl and bowed again. 'I apologise,' she said. 'I did think of killing myself but I had Helga to care for.'

Karl took two tiny steps forward, bowed in return and clicked his heels, not in his usual half-conscious manner, but sharply, with the authoritative *click* of the German Army.

'You do our family, our country, and our race honour, Sister.' He kissed Omi's hands and gave her the documents. 'Keep these safe.'

'On my life,' Omi said.

'And I will meet you tomorrow, in Germany. Our Germany.'

'Ours. Yes. And now I say good-night.'

Omi walked into her bedroom and the door closed behind her. Karl turned and looked at the appalled Norderns, appalled except for Bodo who did not seem too concerned.

'Your Friends,' Karl said acidly. '*Untermenschen.*' He walked to the window. 'Excuse me,' he said, with a ghastly parody of good manners. He opened the window and called into the street and a harsh voice answered.

Karl flashed his vulpine smile. 'My driver. He is coming up to meet me.' He addressed Bodo. 'To help me down the stairs, you know. We don't want an unfortunate accident, do we? You know, elderly gentleman, has a drink or two, falls downstairs and breaks his neck.' He snapped his fingers with a certain relish. 'It would be a most undignified end.'

There was a heavy rap at the door and Karl picked up his hat. 'Time to go but . . . ' he looked around contemptuously. 'I should say that if my sister does not arrive tomorrow with the documents you will be sorry. I have planted one or two time bombs which will certainly explode if anything goes wrong.'

'Time bombs?' Bodo said.

'Photostats.' Karl grinned without mirth. 'They would not satisfy my associates but your Police would appreciate them.'

'Very thorough,' Bodo said.

'Yes, of course.'

'Everything foreseen and provided for.'

'Quite. A good German training. So. I doubt if we shall ever meet again, but who knows?' Karl walked to the door and gave a last glance at the family. 'Heil Hitler!' he mocked, raised his hand in a foul salute, and then Uncle Karl was gone, four weeks almost to the minute since he had arrived.

In the street a car door was slammed, an engine purred smoothly, a car drove away, and in the flat the telephone rang again.

No one moved to answer it until Bodo said, 'Might as well.'

He took the phone, listened, and made a reassuring gesture. 'Yes,' he said. 'Yes, everything's fine. O.K. No, stay there, I'll be over right away.'

'Paul,' he said. 'I'd better go over. I'll keep him with me tonight but I'll have to bring him to Friedrichstrasse tomorrow or he'll smell something fishy. That all right?'

He wasn't answered. The family stayed silent, locked in their misery.

'O.K.' Bodo shrugged into his leather jacket. 'I'll ring you later.'

He stood at the door, for the first time in the years Erika had known him, looking helpless. Then Herr Nordern muttered something.

'What?' Bodo tilted his head. 'Didn't catch that.'

'No!' Herr Nordern shouted. 'No!' He strode to the telephone.

'What do you think you're doing?' Bodo asked.

'The swine's not getting away with it.' Herr Nordern blinked through his spectacles. 'I'm calling the Police.'

Bodo gave a cry of genuine alarm. 'Cut that out.' He barged across the room and clamped his hand over the receiver. 'Don't even think of it.'

The two brothers stood face to face, fury against determination. 'Move away,' Herr Nordern said.

'Nothing doing.' Bodo shook his head. 'Make that call and we'll be inside the nick in an hour—and we won't be coming out.'

'He's not getting away with it.' Herr Nordern's voice cracked with rage.

'Hans.' Bodo placed his hand on his brother's chest. 'He *has* got away with it.'

'No! Wait!' Herr Nordern smacked his fist. 'Got it! We'll burn the papers and then turn him in. . . .'

'Sure,' Bodo said drily. 'Burn the proof. And remember what he said? About leaving a few time bombs behind?'

'Bluff,' Herr Nordern said.

'Maybe,' Bodo said. 'But are you going to stake your life on it?'

'We'll be doing that anyway,' Herr Nordern said. 'If Omi goes.'

'I'm not so sure.' Bodo was thoughtful. 'I think that she'll go through on the nod, like Karl said.'

'You think so?' Beads of sweat trickled down Herr Nordern's neck as he grasped at the idea.

Bodo bit at his thumb. 'I don't see why not. Anyway, it's the best chance we've got.'

Herr Nordern's shoulders slumped. 'All right,' he said, bitter resignation in his voice. 'We'll leave it at that, then. It's a hard thing to swallow, though.'

'It is that.' Bodo lightly patted his brother on the cheek. 'But we'll get through it. So long, Helga, Erika. Just remember—keep your mouths shut.' Then he, too, was gone.

Herr Nordern stared vacantly around the flat as if still looking for Karl or Bodo, then sank on to the settee. 'I can hardly stand. And to think, this time yesterday. . . . Helga, you look shattered. Perhaps if you lay down for a while.' He looked helplessly at Erika.

'Yes, come along, Mother.' Erika was glad to do something, anything, rather than sit with her thoughts. She took her mother's arm. 'Just lie down for a little while. You'll feel better.'

'Better?' Frau Nordern said. 'Better?' But like a child she yielded to Erika's gentle tugging and walked with her into the bedroom.

'There,' Erika helped her mother on to the bed. 'Just lie still.' She pulled the coverlet up. 'Don't cry. Please don't cry. Tomorrow it will all be over.'

'It will never be over,' Frau Nordern said. 'Never.'

She lay unresisting as Erika dabbed her face. 'Try and sleep,' Erika said. 'Just for a while. Close your eyes.'

Frau Nordern did close her eyes and Erika sat with her in the dark bedroom as, to her inexpressible relief, her mother drifted off into an uneasy and restless doze.

Erika tiptoed into the sitting-room where her father was sitting, a glass in his hand. 'She's sleeping,' she said.

'Thank God for that.' Herr Nordern lighted one of his small cigars. 'I've heard of soldiers doing it, falling asleep in the middle of a battle. He'll be through the check-point now, as free as a bird. But I'll get him. Somehow I'll get him. I swear it.'

'Yes, you will.' Erika was as soothing to her father as she had been to her mother.

Herr Nordern shook a baffled head. 'It's endless. Endless. Forty years since the war ended, forty years! And still . . . still. . . . You think that the past is dead and buried but the ghosts come back, and back, and back.' He swigged at his schnapps and brooded over the glass. 'I didn't know about Omi.' He sounded as if he were speaking to himself. 'In all those years I never guessed—no, that's a lie, too. Everyone knew what happened. . . .' His voice died as he stared into the atrocious past. 'I'm sorry, Erika,' he said at last, 'that you heard.'

'It's all right, Father.' Erika's voice was that of a ghost. 'It wasn't your fault.'

'No? That's what we keep telling ourselves,' Herr Nordern said. 'But it happened, when the Russians came in . . . the women . . . it did happen. It was part of our past and we denied it. We haven't told the truth, really. But what else could we do? And now this. . . .' He poured yet another drink, waving away Erika's small gesture of disapproval. 'They'd been through it, the Russians. When you think what happened to their country, and the troops—the Red Army— they'd seen it, and they didn't get leave, you know. Some of them had spent three years in the front line. Not that it excuses—oh God. Oh God Almighty.'

'You should have some food.' Erika stood up, desperate to do something.

'Not for me. And don't wake your mother. You have some though.'

Erika shook her head. 'I'll give Omi something.'

She made hot milk, put cake on a tray, and took it into her room. Omi was sitting bolt upright in the darkness, staring through the window into the night.

'Omi.' Erika touched her shoulder. 'Some food.'

Without turning, Omi shook her head, but Erika persisted. 'Please, you must have something. Have the milk, at least.'

At least Omi did not refuse the milk outright. Erika took a glass and sat on the edge of her bed and, after a little while, Omi reached out for her milk.

'I'm sorry, child.' Her old, thin voice drifted across the room.

'Yes.' Erika could find nothing else to say, and what, indeed, could one say? What words could one possibly find which could ameliorate the anguish, grief, and terror of the day?

Snow fell, the flakes spinning past the window as if so many multitudinous dead souls were peering incuriously into number 13, Klara-Lettkin-Strasse. Down came the snow in a strange, incomprehensible dance, and then Omi spoke again.

'I should not have told. I vowed never to. And yet not telling was a lie, too. It is hard to live with a lie.'

Erika could find nothing to say to that, either. A car went

past, a scooter, a tug called far away: ordinary people going about ordinary, hum-drum affairs. Erika felt a tearing envy for them, for everyone in the city who had nothing to think about but the everyday problems of everyday life.

'If I hadn't seen,' she thought. 'If I hadn't tried to help. If only I had never been born.' And, although she had thought that she would never weep again, she did, sitting in the dark with Omi.

'Don't cry, child,' Omi said. 'What's done is done. All the tears in the salt sea will not wash it away.'

'Omi,' blinded by her tears Erika groped for her grand-mother's hands. 'Won't you think again? Won't you—'

'No!' Omi was harsh, as if there were another Omi inside her frail bones, as if another person were speaking through her mouth. 'Enough!'

Wiping her eyes with the back of her hand, Erika made a last effort. 'Omi.' She spoke to the unyielding back. 'Omi, you told me, just a week ago. . . .'

'Yes. Speak up, child.'

'You said that you would never do anything to hurt me. Ever.'

Omi was silent for a while and then she said, 'That was foolish of me. Never is too long a time to speak of. What I said tonight . . .' she made a fretful movement, 'for that may God forgive me. But I will never hurt you again. I will die first.'

'I don't want you to die,' Erika cried. 'I love you! Love you! But if you get caught tomorrow. . . .'

'Caught?' Omi sounded hurt and imperious at the same time. 'There is nothing to be caught with. Karl told me.'

'But Karl—' Erika began, only to be chopped off.

'Karl is my brother. A man of honour. I knew him before you were born. Before. . . . But you would not understand, child. Too much has happened.'

Amazingly, Omi's voice changed, it became warm and affectionate, the voice of the woman of a few hours ago. 'I should like to go to bed, *Liebchen*. Will you help me?'

'Of course.' Despite everything that had happened during the agonising day Erika felt wounded, not by Omi's request, but by the way in which it was put, as if Omi had half-

338

expected a refusal. She helped Omi off with her clothes, slid a night-gown over her, and with the skill of years, and with the strength of her young arms, eased Omi into bed.

'Bless you, *Liebchen*.' Clutching the documents Omi lay propped on her pillows. 'I shall be back soon, you know.' She was bright, conversational, even. 'I'm only going on a visit. There is nothing wrong in that, is there?'

'No,' Erika said hopelessly. 'Nothing. Should I sit with you?'

'Thank you, but no,' Omi said. 'You must be tired yourself, child.'

'A little.' Erika dragged the words from a bottomless well of exhaustion. 'Do you want your Watchwords?'

'Not tonight. I'm rather tired.' Omi's voice sounded as if it came from another place, and another time, and another world. 'Leave me, *Liebchen*.'

'Yes.' Hardly knowing what she was doing, Erika bent and kissed the withered cheek and left Omi in that other place, and that other time, and other world, and went into the sitting-room into her own world.

The sitting-room was in darkness and she flicked on a side-light, which illuminated the ivy, and the bamboo, and her father, sitting in his chair, an empty bottle by its side, and a half-full one in his hand.

'Not drunk,' Herr Nordern said, as if he had been accused. 'I wish I were.' He downed his schnapps. 'How is she?'

'In bed.' Erika sat on the settee. 'Father, I don't understand her.' Her voice quavered and she fought to control it, to be a sensible, responsible person; and she needed to be, she thought, with her mother on the edge of hysteria and her father drinking like a fish. 'Omi, she—she's like two different people. One minute, one minute she's like, well, like Omi, and then—I don't know—like someone else. I don't understand it.'

She looked at her father, hoping against hope that he would, as he had done all her life, bring, in his own shy, diffident way, comfort once again. But there was no comfort. Not this night.

'I don't understand it myself,' her father said. 'I don't understand anything any more.' He wiped his mouth with his shirt sleeve, a gesture which, for reasons she could not understand, distressed Erika. 'All my life,' he said. 'All my life I've tried to be decent. I have, you know—'

'I know you have, Papa,' Erika said. She would have liked to have cried but now, at last, there were no tears left.

'To be decent,' Herr Nordern repeated. 'I know this—where we live—it's not Utopia. In the bar, when that poor devil was blown up on the A.F.B.—I said then, he deserved it. But I didn't mean it. Not really. But still, I thought we were trying out something worthwhile—and now. What does a man do?'

It was a day of unanswerable questions, and there was no answer to that one either.

'I'll look at Mother,' Erika said.

'She's asleep. I found those sleeping-pills she had after her operation. She'll be knocked out until tomorrow.' Herr Nordern offered Erika some tablets in a grubby hand. 'Do you want some?'

'No!' Erika recoiled.

'No more do I,' Herr Nordern said.

'I could warm you some soup,' Erika offered.

'No,' Herr Nordern shook his head. 'It would choke me. But you have some. Go on,' he urged.

'I don't want any.'

'Then have some coffee, or wine. It won't hurt you.'

It might have been the mention of wine but Erika suddenly felt parched, as if her throat were full of dust and her tongue made of sandpaper. She went into the kitchen and drank a glass of water, and another, and she was pouring another when the phone rang.

It was Bodo and his reassuring voice came down the line. 'How are things?'

'Well, you know,' Erika said.

'Yeah, I can guess. Get Hans, will you.'

Erika handed over the phone to her father. 'Yes?' he said. 'Yes, no, she's asleep. I understand . . . all right. Tomorrow.'

He handed the receiver back. 'He wants to talk to you.'

'Uncle Bodo?'

'Keep your eye on things,' Bodo said. 'I'd stay with you but it's Paul. We're in a club I know. He's O.K. Just make sure no one does anything foolish. You understand?'

'Yes, I understand,' Erika said.

'Good girl.' Bodo paused and then spoke again but in an uncharacteristically diffident manner. 'Er, Erika . . . about Omi. What she said, about what happened to her. . . .'

'Yes?' Erika said.

'Well, just try not to let it upset you too much. You know, it was a long time ago and. . . .'

'I know.' Erika was deeply touched by Bodo's awkward kindness. 'Thank you.'

'Right.' Bodo became practical. 'You're a good kid, Erika, and a lot depends on you now. Make sure Omi's at Friedrichstrasse tomorrow. I'll be there. 10.00 a.m. Got it?'

'Got it,' Erika said.

'Good. It'll be all right. So long now.'

Bodo rang off and Erika turned to her father. 'He says to make sure Omi's at the station tomorrow.'

'Yes,' Herr Nordern emptied his second bottle. 'He's right. If she doesn't go. . . .'

Erika understood. If Omi didn't, then Karl would spring his trap, and it was perfect; polished, refined, and worked out to the last degree of tolerance. 'You should go to bed, Father.'

'I'll sleep in here.' Herr Nordern peered at Erika like a man staring through a fog. 'Don't want to disturb Helga. You go. Try and sleep. A few hours and it will be over. We'll get over it. Somehow.'

'Yes, somehow.'

For once in her life Erika did not shower before she went to bed. Whether Omi was asleep or awake she could not tell and did not ask. She lay in her narrow bed as the snow came down, burdening the beech tree and the war memorial. It layered the streets of the city and the fields of Germany, covering the watch-towers of the Wall and the death-trap of the Anti-Fascist Barrier, turning the savage spikes into harmless balls of cotton wool, and, hushing the continent, it fell on the rockets which, by the thousand, pointed at the innocent heavens.

The owl screeched, the night train moaned. In the sitting-room her father bumped the settee down and the flat fell into a gloomy and depressing silence.

Erika stared at the ceiling, her thoughts going round and round, her mind turning them over like a guinea-pig on a tread-wheel until, like an animal, it grew exhausted and stopped, and she fell into a merciful sleep; except that in her sleep she dreamed. She dreamed that she was in the Anti-Fascist Barrier, running between two huge walls of concrete. Lights blazed on her as she ran until she came to a dead end, then she turned and ran back and met another wall. Up and down she ran, while dogs snarled, and guards, all of whom were Uncle Karl, laughed and jeered and cried, 'Jump! Jump! You're a champion.' And she tried. She jumped as she had never jumped before, but each time she fell back, trapped in the grey concrete.

Chapter 29

ERIKA OPENED gummy eyes to a black, bleak morning, and wished that she was still in her nightmare instead of a world where nightmares were real.

Sick to the pit of her stomach Erika slid from her bed and flicked the side-light on. Omi was awake, propped on her pillows, looking as though she had not slept all night, her fine face rigid and unyielding—and she was still clutching the documents.

'Omi.' Erika could not bring herself to say, 'Good morning'.

'Child.' Omi's voice was as unyielding as her face.

Erika shrugged helplessly and went into the sitting-room. Her father was not there, but there were noises in her parents' room. Listlessly, Erika showered, put on the coffee, then went back into her bedroom. Omi was struggling to get up. Erika helped and wrapped a dressing-gown around her. Then Omi spoke:

'You think that I am doing wrong, don't you, child?'

Erika froze, hoping that perhaps a miracle had happened and that Omi would say that she had changed her mind, but miracles were not taking place that day, not in Klara-Lettkin-Strasse anyway.

'That is what you think, and Helga and Hans,' Omi said. 'But I am not. I have prayed all night long and I know that I am doing right.'

'Has God told you that?' Erika demanded.

'Yes.'

'Then your God is wicked and evil. If he exists.' They were the first harsh words Erika had ever said to Omi, and as she said them she knew that they were irrevocable. They could never be unsaid and by her saying them the strands of love and trust and kindness which had bound them together for fifteen years had been severed for ever. And what was more horrifying was that not one tear rose to Erika's eyes. But still she laid out Omi's clothes and when she had come back from the bathroom, dressed her.

In all that time Omi did not utter a word but when she was dressed and in her chair she said, 'One day you will understand, child.'

'I'll never understand it,' Erika said. 'I don't want to, either.'

'You will,' Omi said. 'When you are old.'

'Then I would sooner die young,' Erika said.

She went into the kitchen and made coffee and laid out plates. Her father came in, bleary and unshaven. He looked enquiringly at Erika who shook her head.

'Well,' he said, 'she has to go, anyway.' He rubbed his chin. 'Must shave. Keep up appearances.'

'How is Mother?' Erika asked.

'A little better, I think. She slept, anyway, which is more than I did.'

Herr Nordern shuffled to the bathroom and Erika took coffee into the bedroom. Frau Nordern was lying on the bed, her face puffy, and looking ten years older. At Erika's urging she took the coffee, first sipping then gulping it down greedily.

'Has she . . . ?' Frau Nordern's voice was hoarse and cracked as if, like Omi, another person were speaking inside her.

'No.' Erika did not need the sentence to be completed. 'She says God has told her that she is right.'

'God?' Frau Nordern half-laughed. 'What God could let this happen?'

'I don't know,' Erika said.

'God.' Frau Nordern stared vacantly into her cup. 'I knew, of course. About what happened to her. Oh yes. It happened to all the women. But I thought that it was done with. It was forty years ago.'

'But yesterday, you said you didn't know.'

'Yes.' Frau Nordern looked into Erika's shocked face. 'I

didn't want it said, though, made real. There are things you don't want to know. Lies you want to live with. Like your Grandfather Ritter.'

'Grandfather?' Erika felt like a figure in some monstrous myth being dragged down into a labyrinth which had no end and which grew darker and more terrible with every step.

'Yes,' Frau Nordern said. 'You might as well know that, too. How he died.'

'But I know,' Erika said. 'He was killed in action.'

'No he wasn't.' Frau Nordern dropped the cup on to the bed. 'He was shot. He surrendered and he was walking in a field and a drunken Russian soldier shot him. Just like that. There was no reason. And the War ended the next day.'

Erika could hardly bring herself to speak. 'Does Omi know that?'

'No. Hans found out but we never told her. That was our secret. Our lie. We had ours and she had hers, too. But we lived with them. We survived. We had our life, you, Paul, a future of sorts. And now.' She dabbed fretfully at her stained night-gown.

'And all because of Karl,' Erika said.

'Not just that,' Frau Nordern said. 'It's the past. Maybe it's true what Hans said, about Hitler building the Wall. They had a rally in Bromberg. Omi told me. They were there with their banners and swastikas and singing the Horst Wessel song. They sent an S.S. squad, all blond hair and blue eyes, and, dear Christ, what they were doing. And we let them, let them do it, because they were doing it to other people. Getting rid of trouble-makers, we said, agitators; bringing order. Yes, we said that and let them murder and torture and now we're paying for it, over and over. And they say that in the West some kids admire them. Dear God.'

'Yes.' Erika did not want to hear any more or think any more. 'You ought to get dressed, Mother.'

'What for?' Frau Nordern asked.

'Because. . . .' Erika was at a loss for words. 'We have to go to the station.'

'I'm not going,' Frau Nordern said.

'You're not seeing her off?'

Frau Nordern shook her head. 'I don't want to see her at all.'

Although she had thought that she was drained of all emotion, Erika was shocked. 'But she's your mother,' she cried.

'Is she? I've only her word on that.' Frau Nordern waved her hand, at once contemptuous and dismissive. 'Let her go. And leave me. Leave me alone.'

As if in a trance, Erika walked to the door, but there she paused. 'Mother,' she said, 'are there any more secrets?' But Frau Nordern did not answer that question.

Herr Nordern was in the kitchen, standing and chewing a piece of black bread. 'Have you eaten?' he asked. 'You must have something. And Omi.'

'I'll see to it,' Erika said. 'Mother says that she's not coming.'

'I know.'

'Aren't you going to make her?'

'No.' Herr Nordern dropped his crust into the sink. 'What's the point? I'm through with arguing. If she wants to stay, let her. Are you coming?'

'Yes.' It had never occurred to Erika that she would not go.

'All right.' Herr Nordern sounded as if he did not care either way.

Erika took a tray into her bedroom, offered it to Omi and received a formal 'thank you'.

'It's all right,' Erika said, meaninglessly. She dressed rapidly, went into the kitchen and forced herself to eat. The phone rang and her father, dressed in his heavy black suit, came from the bedroom and took it.

'Yes,' he said, curtly. 'Yes.' He put the phone down. 'Bodo. Just making sure. He'll be there with Paul. I'd better ring the office, I suppose.'

He phoned in saying that he would be late. 'A family matter,' he said. 'Urgent. Yes, my reasons in writing. Of course.' He put the phone down. 'I'd better ring the Welfare Office, too.' He did so, saying that Frau Nordern was not well and would not be seeing any mothers that day. 'I don't blame her,' he said. 'We've enough problems of our own. You don't think that you should stay with her? She's not in a good way.'

346

'I'll come straight back from the station,' Erika said. 'Paul can explain at school.'

'I'm sorry about that,' Herr Nordern said. 'Really sorry. It should be your day at school. You'd be the heroine.'

Erika dismissed that. 'I couldn't face it,' she said.

'No. Well.' Herr Nordern shrugged. 'We just wait, I suppose. I'll sit with Helga.'

Erika went into her room and picked up the tray. Omi turned. 'That was a terrible thing you said, child. Cursing God.'

'Not as terrible a thing as you are doing, Omi,' Erika said.

'Don't hate me,' Omi murmured. 'Please.'

'It's Karl I hate,' Erika said.

Omi's hands trembled. 'No. Don't say that.'

'I do hate him,' Erika said. 'I hate him and despise him. Why couldn't he have died!' She raised her hand as if she could strike him dead there and then; as if she held a lightning bolt which could reach and fell him as he sat in his fine clothes in a fine hotel, waiting, in the West, and gloating.

She let her hand fall and left the room and sat down, waiting, waiting, until Herr Nordern said, flatly, 'Time to go.'

He put on his coat, Erika hers, and Omi was helped into hers but, old and gnarled though her fingers were, and awkward though it was, she kept a grip on her suitcase that could not be broken.

'So.' Herr Nordern gestured to the door but Omi did not move.

'Where is my daughter?' she demanded.

Herr Nordern was gruff. 'She doesn't want to see you.'

'Not see me?' Omi was at her most regal. 'Tell her that I am leaving and that she is to come and bid me farewell.'

'All right. I'll tell her.' Herr Nordern went into the bedroom and, to Erika's surprise, he came out with Frau Nordern.

'You want me?' Frau Nordern asked.

'Of course,' Omi said. 'You are to say goodbye to me.'

'All right.' Frau Nordern agreed as if she were in some terrible farce. 'Goodbye.'

'That is correct,' Omi said. She held out her gloved hand and, amazingly, Frau Nordern took it and kissed it.

'Good.' Omi nodded. And with that and without a backward glance she turned and left the flat.

As Omi and Erika waited in the entrance for Herr Nordern to bring the Lada round a yellow van pulled up and three men got out.

''Morning gnädige Frau, Fräulein,' one of them said, pulling a chain-saw out of the van.

''Morning,' Erika responded automatically, and then something clicked in her mind. 'What are you doing?' she asked.

'Bringing that tree down,' the man said, cheerfully. 'The big beech. A new building is going there. Pity, isn't it? Still, we'll plant another.' He laughed. 'I won't see it grow but you will.'

It was a final blow and Erika sat, stunned, in the back of the car as they drove into central Berlin, past the Palast, over the Spree, by the great museums and the Police Barracks until, under a railway bridge, Herr Nordern pulled up.

'As near as I can get,' he said. 'Two minutes' walk.' He hesitated, then turned to Omi. 'I must ask you something,' he began.

'No!' Omi cracked the word out.

'Wait, I don't mean that.' Herr Nordern banged his fist on the steering-wheel. 'I just want you to promise me one thing. Just one.'

'And what is that?' Omi demanded.

'Just promise you won't tell Paul anything about . . . about this.'

'That does not need an answer,' Omi said. 'And no Prussian would have asked it.'

In silence they climbed out of the car. Omi clutching Erika as they walked across the icy cobble-stones, under the bridge, and on to Friedrichstrasse, but, still, despite the difficulty of walking, Omi kept the suitcase.

Friedrichstrasse had always been Erika's favourite street in the city, indeed it was one of the few that looked like a city street, with its shops and kiosks and bars, Kabarett Distel, and the flower sellers who always did a good trade, not least in small bouquets which the more daring Berliners placed on the graves of the artists who lay buried in the small graveyard tucked away behind the Berliner Ensemble Theatre. And there was an agreeable bustle to the street as people used the great station which not only served the city and the G.D.R., but was also the rail crossing point to the West, and from which, every day at 12.00, the International Train left on its exotic journey to West Berlin, Hanover, and the Hook of Holland. Yes, a vivid, attractive street, but as they waited to cross it, Erika thought that she would never care for it again.

The traffic-lights changed and they crossed the street to where the station steps led up to the *S-Bahn* and where, leaning casually against the wall, Bodo was waiting with Paul.

'Hi!' Bodo shook hands all round and Paul stepped forward, excited at the thought of Omi going to the West and, the new, reformed Paul very much in evidence, offering her a tiny posy of violets.

'Thank you,' she gazed at the flowers and for one moment Erika thought that Omi would crack, would say that she would not go, and that thought terrified her too, but Omi merely smiled.

'Thank you, Paul. Will you put it in my buttonhole for me?'

'Sure.' With a look of grim determination Paul attacked Omi's lapel and Bodo took the opportunity to draw Herr Nordern and Erika to one side.

'O.K.,' he muttered. 'A bit of luck. First they're busy today—lots of people going over—and second, listen—last night I got hold of a man I know. He's got a cousin in the Border Police and *he* knows a man who's on duty up there this morning.'

'What!' Herr Nordern went white with relief. 'You mean he'll—'

'I don't mean anything,' Bodo said. 'I don't even know the man. But he's going to push Omi to the front of the queue, tip the wink to the Inspector, and she should get through.'

'Can he do that?' Herr Nordern was not asking for details of the workings of the Border Police but for confirmation of his new-found hopes.

'I don't see why not,' Bodo said. 'They're all in some racket or other.'

'Ah,' Herr Nordern gripped Bodo's arm. 'Thank God for you, Bodo. I'll never forget this. Never.'

'Nor will I,' Bodo said. 'I stuck my neck out last night.

Right on to the chopping-block. And, Jesus, what it cost—'

'Never mind what it cost,' Herr Nordern said. 'I'll pay everything, if it takes ten years.'

'More like twenty,' Bodo said. 'Anyway, let's get going.'

'Right.' Herr Nordern, relief flooding his face, took Omi by the elbow as Erika deftly re-pinned the posy on Omi's lapel, replacing Paul's effort which had the flowers upside-down.

'Come along, everyone,' Herr Nordern said, almost jovially. 'No point waiting in the cold.'

They moved from the steps and walked along the side-street which led to the ramp, at the head of which was the customs hall of the station.

There was a queue on the ramp: people, nearly all of them old, shuffling slowly upwards, pushing their suitcases, like a line of refugees. The Norderns joined the queue. Herr Nordern looked meaningfully at Bodo but he shook his head. 'Not yet,' he said. 'In the hall.'

Step by step the queue moved forward. There was no talking, no laughing, only the silent file of a few foreigners and many old Germans, clutching their passports and exit forms, silent, as if holding their breath in expectation—of hope or fear.

But after fifteen minutes, during which they advanced only a very short way, Omi spoke in a clear, commanding voice which made heads turn, and then turn away, as if looking at a person who spoke so loudly might imperil them. 'How long is this going to go on?' Omi demanded. 'Such inefficiency! I have a train to catch.'

'Omi,' Herr Nordern whispered. 'Please—'

But he, in turn, was silenced by Bodo. 'Leave it,' Bodo growled. 'Shows a clear conscience. Get it?'

Herr Nordern got it and remained silent as, slowly, they ascended the ramp and came close to the first barrier, a wooden structure, rather like a Punch and Judy booth, with a blank-faced man inside it, perched well above eye-level.

'O.K.,' Bodo said, as only two or three people stood between them and the blank-faced man. 'Be with you in a second.' He winked at Paul. 'Just going to use some influence, kid.'

'Wow!' Paul gasped in admiration. 'Is there *nothing* you can't do, Uncle Bodo?'

'Can't fly,' Bodo said.

The Norderns watched as Bodo went to the gate which led to the next stage of departure. A cream painted hall with a glass roof, opaque with snow, and punctuated at its far end with a row of narrow, ominous looking brown doors towards which there crept, under the watchful eyes of the Border Police, the privileged: foreigners, the very young, and the aged; those free to leave the German Democratic Republic.

Bodo stood casually at the barrier, his hands in his pockets, a picture of innocence, blandly meeting the eyes of the Police. An old man crept past him, and an old woman. The policeman at the barrier demanded to know if they had any G.D.R. money. No, they had not and were waved through. 'Any door,' the policeman said helpfully, as if there were any point in choosing.

Another old woman crept to the gate. She had no marks either and was waved through. A Turk passed the barrier, and a bearded foreigner arrived dressed in a vast brown overcoat and a black hat with the brim turned down melodramatically, like a parody of a spy.

Bodo looked over his shoulder. Omi was being given back her passport by the man in the booth.

'*Scheisse!*' Bodo cursed under his breath as the sinister looking foreigner, challenged by the policeman, produced with a flourish a handful of coins, worth perhaps twenty pence.

'Keep them,' the policeman said, not without irony. 'A souvenir.'

Behind Bodo, Omi was saying goodbye to her family, kissing Erika and Paul in a fair imitation of regretful departure. Bodo began to sweat and his hands grew clammy—and then another policeman wandered to the barrier, had a word with the policeman there, leaned over the railings, put a handkerchief to his face as if blowing his nose, and whispered, 'Nordern?'

'*Götterdämmerung!*' Bodo muttered. 'You kept that back.'

'That the lady?' the policeman mumbled through his handkerchief.

'Yes.'

The policeman blew his nose vigorously. 'Right,' he said. 'This way, gnädige Frau.'

On their side of the gate Omi halted and looked at her family. 'So,' she said. 'Goodbye. Remember me, and remember your Maker. And Erika, remember the Lord's Prayer. "Forgive us our trespasses as we—"'

At the barrier the policeman nudged Bodo. 'For Christ's sake what is this?' he whispered. 'A *verdammt* prayer-meeting? Get the old bag through here, now, or the deal's off.'

'Right.' Bodo stepped forward, shoving his bulk between Omi and the family. 'Got to go now.' He elbowed a bemused Paul out of the way and unceremoniously shoved Omi through the barrier. 'Go on, Omi,' he bellowed cheerfully. 'Have a good time. Telephone us, don't forget now— straightaway. Our love to Karl!'

He waved vigorously and elbowed Herr Nordern who took his cue and waved also as the policeman hoisted Omi's bag and took her by the elbow.

'It's all right, Omi,' Bodo said. 'You're going the quick route, seeing as you're not well—' adding, *sotto voce*, as Omi was hustled by the policeman past a resentful but unprotesting queue to a door— 'I hope to Christ.'

The Norderns waited as the policeman shoved aside one or two old people, and then as a brown door opened, Omi stopped.

'Go,' Bodo breathed. 'Sweet Jesus, go.'

For one heart-stopping moment it seemed as if Omi would not go after all, but then she raised a quivering hand, went through the door, and it slammed behind her.

'And now,' Herr Nordern began, but was brutally shut up by Bodo.

'Keep your mouth shut,' he said. 'Just for five minutes keep it shut.'

'Five minutes,' Erika thought. 'A mere five minutes.' She looked at her watch. The seconds glowed on, off, on, off, as if they were hours, days, but the minute digit had not flashed 'two' before the policeman strolled up to the barrier, gave Bodo an unobtrusive thumbs up and, in a prison voice, speaking without moving his mouth, said, 'O.K. She's through. Now beat it.'

Bodo did not need telling twice. He turned and with a huge sweep of his hands drove the Norderns down the ramp, urged them across Friedrichstrasse, and into the Bar Mozart, where, greeted on all sides, he ordered rum for two and Cola for two, lighted a cigarette, and sank back into his seat.

'Sorry to rush you,' he said. 'Couldn't stay around.' He downed his rum in one mouthful and, as seemed to be the case with him wherever he went, another appeared immediately.

'Sorry!' Herr Nordern laughed. 'What can I say, Bodo? What *can* I say? She's through. She's—'

He stopped abruptly as Erika kicked him under the table. 'Ah, yes,' he said, collecting himself. 'Paul, you must be wondering, it's just that Bodo has saved Omi a long wait in the queue, and so we're all pleased, naturally. Ha! ha! But—' he looked at his watch— 'you should be at school.'

'No, leave it,' Bodo said, earning Paul's undying gratitude. 'We might as well all wait. You can hear the International Train go out in here.' He pointed to the ceiling. 'Goes right overhead. Half an hour to go. Let's relax a bit.'

'Yes, quite right.' Herr Nordern looked around at the agreeable warm interior of the bar, the more agreeable and warm by contrast with the snowy street. 'We might even stay and have lunch here. Is the food good, Bodo?'

Bodo grinned cynically. 'Terrific. Where are you going, Erika? The "Ladies" is on the left.'

Erika smiled. 'Not that, Bodo. I'm going to phone Mother.'

'Right. Good girl. Trust you to think of that. Mention my name at the bar, they'll let you use the house-phone.'

Erika shook her head. 'Is there anyone in Berlin you don't know?'

'Plenty I wish I didn't,' Bodo said, as more rums came. 'Hey, Paul. Get me a paper will you, there's a stall just down the street.'

Paul, ready to run to the Polish border for Bodo, dashed out.

'O.K.,' Bodo said to his brother. 'Let off steam, Hans.'

Herr Nordern gulped at his rum. 'What can I say? I know

it's not over, not really, but it feels as if it is. When I think, last night . . . I thought that I was going insane.'

'Yeah, I can imagine.' Bodo nodded. 'At least I was doing something.'

'Something!' Herr Nordern laughed a little hysterically. 'Bodo, if I live to be ninety I can never thank you enough.'

'Forget it,' Bodo said. He waved to a shady looking character at the bar. 'I owe you, Hans. Oh yes.' He nodded, unusually serious. 'Do you remember that time you brought two potatoes home, when we were living in that bombed out house? You gave them both to me. Said I had to build my strength up. Not the only memory I've got, brother.'

To his utter dismay Herr Nordern felt his eyes filling with tears. 'Bodo—'

'Skip it.' Bodo grinned. 'You owe me about 50,000,000 marks—and here's Paul.'

An excited Paul darted back, skipping with excitement, holding up *Neues Deutschland*. 'Erika's in!' he shouted. 'She's in the paper. Look.'

They looked, and there was Erika, mentioned on the front page and a photograph of her on page one of the sports section: Erika soaring over the jump, looking devastating, and with a bold headline: 'A Daughter of the G.D.R.'

'A daughter of the G.D.R.,' Herr Nordern breathed. 'And to think—' he stopped. 'What honour, what honour.' He glowed, heat flowing from him and, as Paul and Bodo pored over the article, he slipped his overcoat off and then his conscience pricked him. 'Will Omi be all right?' he asked. 'Is there a waiting-room up there? Shelter?'

Bodo looked away from the paper which he was waving in the face of a suitably impressed waitress. 'Eh? Don't know.' He glanced at the clock on the wall. 'Won't be long now, anyway.'

'Well,' Herr Nordern, warm himself, inside and out, light-headed with relief, pride, and rum said, taking the paper to look again at his Erika, and patting a bemused Paul fondly on the head, 'despite everything, I hope that she is warm. I really do.'

Chapter 30

UNFORTUNATELY, OMI was not warm at all. After going through the Customs with the aid of the remarkably nice young policeman, and solemnly declaring that she was not taking anything out of the country contrary to the laws of the German Democratic Republic and that the purpose of her departure was, as sworn in her statement, to visit relatives in the Federal Republic of Germany, she had been waved through, her word taken as she had known it would be. But then, disconcertingly, having followed a trail of old people down a gloomy, green-tiled corridor, she was told by a surly railwayman that no, the steps she had painfully limped down led to the subway to West Berlin and the International Line was upstairs, and she had dragged herself and her suitcase back up, fiercely refusing an offer by the foreigner in the black hat to carry her suitcase, and eventually found herself on the right platform.

It was a bleak and inhospitable place. A great glass tunnel through which howled a bitter wind driving snow before it, and the tunnel itself was covered with grey, shoddy plastic sheeting, flapping in the wind. Vaguely Omi wondered why the sheeting was there. Were they cleaning the station? she wondered. Painting it? But it was too cold to stand and wonder. Feebly she tottered down the platform, watched from high in the tunnel by guards in glass cabins, with sub-machine-guns.

Along the platform she hobbled, step by painful step, her hands aching, the dirty plastic rattling in the wind like a hundred kettle drums, the snow filtering through a thousand crannies, and then a voice, harsh and raucous, shouted, 'Halt!'

Omi looked up, frightened, her old heart beating against its frail cage. A border policeman was standing a few yards away, pointing to a line, grimy and barely visible, painted across the platform.

'*Verboten*,' the policeman said. 'Forbidden.'

And then Omi understood. Beyond the line was also beyond the sheeting—and beyond that was a view of the other Berlin. Timidly she moved back and sat on a bench, huddled against the wind. 'I am right to do this,' she said to herself. 'I am, to see Karl one last time.' And it was true what Karl had said, that there would be no problems at the Customs and, that being true, it followed, logically, that everything else he had said was true, also. 'And I will come back,' she whispered. 'I will come back to my Erika. And I will write and tell her how sorry I am for what has happened. How I am truly penitent. And I will write to my daughter, and to Hans, and they will understand.'

And then, von Bromberg though she was, and the widow of a von Ritter, bitter tears filled her dim eyes, and it would not have taken a moment longer for her to have limped back down the gloomy stairs and through the dark green corridor, and to return to the warm, simple familiarity of the flat on Klara-Lettkin-Strasse.

And she nearly did it. She almost left the station and the eerie rattle of its shroud of plastic, and the guards perched with their machine-guns. She almost went back to try and re-bury the past, and its dead. But with a grinding roar the train came in and the foreigner with the black hat, like the one Conrad Viedt used to wear in the old films, was leaning over her, holding the hat in his hand and, in atrocious German, was asking her whether she was all right, and whether she wanted to take the International Train because if so—and *entschuldigen*, excuse him—but the train was now here and all passengers had to form up at the white line.

'Thank you.' Omi bowed as, not without tact, the foreigner, despite his unprepossessing appearance stood back respectfully.

'I think,' he said, in his mangled German, 'I think, gnädige

356

Frau, there will be a delay before they let us on the train. You could sit here for a moment. . . .'

'Thank you.' Omi struggled to her feet, refusing another offer by the foreigner to carry her suitcase. 'It is kind of you,' she said, as the bitter wind whipped her. 'But I am a von Bromberg,' knowing as she spoke that she was talking nonsense, 'I need no assistance.'

'Of course, gnädige Frau.' The foreigner backed away, but he walked discreetly behind her as, shakily, Omi walked to the white line, and beyond that to a little gate, where, with a handful of others, she waited as guards came with huge Alsatians which, as the leads were slipped, darted with unnerving knowledge under the train, and other guards with dogs walked its roof, and yet more guards with dogs and pistols searched the interior, and over all the guards in the glass cabins trained their machine-guns on the foreigners and the aged waiting by the gate.

The search was finished. Men shouted and whistles were blown: no traitors or spies were clinging to the train's axles or lurking in the lavatories. The dogs, eager and snuffling, were led away, the little gate was opened, and the passengers were let through.

One by one they went through the gate and in her turn Omi went through, also. And then a curious thing happened. Just as she was about to climb on board through the door which the courteous foreigner was holding open, a man approached her. He was a rather nice-looking man wearing a good overcoat and an expensive, Russian-style astrakhan hat. He smiled, showing teeth as white and even as Karl's.

'Frau Ritter?' he asked.

'Why yes.' Omi was a little puzzled. How did the man know her name? Then it came to her: of course, he was probably a friend of Karl's. How considerate, and how typical of her brother to send a courier to assist her. And, to be honest, she thought, she would be glad of help. She was feeling rather giddy, as if she had drunk too much champagne, and she felt so cold and yet, oddly, hot, too, and the rattle of the sheeting—why, it sounded for all the world like the rattle of machine-guns such as she had heard in Königsberg when the Russians attacked the city. For a moment she actually thought that the guards were shooting at her.

But that was ridiculous. She was showing weakness, silly fantasies, unworthy of a Bromberg, the daughter of a general, and the wife of a colonel. She raised her head. 'Are you a friend of Karl's?' she asked.

'Karl?' The man smiled again, politely waved the foreigner into the train and slammed the door behind him. And as the train pulled out, Omi saw that behind the pleasant man were two large border policemen with two large dogs, and that there was a border policewoman with them.

The pleasant man touched his astrakhan hat. 'Frau Ritter,' he said. 'My name is Werner, Lieutenant Werner, and I have a warrant for your arrest. Would you please come with me.'

In the Bar Mozart, Erika, on the phone, after interminable delays, had finally got through to her mother. Yes, she was assuring her, all was well. Really well. Bodo had fixed everything and Omi was on the train—it was going out now, at that very moment, she could hear it. She actually held the receiver up as if her mother could hear the friendly rumble—and, despite everything, and although there were of *course* many problems to be faced they *could* be faced—and solved, and murmuring other consoling and heartfelt thoughts and adding that she would be home in half an hour, 'So goodbye for now, Mother,' she said. 'All will be well. Really.'

She hung up, thanked the manager of the bar, who refused her offer of payment for the call, wriggled through the crowd of workmen who were drinking rum and eating sausage, and, her heart as light as her step, went back to the table.

And there, immobile as waxworks, and as white, were her father, Bodo, and Paul, and with them was a stubby man with bloodshot eyes, smoking a reeking cigar who, as Erika reached the table, said, 'Fräulein Erika Nordern? Good. Now the party is complete. All of you come along with me, please. Let's do it quietly, shall we? No fuss. That's the way.' Laughing as he ushered the Nordern family into the cheerful, snowy, noonday bustle of the street.